"Daniel Logan, put me down! Whatever will those people back there think about us?"

"They'll think that you just like my arms around you. The women will wish it were them, and the men, ah, darling, don't ask me what the men are thinking now. I don't think you're ready for that. Take us around the lake, driver."

Daniel settled back with his arm across the back of the open carriage. Portia looked up and saw his eyes filled with mischief. He was openly staring at her, and as their eyes met, his expression turned into something so powerful that she couldn't look away. Every part of her body caught fire, and she shivered uncontrollably.

"I'm going to kiss you, little one." He said it gently, and she knew she wouldn't stop him, she wouldn't even try . . .

Sweetwater

SANDRA CHASTAIN

WARNER BOOKS

A Warner Communications Company

WARNER BOOKS EDITION

Copyright © 1990 by Sandra Chastain

Cover illustration by Robert McGinnis
Hand lettering by Carl Dellacroce
Cover design by Anne Twomey

Warner Books, Inc.
666 Fifth Avenue
New York, N.Y. 10103

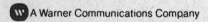 A Warner Communications Company

Printed in the United States of America

First Printing: September, 1990

10 9 8 7 6 5 4 3 2 1

For Nancy and Donna, who are always there when I need them. And for Pat and Anne who loved Portia and Daniel almost as much as I did, and encouraged me to give their story my best.

But most of all,
this is for Adele Leone
who made me believe in myself.

I acknowledge, most gratefully, the suggestions and use of reference material from Gleda James, local historian, who in 1983 spearheaded a movement to buy and re-vitalize the original Springs. Through Gleda's efforts and a resurgence of belief in the natural healing properties of the Springs, she is now marketing the lithium water worldwide. In addition to being president of the Lithia Springs Water Company, she has also restored and opened Dr. Christopher Columbus Garrett's medical office as a museum on the original site of the Springs in present day Lithia Springs, Georgia.

One

PORTIA MacIntosh surveyed the empty railcar and swore. "Fiona! Wake up! Where's Papa?"

Fiona sat up slowly, wiped the sleep from her china-blue eyes and glared at her twin sister. "How should I know? He said he was just going to step outside for a smoke while the train stopped."

"Oh blast! Hell fire and little fishes! Why does he do this? I knew I shouldn't have gone back to the troupe car and left him here alone. You should have gone after him."

"Me? Go outside, alone, and look for Papa?"

The train, creaking and lumbering along like a crotchety old man, began to pick up speed. Portia caught the back of one of the high-backed red serge seats for support. "For goodness sake, Fiona. This is 1890. The last stop was the Atlanta Terminal Station. There were people everywhere."

"Well I don't know anything about Atlanta, Georgia," Fiona said crossly. "And I certainly don't know why we're going to some church training school to perform. We're Shakespearean actors, not school children!"

Portia buttoned the man's jacket she was wearing, tucked her strawberry blonde hair beneath the gentlemen's driving

• 1 •

cap she habitually wore and glanced down. Brown corduroy trousers hugged her slim boyish hips and legs, ending in scuffed knee high leather boots.

"It isn't a Sunday School, Fiona. Papa says The Sweetwater Hotel is some kind of fine resort like Saratoga Springs. People go there to take the mineral baths and drink the water."

"But, we aren't going to the hotel, are we?" Fiona drew herself into a little ball and covered her legs with a blanket. "Oh, Portia, I'm tired of living like a gypsy. I want a real house and a husband."

"I know, Fee, I know." Portia's patience was growing thin. She knew they were all hungry and tired. Still she tried to reassure her sister. "The Chautauqua is the place where we perform. It's a kind of school for adults. They teach language and art, and . . ." Portia moved to the front of the car, opened the door and peered out. ". . . Oh, I don't know, Fee. We'll see when we get there. I've got to go look for Papa."

"What makes you think Papa is still on the train?"

"You know Papa isn't going to get left behind. He's probably found one of those dining cars and some wealthy matron to listen to his tall tales. I'll find him."

"You aren't going to look for him dressed like that, are you?" Fiona's voice registered her distress.

"Don't I always travel like this? Oh, Fee, nobody would listen to me if I didn't dress like a man. You know I have to look after Papa and the rest of the troupe. With Papa slipping away to have a spot of something or other every time I turn my back, and you afraid to get off the train in the dark, who else is going to do it? Can't you see me unloading scenery in a velvet gown? Or maybe I'll throw out a heckler while I'm cinched up in a corset and carrying a parasol. No thanks. Only a man has real power."

Portia glanced at her sister in irritation, then changed her expression into a more gentle rebuke. Not only did Fiona have to tolerate a lifestyle she abhorred, but she was constantly reminded of her sad plight by watching her mirror image attired in men's clothing, and acting like some tough-talking Molly. Poor Fee. Being a twin was harder on her.

"Portia, don't you ever want to fall in love? Get married? Have a family?"

"Me? Of course not; that's the last thing I would ever want to do—give any man control over my life. I like things just the way they are. Besides, I have you and Papa."

"But how will I ever find a proper husband, a real gentleman with you sounding and looking like some tinker's son, and Papa . . .''

Sweet Fiona. She wasn't born to live in such a family. She deserved a fine young gentleman who'd treasure her quiet beauty and gentle nature. Indeed, neither of them deserved a father who was a ne'er-do-well, impoverished fake, but that's what they had. Horatio MacIntosh was a charming rogue, who left the running of the acting troupe to Portia, knowing that by hook or crook she'd figure how to solve their problems.

Marry? Not she. She'd never understood Fiona's desire to belong to anybody. Portia had her family and the troupe. They depended on her and they were all she'd ever need. She'd seen enough of marriage to know what happened to women who blindly gave themselves over to their husbands. They ceased to exist, becoming instead an appendage to the man.

Mama used to shake her head and say that it was too bad that Portia didn't have some of Fiona's sweet gentleness, while Fiona could have used a little of Portia's backbone. But there were two of them and somehow everything got parceled out so that even though they looked alike, they were very different. If there were times late at night when Portia allowed herself to fantasize a bit about settling down in one place, the light of day always brought her back to reality.

Other than Papa's little lapses, Portia liked life just the way it was. Except that now Papa had disappeared.

Portia knew that after her father's last disastrous night on the town before they left Philadelphia, their survival was more likely to depend on crook rather than hook. What money they had left would just cover housing and food for the troupe. Horatio, that lovable rake who wasn't above picking a pocket or two along the way if need be. Secretly Portia hoped that for once he'd be successful and find a pocket filled with money. She was hungry, too.

Opening the door at the end of the rail car, Portia stood on the swaying platform where one car was fastened to the next by a bolted tongue. She could see straight ahead into the car beyond. The train, now running at full speed, was bumping and jerking along as if some giant child were pulling it on a string.

Taking the time to get her balance, Portia leapt across the space between. She opened the door to the adjacent car, brightly lit and packed with lavishly dressed guests chatting gaily. She threaded her way down the aisle between the seats of the elegant car searching for Horatio.

"Boy! What are you doing in here?" the black-suited conductor at the end of the aisle questioned sharply, eyeing her with disapproval. "This isn't your car."

"You're right, sir," Portia agreed, lifting her cap, allowing the mass of rosy golden curls to cascade down her back. This was one of the few times when being a woman could be an advantage. "I seem to have lost my father and I was wondering if you'd seen him." She put a soft wheedle in her voice and approached him. After all, she was an actress, a very good one.

"Just who is your father?" The conductor backed uneasily away from Portia down the corridor until his back was against the glass in the door behind him.

"My father is Captain Horatio MacIntosh, the Shakespearean actor. Surely you must have seen him."

"No. I don't think so, not since you boarded the train. The only cars left are the private cars of Mr. Simon Fordham, next in line, and that of Mr. Daniel Logan beyond, and you may not enter them." The conductor leaned against the door as though he thought she might fling him aside and rip it from its hinges.

Portia studied the toady little man. He didn't have to answer her. She could see past him into the window of the door of the private car beyond. The overhead light cast a golden halo on the men around the table, gambling, she judged, from the look of the cards and stack of money in the center of the light.

At that moment a plump, gold-ringed hand threw out a card, and Portia's heart sank. Stage jewelry. She'd found her father. Horatio was in a poker game with wealthy men who were wearing real gold jewelry with real precious stones. Her father's hand was trembling and she could tell that he was worried. She also knew there was no way in the world she'd be able to get into that car and get him away. She'd wait, right where she was.

"Now, boy—er—I mean, miss, I insist that you return to your own car." The conductor glanced anxiously behind her. She didn't have to see the frowns on the faces of the passengers to know that they were there. The displeasure was evident in the man's expression as he gathered his wits and stiffened his back.

"Yes sir. Oh! I don't feel well." Portia gave a dramatically wrenching cry of pain and clasped her forehead. "I'm afraid I'm going to faint. It must be this constant motion . . . train sickness . . ." She began to sway.

"Oh—Oh my goodness. Don't faint—not in here." The conductor caught her arm and supported her as she collapsed into an empty seat facing the exit.

"Thank you," she managed, her performance calculated to elicit great compassion from the railroad employee. Her results were sufficiently rewarded as evidenced by the worried look on his face. Perfect. She could see out the door into the next car. "I'll just sit here for a moment until my head stops swimming. How long until the next station?"

The conductor pulled a silver watch from his pocket and

strained to read it in the wavering light. "Less than twenty minutes. Austell Station will be the end of the line. Can you possibly wait until we get there before you faint?"

Portia bit back a smile. She could probably wait forever. She'd never fainted in her life—except on stage. "I think so," she whispered, leaning her head on the back of the seat. "If you'll just let me sit quietly, I'll be all right. Go on with what you have to do."

"Fine! Fine!" The little man scurried away, eager to separate himself from a potential problem.

Portia studied the door into the next car. Five sets of hands held playing cards around the table. She could get a clear picture of only one person: a thin-faced man who sat directly opposite the door, nervously smoking a cigar. His finger was girded with a large diamond ring and his chest was blazing with a satin brocade vest. She watched him reach for his pocket watch, halt his motion in mid-air as if he changed his mind, and let his hand drop back to the table. Probably he was either Simon Fordham or Daniel Logan, one of the two men the conductor had identified.

Any thought of stopping her father died as she realized that there was a lock on the private car, a very large lock. There was to be no association between the men inside and the common passengers, no matter how elegant these people were. Portia fidgeted. She'd have to wait and waiting could be a disaster.

Horatio MacIntosh had the good sense to throw in his next two hands. After several long pauses while glasses were refilled, she saw her father pick up his cards again.

"Please, Papa," she whispered. But this time he didn't fold. Portia glanced outside the window and judged that the train was slowing. She couldn't be certain but the twenty minutes must be almost gone. If only she could reach her father before he did something foolish.

Portia would never have admitted it to Fee, but she was more than a little worried. A nervous tic feathered her left eye as she counted off the seconds with every breath. She should have kept a closer watch on Horatio. He'd been too enthusiastic in describing their next engagement and she more than anyone else knew that meant that he was hiding something.

From the time they'd left upper New York state Portia had stopped fooling herself about Papa's latest scheme. The planned week's stay in Albany had ended abruptly after three nights, bringing in just enough money to get them to Philadelphia. There had been a mix-up in dates there and they'd had to wait over for a week before the theater was free. The hold-over had eaten into their earnings leaving them just enough money to buy passage south. Appearing at a summer resort outside of Atlanta was a new booking for them, and she was worried.

Perspiration beaded up on Portia's forehead as she sat watching. The card players added money to the middle of the green felt table at an alarming rate. The man with the diamond pulled off his ring and tossed it on the pot.

The train was slowing down.

The second man with the long fingers and carefully manicured nails was wearing only one piece of jewelry, a heavy silver ring. His movements were smooth with a graceful rhythm. He discarded one card and accepted another, studied them for a long time, snapped them into a stack and fanned them slowly open again before he finally added a large number of bills to the table and waited.

The next two men threw their cards down, leaving only her father's less steady hands. Those hands wavered and then vanished from sight. There was a long still moment when nobody moved. Portia couldn't tell what her father was doing until he laid a sheet of paper on the pot.

Oh God, Papa, don't give him a marker. If you've lost our money, how will we pay it?

She saw him lay down his hand with a flourish, but she couldn't tell what he was holding. The other man spread his cards, one at a time, and for a long moment nobody moved. At last the graceful, sinewy fingers wearing the heavy silver ring began to gather all the money and pull it toward his side of the table. Portia's heart thudded to the bottom of her boot. Papa didn't have to tell her; she knew he'd lost.

At that point the train shuddered to a stop.

The conductor spoke in a bored sing-song voice. "Ladies and gentlemen, we've arrived at Austell Station. Those of you going on to the resorts nearer the springs may take the miniature system called the Dummy Line which will be arriving shortly to transport you. In the meantime you may remain on board or step outside to stretch your legs."

Portia ran her tongue along her upper lip nervously. *Oh, Papa, how could you let yourself get into a game with those men. A little game with the stagehands is one thing, but you couldn't hope to keep up with millionaires.*

Portia glanced around. The conductor was at the other end of the car. As the train came to a full stop she opened the back door and leapt forward to the next car. She tried the lock. It wouldn't open. Inside the men were watching her father exit the back door. Desperately she jumped off the train and sprinted down the graveled roadbed to the other end of the car, just as her father was coming unsteadily down the steps.

"Papa!"

"Portia." His voice was strained. He caught at his stomach and groaned. She couldn't tell whether or not he was actually in distress. Horatio was the finest actor in the troupe and this wouldn't be the first time he'd diverted attention from his misdeeds.

"Papa, how could you?" Portia took his arm and felt him lean on her. His color wasn't good and his breathing was irregular. If he was faking, he was doing a good job of it.

"Portia, I've done it this time. I've lost it, lost it all. What will happen to my darling daughters? Oh! Oh! This is the end."

"Nonsense, Papa, whatever you've done, this isn't the end." They were walking through the darkness beside the train, Portia forced to support his weight more than she'd expected. "What do you mean all? You couldn't have lost much money. We don't have much money."

"Not the money, darlin'. I've lost it all—the show—the troupe." He sagged.

"The MacIntosh Shakespearean Theatrical Group? You've lost our company?" Portia had expected anything but that. She was stunned. For most of her twenty-two years she'd devoted herself to looking after her father and the troupe and now he'd lost it in a card game? She stood there, white-faced and speechless, the breath sucked out of her with the acceptance of his words. Papa had bet their livelihood?

"I had three kings, Portia. And there was all that money there. The idiot in the brocade vest I could have handled, but the other one, he wouldn't fold. Tough as steel he is, rich, some silver miner from Nevada. You should have seen the ring on his finger, made from one solid chunk of silver. There was already a diamond ring on the table and I thought he'd throw his in the pot and we'd be set for life."

"Who, Papa? Who won the company?"

"Logan, Daniel Logan owns us all."

Portia helped her father into the railcar where an alarmed Fiona was waiting. Portia prided herself on her control. This couldn't be happening. There had to be an answer. She could handle it. But how? She couldn't formulate her thoughts any further.

"What's wrong, Portia? What's wrong with Papa?"

"He's just gambled away the company, Fee. Stay here and look after him until I get back."

"Where are you going now?"

"I'm going to find the low-down swine who took advantage of a foolish old man—our new employer, Mr. Daniel Logan."

Captain Horatio MacIntosh breathed deeply and leaned his

head back on the seat. "Be careful, child. He's a very powerful man."

"What are you going to do?" Fiona asked breathlessly.

"Simple," Portia answered desperately. "I'm going to do whatever I have to, just as I've always done."

Two

"**D**RAT!'' This had to be Daniel Logan's car and it was dark. Either he wasn't in his own car, or he was already asleep. What would happen to the private cars when the train pulled out heading back to Atlanta? Would they be moved out to the resort, or would they remain here until the owners elected to return to wherever they'd come from?

Portia looked around, considering her next move. She had to find Mr. Daniel Logan and get back to the troupe quickly. Rowdy, the actor who also served as head grip, would see that the troupe unloaded the sets and costumes, but they'd wait for her to get them to the Chautauqua College, wherever that was.

Across the tracks, Portia could see a row of gas lights illuminating several small hotels and boarding establishments. Passengers were beginning to cross the tracks and she could hear the unloading of the luggage down the track behind her. It was late. She had to do something quickly. The chances were that Mr. Logan and Mr. Fordham were still in Mr. Fordham's car celebrating their victory over a foolish old man. Portia mounted the steps and tried the door to Daniel Logan's car. Locked.

She heard footsteps.

A railroad employee walked down the road bed adjacent to the train, shining a lantern here and there as if he were making rounds. Portia hugged the doorway and held her breath until he moved away again. She couldn't stay out here waiting. Quickly she scurried to the ground, knelt down and felt in the darkness until she found a good sized rock. Wrapping the rock in her cap she swung it hard against the glass in the door, shattering it. The sound made a loud crash in the night.

Portia took out the rock, shook her cap, replaced it and held her breath. Was Daniel Logan inside? No. Had anyone heard? Apparently not.

After a long heart-thumping moment she reached through the jagged opening and turned the knob. The door opened silently and she slipped inside hearing the crunch of glass beneath her boot. She'd find a place to hide. When he came in the door she'd use her rock to . . . to . . .

"All right. That's far enough."

From the inner darkness two arms slid around her in a quick motion that squeezed the air from her chest. The blackness seemed suddenly pinpointed with little sparkles of light and she began to feel fuzzy-headed as she tried to breathe. Her back was jerked up against a very masculine chest encased in rich velvet and smelling faintly of cigar smoke and expensive brandy.

Desperately she yelled and let loose a stream of curses she'd only heard used by the stage hands along their travels, momentarily startling her captor. "Let me go," she growled, thrashing violently under his iron-clad grip.

Portia would have screamed a second time, but one hand twisted her arm up painfully behind her and the other hand clamped her mouth forcing her to drop the rock and swallow the words she'd been about to shout.

Portia knew that he was stronger. She only had one chance. Pretending to weaken, she moaned and went limp in his arms. The man relaxed his grip.

"That's better," he said.

Seizing the opportunity, Portia whirled around and punched her captor's face as hard as she could.

"Awwk! You little thief. You hit me!" Her assailant lunged, taking a new hold, dragging his arm across her upper body in a grip of death. "I wasn't trying to hurt you before. I may pinch your scrawny head off now."

At that moment, Portia leaned down and bit the hand now holding her left breast.

Whether it was due to the shock of his hand touching a breast or the pain of being bitten, the man swore an oath, and slung her across the car where she tumbled in a heap on a great velvet-covered bed.

"If you're a thief, you're out of luck, darling. If you're a railroad dolly looking for a friend, I'm not interested."

He lit the lamp on the small table by the window and turned back to face Portia.

"You black-hearted, card-cheating wretch! You nearly strangled me."

"Well, between breaking my nose and biting my hand, I'd say you did a pretty fair job of protecting yourself. Who are you?"

Portia gasped. She'd bloodied his nose. Beneath the wine colored velvet dressing gown his white linen shirt was spattered with bright red drops. He had to be Daniel Logan, this devil with great black eyes, a dapper mustache, and thick dark hair that fell rakishly forward across his face. Mr. Logan was very angry.

"You're bleeding." She raised her chin stubbornly. "Well, dash it all, it's your own fault. If you hadn't tried to strangle me . . ."

Daniel glared at her. Definitely a girl, he thought, wearing a man's coat and trousers. With her hair tucked up beneath a man's driving cap, her lips drawn into a daring frown of defiance, and that tough, husky voice she could easily be mistaken for a boy.

At first glance she might look and sound like a slim young

lad, but Daniel knew better. He'd felt those firm breasts and there was nothing wrong with his body's response to the touch of her against him.

In the struggle her cap had loosened allowing a strand of light colored hair to escape and hang down behind her ear. Cheeks flushed, chest heaving and blue eyes flashing, the girl on his bed was just about the most enchanting creature he'd seen in a very long time. She was like a tawny barnyard kitten, cornered and spitting fire. He had no doubt that, given the chance, she'd spring up, attack him and be out of his car before he knew what had happened.

"Who are you?" he asked, pulling a fine linen handkerchief from a chest behind him and applying it gingerly to his nose and then to his bloody hand.

Portia's eyes were drawn to the silver ring she'd first seen through the railcar window. This was the man who'd won the final hand in the card game. If she hadn't been certain before, she was now. "My name, sir, is MacIntosh and I've come to discuss a matter of business with you. You met my father earlier this evening?"

"That wily old crook at the card table was your father?" It figured. He'd known that Horatio MacIntosh was in over his head from the moment he bluffed his way into the car and the game. "Well, it's his own fault. I tried to talk him into dropping out, even managed to . . ." Daniel swallowed his admission that for a time, he'd even dealt him enough good cards to keep him from losing everything.

"Crook? Papa never loses," Portia lied valiantly, in what she hoped was a convincing show of indignation. "You took advantage of an old man. You ought to be ashamed of yourself."

Daniel glanced down at his hand, conscious of the painful set of teeth prints in the space between his thumb and forefinger. Damn the little witch.

He'd been able to protect MacIntosh for a while. Daniel never cheated for himself. He didn't have to. One thing he had learned during his years in the gold field saloons and gambling halls was *how* to do it when the occasion arose. That skill, along with the kind of mind that recorded and remembered everything he saw made Daniel Logan a formidable gambler, though he rarely consciously used his eidetic memory. He'd learned long ago that it was better to conceal that peculiar talent.

But MacIntosh wouldn't listen and once the deal changed hands Daniel couldn't cover for the old man. When MacIntosh had lost everything else, Daniel had no choice but to out-bluff all the other players until only the two of them were left. He'd known that the old man couldn't raise his bid and he'd forced the Captain into losing only to protect him.

The last thing he wanted was to own a traveling show. He'd spent the past three years convincing the world that he was respectable, and there was nothing respectable about an acting company, even if they were performing the plays of Mr. Shakespeare. The Captain had failed to mention that along with the troupe Daniel would have a wild woman-child to deal with—as if he wasn't already frustrated by his lack of progress on his assignment at the Sweetwater.

God knows, he thought rubbing his throbbing hand, the last thing he needed tonight was to respond to this girl. He stared at the feisty, vagabond-looking creature shooting invisible spears of fire from across the room. But he was responding, and he knew that this mental encounter was as physical as the rout they'd both experienced a few moments ago. He just wasn't sure that she knew it yet.

Daniel Logan reached behind him and locked the door. He turned toward the woman sprawled across his bed. "I never cheat for myself, only when I am trying to protect someone who needs . . . never mind," he said in a soft quiet voice. "I think, my dear, that we'd better do some serious negotiating."

"Fine," Portia agreed bravely. "I've done this kind of thing before."

Daniel glared at her in astonishment. "Well, you certainly pick an odd way of dressing for it."

"Oh, no . . . you don't understand," she stammered, confused by the directness of his gaze. His expression changed from surprise to a kind of suppressed laughter, though there was still a seriousness there that said clearly that he was misunderstanding her attempt to negotiate. She blushed.

"Hell fire and little fishes!" Portia shook her head and jutted her chin. "What I'm trying to say is that I'm ready to work out an acceptable payment plan to take care of my father's debt. I'm sure we can come to some agreement."

"Maybe," Daniel said, knowing that there was no way she could come up with the amount of money her father had bet. "If I don't bleed to death first. At the moment I think your first move ought to be seeing to the wounds you inflicted on me."

He sat down in a chair by the window and leaned his head back against the crushed velvet cushion. He needed to put some time and space between them, to give himself a moment to consider his next move. Damn! He frowned. The little hellcat had socked him in the nose, but now his whole head ached.

Portia, on the bed, saw his grimace, and flinched. He was so big and strong. She was alone in a half dark railcar with this man, completely at his mercy. That foppish velvet dressing gown hadn't concealed the rock hard body beneath it. She'd come here to find a way to shame him into returning the troupe, yet all she'd done was attack him. Caring and nursing had always been Fiona's department. Portia didn't even know how. But it looked as if she was going to have to try.

On the table near the bed she saw a basin and pitcher. On the shelf above lay his straight razor and shaving mug, his shaving strop, towels and wash cloths. Water. The pitcher would contain water, and she'd clean his face.

Quickly she came to her feet and crossed the room. The sooner she repaired the damage she'd caused, the sooner she'd get back to the business of reclaiming her troupe.

Pouring water into the bowl, she lifted the razor, wishing

there was a way she could slide it into her coat, then sighed, laid it aside and wet the cloth.

"You're not planning to use my razor on me now, are you?"

She turned her gaze back to the man whose eyes were open now, eyeing her warily. "I think you ought to know that I would, if I thought I had to."

"I don't doubt it for a moment. I think that old reprobate is lucky to have a defender like you. Do you always take charge?"

"The troupe depends on me, yes. One way or another, I manage to handle things."

"Yes, and if my nose is an example of your methods I'm not sure that I trust you. Be gentle with me." His voice was a suggestive whisper, filled with mischief, and she realized that he was enjoying her discomfort.

She covered her agitation by violently wringing out the cloth.

"I won't say I'm not still tempted to strangle you, but I'll try not to hurt you, at least not yet." Putting aside the urge she had to look away, she held the cloth out before her like a cross before a condemned prisoner.

"That sounds like a threat."

"I never make threats."

The cold cloth made Daniel flinch as she began to wipe the dried blood from his upper lip. She used quick, rough little motions, like a cat cleaning herself. There was something erotic about the touch of her small callused hands on his face as she worked.

"You have very rough hands for a woman." He caught her hand for a moment and held it open against his cheek and neck. He hadn't met anyone like her since he'd left Virginia City. "Why do you dress like a man? A woman ought to be soft and sweet natured."

Portia swore between clenched teeth. There was no mistaking the rapid beat of his pulse beneath her fingertips. "Because it's necessary. People don't respect soft, sweet women very much. Being soft only allows them to take advantage of you. I've found this is better.''

Portia's voice cracked. She'd never touched a man so intimately before. "Please don't misunderstand," she stammered as she wiped. "No matter what you may think, I'm not very experienced at—this sort of thing. I don't think you'd find me at all interesting."

"You're wrong. I find you very interesting." Truthfully, Daniel didn't know what in Hades he was doing. The girl was proud. She'd come there to bargain for her father's company. He knew that this wasn't the first time she'd pulled her father out of some scrape or other. And knowing the temptations ahead at Sweetwater for a gambling man with high hopes, it probably wouldn't be the last time.

But there was something in the girl's face that reached out to him, something proud and indomitable. She might have been his mother, or his sister, or some part of himself from the past.

The one motivating factor of Daniel Logan's life was his ongoing attempt to make up for a past he couldn't change. Oh yes, he understood what she was doing and he couldn't turn his back on her own brave attempt to make things right. The desperate look in her eyes was a reflection of his own all those years ago in Nevada. He couldn't change anything then, but over and over, for the rest of his life, he allowed himself to be taken by any honest plea for help.

Daniel closed his eyes wearily. He could almost hear Ian Gaunt, his best friend and business associate, berate him when he got to the resort and tried to explain how he'd tried to save a flim-flam man who got in over his head, and ended up with a bloody nose delivered by the thief's tough-talking daughter.

Why take in a ragged, down-on-their luck group of actors? Ian would ask at the same time he was offering his own assistance. Strangers considered Ian cold and a bit aloof. He wasn't. Only Daniel understood Ian's fierce loyalty and quiet strength. For almost fifteen years they'd been together and

Ian knew him very well. Still, even to Ian Daniel might have a hard time trying to explain taking on this little spitfire.

What he ought to do was throw this girl and her father's acting troupe out and get to bed. Tomorrow he'd return to the Sweetwater, ready to set a trap for a jewel thief. Daniel's first two weeks at the resort had been an exercise in frustration. The thief he was after either wasn't there yet or he was smart—too smart.

Originally, Daniel planned to establish his presence at the resort by hinting that he'd come to select a wife. That way he could circulate and ask questions, questions that the guests would be more than willing to answer. The patrons of Sweetwater quickly learned that he was wealthy and eligible. Soon he was unable to move freely about the resort without being besieged by mothers and fathers with marriageable daughters, unable to ask the questions he needed to ask. Finally Ian suggested that Daniel pretend to take a business trip to give himself breathing room.

Now this girl had come along. And in spite of his duty to the assignment he'd accepted, she made him remember himself when he was a determined young lad, left alone on a worked-out mining claim. The acting troupe was no mining claim, but Daniel knew that he couldn't turn his back on them.

There'd been someone who helped him, once, someone who hadn't turned her back on him when he was in need. If Belle hadn't come along and taken him in, he might have . . .

Well, he'd been lucky. Someone had come along to shield and protect him, and now he was in a position to do the same thing for someone else. But the girl wouldn't understand. She'd been in charge too long to accept his protection. She was too proud.

"Tell me about the troupe." Daniel realized he was still holding her hand and released it with reluctance.

"We perform Shakespearean plays," she said, releasing a pent up breath of relief at his letting go. "We have our own sets and costumes. There are twelve of us in all. We've played

New York, Boston, New Orleans, all over." Her voice was too quick and breathless and she took a long minute to calm herself as she rinsed the cloth and wiped his chin and down his neck toward his chest where the blood had dripped.

"And your father? Does he often gamble it away?"

"No. This is the first time he's ever . . ."

Her voice trailed off, and Daniel felt her despair.

"I came here to bargain with you, Mr. Logan. We have no more money, but once we get to the Sweetwater, we intend to perform at the Piedmont Chautauqua College.

"As the owner, you will have all our income, other than the expense of keeping the troupe. But I . . . I'll find other means to earn extra income to pay off Papa's debt. How much does he owe you?"

That look came into her eyes again, that desperate look of determination. It was obvious that her father hadn't told her the amount of his wager. Neither could he. "Five thousand dollars," he lied convincingly.

When Daniel named the figure Portia's face blanched. Damn, he should have made the figure lower. She would have had no idea how much money was involved when her father recklessly used his company as security to cover the pot. Daniel wanted to thrash Captain MacIntosh for his careless action. Five thousand dollars might not be a large sum of money to him, but to the girl, the figure announced the end of her world. Hell, he didn't need all this.

Daniel felt her anguish as she swallowed hard and returned to her task of wiping away the blood. How could she hope to earn extra money? It would take her years to pay off her father's debt.

Twelve players . . . Daniel thought back to MacIntosh's exaggerated claim of a one-hundred-member traveling company. Five thousand dollars might even be a generous evaluation for the group! He watched as the girl rinsed the cloth in the water and hung it on the towel rack. Now she was standing quietly, poised like some frightened bird, ready to fly away if he moved.

"Listen, little one," he said kindly, "I don't want your show. But I know a bit about men like your father. It might not be safe to return your troupe to him just yet. For your own good I think I'll hold on to it until the end of the season. Then I'll consider giving it back to you."

"You will? Oh, thank you." The relief on her face was short-lived. "But why?" She eyed him warily. What did he expect in return? The men she'd been forced to deal with in recent years always had an ulterior motive. Generosity was a quality she'd not found, outside of her own family! Genuinely bewildered, Portia folded one arm across her body and clenched her arm.

"What exactly do you expect in return?" she questioned warily.

"I don't expect anything. I'm in a position to help you and I will." He could tell from the proud expression on her face that taking his help freely would be hard, if not impossible. He didn't want to force her compliance. There'd been a time when he'd seen his own mother resort to doing whatever was necessary to protect him and his sister, and that kind of sacrifice had ultimately killed her.

"Unless . . . Wait a minute." Daniel came to his feet and began to pace. He was beginning to see a way out that would save face for both of them. "I may have an answer. For the last two weeks I've been chased by every single woman in the state of Georgia. I don't have a minute's peace at the resort because of the interference of their mothers."

"Some men wouldn't consider that a problem."

"Maybe, but I'm trying to—well I have important business there and these foolish women are throwing their unmarried daughters at me in full force."

"Why would they do that?" Portia asked, glancing at him warily. After all, he was the kind of man that women would naturally gravitate toward. Even she recognized the pure animal attraction the man exuded.

"Because I made the mistake of telling them that I was looking for a wife. I thought I would be better off to conceal the real reasons why I came, financial reasons, that is, so I said I was wife-hunting. I'm not, but if I were, I wouldn't pick one of those empty-headed little wenches who never had an original idea, or a thought about being a real woman.''

"Just like a man. Shopping for a wife the way a woman would buy a roast of beef,'' she said acidly. "But, what does that have to do with me?''

"I think I have a way that you could earn the full release of your father's troupe, if you're willing.''

"Anything,'' she promised eagerly. "I mean, almost anything.'' Portia might put conditions on her involvement with Daniel Logan, but she knew that she had no choice but to agree, whatever the stipulations. She'd even . . . well she wasn't quite sure what he was asking, but she knew that she would do it. The rest of the crew, her father, and Fiona depended on her.

Making deals and working out problems was nothing new. The Captain had always relied on her business sense and natural diplomacy. Gradually she'd taken on more and more of the every day operation of the group.

Horatio's talent lay in his charm and quick wit. For years he'd been able to convince the local boarding house proprietors to house and feed his troupe. Theater managers miraculously agreed to promote their appearances and somehow they'd managed to survive—until now.

Portia and Fiona's lives might have been different if their mother hadn't died giving birth to their younger brother, a tiny little thing who never took a first breath. So long as Kathryn MacIntosh had lived, Horatio had held himself in restraint. Afterward, year by year, Portia had seen their bookings fall, their costumes lose their beauty and their numbers dwindle. In the last year Horatio had lost their private railcar and now, he'd lost the troupe. Tonight might be the biggest test she'd ever face.

Portia shook off a sense of impending doom, gathering the inner strength that had carried her through all the dark times in her life and tried to formulate a rebuttal. But this time nothing came. There were no more answers. Perhaps the finale had come with this black-eyed stranger who seemed intent on bringing to an end the life she'd promised her mother she'd protect.

Daniel, sensing her resignation, made a gesture of appeasement. "This proposition is a purely honorable arrangement, my dear. It's the only answer I have, and it might just save us both. I'd like you to pretend to be my fiancee."

"Me? Be your fiancee?" Whatever she'd been expecting —that wasn't it. "Listen, Mr. Logan. I don't think you know what you're asking. You can't possibly be serious—I know nothing about how to act at a fancy hotel. I'd only embarrass you."

"Possibly, but I've been embarrassed before. Besides, what you don't know, I'll teach you."

"You'll teach me how to be a lady? Hell fire and little fishes, Logan. You don't have enough years left to accomplish that."

"Well, maybe. But I'll give it my best shot." Daniel swallowed hard, trying to picture this little hellcat trying to be prim and proper. "You won't have to do much. Just make a few appearances at dinner so that the other hotel guests are convinced that you exist, and then you can go on about your business of acting."

"Won't they wonder where I'm staying?"

"They'll be told that you're staying at one of the other hotels."

"Suppose they attend one of our plays and recognize me?"

He gave Portia a long look. "I doubt they'll recognize you when I'm finished."

Portia took a deep breath. She had a glimmering of understanding that the man she was facing was much more complex than he appeared. He hadn't actually compromised her. And he was right. She didn't have any choice.

Drawing herself up to her full height, and jutting her chin

forward, Portia bargained warily. "If I supply you with a fiancee long enough for those women to call off their attack, you'll give back our troupe?"

"Yes. You have my word."

Dare she trust him? In spite of the fact that she didn't want to, there was something about him that made her believe in his honesty. She stared openly at her enemy, captured by the intensity of his brown eyes.

The rakish fall of dark hair and his neatly trimmed mustache gave him a devil-may-care look that made her uncomfortable and she didn't know why. She was acutely aware of Daniel Logan as a man. The feeling was new and disturbing. How long had she been staring at him without answering his question?

"All I have to do is pretend to be your fiancee?" she finally stammered.

"That is correct."

"All right, Mr. Logan. Done. So long as the arrangement is only a business deal and temporary. If that is acceptable to you, I have no choice but to agree."

"Fine. That's settled. There's just one thing."

"Yes, what now?"

"What's your name?"

"I'm . . ." Portia choked. She couldn't say her name. That somehow committed her, committed Portia MacIntosh to do something that made her lose control of her own fate, something she'd sworn she'd never do. Then the answer came to her, an answer that made her suddenly giddy with inspiration and secret glee.

There was no practical way that she could be Daniel Logan's fiancee. Not only would she do something awful, but some sixth sense told her that the less she saw of the man the better off she'd be. He unsettled her and she didn't know why.

Fiona always played the demure, ingenue roles. Her manners were the reflection of every great stage lady she'd ever portrayed. Soft, gentle, Fiona would be perfect as Daniel

Logan's fiancee and for once she'd be forced to grow up and do her part in pulling their father out of another of his predicaments. Fiona had always wanted to be a lady and find a real husband. This would be her chance.

Daniel Logan would never know the difference. Other than a slight variation in their hair color, and the fact that Portia's eyes were a bit bluer than Fiona's, they were physically identical. Besides the railcar was too dark for him to see her clearly.

"My name . . ." Portia softened her voice and gave the stranger a staged, timid smile. "Your fiancee's name is—Fiona."

"Very well, Fiona," Daniel said seriously. "As far as the world is concerned, we are engaged. Take your troupe to one of the small hotels across the street from the depot and spend the night. I'll make arrangements for your move to the Chautauqua quarters, and pay your bill in the morning."

Morning? Good heavens it was after midnight now. She'd been in Daniel Logan's railcar much too long. Portia lowered her head and moved quickly to the door. She stopped, turned, and held out her small hand, prepared to shake on their agreement. "Very well. Good night, Mr. Logan."

Daniel followed her lead, clasped her hand in his large one, and, lifting her chin with his finger, lowered his lips to drop a soft, sweet kiss on Portia's startled mouth.

Portia gasped and tilted her head back staring at him in disbelief. *He'd kissed her.* His lips had been a gentle caress that warmed her face and drained the little remaining strength from her legs. She was trembling so that she knew he felt her shake. This wasn't part of their bargain. Portia jerked her hand away and pushed against his chest, afraid he might kiss her again.

"You kissed me!"

"I did, didn't I?"

"But you shouldn't have." Portia's heart was pounding.

Daniel could see the pulse point in her neck quivering as she drew in a deep breath. "Why not? It's considered customary for two people who just got engaged." His own pulse wasn't behaving any more reasonably.

"But the engagement isn't real. It's only pretend, to make the world think that you are affianced. There is nobody here but the two of us."

Daniel groaned inwardly. He hadn't intended to kiss her. He looked at her for a long, silent moment, remembering how she'd drawn back and hit him in the nose. "You're right. I'm sorry. I didn't mean to frighten you."

"I wasn't frightened. I've been kissed before," she protested bravely, willing the stamina to restrain her trembling leg muscles. "I was only . . . surprised. But I don't think that you should do this again."

"I know." He stepped away, unlocked the door, and sliding his hand beneath her elbow, gently ushered her out into the night. "Good night, Fiona MacIntosh. Sleep well, and tomorrow—buy yourself a proper dress."

Long after she'd gone, Daniel stood on the platform outside of his railcar, smoking. The Dummy Line train, with its narrow rails and miniature cars arrived to ferry the passengers to their lodgings along the three miles of track connecting the resorts built around the famous mineral springs. Soon the depot was quiet.

Daniel wasn't sure why he'd bought himself a railcar. He'd arrived by carriage the first time. If he'd taken the carriage today he might never have joined Simon Fordham's poker game. He would never have gotten caught up in the agreement he'd just made. But then, he might never have met Fiona MacIntosh either.

Owning and operating a traveling show was not something Daniel was a stranger to. From the mined-out gold fields of California to the silver mines of Nevada, he'd traveled with Belle's girls after she'd taken him in. Their performances had been on makeshift tent stages in the gold fields, in bars and saloons, and he learned about handling people and how to promote them. Later, when Belle had grown old and retired to run a boarding house in Denver, he'd expanded his business to include gambling, food and supplies.

At twenty-five he'd built his first hotel in Nevada. Now he owned an even finer hotel in New York City. Still, he couldn't resist the lure of wild, untamed land, secretly acquiring great sections of land in Alaska. It had taken him twenty years, but he'd become wealthy, very wealthy.

Daniel looked out over the line of darkened railcars and wondered why his mission to stop a jewel thief was so important. He couldn't explain his sense of being violated five years ago when he'd been outsmarted by thieves. They staged a fire and in the confusion stole the hotel safe containing the jewels that had been entrusted to his safekeeping by the guests in his own hotel. It wasn't just the lost jewels. He'd replaced them and repaired the hotel. But he'd been invaded in his own world and he couldn't let the thief go unpunished.

He'd hired the Pinkerton Brothers Agency, and joined them in tracking down the culprits. Matching wits with the thieves had been so satisfying that Daniel had agreed to play detective for the Pinkerton firm whenever a situation came up that demanded a private detective who could blend with the rich and famous.

This time he'd been called in after thieves had used the same burn-and-steal method at the famous Saratoga Springs. The Pinkerton Brothers had a tip that the next target would be the Sweetwater. Daniel and Ian Gaunt had set out for the resort expecting to find the same thieves that had hit his own place. But so far there was no sign of that old gang.

The wife-hunting cover story was wearing thin and Daniel was no nearer finding the criminals than he'd been two weeks ago. The thieves were surely there, posing as guests, waiting, biding their time until the resort was filled with wealthy summer residents. But which of the guests was he after?

Daniel had watched them all circulate, met most of them over coffee and at the dinner table. So far he hadn't a clue. And he wasn't likely to find one until he announced that he'd selected the wife he was supposed to be seeking. This girl would solve the problem.

Miss Fiona MacIntosh would provide breathing room, he told himself, then he'd release her from her promise and back away without recriminations. She was one woman who wouldn't take her assignment as a future bride seriously. That made her the perfect choice.

Daniel knew that he was doing a selling job on himself. The truth was that the last thing he needed right now was the distraction of a traveling acting troupe or a young woman with eyes that spoke to him of his past. But he couldn't turn his back on the girl. He might just as well get on over to the Sweetwater and check out their arrangements.

Life was ironic. He'd come full circle. Shakespearean actors might be different from Belle's dance hall girls, and a tent saloon, but people were people and the paying customer was pretty much the same the world over. An acting troupe might even be fun. Daniel realized in pleasant surprise that for the first time in a long time, he felt an excitement about tomorrow.

Long after Portia had moved the tired crew members to the hotel and reported back to her shaken but recovering father that she'd worked out a deal for the return of the troupe, she stood at the window of her room considering the bargain.

The Captain hadn't asked her how she'd managed. He rarely did anymore. He was simply content to let her handle the problem. Fiona's participation in the return of the troupe might be a bit harder to rationalize. The hour was late. Time enough tomorrow to explain to Fiona that she would have to pretend to be Daniel Logan's fiancee.

But sleep wouldn't come to Portia. She couldn't find a way to erase Daniel Logan from her mind. He'd held her hand, gently as a real suitor might. Then, he'd done the unthinkable. He'd kissed her. He could have demanded much more from her. He could even have forced her to . . . her mind couldn't take that line of thought any further. She knew that her fate was in his hands. But for tonight, he'd let her go.

The next time she might not be able to get away. Except that it wouldn't be she, it would be Fiona that she'd delivered into the arms of that handsome rake. Suppose he found out the truth? Surely he wouldn't care which of the MacIntosh sisters pretended to be his fiancee. But she suspected that he wouldn't take it lightly that she'd tricked him. Suppose he kissed Fiona?

Portia felt as if she were standing on some high cliff being buffeted by the wind. Little jolts of energy seemed to be bursting inside her body, like the bubbles she'd seen in the champagne being drunk during intermission in the great opera house where they'd once played.

She couldn't stop thinking about Daniel Logan. For the first time vague, unnamed sensations were flitting through her mind, skittering down her backbone and shooting little tremors of energy outward beneath her skin. It wasn't the situation that was responsible for her restlessness, it was the man. She wondered if she'd mortgaged her soul to the devil, knowing that even if she had, it was too late to back out.

Three

DANIEL Logan crossed the great expanse of brightly lit hotel grounds and walked toward the stark white Moorish towers that housed the Piedmont Chautauqua College. It was very late but he needed to discuss the arrangements for the acting troupe before their arrival tomorrow. For the moment he didn't want to make his ownership public. Keeping the image he'd projected among the guests was imperative.

He knew that it would only be a matter of time until they found out who his fiancee was, but with any luck he'd only need a few more days to set his trap and catch the thief or thieves. If they wondered a bit, all the better. He could question them while they were being curious.

He took in a deep breath of the fragrant air. The Sweetwater Hotel was truly a wonder. Nowhere else in the world had he seen such lavish surroundings and accoutrements. His first hotel, The Lodestone, had been a grand establishment in Virginia City, Nevada, but neither it, Saratoga Springs, nor his latest acquisition, The Crown in New York City, with all its attention to wealth and detail, could compare with the grand scale of the Sweetwater and its lithium springs. Too bad the resort wasn't for sale.

Daniel had read of the calming effect of the chemical lithium. The Cherokees had known and made use of the springs long before the white man claimed the land on which they were located. But only in the last seventy years had the scientific world learned of its medical value.

Now there was a sanitarium across from the springs to treat opium addicts and alcoholics, and visitors from all over the world came to the Sweetwater to drink the water and take the baths. Or, so they said. Daniel smiled. He understood the gay, wealthy patrons of the hotel who wanted to rub shoulders with the Astors and the Vanderbilts.

But the Chautauqua College built on land adjacent to the hotel, just gearing up for its annual summer session, was a new concept. A program conceived to bring learning to the masses was a grand idea.

Daniel admired anybody who tried to learn and better himself. He only wished there'd been such a place in Nevada. There had been a time when he wanted desperately to learn. Belle had taught him to read. After that there was no stopping him. Like a sponge he absorbed everything he heard and every book he came in contact with. He'd been almost grown before he'd realized that everybody who learned to read didn't have his unique talent for retaining every word.

As far as he could tell from the literature the desk clerk had given him, this school wasn't offering anything that he didn't already know, other than religious training for church workers, and he'd had his share of bible thumpers trying to close down their traveling shows.

In the darkness the college looked like some Islamic mosque, with its great towers shining white and pure in the moonlight. Because of the late hour Daniel had sent a messenger ahead to warn the Chautauqua director of his arrival.

Daniel was shown immediately into the office of Mr. William T. Long. While the Sweetwater gleamed with the new incandescent electric lighting, the offices of the assistant director of the Piedmont Chautauqua Summer College still used the traditional gas lights, and the room appeared austere in the poor light.

"Mr. Logan? Please come in. Your messenger said that you insisted on speaking with me this very night."

Clearly the man behind the desk had already retired for the evening and just as clearly he was puzzled by the request of the man considered by the hotel staff to be the wealthiest, most eligible new member of the Sweetwater elite.

"Please forgive me for disturbing you so late, but I have unexpectedly become the new owner of the MacIntosh Shakespearean Theatrical Company, and I understand that they're scheduled to be a part of your summer session."

The puzzled expression on Mr. Long's face turned to one of complete bewilderment. "I don't know what you're talking about. Someone must be playing a practical joke, Mr. Logan. I'm afraid I've never heard of the MacIntosh . . . Shakespearean troupe. And I have my doubts that the directors of the college would allow plays to be performed on the same arena where the great sermons are to be preached. You understand that some of our staff members are missionaries and very devout people."

Somehow Daniel Logan wasn't surprised to learn that the troupe wasn't expected.

The picture of the proud, feisty young woman standing her ground before him in his parlor car flashed across his mind. She'd been lied to by her father, and he'd bet it wasn't the first time either. That old fool—he'd probably planned to march in here and bamboozle this man into giving them summer employment. After having seen him work the other men at the poker table, Daniel had little doubt that Horatio might have done it.

"I see," Daniel said slowly, glancing around the office filled with bibles, fliers and what appeared to be lesson plans. "Just what do you have on the agenda for the summer college this year? I believe you do offer certain programs in the arts?"

"Oh yes. Well, I have to explain. You see, since Mr.

Henry W. Grady, our most influential patron, passed away, we've had to refocus our direction and cut back on some of our original plans. Finances have dropped off, you understand.''

"And the original plans were?"

"Mr. Logan, I can't quite see how our curriculum will interest you, and it is very late.''

"Please, Mr. Long, indulge me. I assume that you do offer the same kind of instructions that the original summer college offered in upper New York state. I mean, you do offer more than just a Sunday School and religious instructions don't you?''

"Oh, yes. Mr. Grady was very insistent on our fulfilling our commitment to educate the masses by providing inexpensive short term classes in the summer time where they can combine a vacation with learning.''

"Go on," Daniel instructed.

"Well, along with our training of Sunday School teachers, we offer courses in language, science, history, mathematics, and the arts. Originally we had planned to bring in artists to present the great works of music and opera, but sadly, the cost of building the center hasn't yet been recouped, and we simply haven't the funds to offer more than a few classes in music appreciation.''

Daniel was beginning to get an idea. "So these people who attend your school actually stay here?''

"Yes, on the grounds we have tents and cabins. There are also cheap hotels and boarding houses in Salt Springs and of course there is the Sweetwater.''

"So your opposition to presenting the plays of Mr. Shakespeare isn't moral, as you suggested. It's financial, isn't it? And you'd use the MacIntoshes if you could afford them?''

"Yes, I'm afraid so. While we have space to house the troupe in our special dormitories, we simply haven't the money to either finance their housing or pay them. Pity.''

"Yes. It is a pity. Let me make you a proposition, Mr.

Long. You arrange proper food and housing for my troupe and set up a schedule for the performances, and I'll pay the cost."

"You'll what?" Mr. Long's tone expressed his incredulity. "I've spent the better part of the year unsuccessfully soliciting funds for the operation of the college. Then, out of the blue, comes endowment for an arts program from a man I never even approached!"

"Then it is possible?"

"Of course. How wonderfully generous of you, Mr. Logan. Will these be paid performances for all who wish to purchase a ticket, or will they be part of the free evening offerings of the college?"

Daniel considered the question. Paid performances would replenish Horatio's lost gambling funds. On the other hand, the purpose of an institute, a college set up to educate the masses, intrigued him.

"I propose that at the end of the summer, the troupe receive a fee for their services, which I'll provide. They will believe that you are paying them. The plays will then be offered to the public free of charge. I have only two requests."

A beaming Mr. Long stood and rubbed his hands together in glee. "Of course, Mr. Logan, whatever you say sir."

"First, neither Horatio MacIntosh, nor any member of the company is to know about our little bargain. There will be five performances per week which will end no later than ten o'clock in the evening. Agreed?"

"Agreed. This is most generous of you Mr. Logan. The members of the college, the guests of the Sweetwater, and the people who come to the sessions will benefit greatly from your gift."

But it wasn't any of those people Daniel was thinking of as he crossed the landscaped grounds, and returned to the hotel. He took the stairs, passing the new electric lights mounted on the walls along the massive stairway to the second floor without a thought to the wonder of this novel illumination.

His gift wasn't being offered to the masses. His gift was to a stiff-necked girl whose teethmarks still brought a tinge of pain to his hand, and a blustering old man who reminded him of Belle.

"Yuck! That tastes funny!" Fiona made a grim face and swallowed the water. "What's wrong with it?"

"Fiona, my darling daughter, that's the mineral content. It's miracle water you're drinking. It'll cure opium addiction, calm the mentally deranged and—it'll restore your father's youth." Horatio MacIntosh took another drink from his glass and beamed at his troupe seated around the late morning breakfast table in the near empty dining hall. "What did I tell you, Portia, isn't this fine?"

"I have to hand it to you, Papa," Portia agreed, still not believing the ease with which they'd moved from the hotel to the dormitory housing the Chautauqua staff. They'd worked their way across the country and back, but never had they been treated with such respect by staff members. It didn't make sense. "This is more than I ever expected."

"Excuse me?" A young man wearing black trousers and a white jacket with the name Sweetwater embroidered on the sleeve, stood hesitantly beside their table. "I have a letter for a Miss Fiona MacIntosh?"

"Me?" Fiona looked at Portia with question marks in her eyes.

"Are you Miss MacIntosh?" He moved immediately to Fiona's elbow and held out a silver tray on which a butter-colored envelope was lying.

"Yes. I suppose I am, I mean, of course I am. Are you certain that this is for me?"

"Yes ma'am." The servant continued to hold out the tray until Fiona took the envelope. After an unacknowledged glance at Horatio, the boy turned and left the room.

"Well, open it Fee," Horatio commanded. "Probably from some secret admirer who's heard that you've arrived."

Portia decided that the note was probably meant for her.

It was more likely to be from a merchant requesting payment for one of the debts they'd left behind when Horatio had arranged their hasty escape in the middle of the night.

Fiona opened the envelope and slowly read the contents once, then a second time. "I don't understand," she finally said, handing the message to Portia. "A Mister Daniel Logan is asking—no—commanding my presence at dinner this evening. How can that be?"

Portia took the note, knowing already what she was going to read. She had yet to explain the details of her agreement with Daniel Logan to either her sister or her father. She'd hoped to delay the truth for a few days until she could see some kind of solution to a summer under Daniel Logan's control. But any delay was going to be out of the question now.

"Read the note, Portia," Horatio commanded.

Portia took a deep breath and read. "The note is a request that Miss Fiona MacIntosh join Mr. Daniel Logan for dinner in the Sweetwater Dining Room this evening at eight o'clock."

"Me? Whatever for?" Fiona stood up, prepared to leave the table in her distress. "I will not go out with some rich stage-door Johnny who expects heaven knows what."

"Fee . . ." Portia said.

"Rather presumptuous of Mr. Logan, Portia, my dear," Horatio observed and helped himself to another biscuit with ham.

Fiona looked from her father to Portia and back again. "Why, I don't even know this Mr. Logan. I mean, surely you didn't make me part of your bet, did you, Papa?"

"Fee," Portia began again.

"Well, I won't do it, Portia. Tell him. You always straighten out Papa's little indiscretions."

"Fee, shut up!" Portia said quietly with that ring of authority that the entire cast recognized. "There is no reason to let the rest of the cast know about this just yet. Papa didn't do it. I did. You have no choice."

Fiona glanced around at the other cast members seated at the other tables. She sat down and stared at her identical twin in surprise. "What do you mean?"

"I hadn't told you everything. You were tired, Fiona. And Papa, you weren't feeling well. I thought that a good night's rest might make the truth easier to take."

"Tell us now, Portia," Horatio directed, knowing that whatever Portia had done was better than he deserved.

"Well, you already know that Daniel Logan is our new employer. Papa lost the troupe to him in that card game last night, and . . . well, he agreed to return it if we meet certain conditions."

"What conditions? I don't understand." Fee leaned forward in her chair and clung to the arms as though she was restraining herself from running away.

"I had to bargain with him, Fiona. He only agreed to relinquish ownership if I pretended to be his fiancee while he is staying at the hotel."

Fiona's mouth dropped open in astonishment. "Why on Earth would he want *you* to pretend to be his fiancee? You've never even had a beau."

"So that the women at the hotel will leave him alone. It seems he is in great demand."

"Oh, then he meant to send the invitation to you?" Fiona's relief exceeded her shock. She was still eyeing Portia suspiciously.

"Well yes," Portia agreed. "It was me he asked. But," she paused, wondering how to explain her impulsive behavior of the night before, "but, he thinks that I'm you, Fiona."

"Why? We may look alike, but unless the two of us are together nobody would ever know it, the way you act and dress, Portia."

"That's true. Explain yourself daughter," Horatio demanded.

"Maybe it was a bad bargain," Portia admitted. "I was tired. I simply couldn't think of another answer. We all know that I'm no lady. I've never even played one on the stage.

There is no way that I can go out to dinner with Daniel Logan. He'd expect me to act like a fiancee. I just can't do it. It was a desperation move, pure and simple. I told him I was you, Fiona.''

"You told him you were me? How could you do such a thing, Portia? He actually thought you were me? That's disgraceful and I won't do it." Fiona's voice held the threat of tears.

"Yes you will, Fee. For years I've done everything in my power to keep us going and solve our problems." Portia's voice was firm and her tone allowed no room for argument. "Now, it's your turn. You're going to have to go to dinner with the man who controls our future. There is no other way."

There was a long silence as Fiona simply shook her head from side to side.

"I'm afraid she's right. You'll have to go, Fiona, dear," Horatio agreed, with a deep sigh. "But not just because of a foolish old man's weakness. This is your chance, my daughter, to do something you've always wanted to do, be a real lady. If it buys us a little time to figure out how to reclaim the troupe, that's the way it will have to be."

"But, Papa . . ." Portia began, having seond thoughts about the bargain she'd made.

Horatio smiled as though he'd reached a favorable decision freely. "Stop worrying, Portia, I'm sure Fiona will carry out your agreement nicely. After all she's a first class actress, and a MacIntosh."

Fiona stood and stamped her foot. "No, I won't. I've never been to a fancy place like that. Acting on the stage isn't like playing a role with a real man. I'd be too afraid. He's probably some red-faced lecher."

"No, Fiona," Portia said softly, "he's very handsome. I think you'll be impressed."

"But, I'll be too afraid," Fiona argued. "I can't do it. I will not go alone. Portia must come too."

"I can't, Fiona. He'll recognize me and know that I lied to him. I don't think this is a man who'll tolerate a lie. At least you've played the proper lady's roles on stage. I'm always the young lad.''

''Why would it matter to Mr. Logan? There are two of us. We're twins. If I play the part, why should he care? If you don't go, then I won't go,'' Fiona declared, lifting her chin in her best prim, put-upon gesture as she left the table. ''And you can't make me.''

''Oh, Papa,'' Portia cried in despair. ''I never should have agreed to his proposal. There must have been another way. I just couldn't think of one. What are we going to do? We'll be thrown out and we have no money.''

Horatio had never seen Portia quite so distraught over a situation. Usually she was a rock. This time something had thrown her and he didn't think it was just his own foolish mistake. She simply didn't want to be involved with Daniel Logan and she was trying desperately to find a way out. Still, a bargain was a bargain and the MacIntoshes always kept their word—or almost always.

''Wait a minute, girls. Twins—that's it. I see the answer.'' Horatio slapped his plump thighs in glee.

Portia wasn't sure she wanted to hear his idea. More often than not, Papa's ideas led to disaster. He was like a leprechaun, with his way of making things complicated when the truth was always simpler. But they'd never been in a situation like this before and she hadn't a glimmer of a way out. ''Tell me, Papa.''

''Other than an occasional matron, you've always played the young lad. That's what you do best and that's what you'll do now. If Fiona is to act her greatest role as the intended wife of Mr. Daniel Logan, then you'll give your greatest perfomance as the lady's twin brother, Phillip. That way you can keep an eye on Fiona and make certain that she isn't taken advantage of.''

Taken advantage of? Portia's inclination to refuse died as she recognized the truth of her real concern. Daniel had kissed her. She'd tried to deny how his kiss felt, but she couldn't. *What if he tried to kiss Fiona?* She was worried and she couldn't confess her reservations. She'd have to do something, to protect her sister's virtue from a man she herself couldn't trust.

Still, pretending to be Fiona's twin brother seemed much too complicated. "There has to be another way. I don't want to have to worry about which fork to use and when to wipe my mouth. I wouldn't fit in. That's why I used Fiona's name in the first place."

Portia looked away from her father's intent gaze. That wasn't why she used Fiona's name. It wasn't like her to lie to herself. She'd put Fiona in her place because she was plain scared of Daniel Logan. "I can't do it," she whispered desperately.

Portia looked at him now and caught the full force of the shocked expression on his face. She was behaving irrationally. She'd always done whatever was necessary to take care of business. Now suddenly she sounded like Fiona when she was forced to do something she didn't want to do. What was she really worried about, the proper fork, or the man? One problem was as bad as the other.

"Well," Horatio dabbed his napkin to his lips, "I suppose I'll just have to go up and challenge Mr. Logan to a new bet. We'll play a round of billiards. I understand the hotel has a grand game room. I'd planned to check it out, and this will give me an excellent opportunity. If he wins, I leave. If I win, he gives up his claim to the company."

"Billiards? Hell fire and little fishes, Papa. No! Wait. You can't go, Papa. I'll think of something."

"Oh? What? You promised Mr. Logan a fiancee and Fiona won't go without you."

"All right. I'll do it." Portia knew she was making a mistake, but she couldn't seem to think clearly enough to come up with another solution.

Whatever happened, she couldn't take a chance on her father making any more bets, or allowing Fiona to be alone with Daniel Logan. There was no reason under the sun for Daniel Logan to agree to her father's billiards challenge, but he might. There was too good a chance that Papa would lose. She couldn't allow that to happen—not again. If possible, she intended to keep Horatio MacIntosh and Fiona away from Daniel Logan entirely.

"You look absolutely beautiful, Fee." Portia, preparing for the ordeal ahead, had already dropped into the lower voice she used on stage to project the image of a young male.

"I've never seen a dress so lovely," Fiona whispered, gazing awe-struck at the reflection in the mirror. "How could he know my exact size?"

"Probably just a good guess," Fiona answered with a hot blush. The man probably had enough experience with women to be able to calculate her measurements by simply holding her in his arms.

The gown was of white silk, embroidered at the hem with silk thread of the same color. The soft fabric clung to her body and formed a train behind her as she walked. The bodice of tight-fitting white velvet was draped with swirls of shimmering silk, gathered by clusters of pearls at the bustline and allowed to fall gently to the floor. Fiona had piled her honey colored hair high on her head, entwined it with pearls and inserted two silvery white feathers giving her the look of subdued royalty. Mrs. John Jacob Astor couldn't have been more regal.

From the moment Fiona left the dormitory and started down the steps to the foyer she began taking on the characteristics of the lady she was dressed to portray. No matter how shy Fiona was, she was a fine actress. By the time they reached the foyer, Portia knew that her decision had been a wise one. In spite of her insecurities, Fiona would have a grand time and Daniel Logan would be able to say that his choice of a fiancee was perfect.

"Who will you be tonight, Portia?" Fiona asked eagerly. They were traveling the short distance between the Chautauqua grounds to the hotel by special carriage dispatched from the hotel.

"Be? What do you mean? I'll be Phillip, your twin brother, of course."

"No, I'm not Fiona. I shall play Ophelia. That way I won't be so very nervous."

"Well, if you're Ophelia, I suppose I'll be Prince Hal."

"But Prince Hal was a dandy, Portia. I'm not sure I want my brother to be like that."

"So much the better. If I forget and become myself, your fiance won't suspect anything."

"I wondered why you were dressed so foppishly."

Portia looked down at the maroon velvet frock coat and cream colored trousers she was wearing. They were the finest garments from their wardrobe that could pass for current fashion. She hadn't considered the picture she presented. The only problem she'd had was her hair. Finally Papa had located a modern wig which had sufficiently covered her own tresses, providing she wasn't subject to close scrutiny.

As the carriage circled through the brightly lit grounds, they passed elegantly attired couples out for an evening stroll. Everywhere was the sound of music. Violinists strolled through the soft night air, pausing here and there to serenade the guests. Atop a huge rose covered mound was a gazebo where a stringed quartet was playing Mozart. From the hotel itself they could hear the lilt of a polka from still another orchestra.

Portia was glad that Daniel hadn't come for them. Arriving alone would make a much more dramatic entrance and the carriage ride gave both of them time to get into their roles more slowly. Never again would either sister have such a stage to play on, nor would they play for stakes quite so high.

The Sweetwater was the proper surroundings for a man like Daniel Logan. Everything about the man and the hotel complemented each other. Portia sighed, wishing the evening was at an end, and that the obligation she'd made had been fulfilled. Tomorrow morning she would start the troupe rehearsing, get the costumes repaired and the sets in order. The supplies they'd been using might be all right for a dark stage, but here everything was so light. It would be very difficult to hide their shabbiness.

"What's he like, Portia?"

"Who?"

"Daniel Logan?"

"He's . . . He's tall, handsome, and very elegant." And he has a smile like the devil, Portia could have added. And his hands are strong and his lips are . . .

"I'm afraid, Portia. I still don't know why you ever agreed to have me act as his fiancee. I'm sure we're going to be found out and disgraced." Fiona opened and snapped closed the lacy stage fan she was holding.

"Nonsense. All I've ever heard from you was that you wanted to be a proper lady and find a husband who wasn't an actor. Here, my other self, is your opportunity. For once in your life, Fiona MacIntosh, you can be that lady and nobody will ever know that you aren't."

"Do you think so? I'm not sure. Suppose I don't know the proper fork to use, or what to order, or . . ."

"Hell's fire and little fishes, I'm sure that I don't know one fork from another either. We'll just watch everybody else and do what they do."

"But I'm not like you, Portia. I'm not very brave. Suppose I make some horrible error?"

"You won't, Fee. Buck up. We'll get each other through this."

"I know what I've always said, Portia, but I'm not a real lady. I'm just a pretend lady. Everything about us is pretend, Portia."

"Nonsense. You don't have to be a real lady, Fee. You're not Juliet when you're on the stage either. But there isn't anyone in the audience who knows that after they've watched you perform. Just underplay your role as the loving fiancee tonight and you'll be perfect."

The carriage was approaching the crest of the drive and the doorway of the massive white wooden structure that rose three stories. An open porch with wooden pillars to support the roof ran around the building and sheltered the great rocking chairs and swings in which the guests could chat by the hour.

"La! Will you look at this place." Fiona's eyes were filled with wonder. "It looks like a birthday cake with a thousand candles all lighting up the sky."

"This is where the rich play, Fiona, where our new owner, Mr. Daniel Logan, has come to find a wife. Papa's pamphlet said there are three hundred rooms, and lounges, with dining halls and a ballroom on the top floor. There's even a bath house on the roof where the guests can take the waters without leaving the hotel. Nothing like it in the world."

Even Portia was impressed with the Sweetwater. For once in his life, Papa hadn't exaggerated. She wished just for a moment that she was more like Fiona, like her mother, that she too could be a great lady. But she wasn't. It had taken Portia a long time to be comfortable with being compared with Fiona, who looked exactly like her on the outside, but who was so very different.

Portia had tried to be sweet and gentle as her mother Kathryn expected her to be. It seemed that all she did was make mistakes after which she'd feel miserable and out of place. Then her mother died and Portia learned that those qualities that had so despaired her mother served her well in filling Kathryn MacIntosh's shoes. The family needed her and that need filled Portia's life and made her complete in return.

The carriage stopped, and the doorman stepped forward to assist Fiona from the carriage. *Just as well*, Portia thought. *The first thing I'm supposed to do as a man and I'm sitting here like some country bumpkin with my mouth hanging open*. Being a lad on the stage was one thing, she decided, but being one in real life tonight might turn out to be an exercise in foolishness. Being her sister's brother was even more bizarre.

And then she looked up at the hotel and she knew it wasn't the role or the play that was giving her the first case of stage fright she'd ever known. It was Daniel Logan who was making her doubt what she was.

Four

"GOOD evening, my dear." Daniel Logan stepped forward to meet Fiona, extending his hand to take her smaller one and lift it to his lips. "You are enchanting."

Portia was glad that Fiona was in front. Daniel Logan quite took her voice away. He was wearing a black cashmere dinner coat buttoned at the waist, sharply creased striped trousers, and a pleated white shirt. A scarlet band of satin wrapped round his waist and hung down his right leg like the costume of some royal figure. His dark hair was parted neatly on one side and his starched white collar made a picture frame for his deep eyes and dark lashes.

As Daniel raised his eyes he caught sight of Portia lagging behind and lifted a puzzled eyebrow at Fiona. "You brought someone with you?"

"Uh, yes. Papa felt it wasn't proper for me to meet you here without a family member along." She lowered her eyes prettily. "I hope you don't mind. This is my brother, my brother . . ."

Portia could see that she'd forgotten the name they'd settled on. "Phillip," she supplied, stepping forward to shake Daniel's hand with false gusto. "Phillip MacIntosh, Fiona's brother. And you're Daniel Logan?"

Daniel continued to shake Portia's hand for a long moment while he looked from Fiona to Portia and back again. "Of course," he finally said with an odd smile. "I'd have known that you were brother and sister anywhere. You're very alike, aren't you?"

"Uh, yes," Portia agreed, glancing around at the beautiful women and men staring openly at them. "I say, Daniel, I believe we're blocking the way here!"

"Yes, and I think by this time the news of the arrival of my fiancee will have been announced to the world. Shall we go in to dinner, my dear? You too, Phillip. I'm sure the maître d' will be able to change my reservation to accommodate three instead of two."

She was too short to be a man. Portia hadn't thought about that until she was standing beside Daniel Logan. He made her feel like a midget at a side show. She was uncomfortable. She wished she'd never seen the man before.

Walking behind Daniel and Fiona into that dining room was the most uncomfortable stage entrance she'd ever made. There was an obvious hush from the guests watching their arrival. Portia had never sought center stage; now every eye in the room was focused on her and Fiona.

Portia tried not to see the way Daniel's coat hugged his broad back, or the trim cut of his trousers over long firm legs that moved with the rhythm of some wild creature in the forest. A leopard. If Bertha the wardrobe mistress were telling fortunes, and she were giving Daniel Logan the soul of an animal as she often did, a leopard would be the animal she'd choose. Portia shook off her obsession with the man and turned to concentrate on the hotel.

"The hotel will accommodate five hundred guests, Fiona," Daniel was saying. "We'll eat in the grand dining room. Not only is the food excellent but the furnishings are the very latest in the world. The crystal, the china, all the best. I understand that the walls are pure cherry wood."

"And the mirrors are lovely," Fiona was saying in a soft awed voice, "I love the way the light is reflected by the mirrors. It looks like there are thousands of stars inside."

"What do you think of the incandescent electric lights, MacIntosh?" Daniel called politely over his shoulder, all the while holding tightly to Fiona's arm with a possessive grip that bothered Portia more than she had anticipated.

"They're spectacular. These are the first I've seen, though I've read about them."

"Just wait until you taste the food, Fiona, my dear, it is spectacular as well. Most of the chefs are from Europe. The hotel has spared no expense to satisfy the taste of its guests. Oh, good evening, Mrs. Aaron." Daniel paused before a robust woman with steel gray hair and a bosom that seemed to defy the laws of gravity. "I'd like you to meet my fiancee, Miss Fiona MacIntosh, and her brother . . . Phillip."

"Why, Mr. Logan, I had no idea that you were affianced. Miss MacIntosh, you'll make yourself the enemy of half the population of Atlanta by running off with Daniel here."

"Very good," Daniel imparted to Fiona as they passed into the dining room. "By the morning every woman in the hotel will know that I'm out of the running. Thank you my dear. And you too . . . Phillip."

Portia heard snatches of conversation trail off as they passed through the dining room to their table.

"My word, who is the beauty with Daniel?"

"Hello Logan. Nice to see you back."

Daniel was charming. He greeted everybody along their route, carefully holding Fiona's elbow, but not slowing to identify her. By the time they reached their table he'd piqued the interest of everyone, just as he'd intended.

While he didn't make his attention obvious, Portia felt Daniel's eyes on her and there was something in his smile that made her decidedly uncomfortable. Of course, she couldn't blame him for his displeasure in her presence. After all, he hadn't expected to have to entertain a brother.

In the background a string quartet softly played a Strauss waltz. Uniformed waiters and wine stewards scurried about like sleek green ants hurrying to bring food back to the queen. Taffeta rustled, sweet scents of flowers wafted through the air and everywhere there were people moving about. Daniel could barely read his menu for the interruptions of other guests anxious to be introduced.

"By the way, Phillip, how is Captain MacIntosh this evening? I trust he got over his little indisposition?"

"Oh, yes. He's fine now," Portia said stiffly.

The wine steward opened a bottle and poured a small amount into a stemmed glass for Daniel's approval. When he'd tasted and nodded his acceptance, their glasses were then filled.

"Thank you for the lovely gown," Fiona said as she sipped the sparkling liquid. "But I can't imagine how you knew my size."

Portia nearly choked. She didn't have to pretend the coughing attack to divert Daniel's attention from Fiona's innocent question. If there was one thing Daniel Logan did know it was the size of the MacIntosh twins. He'd had first hand experience in their measurements.

Daniel only smiled at Fiona and said he was pleased that the dress fit so beautifully.

They dined on raw oysters, broiled fish, roast turkey and boiled potatoes. They ate baked squash, celery salad, and Neapolitan cake for dessert. Imported coffees and mints followed the meal that Portia thought would never end.

Daniel's polite inquiries to Fiona were met with soft, hesitant replies. Fiona was caught up in the glamour and beauty of the guests around her, just as Portia had known she would be, and the fear of Daniel's attention was quickly forgotten in the excitement of the evening.

Fiona was at home in these surroundings and Portia knew that in spite of her reservations about accompanying Daniel, Fiona was having the time of her life. And Portia realized as never before that her sister belonged in such a setting with a man like Daniel Logan. The knowledge filled Portia with a kind of bittersweet pain.

There was a sudden silence and Portia looked up. Had she missed something in her growing discomfort?

"Phillip, Mr. Logan asked if we'd seen the Barnum and Bailey circus perform?"

"Eh, no. Not yet, though we've followed it in several cities." Her voice broke. She couldn't have managed to sound like a young gentleman so realistically had she not been so nervous.

"I understand they're appearing in Europe now. They were in London in the fall. Are you older or younger than your sister?" Daniel inquired of Phillip.

"Older . . ." Portia began.

"The same . . ." Fiona said with swallowed embarrassment.

"What she means," Portia tried to explain, "is that we're twins and I'm older by a matter of minutes."

"Of course. That explains your very close physical size and resemblance." Daniel pulled out a cigar.

"Yes," Fiona said with a glare at Portia. "We are very much alike. Though Phillip is inclined toward bossiness at times."

"Oh? The privilege of an older brother, I believe. Care for a cigar, Phillip? They're Havana's finest. The hotel has them imported directly."

Portia looked at the cigar and gulped. The thing must have been ten inches long and an inch around. She started to refuse, then looked at the quirk of his lips and the quiet amusement in her host's eyes and changed her mind.

"Thanks, Daniel. Nothing like a good cigar to finish off a fine meal."

She watched as he bit off the tip and twirled the end around in his mouth before striking a match to it and drawing deeply. Copying his actions, she leaned forward to allow him to light hers.

For one second she was certain that she was going to choke to death. For another second she tried to hold back the spasm that racked her throat and chest. She was about to be exposed. Daniel would be humiliated and they'd never get their troupe back. Portia tightened her throat muscles and bent over the table, releasing the smoke in a spasm of coughing.

Daniel Logan leaned forward and asked, "Are you all right, Phillip?" His face seemed innocently troubled, though his eyes were filled with unconcealed mirth.

"I'm fine," she managed, holding on to her wig as she sat up. "Just a tickle in my throat. It must be all this perfume in the air."

"Do have some mineral water," Daniel offered, filling her water glass from a decanter on their table.

"Thank you." Portia took a long swallow of water, frowning and crinkling her lips in displeasure as she drank. "Awwk! That tastes terrible." The water was as bad as the cigar.

"It's lithium water, from the springs. They put a pitcher on every table. It aids in the digestion. It also helps with smoker's cough, I understand. I even put a few drops on a wound I acquired on my hand—worked wonders."

Wound? Portia wouldn't allow herself to look at the man. His comment was normal conversation, nothing more. *Please*, she prayed, *let Fiona pass it off without comment*. "A body would get well in self defense, I imagine," Portia added hastily, taking another deep breath. "I'm sorry about the coughing attack. I'm not used to cigars. Normally I . . . I—chew."

"Oh? But your teeth are so white, so . . . sanitary. I wouldn't have taken you for a chewing . . . man. Would you like me to ask the waiter to bring chewing tobacco?"

Fiona gasped. Portia shook her head. "No, I don't chew in public places, Daniel, but thanks."

"Well, if you're ready to leave, my dear?" Daniel signaled to the waiter, signed his name to the check and waited for Fiona's signal that she too was ready to leave.

"Yes, thank you Mr. Logan. The meal was wonderful." Fiona dropped her eyes shyly. "I thank you for bringing us."

"Nonsense; the pleasure, I assure you, was all mine. Seeing your lovely teeth chewing so daintily on the turkey rather than my hand was ever so much nicer."

Fiona raised her eyes, obvious puzzlement reflected in her glance. Portia groaned. Fiona was a very talented actress but she wasn't quick enough to understand Daniel's teasing with all this talk about teeth.

"Mr. Logan," Portia interrupted hastily, "where do you live when you're not traveling about in your private train car?"

"Live? I have no permanent residence at the moment. I maintain suites in both my hotel in New York and in Virginia City. And I plan to look over some property in Atlanta. Since Mr. Sherman's little bonfire, it has really begun to grow. One day it will be the center of the south and anybody who gets in on the real estate market will prosper. I intend to invest in commerce, land and a hotel or two."

"That sounds very sensible," Fiona observed.

"Sounds dull to me," Portia quipped. "I mean where's the adventure in that?"

"So you like being challenged, do you, Phillip?"

"What Phillip means," Fiona added sharply, "is that he doesn't like staying in one place. My twin—brother prefers traveling."

Daniel glanced across the table at the slight young man and nodded. At least one accurate statement had been made tonight: The two of them were twins. Fiona was absolutely lovely, and Daniel was pleasantly surprised. She was a perfect choice for a fiancee, better than he could have imagined. Sweet, gentle, without the kind of pushy sophistication that he'd grown accustomed to. Fiona would most definitely make some man a fine wife. Some other man.

It was the peculiarly feminine brother sitting beside her that occupied Daniel's attention. He hadn't confirmed his hunch just yet, but he was almost certain that the young man pretending now to be Phillip was in fact the same little wildcat who had come to his railcar ready to do battle for the return of the acting troupe. To learn that there were actually two of these exquisite creatures was beyond his wildest imaginings. Why had *Phillip* given him her sister's name when he'd asked? And what was even more intriguing was—what was Phillip's real name.

Daniel was fascinated, captivated, and totally aware of the feminine body beneath those masculine clothes. After all, he'd held the woman close last night, and she'd been wearing boy's clothing then, too. The only difference was that last night one single strand of strawberry blonde hair had been hanging down beside her delicate pink earlobe. Tonight that hair was stuffed up beneath an odd looking brown wig. Interesting, very interesting. Daniel had planned to take his fiancee to dinner, introduce her around and send her back to the Chautauqua grounds. But suddenly he didn't want the evening to end.

Daniel Logan looked at his hand, flexing it with exaggerated stiffness. The ploy to find himself a wife was a smart move and an intriguing idea. There was really no reason why he shouldn't have a bit of fun along the way. He flexed his hand again and glanced across the table in time to watch Phillip avert his eyes. Oh, yes. The evening had been exciting, and his companions were more stimulating than any of the guests of the resort. He would keep up the charade for the moment and see where it led.

Portia stood. She'd had about as much tension as she could take. Never before had any man shaken her confidence as much as Daniel Logan. The suggestion of a headache played across her forehead and she knew that they were taking a risk in extending the evening.

"Thank you for a lovely evening, Daniel. But my sister and I have had a long journey and we still haven't recovered from the trip. I think we'd better get back to the troupe before one of these other ladies attacks Fiona and scratches her eyes out. Coming, Fiona?"

"Oh, must we Po—Phillip?" Fiona's reluctance was genuine.

"Oh, please. Not yet, my dear." Daniel rose and offered his hand to Fiona. "The evening has only just begun. From here, we could choose the ballroom on the top floor of the Sweetwater, or we can attend the nightly dancing and fireworks at the Pavilion. Of course, Phillip, if you're really tired, we'll excuse you."

"Not tonight, Daniel," Portia hastened to intervene. "I really must insist, Fiona, that we retire."

"No. If you don't wish to accompany us, Phillip," Fiona said with her best stage lady dismissal voice, "we'll just excuse you. After all, a bargain is a bargain, isn't it, Mr. Logan? I believe I'd like to see the Pavilion." She rose and gave him a gracious smile. "Ready?" Fiona took Daniel's arm, swept around her chair, and down the aisle with a flourish.

Well, Fiona was asserting herself for once. Portia, as angry as she was, had to admire her sister's rare show of authority. All right, if Fiona was enjoying herself, she'd let her have her night. Every man in the place had his eyes glued on Fiona as she walked out of the dining hall with all the grace and beauty of the world's best actress leaving her lover on stage. At any moment Portia expected the thunder of applause.

But Portia wasn't sure what it was that she was feeling as she brought up the rear: calm anger that Fiona wasn't following her instructions, concern that she was losing control of a potentially dangerous situation, even a bit of jealousy perhaps.

The last thing in the world Portia wanted was to be one of these women, dressed up like some member of royalty, forced to smile and be gawked at as Fiona had been for the last hour.

Perhaps she was just worried about Fiona. Portia didn't want this evening to make Fiona more dissatisfied with their simple life than she'd been before. But seeing how naturally she fit into such a setting, Portia knew that Fiona belonged here in a way she herself never could.

What would Daniel Logan do now? Even if he discovered their little ruse, what could he do about it? He'd wanted a fiancee and she'd given him one, a proper one who could play the role as it should be played.

Why then did she get the feeling that he was improvising a new direction for this play? Had she opened a Pandora's box that was drawing them into uncharted territory? Portia shivered. The warm summer breeze was cool against the cheek that she rubbed absently. Every muscle in her face ached from smiling.

Acting on the stage was one thing, but acting a role in real life was very different. She didn't know her lines here and she was in constant fear that she was the one who was about to make a mistake. She could only hope that she could bring this evening to a close as quickly as possible.

Just ahead, down the wide expanse of graveled pathway, Daniel had taken Fiona's arm gracefully in his. He was pointing out first one attraction then another. If Fiona was ill at ease Portia could see no signs of it. In fact, her sister seemed to be blooming under Daniel's attention. God, what if Fiona took all this seriously? *She mustn't fall in love with Daniel.* That would be disaster.

Fiona could never control a man like Daniel, with fire in his blood, and such gentleness in his kiss. Not Fiona. It would take a more experienced woman to handle Daniel Logan, someone with even greater fire and a great deal of control. Portia sighed and hurried her step. Not being close enough to hear their conversation was worse than hearing.

Where on Earth was Daniel Logan taking them now?

As they walked around the edge of the sparkling water, Portia could smell the scent of early flowering roses. In the distance she could see the Pavilion, sparkling with lights and literally packed with people. Everywhere vendors hawked their wares while people milled around the lake and walked about the paths through the gardens, pausing to sit in the swings and on the benches by the water. The sound of laughter and low conversations filled the soft night air. The evening was magic, the kind of magic that neither Fiona nor Portia had ever experienced.

The Pavilion was a white lacy structure built over the lake. The dancers were moving gracefully across the floor like some fantasy shadow players in a daydream.

"Would you care to dance?" Daniel inclined his head and waited for Fiona to reply.

"Yes, thank you. I'd love to." Fiona bowed slightly and stepped out onto the floor, completely enchanted by the music and the night.

Daniel turned back to Portia. "Find yourself a lady, Phillip, and join the fun."

"No thanks," Portia managed, "I'll just watch the two of you."

"Whatever you say," Daniel said with a rakish glance, swirling Fiona away in a rustle of silk and satin. "But you're missing all the fun . . . boy."

"Hell fire!" Portia said under her breath. Of course he would expect her to dance. To Daniel Logan she was a man—no, not a man, a youth who couldn't even smoke a cigar without making a fool of himself. Fiona had been right. This evening was turning into a disaster but Portia was the one who was uncomfortable and out of place. She started back toward the white lacy framework that made up the walls of the structure. If she could just get into the shadows she'd wait until the end of this dance and insist that they return to the dormitory.

Propping herself against the rail Portia searched the crowd until she found Daniel and Fiona gliding through the other dancers like graceful music box figures. When the waltz came to an end they made their way back to the spot where Portia was waiting.

Just as they reached her, they were intercepted by a woman wearing more jewels than Portia had ever seen. And she doubted these jewels were made of stage paste or colored glass. She was wearing a rose colored dress covered with yards of black lace, the hem of which had been caught up and attached by a band to her wrist. Behind the sparkling woman was a tall, thin serious young man with the gentle, beautiful face of a museum sculpture of a young Greek philosopher.

"Daniel, I heard about your engagement," the woman said with a warm smile. "Is this the young lady?"

"Lady Evelyna," Daniel greeted her, and took the hand offered. He touched his lips to her fingertips and planted another light kiss on her cheeks. "Of course. I'd like you to meet Fiona MacIntosh, my fiancee. Fiona, this is Lady Evelyna Delecort, the Countess of Hidemarch."

"How lovely you are," Lady Delecort exclaimed. "And this is my son, Edward."

Daniel led Fiona forward, waiting for her to acknowledge Lady Evelyna's compliment. But Portia quickly realized that Fiona hadn't heard a word that either Lady Delecort or Daniel had said. She was staring openly and breathlessly at Edward, who was staring just as intently at Fiona in return.

Portia felt her heart do a somersault. Fiona had forgotten where she was and what role she'd been assigned. Daniel was glancing in chagrin at Lady Delecort, who was frowning at Edward, whose eyes were locked on the bemused Fiona with unmistakable ardor. Portia decided that she had to do something, quick. Incurring Daniel's displeasure could carry a consequence she didn't want to contemplate.

"And I'm Po . . . Phillip MacIntosh, Fiona's brother, Lady Delecort. We're so pleased to meet you." Portia came quickly forward behind Fiona, giving her sister a quick sharp kick to the ankle and a nudge with her elbow, as she followed Daniel's example and planted a kiss on the Countess's still outstretched hand. "Aren't we, Fiona?"

But Fiona was caught up in the unwavering gaze of the young man who was asking her to dance. Portia could see their livelihood dissolving in the warm glow of interest reflected in Fiona's eyes as she moved out onto the floor and into the circle of Edward Delecort's arms. She could sense Daniel, tense and glowering beside her.

It was obvious that Fiona had forgotten about Daniel. Fiona and Edward glided across the dance floor as though they'd been made to fit together. They dipped and whirled to the music on a cloud of enchantment. For once in her life Portia was completely flabbergasted. She looked helplessly at Daniel and Lady Delecort, the other two players in the drama who were eyeing the dancers with the same dumbfounded air.

"Well," Lady Evelyna finally managed. "I am sorry for the bad manners of my son, Mr. Logan. He's never . . . I mean, I assure you he didn't mean to be rude by . . ."

"Quite all right, Lady Delecort. I'm fully aware of the beauty of my fiancee. Few men can resist her. Edward isn't the first one to be charmed by a MacIntosh. The entire family is rather interesting." Daniel glanced at Portia with barely concealed anger. "They are not always what they seem. Though I'll admit, this is an unexpected train of events."

"Yes," the English dowager agreed. "Edward hasn't had much experience with women, I'm afraid. He's always been a dreamer, a tinkerer, interested in mechanical things utterly beneath his station."

"Oh, how exciting," Portia said, feigning interest in the Countess's son, anything to keep some semblance of conversation going that would divert attention away from Fiona's defection. "What brings you to the Sweetwater?"

"I am an American by birth. I wanted Edward to see something of my own country before he takes over his birthright. The voyage over put him a bit under the weather so we came here to take the waters, although I've had a time getting him to the Springs. He's quite taken with the new incandescent lights and the hotel's communication system. Can you imagine—he wants to rush back to England and introduce the telephone system there?"

"How interesting. I'm going to look into the new process

of illumination myself," Portia agreed with growing desperation. "Don't you find the system unique, Logan?" Portia
felt as if she were on stage with a cast of actors who'd
forgotten their lines.

"Oh, indeed," Logan said, staring at Portia with a strange
expression of half amusement and half controlled anger.

"Indeed," Portia echoed quickly, trying to remember to
keep her voice pitched low. "Maybe Edward ought not to
be dancing if he isn't well. He ought not to take a chance on
overdoing." Portia realized that she had to step in and bring
the obvious attraction between Fiona and Edward to an immediate end. "I'll just cut in on them, Logan, and bring my
sister back. It's time we retired as well."

"Oh? By all means, Phillip. Cut in."

Daniel's surprise at Portia's quick recovery from the awkward situation was second only to his surprise at watching
her firm intervention between Fiona and Edward. Portia
tapped Edward on the shoulder. "I'd like to cut in, sir."

Edward ignored Portia's request.

"Lord Delecort," Portia spoke firmly, as she stepped between the two dancers. "I would like a word with my sister."

"Portia, go away!" Fiona cried, trying to jerk out of her
sister's grip. "You're making a spectacle out of both of us
in front of Edward."

"Shut up, Fee. Dance!" Portia awkwardly turned Fiona
away, concealing them in the flurry of dancers.

"Portia MacIntosh, let go of me, or I'm going to scream."

"Scream? And you're worried about me making a spectacle
of us? Fiona, I swear if you don't stop playing the fool this
minute I'm going to slap your face and really give you a
reason to scream. What do you mean by ruining our chances
to reclaim the company from Daniel Logan? Do you realize
how furious he is? What were you doing, dancing off, moon-
faced and pie-eyed over another man?"

"I . . . I . . . oh my goodness, Portia—what did I do? I
didn't think."

"You may have cost us the troupe, Fiona. Why on earth are you acting like some lovesick dolly over Edward Delecort?"

"Oh, Portia." Fiona's voice quivered with a mixture of pain and fear. "Portia, I never knew. I never thought that it would happen. But I think I've fallen in love."

Five

DANIEL signaled for a carriage and assisted a silent Fiona and a worried Portia into the open conveyance.

"The Chautauqua dormitory," he instructed the driver, climbed inside and sat across from the sisters.

Portia waited with growing dread. He had every right to be furious. Fiona was to have played the role of his fiancee and she'd embarrassed and disgraced him, the man who held their fate in his hands.

"Mr. Logan," Portia began desperately, "I mean Daniel. I just want you to know that I'm ashamed of Fiona's behavior tonight. I know she embarrassed you in front of your friends and I assure you, it won't happen again."

"I am truly sorry," Fiona said softly.

Daniel continued to stare, not at Fiona who was sniffling into her handkerchief, but at Portia whose tight expression said better than words that she wanted to vault over the side of the carriage and disappear into the night.

"Fiona didn't embarrass me," Daniel finally offered. "She couldn't have known what to expect. This whole charade was unfair. There are times when fate intervenes and forces one to change direction. I of all people ought to know that."

Portia fingered her wig. The way he was staring at her made her wonder if her hair was slipping from its hiding place. Her starched man's collar was digging into her chin and she felt a headache rumbling behind her right eye.

"I don't know what you mean, Daniel. A person should always be in control of his actions, always."

"Mr. Logan." Fiona's soft voice was almost a sob as she spoke. "I do apologize. I don't know what got into me. I've never acted like that before. If I caused you any embarrassment, I'm sorry. I tried to tell Po . . . Phillip that this evening was a mistake, but nobody would listen to me."

"Fiona, dear." Daniel took her hand and brought it to his lips. "You were exactly what I needed to give those old battle-axes the message to leave me alone. What happened at the Pavilion was—is—forgotten."

"Then you're not going to . . . to punish the troupe?" Fiona's distress was genuine. Both she and Portia knew that Daniel had every right to do whatever he wanted to.

"No, Fiona," he said softly. "I'm not going to punish anybody. We'll have dinner tomorrow evening, just like we did tonight. That ought to set any wagging tongues to rest."

He wasn't angry anymore. Portia let out a sigh of relief and waited for Fiona to agree. After an embarrassing silence Portia decided that she was waiting in vain, and answered for Fiona. "Of course she will, Daniel, won't you, Fiona?"

But they were both saved from Fiona's answer.

As the carriage pulled up before the dormitory Rowdy and Bertha, the wardrobe mistress came running out. "Fiona, P—Phillip, come quick. It's the Captain. He's been taken ill. The doctor is with him now."

This time Portia did vault over the side of the carriage, taking the steps to the Captain's room two at a time. A huge barrel-chested man with black sideburns and a bushy mustache was backing out of the room and closing the door.

"Doctor? Captain MacIntosh is my father. What's wrong?"

The doctor took in Portia's attire and shook his head in confusion. "I need to speak with Portia. Where is she?"

Portia looked around. Several members of the Chautauqua staff were gathered at the end of the hall. Daniel and Fiona had reached the top of the steps behind. Had he heard their exchange? No matter. It was too late to worry about revealing the truth now. "I'm Portia, Doctor," she agreed urgently. "Please, tell me what's wrong?"

"Captain MacIntosh had an attack with his stomach. He was taken quite severely with pain, and vomiting blood. I've given him a relaxing draft of medication and he's resting quietly now."

"Blood?" Fiona repeated in alarm. "Will he be all right?"

"Yes, for the moment. Your father has lived rather an excessive life," the doctor said gravely. "Too many hard spirits, too much food, and too little care. I suspect that he may have a bleeding stomach ulcer. Besides the stomach problem he has a minor heart condition which he apparently has had for some time. The pain frightened him. We know that stress and worry affect a heart condition. So we have to deal with problems that aggravate each other."

"Can you treat him, Doctor?" Portia inquired with a tremor of fear in her voice. He couldn't die. She'd had to take care of her father; she'd promised her mother that she'd look after the Captain. Now . . .

"Treat him? Yes. Fortunately, he's in the best place he could be to have his condition treated. He needs rest and complete relaxation. I've prescribed a special diet beginning tomorrow morning, and a program whereby he will both drink and bathe in the lithium waters."

"But I don't understand," Fiona said tearfully. "How will taking baths in mineral water and drinking it help Papa?"

"The mineral water has the highest percentage of lithium of any natural source in the world. The lithium calms the stomach and allows nature to repair itself."

"Are you certain, Doctor?"

"I'm sure, young, eh . . . lady. When this part of the state was first settled, Chief Amakanasta and the Cherokees believed the Great Spirit of the Springs healed their ills."

The doctor pulled his pocket watch from his vest and took a quick look at the time before he continued. "Physicians soon realized the medicinal properties of the water and in no time it was prescribed all over the world. Three years ago we were honored to hold an International Congress of Physicians right here at the Springs."

"That's very good news, Doctor . . . ?" Daniel Logan stepped forward.

The doctor returned his watch to its pocket and held out his hand. "Garrett, Christopher Columbus Garrett, sir. I'm the resident physician here at the Springs. And you are?"

"Daniel Logan, I'm Miss Fiona MacIntosh's fiance. "We'll see that her father isn't subjected to any further stress and that he follows your instructions."

"Logan, yes. Captain MacIntosh insisted on speaking with you as soon as you arrived. I think he'll rest rather easier if you'll go on in and get it over with."

"No!" Portia said sharply. "I should speak with my father first. I am responsible for his care."

Daniel raised an eyebrow, hesitated a moment, then simply brushed past Dr. Garrett and Portia, closing the door behind him. When Portia heard the click of the lock she was furious. How dare he take over and make decisions that weren't his to make? She'd looked after her father for too long to allow some dark-eyed stranger to barge in and assume responsibility for them.

Dealing with scrapes with the law, impatient creditors and occasional women friends of her father who had believed his tall tales had become second nature to Portia. But this was different; this was her father's health and she didn't know what to do.

"No stress, ladies, remember," Dr. Garrett was saying, shaking his head in perplexity as he looked from Portia to Fiona and back again. "I'll have to be getting back to the hotel. See that your father starts on the spring water first thing in the morning.'' He tipped his bowler hat, picked up his black medical bag from the floor and started down the hallway.

"Yes, Doctor," Portia called out. "Please have your bill prepared and I'll take care of it." She didn't add *somehow*, for she hadn't any idea how she could come up with his fee, no matter what it was.

The doctor stopped. "Don't worry, Portia is it? Your father explained that Mr. Logan is in charge and that the bill should be sent to him. You're fortunate to have someone to step in and take care of your group until your father is better."

"Logan! I don't think you quite understand, Doctor Garrett, *I* look after this family. Mr. Logan may technically own the *troupe* but *this family* doesn't belong to him."

Fiona stepped forward and laid a restraining hand on Portia's arm. "We're sorry, Dr. Garrett. We don't mean to be ungrateful, but you understand that this is such a shock. Thank you for coming out at this hour."

Doctor Garrett nodded his head. "You're very welcome, my dears." He frowned once more at Portia and walked away.

Portia shook off Fiona's hand, pulled off her cap and slapped it against her thigh as she considered what she should do. The first thing she had to know was how Dr. Garrett was called in. "Rowdy, what happened?" Portia cornered the actor-roustabout and waited for his answer.

Rowdy scratched his shock of carrot red hair and cleared his throat. "Well, the Captain, he found a bottle of brandy —somewhere—and we were just having a little game of poker when he began to have stomach pain. We thought he was just putting on like he does when he's losing, but when he keeled over we knew it was serious. Lawson Paine and I brought him to his bed and one of them Sunday School teachers called the doctor."

"Didn't it occur to you two that he'd already had a shock last night. He's an old man and—"

"I'm sorry, Portia. We didn't know he wasn't well—I

mean he's always . . ." Rowdy's voice trailed off in obvious embarrassment.

Portia knew she was being sharp with the man because she was worried. What was Daniel Logan doing in there with her father?

"Portia, what will we do if something happens to Papa?" Fiona's voice was stricken with pain. She stood like a porcelain statue in the light of the moon shining through the window by the men's dormitory door, her face pale with worry.

"Stop talking like that, Fiona. Papa is going to be fine. You go and find the person who called the doctor and thank him properly. Then go on to bed. I'll wait here for Daniel Logan to come out and then I'll see to Papa myself."

Portia watched as Bertha led Fiona away, leaving only Rowdy behind. Portia considered knocking on the door and insisting on seeing her father. But she couldn't do that. She couldn't talk to him about what was happening. He was a sick man. Her father had a heart condition and an ulcer that she hadn't even known about.

Beyond the door Horatio MacIntosh lay, his eyes closed, thinking. The attack he'd had leaving Daniel Logan's railcar had been bad, but he'd passed it off as too much excitement. Tonight, when he'd felt his insides twist with pain he'd known that this was real. His mortality flashed before him and he knew that he had to make plans to take care of Portia and Fiona. Portia meant well. She'd been able to take care of the troupe up to now. But she didn't have the means to supply their needs and Daniel Logan did.

Horatio had heard the door open and close and he knew that Daniel Logan had to be the person waiting in the dim light.

"Captain MacIntosh, you wanted to see me?"

It was Logan. The doctor had followed his instructions. "Thank you for coming," Horatio said slowly, formulating his plan as he spoke. "Tell me, Mr. Logan, did you enjoy the evening?"

"Yes, the evening was most—unusual. But what's this all about?"

"I seem to have taken a turn I didn't count on. That's what I want to discuss with you. I hadn't intended to bring you further into my little family and our problems, Logan, but I think that I'd like some answers from you."

"Of course, Captain. What do you wish to know?" Daniel dragged a chair up to the bed and sat down. The old gentleman was speaking slowly and with great effort. The attack had apparently been bad enough to put the fear of God into him.

"I thought I was dying tonight, Logan, and I became very afraid for my girls. You now own my troupe and I think that I trust you. What I want is—what I'd like you to do is— take care of Fiona and Portia if something happens to me."

"Ah . . . Portia. So that's her name. Portia, that's a damn sight better name than Phillip. I thought I heard your man call her by that name when we arrived back here tonight."

"So? You already knew?" Horatio smiled. He'd have liked to have been there to see how Portia had given herself away. She'd be furious to find out she'd failed to fool him.

"Oh yes, I knew immediately. Fiona is a lovely young woman. But she wasn't the woman in my railcar. She hasn't the spunk to sock me in the nose."

"Is Portia aware that you know about our little ruse?"

"No, not yet. She was working so hard to keep her identity hidden that it seemed a shame to tell her. I think I'll just let her go on being Phillip until she decides to end her masquerade."

Horatio caught the amusement in Daniel's voice and chuckled under his breath, catching his stomach in exaggerated pain. He'd been right. There was something brewing between Daniel Logan and Portia. Neither might know it yet, but it was there. Maybe Daniel Logan was the answer to their problems in more ways than one.

"Will you look after the troupe and the girls until I get myself together again? I know the company belongs to you, but I'd like to think that you appreciate what you have."

"I think I do, Captain MacIntosh. You don't worry about a thing." He stood. "And don't let *Phillip* know that I'm on to her . . . him. Letting Portia pretend to be her own brother will keep her confused enough so that I can assume the responsibility for your troupe without having to argue with her every step of the way."

"I don't know about that, Daniel. Portia would argue with a fence post if she thought she was right. I don't think being Phillip will stop her."

"I don't doubt that for a moment, but at least it will give her something to think about other than feeling that I've usurped her rightful place. Besides, it will be great fun to see how far this little charade will go. Good night, Captain MacIntosh. Sleep well."

Horatio closed his eyes. Logan was the right choice. Something about the man reminded Horatio of himself a long time ago. Yes, heading for the Sweetwater had been a capital idea. He should have thought of it sooner.

Outside Horatio's door Portia paced back and forth. Whether she wanted to or not, she'd have to go along with Daniel Logan. Her father needed treatment and that treatment depended on Daniel Logan. Portia had no choice but to wait patiently.

Getting the troupe back was no longer the most important fact. Her great plan to win Daniel over by having Fiona pretend to be his fiancee might already be blown. And Rowdy had called her Portia when she ran up the stairs.

If Daniel Logan heard and remembered the slip, she'd have to tell him the truth. She hadn't wanted to pretend to be Phillip MacIntosh in the first place. They'd fulfilled Daniel's request for a pretend fiancee already, even if the evening had ended badly. He couldn't argue with that, could he?

He could, she decided. He could do just about anything

he wanted. Portia couldn't see an answer. She only knew that she was responsible for keeping in Daniel's good graces. Where it had been simply caring for the troupe in the beginning, now the Captain's life might depend on it.

The door opened and Daniel appeared.

"He's sleeping now. Come walk with me, Phillip. We have decisions to make."

Portia glanced inside the room and saw her father lying quietly on the bed. She saw the covers rise and fall and, satisfied that he was resting, reluctantly allowed herself to be led away.

"Rowdy, stay with him," she called over her shoulder as she followed Daniel Logan back outside and into the night. It was just as well to have the coming ordeal over with so that she could get out of wig and get back to being Portia MacIntosh.

The tall Moorish columns that stood at either end of the Chautauqua structure looked suddenly ghostly as the tree limbs moved back and forth, casting spidery shadows across the walls.

"Mr. Logan, I think it's time we were honest with each other," Portia began.

"My feelings exactly. Your father is worried about you and your sister. He wants me to take personal charge of you along with the troupe. That's what I'd like to discuss with you."

"Take personal charge of us?" Portia was dumbfounded. Her father was handing their care over to this dominating yet oddly gentle stranger. "I don't think so, Mr. Logan. I've always looked after us and I'll keep doing so. I thank you for your concern, but we'll manage on our own."

"And I'm sure you can—Phillip," Daniel agreed, watching her gravely, taking in the proud tilt of her head and the tremble of lips pressed tightly together. "But maybe, for the sake of your father, you'll allow me to help. I promised the Captain."

"But . . . I don't understand why he would turn to you— a stranger." Portia was torn between relief that he apparently hadn't heard her called by her real name, and consternation at the unexpected turn of events.

"Nevertheless he did. For now, I think we will have to abide by his wishes. Won't we?"

The man was right. She couldn't make a scene, no matter how much she wanted to claim her rightful identity and bring this charade to an end. Her father had devised the plan to make her Fiona's brother, Phillip, and until the Captain was well enough to face Daniel's possible anger at their deception, she'd be forced to continue.

Daniel watched the changes of expression on the girl's face. He fought a sudden urge to clasp the slight figure in his arms. She was strung to the breaking point, and he was afraid that the wrong move on his part might be just enough to push her over the edge. She was concerned about her father. He didn't need to add to her woes by a confrontation. He'd wait until tomorrow to discuss anything more.

"All right then, Phillip. I'll say good night now. We'll talk tomorrow."

"Good night," Portia answered in a low tight voice. "I expect that when the Captain feels better he will think differently about asking you to give up any of your time to take care of us. Now, if you'll excuse me, I need to get back. Tomorrow I have to see about putting together the necessary sets and props for our first production."

"Yes, you do that. Check out your supplies and report to me in the morning about ten. I think we'll set a conference daily for that same time."

"Report to you? Why? You wanted a fiancee in exchange for returning our troupe. Fiona gave a magnificent performance just as you'd requested. I see no need to carry this further." Portia turned and walked away.

"Just a minute, Phillip." Daniel strode after Portia and caught her by the shoulder, turning her back to face him. "I understand how this must make you feel, but I'm only following your father's wishes."

Portia stared at Daniel silently. Her eyes were wary and her mouth was trembling in exhaustion. Horatio had given them over to Daniel. She couldn't believe her father's action yet she couldn't defy him.

Daniel felt her confusion. He had won the contest of wills, but at what price? She was proud, too proud, just as he had been when Belle had found him standing rebelliously inside her ladies' tent. He'd gone there to steal food and find a warm place to sleep. Belle listened to him as he extolled his talents as a potential bouncer and protector of women. She hadn't laughed at his bravado. Instead she'd nodded and hired him on the spot. Now he was in the same position as Belle. Could he be as kind?

"P . . . Phillip," Daniel began, "your father is ill and he is concerned for you and your sister. He wants me to take care of you and for the moment that's what I intend to do. I apologize if it seems that you're being tossed aside. I assure you that I know how important you are to the troupe. But I gave your father my word and I intend to honor it. Let's not fight any more tonight. When your father gets better, we'll talk about what he wants to do."

Daniel started back toward the dormitory, paused and waited for Portia to walk with him. "Your father trusts me. Won't you trust me, too?"

He raised his arm and Portia thought for a moment that he was about to touch her. Then he held out his hand to shake hers in what was obviously meant as a truce.

Daniel's hand was warm and gentle. He held hers for a long moment without speaking, then turned and walked away. "In the morning at ten, Phillip," he called over his shoulder. "We'll make a list of the new supplies you'll need. Can't have my troupe looking shabby before the gentry, can I?"

"I—I—*my* troupe." Portia muttered all the way upstairs to the women's dormitory. She marched into the room and slammed the door behind her. "Can you imagine? He called it *his* troupe."

"Who?" Fiona, already in her night clothes, was sitting on the edge of her cot while Bertha brushed her hair. "What are you mumbling about, Portia. Is Papa all right?"

"He's sleeping. It's Daniel Logan. Can you imagine? He's commanded that I report to him in the morning with a list of all the supplies we need. He doesn't want *his* troupe to look shabby in front of his fine friends."

"Oh? Do you mean we'll have new costumes and sets?" Fiona rose and danced about the long narrow dormitory room. "Oh, Bertha. We're going to have new costumes and sets. Isn't it wonderful?"

"Is it true?" The other women members of the cast sharing the dormitory room left their cots, and came eagerly forward to share in the good news.

"Portia, how did you manage it?"

"Stop getting so excited. I don't intend to let Mr. Logan make our decisions," Portia said sharply. "Daniel Logan does not own this troupe, no matter what he thinks, and he is not going to supply us with anything!"

Portia tore off her wig and flung the offending thing into the open trunk at the foot of her bed. She peeled the maroon morning coat off and slung it on the bed. She didn't know why she was having such trouble accepting Daniel's help. He had offered it sincerely. The troupe needed new costumes and the show needed new sets. It wasn't the help that was bothering her, it was—the man.

"But Portia," Fiona asked in dismay, "why would you turn down such a generous offer? Did you think of what it means to the troupe? Lawson Paine might even stop threatening to quit."

"She's right, Portia," Bertha agreed. "Lawson is getting restless. He's the only lead actor we have. The Captain's too old and Portia's too young. This resort and new costumes and sets might keep Mr. Paine happy. Besides," Bertha agreed, "the Captain wouldn't have made the arrangements with Mr. Logan if he hadn't thought it best."

Portia looked around at the disappointed faces. Fiona was

right. Whatever she did must be what was best for the troupe, not what she wanted personally. What she wanted personally was to forget she'd ever laid eyes on Daniel Logan, forget the smell and touch of the man, forget the way his mustache covered that little half smile that made her want to draw back and slap his face. Most of all she wanted to go back to her nice safe world where she knew the boundaries and was still in charge of her fate.

Long after the others were in bed, Portia stood looking out at the empty gardens and moonlit courtyards. In the distance she could see the Sweetwater Hotel sitting above them in the moonlight like a jeweled crown. It was still lit up as bright as day and the silence was eerie and artificial.

In the end she realized that she had no choice but to go along with Daniel. He controlled her whether she wanted to admit it or not. Portia felt a cold sense of dread ripple through her. What was going to happen to them? Papa wasn't getting any younger. Now, he might die.

As for Fiona? Fiona wanted to marry a real gentleman and become a lady. She didn't think for one minute that an English lord like Edward Delecort would seriously be interested in her sister. But was it fair to interfere with Fiona's chance at real happiness?

Their costumes were shabby and their props broken and patched. In the dark little theaters they'd played across the eastern states, it hadn't mattered. Nine times out of ten their audience didn't know what they were saying anyway. Would new sets and costumes save the troupe? Portia didn't know, but she knew it was the only chance she had of keeping her family together.

Perhaps she should confess her deception to Daniel. What could he do? What *would* he do? The truth would free Fiona to follow her heart. But there was still the Captain's health to consider. She'd figure out something. She always had. If only she could forget the kiss in Daniel's railcar, the kiss he intended for Fiona—not for her.

* * *

"Did you have a pleasant evening?" Ian Gaunt looked up as Daniel tossed his hat expertly on one of the hooks of the brass coat rack.

"Let's just say it was interesting, Ian. Did you see her at dinner?"

"I saw her. She's very lovely, old friend."

"She's more than lovely. She's probably the most intriguing woman I've ever met."

"I must say Dan, I'm surprised you found someone like that in a run-down traveling show. The gown appeared to be a perfect fit."

Daniel unwound the satin scarf, unfastened his shirt and dropped it across the chair. "Oh, I don't mean Fiona, though she is beautiful. It's her twin sister, Portia, I'm referring to. They're twins, women. Portia is also an actress. She's just pretending to be a man for some reason."

"Two of them? Identical twins? Why would one of them pretend to be a man? I don't understand, Dan."

"Neither do I, Ian. I've had women from the docks of San Francisco to the silver mining fields in Nevada, but this one intrigues me greatly. I haven't had this kind of fun since the early days in Virginia City."

Ian retrieved Daniel's jacket and hung it in the ornate chifforobe by the door as he considered the carefree manner of his old friend. He was right. In the last few years Daniel hadn't seemed this lively.

"You know, Daniel, in spite of all your accomplishments, I can't remember you ever having much fun. Maybe it's this place. Maybe you ought to stay. I don't understand why you keep working for the Pinkertons when you can afford to come here as a real guest."

Daniel considered Ian's words. His observation was true. For the last years he'd moved up the ladder of success, polished his image and played the part of a gentleman. But playing had been all it was. He was still Daniel Logan, the son of a washed-up miner, and a mother who never had a home.

"Until now," he answered Ian, "the challenge of finding the thief has been more exciting than any of the people I've met, or the places I've been. But this time—hell, this assignment may be better than my first royal flush and a damn sight more interesting. Let's get to bed, Ian. I have a date with a lady in my chambers in the morning."

"Oh, do you want me to disappear?"

"Hell no. I want me to see her up close, Ian. Tell me what you think. Stick around, I don't want to scare her to death just yet."

"Somehow I doubt that a girl like her will scare easily."

"Oh, but I do, and that's what makes the possibilities so interesting. I think I'll let her go on being Phillip for the time being. Would you order breakfast for two, here on the balcony, for about ten o'clock?"

"Breakfast? Fine, *sir*. What will you want?"

"I think she'd like strawberries, Ian. Order strawberries, and cream, and soft cooked eggs with bacon, and bread. And coffee, or do you think she'd prefer tea? Hell, get both."

Ian shook his head. His exaggerated attempt at servitude had gone right over Daniel's head. Ian wasn't sure he liked this turn of events. He'd been with Daniel for ten years and though Daniel had given aid to strays from Virginia City to New York, he'd never seen him lose sight of his objective before. He hadn't even asked Ian for a report. He seemed to have focused all his attention on these actresses and that wasn't like him. Unless Logan thought that the acting troupe might be responsible for the hotel burglaries they were investigating. Maybe . . .

Ian spoke into the receiver of the hotel's new communications system.

After a series of crackles a tinny voice answered. "Yes? This is the restaurant. May I assist you?"

Ian gave the order for breakfast, insisting that if it took a special trip into the countryside, strawberries were definitely necessary.

"I don't like you bringing a woman into this, Daniel,"

Ian said as he turned away from the telephone. "Getting involved with her is risky. Suppose she finds out something and gives us away?"

"Gives us away how, Ian? She doesn't know anything. What can she do?"

"Has it occurred to you, my friend, that we could be the ones being used? What better cover could a thief have than an acting troupe that moves around the country? The good Captain gets into your card game, loses the troupe in a bet, then he's legitimately under the protection of the wealthiest man at the resort."

Daniel smiled. "Oh, that occurred to me right away. Our Captain MacIntosh is quite capable of being the mastermind behind our little gang of thieves. If he is, he's playing right into our hands. What better way to keep a watch on the rooster than to be in the hen house?"

"Hen house, maybe, but I think you're asking for trouble. Careful that you don't end up married to one of the chicks."

"What's the matter, Ian, don't you think I would make a good husband?"

"I think that you'd make a very good husband, Daniel Logan, if you found the right woman."

Daniel stroked his mustache with his forefinger thoughtfully. "I'm going to telegraph William Pinkerton and have him check the Saratoga. I want to know if the MacIntosh Shakespearean Acting Troupe was in the vicinity when the robbery occurred."

"Good idea," Ian agreed and said good night, leaving Daniel to consider his associate's reservations. Ian was a good friend whose opinions Daniel valued.

The first time Daniel had seen Ian was in a gold-town saloon just above Virginia City. Ian had been the bartender in a cheap little tent bar, down on his luck and wondering out loud what had ever prompted him to leave California to prospect for gold in Nevada. He'd been in danger of being hung up by his heels by a drunken miner who'd accused Ian of watering his drink. Daniel had rescued Ian from the irate miner, given him a job at the Lodestone and they'd been together ever since.

When Daniel had bought the Crown Hotel in New York Ian had become the new general manager. Then, three years ago, the hotel had been robbed. Afterward, Daniel insisted on becoming part of the Pinkerton team investigating the robbery. Ian turned over the management of the hotel to his assistant and followed Daniel without question.

Daniel liked the challenge of matching wits with the kind of criminal who robbed the wealthy, and he'd been good at it. They'd continued to take special assignments, traveling for the Pinkerton Agency ever since, Daniel as the silver miner and hotel owner from Nevada, and Ian as his business associate.

Though Daniel insisted they were simply friends, Ian continued to treat their relationship more like that of employee and employer. Moving in and out of the homes and lives of the wealthy as if they belonged, they'd worked well together. The measure of their success was that they had never been identified as Pinkerton men and they'd never failed to fulfill an assignment.

Tall, thin, with sandy brown hair, and an air of mysterious elegance, Ian appeared oblivious to the admiring glances he received from the women guests. Daniel suspected that Ian, a very private person, had never had a close lady friend. He seemed completely unaware of his cool, aristocratic demeanor and good looks.

Ian didn't approve of Daniel's plan to use his supposed search for a wife as their cover. What Ian didn't know was that Daniel had been half serious. A wife and family had a certain amount of appeal that Daniel was beginning to acknowledge.

Still, more often than not, Ian was right. The search for a wife had been a half-hearted pursuit that became more and more boring as each new prospect was paraded before him, until Portia came into the picture. Though definitely not wife material, she was lively, and if truth be known, appealing in an earthy way.

Admitting his interest was one thing, but Daniel couldn't let his fascination with a wench from a traveling Shakespearean troupe come between him and his assignment. Daniel wasn't sure how much of his interest was professional and how much was personal. So far Portia MacIntosh was the only real woman he'd met. The kind of women Daniel had seen at the Sweetwater would probably swoon as soon as he tried to bed them. Had he been serious about marrying, the only children he'd get would be from some scullery maid on the wrong side of the sheets.

Daniel sighed. Portia had courage and he liked that. Now that he'd learned that Portia and Fiona were identical twins he wanted more than ever to know the woman who wore men's clothing and called herself Phillip.

Daniel began to smile. Portia would report to his room in the morning. He'd make certain that they wouldn't be disturbed until he found out all he needed to know about the MacIntosh Shakespearean troupe. That was part of his job. If he found out more about Portia at the same time, all the better.

Daniel Logan went to bed, planning his session with Portia the next morning. He chuckled out loud as he recalled her determined effort to dance Fiona off the floor at the Pavilion. Oh yes, Portia MacIntosh was determined. And so was he. Sooner or later he'd see her as a woman, and this time when he kissed her, she'd kiss him back.

Six

PORTIA strode back and forth outside Daniel Logan's bedroom, slapping a folded sheet of paper against her thigh and swearing under her breath. She knew she was early, but the sooner she knocked on that door, made her report and got out, the better. With a tug on her driving cap she jutted her chin forward and tapped.

"Come in," Daniel Logan commanded. "Did the kitchen find the strawberries I ordered?"

There was a long silence while the door opened and closed. Daniel Logan, wearing only his trousers, inserted the bristled brush into his shaving mug, swirled it around and applied thick globs of white lather to his face.

There was more silence.

"Ouch! I seem to have grown an extra thumb this morning, Ian. My nose is still sore and now I've tried to cut it off."

Portia gasped. Nose? She'd done that to Daniel Logan?

Daniel heard her startled breath, glanced into the mirror and caught sight of the slight figure standing hesitantly at the edge of the oriental screen separating his tub and wash stand from the rest of the bedroom. It was Portia. She was early.

Again wearing her boy's clothing she stood there, meeting his eyes in the mirror with big-eyed bravado.

Daniel's first inclination was to order her away and reach for the red velvet dressing gown lying on the bed behind him. He didn't. The disguise was her idea. Let *her* give it up. With some perverse need that he couldn't define, he continued with his shaving.

Wearing only his trousers, his feet and chest bare, Daniel cleaned the soap from his straight razor on the towel he had draped around his neck. She didn't turn away. His admiration for her grew as he took in the stubborn thrust of her chin and the determined way she refused to give in to embarrassment.

"Good morning, Daniel," Portia managed, her voice squeaking miserably. "I'll just come back, when you're dressed."

"Oh, P . . . Phillip. Nonsense. There's only the two of us men. I'll be done here in just a minute." A muscle twitched in Daniel's face as he turned and gave Portia a deliberate look of camaraderie. "How is the Captain this morning?"

"Feeling better. I left him drinking mineral water. Uh, Daniel, that's what I wanted to talk with you about, the Captain's condition."

"Don't worry, Phillip. I made it a point to find out that Dr. Garrett is an excellent physician. He will look in on your father daily."

"I appreciate your concern, but my father is my responsibility and I'll make any future arrangements."

"Very well," Daniel agreed easily. If he planned to work with Portia in any reasonably friendly way, he'd better at least let her think that she was in charge. Otherwise she would bristle up and he'd never be able to help her or learn anything about the troupe's past activities. He turned back to the mirror.

"I thought you were my associate, Ian Gaunt. I hate shaving. Back in Virginia City I'd forget about shaving and grow a beard. Of course, in New York, a man has to be damned uncomfortable if he's going to be fashionable. What do you think, would Fiona rather I be clean shaven?''

"Yes, I suppose. I mean I'm sure she'd like you, either way.''

"Good, I'm glad to hear that. Fiona is a perfect choice for my fiancee. I never would have guessed when she broke into my rail car that she'd be so lovely in an evening gown. Did she like the dress?''

"Uh, yes sir. Fiona very much liked the dress." Portia glanced around the room. This wasn't going to work. She was miserable. She tried to look at anything but the man shaving himself. She hadn't wanted to come here but she hadn't known it would be this bad.

Daniel's tall, powerful frame was magnificently handsome. His shoulders flexed as he moved and she felt her stomach flutter. She supposed that he was the kind of man women secretly dreamed of. Forcing herself to uncurl her fists she tried to understand her response to Daniel Logan. He was no different from Rowdy, or Lawson Paine. Both were considered to be quite attractive by the ladies in their audiences.

Rowdy was powerful. Lawson was handsome. Daniel was neither, yet he was both. Portia tightened her stomach muscles and turned her eyes defiantly to the dark red oriental rug on the floor.

"I've ordered breakfast. It should be here momentarily. In the meantime, we can talk while I finish shaving." Daniel caught her expression of misery as she stared at the floor. He didn't know why he was putting Portia through this. He figured that sooner or later she'd have to admit her little masquerade and then he could meet her as the woman she was. But so far she was gamely going through with her role. And the more she pretended, the more he badgered her.

"Breakfast?" Portia hadn't expected that. She opened her mouth to protest and caught sight of Daniel's lips holding back a smile.

At least he had her attention again. Daniel set the razor on the side of his face just below his cheekbone and made a slow, wiggly motion, leaving a trail of fresh smooth skin down his face toward his chin. He wiped the foam from the blade with the edge of his towel and leaned forward, making the same motion on the other cheek.

"Yes. You do eat breakfast, don't you?"

"Well, yes, but I . . ."

"Where have you performed?" Daniel asked, cutting off her attempt to refuse his offer.

"Just about everywhere I suppose. We never stop."

"Don't you have a home some where?"

"A home?" Portia frowned and looked down at her hands, now tightly clasped again. "No, we don't have a home."

"Neither do I," Daniel admitted with a scowl on his face, "but I intend to some day." How had he allowed the conversation to turn to homes and his future plans? There was a wistfulness in his voice that he covered abruptly with a clearing of his throat.

The picture of a lonely cabin in the high country, piled high with snow, flashed into his mind and vanished just as quickly. He was past that kind of longing. A suite of rooms in his hotel, comfortable and private, was right for him, very private and very quiet.

"Have you ever played one of the New York theaters?"

"Yes, last month. Before that we were at Ford's Theater in Washington, D.C. We've played Boston, Philadelphia, St. Louis—every place that has a railroad and a stage."

"Have you ever played Saratoga Springs?" he asked casually.

"No, the closest we've come was Albany."

Albany. Daniel felt a tightening in his chest. Albany was close enough to Saratoga Springs. "I guess that the Captain disappeared as usual, probably met up with some of the guests from the Springs and went back with them for a late night dinner?"

"No, if there were any guests from the Springs in the audience I didn't know it."

"But he does make a habit of disappearing in the evenings, doesn't he?" He was trying to keep his voice casual. Even so, she looked at him curiously. He was afraid he'd pressed too hard.

"Sometimes my father likes to have fun. And he gambles from time to time as you already know. Or at least he did. Of course, he's giving all that up now."

Daniel heard the strain in her voice. The old bandit. He'd bet that Horatio was harder to keep up with than a street thief and if he really gave up the kind of life he'd been leading, Daniel would shave his mustache and grow a beard. He didn't believe a word Portia was saying. For now, he'd go along, at least until he got the report from the Pinkerton office.

"Must be hard on you, keeping up with your father and looking after the troupe. I'll bet he wins more often than he loses. Must be good when he's able to bring home money, jewels, or other prizes after a night out with the boys."

"I wish," Portia said wistfully. "You've played with my father; he used to win, but lately . . ." Her voice trailed off and she let out a deep breath before she added. "Papa only gambles when we need money."

It came to him that Portia would never criticize her father and she would never give in to the embarrassment of admitting that he was irresponsible. She was taking what must be an awkward situation and handling it with great self-control.

Also, based on their present situation, she was probably no stranger to half-dressed male bodies. He guessed that she'd made too many costume changes in hallways and make-do dressing rooms to be totally ignorant. Through his early years he'd experienced the same kind of togetherness as he traveled with Belle and their own troupe of dance hall girls.

Being here in his hotel room had to be more awkward for her than it was for him. The corner of the room where he was performing his morning toilet was larger than most of the dressing rooms in the theaters he'd seen, yet he felt as if they were almost touching, and he was having a difficult time holding his razor steady.

Still, Portia seemed unperturbed. She stood clasping a sheet of paper, gamely waiting for his attention. Rather than feeling good about having her here, he was feeling a little ashamed that he'd insisted she come. He sensed she really wasn't nearly so experienced as he thought she was, or as she pretended to be. He'd better get finished with his shaving before his employee decided to bolt or he cut his own throat.

Portia was wearing her usual ribbed brown trousers and scuffed leather boots. She'd added an oversized vest which more than covered the small firm breasts he'd felt the night he'd captured her in his rail car. With the vest, she was wearing a flowing brown silk tie. He could see her soft white neck above the vee of her shirt, her soft, very feminine white neck.

"I don't suppose you have to do this every day, do you, Phil?" Daniel asked as he walked toward her. "Shave, I mean."

"Eh, no. I mean I don't have much of a beard yet, sir." Portia's voice had dropped into some kind of hushed gravelly tone. There was a bright stiff look about her gaze. He wondered what she would do if he reached out and lifted that absurd cap from her head allowing her golden hair to escape and fall down her shoulders. Instead he forced himself to pass her and step out on the balcony into the bright sunlight. With mirror and scissors in hand he deftly trimmed his mustache.

"What do you think?" Daniel asked as he strode gracefully back into the room, stopping only inches from where she was standing, frozen into a wide-eyed statue. "Is it even?"

Portia gulped. A flush of pink rose from somewhere about the vicinity of the brown silk tie. Heat flooded her face and dampened the roots of her strawberry colored hair concealed beneath her cap.

"Even?" She pretended to examine his efforts and nodded her approval.

Daniel's admiration for the girl grew. She had spunk. He'd known that last night when she gamely cut in on her sister and Edward and insisted on dancing Fiona off the floor. His supposed fiancee and Portia were unmistakably twins, one as beautiful as the other. But it was Portia who intrigued him.

"Uh, Phillip, it's going to be grand having a brother. I don't have any family—anymore, and sharing yours will be great fun."

Fun? The man was a flapdoodle. Whatever arrangement they had was going to be temporary, very temporary. Having him as a member of her family was about as inviting as red ants in her bloomers.

"I don't think we need to go quite that far, Dan," Portia said. "Last night very nearly turned into a disaster as it was. I don't think we'd better repeat that again. Fiona and I don't belong in that kind of setting."

"Well, I'll have to admit that your wardrobe could stand a bit of help. I think I'll send Ian to Atlanta with your measurements and order a few clothes for both you and Fiona, and maybe for the Captain as well."

"Measurements?" Portia's poise seemed to break and she blanched noticeably. "I don't need any clothing, Dan, and I would appreciate it if you'd tell me why I'm here."

"Fine. Let me get a shirt and I'll be ready to get down to business. In the meantime, do step out onto my balcony and have a look at my view of the grounds. I can see straight across the lawn to the ladies' dormitory. You won't tell them, will you?"

Portia whirled and hurried out on the balcony, taking great, deep breaths of air into lungs that felt drained and parched. Ladies' dormitory? Surely he wasn't a peeping Tom. She glanced across the landscaped gardens, emerald green in the late June sunshine. He was right. If you looked up, across the tops of the trees, Daniel's porch was directly across from the Chautauqua dormitory.

The distance was too great for Daniel to identify the figures moving about inside. But the petticoat thrown across the window sill identified the room to her as the one she and

Fiona shared with the other women. Then she saw it, the spy-glass on the floor beside the half wall around the porch. He could surely see that far. What if . . . ? First Portia blushed, then felt a surge of anger.

Wasn't it bad enough that the man was trying to take over their lives? Now he was in a position where he could spy on them, directly. And he proposed to order clothes for the Captain, for Fiona, and for herself. Take her own measurements? Lordy, what would he decide to do next? She'd better get out of there before he brought out the measuring string.

"I'd like to get my report made, Daniel. Fiona will be wondering what has happened to me. I have to make the arrangements to get the Captain over to the Springs to take one of those hot baths."

"Don't worry, Phillip." Daniel raised his voice so that Portia could hear him as he dressed. "I've already ordered a carriage for ten o'clock every morning. It will deliver your father to the bathhouse and back to the dormitory in time for lunch."

"You have? I don't think you know the Captain, Dan. I guess we ought to talk about that. I have to be very watchful of my father."

"Oh?"

The sun was warm. Portia felt beads of perspiration dampen her hair beneath the cap she was wearing. The extra vest was hot and the binding she'd wrapped around her breasts was beginning to chafe.

"The Captain is just as likely to order the driver to take him up here to the hotel for a game of billiards."

"I've taken care of that, Phillip. The staff has been given orders to verify any of the Captain's requests with my associate, Ian Gaunt. They'll keep a very close check on your father."

"Why, Dan? This wasn't part of our bargain. Why are you doing this?"

"Because," he bit back the flippant reply he'd been about to give and answered her more seriously than he'd planned, "there was someone who was very kind to me once. She helped me when I had nobody else to turn to. Maybe this is my chance to do the same thing for somebody else. I think she'd like your father. She'd probably have given him a run for his money. They'd have been a good match."

"Your wife?"

Daniel heard the change in her voice and he glanced up to see the woman on the balcony standing very still as she appeared to be studying the gardens beyond.

"No." Daniel could have laughed at the idea of the sharp-talking older woman who'd been more of a mother to him. "Belle was a friend, a very good friend who took me in and cared for me. She was special. She was a lot like Horatio, you know; loved the theater."

"Was she an actress?"

"Not when I knew her. Belle was . . . well, I wish you'd known Belle."

Daniel Logan fastened his shirt and tucked it into his pants. He'd never told anybody about Belle before. He didn't know why he'd told Portia. She was very easy to talk to, too easy. But he was still bothered by her background.

At the dormitory last night, when Horatio, convinced that he was going to die, had confirmed Daniel's belief that Fiona and Portia were in truth identical twins, Daniel had become totally fascinated with the MacIntoshes. The Captain was a wily old fox. He knew that they'd had no commitment to play a summer season at the Chautauqua. He'd planned to talk his way in. Perhaps he'd done the same thing in Saratoga Springs.

The card game and the phony acting engagement could have been nothing more than a ruse to give the old man a chance to scout the hotel for possible marks. There would be more than one dowager who would fall for his charms. Daniel was certain that Captain Horatio MacIntosh had survived by his wits and his charm as much as by his talent on the stage.

There was another possibility too. He might have known he was ill, might even have deliberately lost that final hand to put his family under Daniel's protection. The pain last night and the doctor's report had confirmed the old man's illness. A heart condition, Dr. Garrett had diagnosed. And a stomach ulcer with the potential for rupture without rest and proper care.

Daniel gave himself a final check in the mirror and grinned. Behind him, reflected in the glass, was Portia, looking decidedly uncomfortable as she glanced at the floor and back into the morning sunshine. She'd seen his spy glass. Fine, he'd intended for her to know that he planned to keep a close watch on them. Horatio had extracted a promise from him to look after them. He wasn't at all sure that the spy glass was what Horatio had in mind, though.

"Belle was special," Daniel went on quietly. "She would give away her last cent if somebody needed it. She could shoot a fly from a tree trunk twenty feet away and tell a joke that would . . . well, never mind about that. She liked music and books. Why, you wouldn't believe the books we had to cart around every time we moved. I probably know as much about Mr. Shakespeare's plays as you do. No, Belle wasn't a lady, but I loved her very much. To a ten-year-old boy, Belle was both mother and friend."

Daniel's voice was very soft and Portia turned to listen. For a moment she forgot her anger. She forgot her reluctance to be there as Daniel talked. There was a sadness in his voice, a loneliness that she knew he hadn't intended her to hear. It was all Portia could do to keep from moving back into the bedroom where the man was dressing and take his hand in compassion.

A gold miner from the west reading Shakespeare? She'd known he was well educated, but there was so much about the man that didn't fit together. He was touched with a past sorrow and somehow she and her family had become caught up in it. *Oh, what a tangled web we weave when first we practice to deceive*. Where had she heard that? How true it was!

"What do you think of this new green morning coat, Phillip?'' Daniel stepped out onto the balcony beside her. "Might be a better color for you with your fair skin. Though you'll need a black or even a white one for evening wear." Daniel smothered a smile at her look of shock when she lifted her eyes and examined the jacket.

"It's very nice, Dan. But I said I'm not interested. The troupe belongs to you, for now, but you aren't responsible for my family. I am. I've looked after my sister and my father for years."

So, she wanted to be the man of the family? Fine. Sooner or later, she'd have to be honest with him. He hoped it would be sooner.

Portia tried to direct her gaze away. The jacket was the most beautiful color she'd ever seen. It fit Daniel's body without a wrinkle. The pale cream colored trousers he was wearing hugged his hips as if they were a second layer of skin. He was a handsome devil, with the sun touching his face with light and lacing his dark hair with tinges of red. Portia had the feeling that Daniel Logan knew that her knees were turning to gruel, and that her heart was racing like a frightened filly facing an aroused stallion. The silence was filled with tension.

She should have told him first thing this morning. She'd intended to march into this room and tell him that she was Portia MacIntosh, right away, before she got involved any deeper. But when she'd seen him, wearing only his trousers, she couldn't speak. Now the time had passed and it was too late. If she admitted that she was a woman, then she also admitted that Daniel was a man, a man who fascinated her. Being interested in a man was new to Portia, new and very frightening. She didn't want to think about the feelings he aroused in her. She didn't want to feel anything at all. All she wanted to do was run, hard, fast, far away.

"Daniel"—Portia's voice cracked and she took a breath, forcing her voice to deepen as she forced her attention to the list she was holding in her hand. "I'd like to give you my report now. I have to get back to the troupe and get started on the adjustments we'll have to make to this stage. You see, we've never acted in an area built for preaching sermons before. The dimensions and the acoustics are very different.''

"I don't understand, Phillip, what do you mean, sermons?''

"Didn't they tell you? They've moved us from the outdoor stage. It didn't have a curtain. In order to present a polished performance for the kind of audience we hope to draw from the resort, we must have a curtain. Besides, Mr. Lane tells me that the religious enlightenment sometimes goes on for hours and we wouldn't be able to begin on time.''

"Religious enlightenment?'' Daniel couldn't keep the incredulous tone from his voice. "You mean you'll be competing with God?''

"Well no, not exactly. The sermons are offered at six-thirty. They should be finished by the time we begin our plays at eight. But the director is insistent that we be finished by ten o'clock, some kind of rule of the Chautauqua. That will be difficult because of shortage of crew members.''

"Oh, how is that?''

"Well, our stage hands and wardrobe people also double as actors. Some of them are good and some are just bodies. That hasn't made a great deal of difference in the past, but now—well, I don't know.''

"Can't you find additional actors?''

"Sure, but that will take time and patience. New actors will have to learn their lines and we'll need costumes.''

"I'm beginning to see what you mean. What do you suggest?''

"I haven't an answer yet. We'll start off with *Romeo and Juliet*. That's our best play. We can manage that, I think. Then, well maybe the Captain will have an idea.''

"*Romeo and Juliet*. Fiona plays Juliet, no doubt. And you?''

"Romeo, of course, I could never be Juliet. She's much too foolish.''

"Perhaps, but I don't think you're Romeo either. You're much too . . . pragmatic."

"Pragmatic? I'm afraid I don't know the word."

"It means that you accept things as they are, and deal with them as you have to. I understand that, Phillip. I understand that very well."

There was a sharp rap on the door.

"Ah, that must be our breakfast now. We'll eat, then I'll have a look at your list." He moved to open the door.

Breakfast? Business? Portia took a hurried step that carried her farther onto the balcony. Heaven only knew what Daniel Logan had planned next. He'd probably come down to the Chautauqua and take a personal inventory of their supplies. Sooner or later somebody with the troupe was sure to give her away.

"Phillip, come and have a look at what Ian found. Sweet, red strawberries. I believe that we have enough for you to take some back to my fiancee. Does Fiona like strawberries?"

"Yes. Fiona is very fond of strawberries." Portia didn't want to have breakfast with Daniel. She wanted to bring this meeting to a close and get away from his overwhelming presence.

"That's one thing to keep in mind, Phillip. Ladies like surprises. Candies and flowers are nice, but fresh, sweet strawberries—that's a gift from the heart. Don't you agree?"

Enough. He'd gone far enough. Troupe or no troupe, strawberries, or no strawberries, she had to get out of Daniel's room before—

"Not all women, Daniel."

"Sure they do. All women love that kind of attention. I see I'm going to have to teach you how to handle the ladies. Come and try a berry."

When she turned Logan was standing behind her, holding out a bowl of bright red berries piled with white crystals of sugar. On his face was a wickedly innocent smile. He was like one actor trying to upstage another actor by ad-libbing.

new lines and unexpected stage positions. He was toying with her, playing the star. She recognized the technique.

Well, Portia knew a thing or two about upstaging an actor. Quickly she forced herself back into the character of the role she'd been assigned to play. All right, he wanted the two of them to be buddies. Apparently she wasn't going to have a choice.

Fine, it would mean that Fiona would be able to see Edward, her father would have proper medical care, and Daniel would underwrite the troupe. She'd pretend to be interested in learning all she could about the well-to-do, and she'd give Mr. Logan a thing or two to think about in the meantime.

Portia reached for one of the berries, and popped it into her mouth, licking the sugar crystals off her lips with her small pink tongue. "Delicious, Daniel," she said, clearing her throat. "Fiona will love them. Do we have coffee or tea for breakfast. I prefer coffee; it's a more manly drink, don't you think?"

"Eh, yes. Oh, and this is my associate, Ian Gaunt." Daniel inclined his head and moved back as Ian stepped into the room. "Ian, shake hands with Phillip. We'll enjoy our breakfast out on the patio."

"Fine. Good morning, Mr. MacIntosh. I'm very pleased to meet you."

Portia shook Ian's hand and watched as the lean, dark-suited man uncovered the wheeled breakfast table. It wasn't bad enough that she was in a hotel room alone with one man, now there were two!

Daniel offered Portia a chair, and pulled up his own seat opposite her. Portia tried not to see the pleased expression on the elegantly attired man sitting across the table from her.

As they ate the berries, Ian reported on his ride into the small town called Salt Springs just beyond the hotel. He'd found a farmer and convinced him to part with the last of his strawberries in return for the promise of tickets to see the play. The farmer had never seen Shakespeare but his wife, who picked the berries, had wanted to go on the stage once.

"Maybe we ought to sign her up." Daniel laughed and passed a plate of sweet rolls. "Phillip says we need more players. What about it, Phil?"

Portia only nodded. It was bad enough that every time she got within five feet of Daniel Logan her innards started an Indian war dance somewhere about her rib cage, and she couldn't think coherently. Now, the intermittent touching of their knees made the situation even more unbearable. What in the world was poor Fiona to do if he began to act like the loving fiancee? She'd better give Daniel the list and get off this balcony and out of his hotel room—quick!

Portia looked down over the balcony rail. Beyond Logan's shoulder she caught a glimpse of shiny blond hair catching the bright morning sunlight. Blond hair and a smiling face, on the pathway below; a familiar smiling face. It was Fiona.

Oh lordy. Fiona, dressed in some ridiculously out of date sailor suit, was riding a bicycle rockily up the trail beneath Daniel's window. The figure following behind on the second cycle was Edward Delecort. Where did she get that costume? What if Daniel saw her? He might not be so tolerant of Fiona's action this morning as he had been last night.

"I say, Logan, mightn't we go inside? I really don't care for any more breakfast and the sun is very bright out here. I fear that it's giving me a dreadful headache." Portia stood and covered her eyes dramatically. *Wonderful, a man with a headache. How silly could she get?* Thank heavens she was supposed to be an actor. People expected stage actors to be a bit odd, otherwise Daniel would wonder about her.

"Of course, Phillip. This sun is warm if you're not dressed for it. Maybe what you need is a good shot of whiskey in that coffee. That will relax you."

It was all Daniel could do to keep from laughing out loud. If the rest of the troupe's acting was as bad as that of the would-be young man pretending to faint on his balcony, heaven help the Chautauqua guests. Giving away the tickets as he'd promised the director might not even guarantee a full audience.

Daniel rose and followed Portia inside, but not before he too had seen Fiona on the riding trail beneath his window. She called out to her companion with a look of total bemusement on her face. Pulling up beside Fiona, Edward Delecort pedaled slowly, the same calf-like look plastered foolishly across his aristocratic features.

Daniel knew that Portia was in a panic. "As a matter of fact, Phillip, I remember once in California I was laid up for a week by the sun. Ian, bring the bourbon."

"Are you sure, Dan? Seems a bit early for spirits." Ian's voice was filled with reproach. It was obvious to Daniel that Ian did not approve of what was taking place. "As I recall, old friend, your illness was in the nature of a fever caught from one of those workmen building the railroad—not from the sun."

"I'm sure, Ian. We can't have poor Phil ill at a time like this. Pour—him—a shot of bourbon in his coffee. Drink up, lad, I don't want you fainting on me before your voice changes."

Voice? Portia glanced helplessly from Daniel Logan to his friend, and back again. She had to keep Logan off the balcony before he saw Fiona. She'd stay inside and drink the bourbon, somehow.

Portia took the steaming liquid, swallowed it, and felt her insides boil with fire.

"Whow!" This time the deep voice wasn't an act. Gasping for breath, she said, "That's pretty potent whiskey, Daniel. I don't think I'd better have any more." Her eyes tearing, she sat the cup carefully down on a table by the doorway and handed her report to the Daniel Logan, who seemed suddenly to be overly concerned with his own coffee. When he made no move to take the sheet of paper, Portia released it a few inches from the waistline of Daniel Logan's green morning jacket. It floated to the floor and settled between his feet.

"This gives you all the information about the first play, Mr. Logan. After *Romeo and Juliet*, we'll probably follow with *Twelfth Night*—if the Captain is well enough to go on stage. Please look it over and you'll see exactly what we're going to need if you expect to be pleased with our production.''

"I'm sure I'll be pleased," Daniel agreed. "And I'll provide whatever assistance you may need." He leaned down and lifted the paper. His movements pulled his trousers tight against his thigh. Portia jerked her eyes away, barely registering his agreeing nod.

"Then you'll allow me to get back to the troupe?" Portia's voice was stretched thin as she inched her way to the door. Her head was truly pounding from the bourbon as well as from nervous tension by this time, and she felt a peculiar weakness in her knees.

"Of course," Logan agreed. "Take this afternoon to get the feel of your stage and make your plans. You can tell me all about *Romeo and Juliet* over dinner."

"Uh . . . no! That wasn't part of our arrangement. You were to introduce Fiona to the guests as your fiancee and that was all. You've done that. We've fulfilled our part of the agreement."

"Nonsense, lad! I gave my word to the Captain that I'd look after you and your sister. Of course, his request alters our original agreement. We will be seeing a great deal of each other, I think. Now, I'll say goodbye, until tonight. Have your sister ready at eight. I'll send the carriage for you both. Tell Fiona that I'm anxious to see her again. I have special plans for after dinner."

"I'm sorry, Daniel, but as you say, Father isn't well. I'm sure that Fiona will insist on staying close by him. Speaking of close, I'd better get a move on. The Captain would bribe the Holy Father and all his nuns to let him go, if he thought he could get away with it and I don't trust him alone."

"Yes, I got a taste of that the night we played cards. He must be a real handful for you and your sister."

"He didn't . . . I mean playing cards was all he did, isn't it? You didn't lose anything, did you?"

"Lose, you mean as in gambling? No."

Daniel couldn't miss the look of relief on Portia's face. So the old crook did bring home other prizes from time to time.

"All right, I'll excuse you tonight, Phillip. I suppose you weren't part of the bargain. After all, you didn't make the deal." Daniel paused and looked at her shrewdly. "But Fiona's time is mine, all of it, now that we're engaged. Your father approves of my plan."

She understood that, all right. Horatio thought it was the right thing to do, giving them over to Daniel's care. And it was obvious that Daniel was taken with Fiona. He wanted to see her again and that didn't have anything to do with an agreement. Well, Portia couldn't blame him for that. Portia wasn't sure that she'd be able to force Fiona to go with Daniel again, now that she'd met Edward Delecort.

Daniel went on smoothly, "The guests will think it odd if my fiancee makes one appearance and disappears. I intend to uphold my end of the agreement and I expect Fiona to carry out hers." The latter was said with a warning in his voice.

"All right," Portia agreed hastily. "Fiona will be there. I promise." Daniel's warning rang in her ears as she hastily said her goodbyes and dashed down the marble steps of the great hotel. Special plans for after dinner? Unwanted images filled her mind as she walked across the green lawns, past the wealthy guests out for a morning stroll, past the Dummy Rail Line ferrying passengers back to the Springs where they would bathe in the mineral waters. She hardly noticed the lake or the vendors hawking their souvenirs and finger foods. The Sweetwater was a place for the idle rich—not for someone like her.

Portia didn't know whether she was more angry with Daniel, Fiona, or herself. Fiona—the very idea of her dashing brazenly out behind Portia's back at the first opportunity and allowing Edward Delecort to take her for a bicycle ride across the resort grounds. What if Daniel Logan had seen her?

Portia brought her rapid pace to a stop as she reached the

Chautauqua grounds and considered her next move. The truth was that in spite of her anger, she knew that Fiona truly belonged in such a setting. There was something gentle about Edward and there was that same gentleness about Fiona. Did she have the right to make commitments that might cost Fiona the honest attentions of a man like Edward Delecort? But were Edward's attentions really honest? That was something she didn't have time to think about.

Damn papa! Poor papa. She was torn between understanding his fear and cursing his solution. On the other hand, if he'd had his attack elsewhere, he might not be getting the care he needed. For once Portia didn't know what to do. Whichever direction she took someone was going to be hurt and she choked back the unbidden thought that for once, it just might be her. She'd have to talk with Fiona. Papa couldn't be bothered until he was well again.

It was well after lunch before Fiona appeared in Papa's room, where Portia was giving her report on her morning meeting and their new owner's latest directive.

"I'll not go out with Mr. Logan again, Papa," Fiona said firmly as she came in the door. "I have other plans. Besides, Daniel Logan isn't really interested in me."

"What do you mean?" Portia snapped. "Of course he is, Fee. He's very handsome. He's wealthy and he wants you to be his fiancée. You've always wanted this kind of life. This is your chance."

"If he is all that interested in me, why did he spend all night asking questions about you?"

"About me?"

"Well, about Phillip, my brother Phillip. I could tell, Portia, the rest of the time he was just acting, like someone saying the right lines, but he didn't mean them, not at all. That's all right. I like Daniel, I really do. But . . ."

"Now, now, girls," Horatio interrupted. "When I talked to Daniel Logan he promised that he'd take care of both of you and the troupe until I could regain my health. He seemed pleased with Fiona even if he did ask a great many questions about you, Portia. You didn't tell him the truth this morning, did you, Portia, about your sister?''

Portia jumped to her feet and began to pace back and forth. ''No, Papa. I couldn't. He still thinks I'm Fiona's brother and now he's decided to introduce me to society as well. While he's courting Fiona, he's going to teach me to be a man. Last night he offered me a cigar, and this morning, in his room, he . . .''

''He what?'' Horatio sat up, swung his legs off the bed, and groaned.

''No, Papa, I didn't mean that he did anything ungentle-manly. It was just that he offered me whiskey to drink. Whis-key, in the middle of the morning! What kind of man would do that?''

''A man who thinks he's talking to another man, of course,'' Fiona said.

''Well now, what's wrong with that, Portia?'' Horatio leaned back on the pillow and sighed deeply. ''Wasn't that what you wanted?''

Portia was going to get no sympathy from her family. She was becoming totally frustrated. ''Yes. No! Oh, I don't know. The man is impossible to understand.''

''Poo!'' Fiona inserted. ''You're exaggerating. He's a man just like any other man. What are you worried about?''

''No he's not. He's a rogue, a ladies man, a real masher, that's what!''

Horatio's expression was subdued and unusually serious. ''It seems to me that Fiona ought to be the one worried about that—not you. You like him, don't you, Portia my girl?''

''Certainly not! I despise the man. I don't even want to think about him.'' That was true enough. She didn't even want to examine the emotions he aroused in her.

''I see.'' Horatio slid his feet back beneath the covers and studied Portia. After a moment he leaned back against the pillow, reached beneath it and drew out a long cigar, one of the same kind of cigars that Daniel Logan had offered her the night before. He sniffed it deeply, then swirled it around in his mouth for a moment.

"Papa!" Fiona came to her feet. "You don't plan to light that, do you? After what the doctor just told you about excesses and your health?"

"She's right," Portia added wearily, "you've got to get better; we need you on stage."

"And I'll be there, never fear." Horatio studied the cigar with envy. "I'm not going to smoke it, but I can smell it every now and again, and imagine." He replaced it in the folds of his robe and smiled. "Ah, Portia, don't worry. From the time you were ten years old I've never known anything or anybody to get the better of you, and I don't think Daniel Logan will be the exception. I'm just sorry that you have such an old fool for a father. Your mother would be very proud of you."

"Oh, Papa. I love you. But you don't understand. Daniel Logan is absolutely the most infuriating man I've ever had the misfortune to come in contact with. The very idea of him dashing about his hotel room half dressed when he had a guest present!"

Horatio MacIntosh's chortle was genuine. "Better there than elsewhere." He slid up in bed and studied the elder twin seriously. She seemed genuinely upset. Had he made a grave mistake about Daniel Logan? No, he smiled and settled back against his pillow. He'd been right.

Daniel Logan was everything that Horatio had hoped for. Last night when Horatio thought the end was near he'd come clean with Daniel about his girls, only to find out that Daniel already knew. Daniel had been amused. Even then Horatio had sensed something more than pure amusement in his manner.

Sooner or later Portia would be forced to admit that she was a woman. In the meantime Horatio would stake his . . . Hell, he was staking his life on Daniel Logan's being the man to teach Portia what she was. Now Fiona had met an English Lord. All in all their engagement at the Chautauqua College was going to be very interesting.

"Well," Portia went on, "I'm not going with Fiona this evening Papa. Sooner or later he'll see through my disguise. I may be able to fool him once a day in his quarters. But I could never hold my own before all those people at the hotel. When he and Fiona have dinner this evening, I'll not be there. I have work to do here with the troupe."

"What do you mean, when Mr. Logan and I have dinner tonight?" Fiona asked. "I did what you asked last night, Portia, but I can't do it again. Tonight, tonight, Edward and I are going dancing on the rose mound. Oh, Papa, it's the most glorious mountain of flowers with a quartet playing music at the top and Edward says that you can see for miles."

"Oh, no you don't, Fee. You almost gave everything away this morning, riding a bicycle directly underneath Daniel Logan's window. You can *not* go with Edward. Just what do you think will happen to us if Daniel Logan's fiancee is seen with another man? What happens to Papa if Mr. Logan decides not to give us the support we need for the troupe?"

"Oh, I didn't think. I don't want to hurt Papa. But, it isn't fair," Fiona said almost in tears. "Please don't make me do this. Besides, Mr. Logan will give us the support we need. He said he would. Edward, I mean, Lord Delecort assures me that Daniel Logan is a man of his word."

"And how would Lord Delecort know about Daniel Logan? They hardly travel in the same circles." Portia knew she was being quarrelsome, but she had to make Fiona see that swooning over Edward was an impossible situation.

"Well he doesn't really know him, Portia, not well. But Edward told me that when he and his mother were in New York everybody talked about Daniel Logan. He's very wealthy, you know. Made his money in silver mines and hotels."

"All right. Daniel Logan is trustworthy but the Mac-

Intoshes keep their word too, Fiona. He is expecting you to have dinner with him this evening and you have to go." Portia sprang to her feet and ripped her cap from her head, swinging a fall of red-blonde curls vigoriously. "For Papa's sake."

Fiona mustn't be allowed to spoil everything. Portia was desperate. Their entire lives depended on keeping Daniel Logan happy. Damn him. Why couldn't he have just used Fiona to announce his engagement and then gone back to his regular life and left them alone?

"No!" Fiona stamped her foot and ran to the bed. She dropped to her knees and rested her head against her father's chest. "Please, Papa, don't let her do this to me. She's always spoiling everything, being so bossy. All my life I've wanted, wished for someone like Edward and now that I've found him, Portia wants to spoil it. Don't let her do it, Papa."

"But Fiona, there's more at stake than what you want, or what I want," Portia argued quietly.

Horatio gave a long, deep sigh and patted his daughter's head. "She's right, Portia. I don't know Edward, but this is Fiona's chance and we can't force her to give it up, even if it does mean that we may lose the troupe. Maybe it's time we gave up all the traveling. I'm getting older. Sooner or later, there'll come a curtain and I won't be able to go on. I got us into this mess and it's up to me to get us out of it. I'll go and talk to Daniel Logan myself."

Portia heard the strain in her father's voice. She heard the wistful despair in Fiona's. And she knew that she had to find another way. It was up to her. It always had been. "No! You can't go, Papa. I'll go."

"What do you mean?" Horatio asked suspiciously.

"I mean that 'Phillip' will have to go and talk to Daniel Logan. I'll tell him that Fiona is indisposed, that she—"

"No, Portia," Fiona interrupted sharply. "I'll do it. It was very selfish of me to refuse. If you tell him that I'm indisposed, he'll only delay it until tomorrow or the next day and sooner or later he'll find out the truth. I'll tell Edward." Fiona came to her feet. Joan of Arc couldn't have given a more soulful performance.

"No," Horatio said. "Neither of us wants to spoil your happiness Fiona. There's really only one answer. Portia, you'll have to do what you should have done in the beginning. You'll have to go with the man, you—not Phillip."

"But . . . but . . ." Portia's voice trailed off as she looked aghast into the faces of her family. She couldn't do it. There was no way she could put on a dress and face Daniel Logan.

"What's wrong, Portia, my girl?" Horatio asked quietly. "You've been my right-hand man for so long. Are you afraid to face Daniel as a woman?"

"Of course not. It's just that I'm sure he'll realize that I'm not Fiona. I mean, I'm not graceful and beautiful, like Fee. I don't know how to make small talk and flirt. I'll feel like a fool."

"Nonsense, you're exactly like Fiona. You're her mirror image. But you're you too, Portia. You're warm and generous, and when Fiona gets through dressing you, I promise you that you'll be beautiful." Horatio beamed his confidence toward a nodding Fiona and her skeptical twin. It was all he could do to keep from smiling. He couldn't have worked the plot out better if he'd planned it himself.

Portia walked to the window of the tower room her father had been assigned after his attack. Her chest was tight and her head ached. Even the great beauty of the grounds had no calming effect on her agitation. She knew her father was right; there was no other way out. But she wasn't sure she could face the world as a woman. Blast! It wasn't even the world she worried about. It was having to be a woman with a man like Daniel Logan. The picture of his bare chest and powerfully muscular arms kept intruding in her mind like a bell ringing over and over.

Below, she could see the courtyard around which the Chautauqua grounds were built, and the stark white Moorish buildings that made a square around the open interior. She could see the building across the way, the class rooms where those who were attending the summer classes took their courses in mathematics and languages.

On the opposite side was the open amphitheater where the crowds gathered to listen to the concerts and the ministers. That theater would hold seven thousand people. Thank goodness they'd been given the smaller stage. With thousands of people coming to the resort daily, they might never have such a large audience again and she'd have to prepare the players carefully so that their small troupe wouldn't be overwhelmed.

If they could do well, new opportunities might be offered. If she could somehow convince Daniel Logan to return the ownership of the troupe to her father they might be able to continue here. Her father would get well and Fiona could spend time with Edward, and she . . .

"All right. I'll do it," she said with resignation in her voice. "But I will not wear a corset or a bustle."

"Oh, Portia." Fiona sprang gaily to her feet. "Bustles are out of style anyway. But a corset? I think you're going to have to wear one if you're going to get into a ball gown. We'll cover those awful hands with gloves and Bertha will do your hair. You'll be beautiful."

Horatio MacIntosh watched as an animated Fiona put her arm around her sister in a surprisingly tender move. They went out the door, discussing the merits of using one of their "great ladies' " dresses from the troupe wardrobe, versus trying to adapt one of Fiona's gowns for the occasion. Bertha would come up with something.

Yes, he nodded to himself. Though his bringing the troupe to Georgia had been a desperation move, the current trend of events might be a much better script than he could have written.

Seven

PORTIA had bathed and washed her hair under Fiona's careful instructions. Now she sat, cross-legged on the open window ledge in the sun drying her hair with a large towel.

As she tried to empty her mind of any thought of the evening to come, she threaded her fingers through the thick strands of her strawberry colored hair, spreading it across the shoulders of her worn Chinese silk kimono. The kimono's once bright splashes of color were faded now and the garment, retired from some earlier stage play, had become her dressing gown.

Outside the dormitory window the pleasant June sunshine washed the pastoral scene with gentle light. Now and then a soft breeze skittered along the tops of the pine trees, sailing in little ripples across the smooth lake water as though it were testing the temperature. A small fat wooden boat moved lazily across the sparkling water, carrying a gentleman carefully dressed in light colored trousers and cotton jacket and a lady bobbing a frilly parasol behind her head like a saucy wink.

What did they find to talk about, these carefree vacationers? What made these women preen and laugh so gaily without looking like simpering fools? She and Fiona were not uneducated women. Their father had seen to their schooling as best he could. They could read and write, though figures seemed a more necessary skill to Portia's practical mind than poetry and serious literature. But carrying on the kind of coy flirtations she'd witnessed at dinner and at the Pavilion the night before were like foreign languages to Portia. She was totally lost.

At least the deception would come to an end this evening. There was no way she could fool Daniel Logan into believing that she was Fiona. He'd see through her in the first five minutes. The end of the charade was at hand.

After Daniel learned the truth she could get her life back under control. What could the man do, dismiss her from the troupe? A horrid thought crossed her mind. What if he decided to get rid of all the MacIntoshes? No, he wouldn't do that. She wouldn't let that happen. She'd figure out a way to make *him* end the pretend engagement without bringing calamity down on the others. But how? For once she needed some of her father's devious thinking.

What she really needed was to concentrate on getting ready for their on-stage performances. Bertha and Rowdy were seeing to the sets and costumes. Scripts were being studied and a quick run-through was scheduled for tomorrow afternoon. Mr. Lane, the Chautauqua director, was preparing a schedule and they'd know by tomorrow when and how often they would be expected to perform. If only her father could regain his health everything would be perfect—except for Daniel Logan, who seemed intent on intruding into every thought she had.

She wondered where Daniel was now and what he was doing. To be able to afford an extended period of time at the Sweetwater, Daniel had to be very well off. She wondered what kind of woman he'd choose to marry. Would she be a grand lady like the ones she'd seen in the hotel? What would Daniel think when he saw her tonight instead of Fiona?

Thoughts of the evening that lay ahead seemed to nudge her mind like the persistent buzz of the great fat bumblebee which seemed determined to make a hole in the wall adjacent to her window ledge. She understood that bee very well. He was desperately trying to fit himself into a situation where he was grossly unsuited. That was what she was about to do. Oh, blast! Why had she ever been foolish enough to break into that railcar?

There was a disturbance in the doorway. As Portia looked up Bertha was heading toward her, her lips pursed angrily. Behind Bertha was a heavy set woman, dressed in black and wearing an expression more forbidding than the mask of the wicked witch in MacBeth.

"Are you Miss MacIntosh, Miss Portia MacIntosh?"

"Yes ma'am." Portia came to her feet and pulled the kimono together, folding her arms across her chest. "Is there something wrong?"

"Yes there is, but I'll wait, while you cover yourself properly."

The woman stopped and turned her head. The absurd picture of one of those ostriches at the Philadelphia zoo flashed into Portia's mind, and she had to bite back a smile. "But I am dressed. This is a Chinese kimono, Mrs. . . . ?"

"I see. Well, I am Mrs. Willard Bartholomew and I represent the women of the Missionary Society. We are very concerned about actors performing stage plays here in our church school."

"Your church school? I'm afraid you don't understand, Mrs. Bartholomew. We perform only Shakespearean plays, not—whatever it is you think we do."

"We've heard about those wicked vaudeville shows in New York City. One of your own men admitted that you'd played there. Perhaps you don't understand that the Piedmont Chautauqua is a school for Sunday School teachers, and missionaries devoted to the spiritual enlightenment of the heathen man."

"I was told," Portia began, remembering that their employment at the Chautauqua was tenuous at best, "that this place was conceived as a means of, of . . ."

". . . broadening the mind of the common man," Fiona finished as she moved over beside Portia and smiled sweetly at the woman towering over both of them.

"Common is the proper word, I'd admit. Just look at you, standing there half dressed, with your hair streaming about like one of those wicked 'stage' actresses."

"Common?" Portia was too angry to reply. Instead she began to walk slowly toward the woman whose cheeks puffed out with every breath, making her resemblance to the ostrich more and more obvious. Before she began to give way to the violent urge she had to giggle, Portia answered slowly. "I suggest, Mrs. Bartholomew, that if you have an objection to our performing, you take it up with whoever is in charge here."

"Oh, my husband, the Reverend Mr. Bartholomew, has already done so. We feel we were grievously misinformed. The summer schedule made no mention of your attendance or Mr. Bartholomew would never have consented to join the staff." The woman's jaw tightened grimly. "We don't deal with your sort!"

Portia heard Bertha's gasp and sensed her movement toward the woman standing lockjawed and righteous in her moment of glory. "Bertha!"

"I see." Bertha shrugged off Portia's warning. "You're a missionary but you don't deal with stage actors, or with people of 'our sort'? My, my, what a Christian attitude you have. Brought your stones along, did you?"

Mrs. Bartholomew was startled. "I beg your pardon?"

Portia stepped between Bertha and the woman. "For your information, Mrs. Bartholomew, my father, Captain Horatio MacIntosh, is an educated man. He used the bible to teach my sister and me how to read."

"That's commendable, I'm sure—" she began, fussing with the purse she had crammed under one arm.

"And one of the passages I recall learning says something about those who are without sin casting stones. I don't see any stones here. I assume that means that we are both in agreement that you are less than perfect, and that we understand each other. Good night, Mrs. Bartholomew.''

A choked intake of breath escaped the woman's lips as she opened and closed her mouth in a search for words. Finally she whirled around and strode toward the door, pausing for one last barb delivered from the hallway. "Don't think that I'm done with this, Miss MacIntosh. You may have bought your way into this school, but I'll see to it that those who come here for the comfort of the ministry won't attend your stage plays.''

"I think that we've made an enemy, Portia." Bertha shook her head and closed the door after the irate Mrs. Bartholomew.

"Maybe you ought not to sit in the window," Fiona said, her bravado suddenly gone. "We don't know who else has the wrong idea about us."

"Nonsense, nobody can see me. Besides, I'm covered." Portia leaned over letting her hair fall forward across her face. She didn't want Bertha and Fiona to see that she was concerned. It wasn't the woman that bothered her, or the fact that someone might see. What bothered Portia was the woman's observation that they weren't on the printed summer program and her statement that they'd bought their way onto the schedule. She'd suspected this from the beginning.

It wouldn't be the first time the Captain had taken them somewhere they weren't expected. This was happening more and more often of late and the day was past when the world was so desperate for entertainment that they'd rally around an acting troupe and welcome their show sight unseen.

This time, if they'd bought their way onto the schedule, it had been Daniel Logan who did it. And the last thing she wanted to do was be more indebted to that man than they already were.

Portia threaded her fingers through her hair and felt the heat of the sun absorb the moisture. She wondered where Daniel was right now. Was he standing across from the dormitory window watching? She flipped her hair back and looked across the tree tops. It wasn't the hotel she was seeing. It was Daniel Logan, who believed that Phillip was a man who wouldn't be offended by another man's body, or any other male thing that he might decide to do.

Portia took a deep breath and closed her eyes. She wouldn't run away from him. She wouldn't admit defeat. The house lights were being lit. It was time for Portia to dress for her greatest performance.

Across the grounds Daniel was leaning against the lacy white rail of the gazebo atop the rose mound that lay between the Sweetwater and the back portion of the Chautauqua buildings. Hundreds of rose bushes were bursting into bloom. They lined the circular walk that led the twenty-five feet to the top, adding their sweet fragrance to the afternoon air. Below, the manicured lawns lay like sheets of emerald held to the Earth's surface by patchwork stitches of bright flowers and green trees. Everything about the place had been designed to appeal to the wealthy and they were responding. It wasn't unusual to have the Astors or the Vanderbilts as guests.

During the next two weeks the hotel would fill up with even more choice prospects for a jewel thief. The guest list was impressive. Everything he'd seen so far made him believe that the thieves he was seeking were either already here at the Sweetwater, or would be here soon.

He wondered what would happen in the future. When the railroads and banking industry began to employ private police to protect themselves, the thieves changed their targets. They realized that there was a fortune to be made in robbing jewelry stores and traveling jewelry salesman. The bank and train robbers gave way to a different kind of criminal.

The retail merchants and the companies that mined the gems were forced to join together for their mutual protection. The Jewel Alliance was formed. The Alliance hired the Pinkerton Brothers to protect their products and hunt down the criminals. That move drove the thieves into the hotels and resorts and brought Daniel and Ian into the picture.

In the past the thrill of the hunt would have been enough. But of late, Daniel found his thoughts going back to the West and those days of struggle and anticipation. He'd thought that was all past, that New York was the measure of his success. But that lifestyle seemed artificial, like life at the Sweetwater. The Astors and the Vanderbilts of New York just had different names here in the South.

More and more he'd begun to look back fondly on the old West and the rowdy, tough crowd of miners who lived life to the fullest and made their fortunes on a turn of the shovel. There was a kind of stubborn honesty about them that he understood.

Portia was a lot like those miners. Portia. She'd crept into his mind again. Instead of concentrating on searching for the jewel thieves he was involving himself with a traveling Shakespearean acting troupe and mooning over a young woman who disguised herself as a boy and professed a liking for chewing tobacco.

He felt an unexpected smile curl the corners of his mouth as he thought about Portia. The girl was just that, a girl—a slim, boyish girl who innocently concealed how beautiful she really was. She was meant only to be a diversion to allow him space to move about the hotel unaccosted. Yet, from the time he'd caught her in his rail car he hadn't been able to get her out of his mind.

Tonight he'd take her and her sister to dinner and for a stroll about the grounds. Daniel would see the girls back to the dormitory. Afterward he intended to look into the gaming tables, the private poker games, and share after-dinner cigars with the gentlemen. It was time to begin seriously compiling a list of candidates for the jewel thief. The thief had to be here.

"Dan?" Ian Gaunt stood quietly at Daniel's elbow, holding out a long black eye glass such as those used by ship captains of old. "Would you care to look through the spy glass?"

"What, I'm sorry, Ian. What did you say?"

"I understand that you can see all the way to Atlanta from here."

Daniel took the slender instrument and placed it against his eye. From the vantage point of the gazebo the sprawling city of Atlanta came readily into view. It was growing in all directions in the years since Sherman had burned it to the ground. He swung the spy glass around, passing the great Stone Mountain and the lesser Kennesaw Mountain in the distance until the white Moorish towers of the Chautauqua dormitory were in his sights.

And then he saw her. Portia. She was sitting in the open window with her eyes closed as she dried her strawberry blond hair in the warm sunshine. Like some old world Rapunzel she sat, her slim young body outlined against the dark room beyond. For a second she opened her eyes and blinked them quickly as if she had gotten a speck of dirt in one of them. When she lifted her hand and shielded her face from the sun he realized that she was looking directly at him. For a moment their eyes seemed to meet and he could see her small tongue slide across her upper lip.

"Damn." She *was* beautiful. His involuntary exclamation drew Ian's attention.

"What's wrong?"

"Nothing Ian. I was just thinking about . . . well, never mind. Have you ever had a woman give you a bloody nose?"

"No, but there was a lady in Seattle once who tried."

"Ah, Ian, you always seem so cool, so composed. Don't you have any problems?"

"Problems? Not really. But I do confess that there are times when I'd like someone to share my life."

"Maybe it should be *you* looking for a wife, Ian. It isn't too late."

"I think it is, Dan. I guess I've just become more skeptical about people. I find it difficult to approach the kind of women that come to a place like this."

Daniel decided that he'd probably be better off if he were

more like Ian. At least he wouldn't be captivated by a gypsy actress who used her teeth as weapons. He couldn't wait to see how she planned to conceal that glorious hair tonight. Daniel snapped the spyglass shut and returned it to his companion.

"Here you are Ian. Wonderful things, these spy glasses. You can certainly see things you might not see otherwise." Daniel felt a broad smile widen his lips as he started down the circular staircase through the roses to the ground.

"I can imagine," Ian said dryly. "Now, what about this hotel guest list? Are you ready to have a look at it?"

"How'd you manage to get the list, Ian? You didn't give us away, did you?"

"Certainly not. Getting the list was no problem. It's posted in one of the downstairs halls, so that the other guests can know who has arrived and who is departing."

"Very convenient. And do you see any interesting prospects?" Daniel began to scan the names printed in a fine hand.

"Outside of the locals, there are several groups who came here from Saratoga Springs and some newcomers from New Orleans and Florida. The only names I question on the list are a Mr. and Mrs. William Trevillion and their daughter Victoria, and of course, the Lady Evelyna Delecort and her son Edward."

"Somehow, Ian, I can't see Edward as a jewel thief. Lady Evelyna? If she were a little younger—maybe. We'll see."

As he descended from the top of the rose mound, Daniel wondered if Edward would whisk Fiona away as he had last night. He'd have to have a little talk with the nobleman. Riding bicycles in the park with Daniel Logan's fiancee openly could jeopardize his plans. If Edward insisted on courting the girl, Daniel would have to make certain that he approached it clandestinely. Nothing like a little guilt and guile to make an affair more appealing.

"Ian, do you think we could find a local seamstress to help out with the costumes and canvas for stage sets?"

"Why, Daniel? That group of actors can fend for itself. Surely you don't intend to let the other guests know you're involved with them, do you?"

"Ian, you're turning into a snob. Don't you know that Harvard University and the renowned newspaperman, Henry Grady, are responsible for the Piedmont Chautauqua being housed here? Half the people you see on the grounds are day visitors, workers, ordinary people. Surely you don't object to being in their company. It's our duty to help those less fortunate."

"I'm aware of the plight of the common man, Daniel," Ian said dryly. "We're probably two of the commonest men here. If we were women we'd be making four dollars a week working in a shoe factory."

"Or acting in a traveling stage play like Captain MacIntosh's daughters."

Ian groaned. "Now we're back to them again. And that's what worries me. You're getting too involved with that woman. I saw how the sparks flew between the two of you. But she's not right for you. And this isn't smart."

Daniel and Ian lifted their hats in greeting to the other guests as they made their way across the lawn and climbed the veranda steps. They claimed a couple of rocking chairs and sat down on the great open porch that wrapped around the hotel like a baby's bib.

"Afternoon, Mr. Logan, Mr. Gaunt," a portly man with high buttoned shoes and a straw hat offered. "Care to join me for a cigar and a glass of Kentucky whiskey?"

Daniel nodded his agreement. "Afternoon, sir. I'm afraid you have the advantage on me. I don't believe we've met."

"You're right. One of those blacksuited hotel helpers pointed you out. William Trevillion, here. Pleased to meet you."

"How do you do? I'll pass on the cigar but a bourbon and mineral water sounds good."

"No mineral water for me, thanks. It would be a damn waste of good drinking whiskey to mix it with any mineral water. I let my wife drag me down here, but this lithia water is worse than that New York spring water. Bathing in it is about as close as I come to that poison.''

"Agreed. But the medicinal attributes of the water have certainly received their share of testimonials. Ian, what about you . . . ?''

But Daniel saw that Ian's attention was totally focused on the approach of a slender young dark-haired girl with a heart-shaped face and mysterious green eyes. Ian looked a bit like Edward had looked the night before when he caught sight of Fiona.

"Oh, Papa.'' The young woman swept across the porch and stopped abruptly as though she hadn't really seen either Daniel or her father. "Mama sent me to fetch you.'' She spoke the words but her attention was totally claimed by Ian.

"I'm sure she did,'' Trevillion observed dryly. "Mr. Logan, Mr. Gaunt, my daughter Victoria, just arrived from finishing school in Europe.''

Daniel groaned inwardly—another prospect was being placed on the matrimonial block. "Very nice to meet you, Miss Treveillion.'' For once he needn't have worried. This startingly beautiful young woman had eyes only for his associate.

"Yes, uh . . . I mean . . .'' Ian stuttered miserably as Victoria focused her attention on him.

"All right, Victoria, now run along and tell your mother . . .''

"Oh, but, Papa, Mama said that I should remind you that it's time to take your French class over at the college.''

"French! Hah! Victoria, you can tell your mother that I'm . . . I'm . . .''

"Joining me,'' Daniel finished smoothly, "for . . .'' He glanced at Ian.

"Archery lessons,'' Ian supplied after an uncomfortable moment of silence while he simply stared at the attractive young woman.

"Quite,'' the portly man agreed firmly. "You tell your

mother that I'm never going to France, that I don't care if I know any wee-wee's or Monsewers, or whatever. These gentlemen and I have other plans.''

''Whatever they are, I'm sure they'll be more interesting than language lessons,'' the young woman said with a demure cast to her eyes, an expression in direct contrast to the suggestion in her voice. ''Do you speak French, Mr. Gaunt?''

Ian accepted a short thick glass filled with an amber liquid from one of the waiters, and brought it to his lips. ''A smattering—here and there, Miss Trevillion. In my travels I've managed to pick up certain skills of communication.''

''How nice.'' The girl dropped her gaze to the glass for a moment, then switched her attention from Ian to Daniel as though she'd just noticed his presence. ''Will we see you two gentlemen at dinner this evening?''

''Of course, madam,'' Ian said in a rather strained voice. ''Mr. Logan and his fiancee will be dining at eight.''

''Fiancee?'' Her eyes widened and moved casually back to Ian. ''And you, sir?'' she said softly. ''Are you . . . affianced?''

''Me?'' Ian's face flushed and he glanced at Daniel for help. ''Certainly not. I'm . . .''

''Available.'' Daniel supplied the answer as he took a sip from his drink. ''I think that Miss Trevillion might be the answer to the problem you mentioned earlier, Ian. I'm sure that you'd be pleased to have Miss Trevillion and her mother and father join you for dinner this evening, wouldn't you, Ian?''

''Uh . . . yes,'' Ian stammered, uneasily. ''I'd be delighted, Miss Trevillion.''

With one last glance at Daniel, the young woman offered her hand to the startled Ian and waited while he lifted it to his lips with old world poise.

''I'd be delighted to join you. However, my mother isn't feeling well. Could you possibly settle for just me? I mean I'll be properly chaperoned by all the other guests here, won't I?''

"Of course," Ian agreed, never taking his gaze from the young woman, who'd taken a step closer. "I'd be delighted to escort you to dinner. Until this evening, Miss Trevillion."

"Until this evening, Mr. . . . Gaunt, is it?"

"Ian, Ian Gaunt," Daniel said in an impish tone, "of the Scottish Gaunts. Ian's family fled from Scotland the year of the 1745 Scottish rebellion and emigrated to Canada where they've been in business," Daniel added, "for over a hundred years."

"And what kind of business does your family have in Canada, Gaunt?" Mr. Trevillion asked indifferently as he pulled a cigar from his inner coat pocket and bit off the end.

"My family is into foreign investments," Ian said smoothly, still holding Victoria's hand.

"Oh, what do you invest?" Victoria made no attempt to remove her hand from his grasp.

"Money. Several years ago I started my own business. I act as a kind of go-between," Ian explained easily. The discussion of business had never been a strain for Ian. "I arrange things."

Victoria's lips parted into a sweet smile. "You mean like a banker?"

"Well, yes, among other things," Daniel finally interrupted. Ian was definitely being caught up in the young lady's spell. It was Fiona and Edward all over again. Ye gods, it must be the water. Everybody was going ga-ga over everybody else. In this case Victoria seemed genuine enough, but William Trevillion didn't match his daughter's polished demeanor. Something wasn't right.

"Better get along now girl," Mr. Trevillion admonished. "If you're going to dinner with Mr. Gaunt here, you'd better start getting ready now, or you'll starve the poor man to death waiting for you."

Victoria stepped back and lowered her eyes prettily. "Yes, Father. And I look forward to this evening, Mr. Gaunt."

The three men watched as the young woman gave a last reluctant smile and turned back inside the hotel. Daniel suspected that she'd gotten the message that he was wife hunting. She'd probably been told to play up to him. But it had been Ian who caught her attention, and that might prove interesting.

Daniel glanced at his friend critically. He'd never thought much about Ian's appearance but he supposed that he was attractive to women. In his cummerbund and afternoon coat he looked like all the other guests of the hotel, prosperous and very proper. If the truth be known, Ian was more of a real gentleman than Daniel had ever pretended to be.

Silent and loyal, Ian's only problem might be that he was becoming downright stuffy. Miss Victoria could be just what Ian needed. Daniel was fairly certain that Victoria Trevillion, for all her schooling, was the kind of woman who went after what she wanted. Ian might not even have to do the pursuing.

Now Ian was staring after the receding figure with a curious puzzled expression on his face. Daniel chuckled to himself. The Sweetwater was certainly fulfilling its promise of entertaining its guests. No reason why Ian shouldn't get himself a woman, a wife even. He had the money, certainly. Daniel had never been miserly to him and Ian had invested his funds cautiously. If the truth be known, Ian's wealth was more than respectable.

When they left Willard Trevillion an hour later, Daniel had determined that Mr. Trevillion had married the money he was spending. And he thought about the fact that the Trevillions had just recently been at Saratoga Springs.

Daniel was invited to join the nightly poker game in one of the suites on the top floor of the hotel, a game by invitation only, for gentlemen who could afford to lose.

Later that evening Ian was berating Daniel for suggesting that he escort Victoria Trevillion to dinner. "Why in the world did you do that, Daniel?" Ian was tying his ascot and adjusting the green cummerbund which he preferred over the traditional brocade vest. "I won't know what to say to a young woman like her. I need to be keeping an eye out for . . ."

"For who, Ian? If you mean the thief, we don't have any idea who we are looking for. William Pinkerton's tip simply said that the burglar is probably acting alone and that he is on his way to the Sweetwater. Something or somebody special drew him here and sooner or later, we'll figure out what he's after. This is the way we've approached every assignment we've taken and sonner or later we've spotted our man. Just relax and have fun.''

"But how will I be able to look for the thief when I have to worry about Victoria?"

"My dear friend, Victoria's father could well be the thief. We already know that he's been at Saratoga Springs, and recently."

"How do you know that wasn't more bragging?"

"Remember how he said that mixing whiskey with mineral was such a waste? Well, he said that the lithia water had the worst taste. He's familiar with the mineral water at Saratoga. And he's outspoken. Just consider this an assignment and pump Miss Victoria about the other guests."

"I suppose I could, couldn't I? But Dan, I confess, I'm afraid that I won't be very good at this. I'll be distracted."

"You and I go back a long way, old friend. We've both worked hard. It's time that we enjoyed some of our wealth. Miss Victoria seems interested in you. You need to find out why. She is very lovely, isn't she?"

"Yes. She's the most beautiful woman I've ever seen. I can't believe that she's on the level."

"Maybe she isn't. Maybe she's the thief. We can't rule out anybody at this point."

"Is that why you're pretending to be so interested in the MacIntosh girls, why you've assigned one of our men to keep an eye on the Captain?"

"Of course," Daniel answered, knowing that his interest in Portia had little or nothing to do with jewel thieves, or the Captain's past.

Ian gave a final pat to his tie, picked up his top hat and handed Daniel his own. Looking in the mirror at the two of them Daniel had to admit that they made a dashing pair. Ian, with his light hair and serious expression was sophisticated and elegantly fashionable. He looked like some old world aristocrat in his gray velvet coat and matching corded breeches. Beside Ian, Daniel's black hair and mustache, his black frock coat and brocade vest made him look like a Mississippi riverboat gambler. Yes, Ian had class. Daniel simply had money.

"Let's get to our ladies, old friend." Daniel clasped Ian about the shoulders, stepped away, gave a sporty tap to his top hat and began to whistle a merry tune as he opened the door. "After you, Mr. Gaunt."

An uneasy Ian Gaunt preceded Daniel out the door and down the winding staircase to the great lobby, nodding at the patrons on the stairs and in the bright expanse of light below.

"You reserved a table for us both?" Daniel inquired as they reached the hallway.

"Yes. My table should be ready now and yours in half an hour."

"Thank you, Ian. Have fun with the lovely Victoria, but watch out for Mama. She could always get well and join you. She's probably two-headed and four-footed."

"I hope not. If so, I may very well come and trade with you." He shook his finger at Daniel and touched it to the brim of his hat. "Perhaps Miss Victoria and I will see you later, at the Pavilion."

"Do you dance, Ian?"

"Certainly. One of your saloon lasses taught me, in Virginia City."

Daniel's lips spread into a knowing curl. "Lasses? I never saw you dancing Ian. When did that take place?"

"The lessons were private, Dan, very private. There are some things a Scotsman never tells." Ian bowed slightly, returned Daniel's smile and turned toward the steps, his walk a bit more jaunty than usual.

Daniel watched as Ian strode away. Perhaps Ian wasn't so staid as he'd suspected. Perhaps Ian had a totally secret life.

Daniel grinned openly. Perhaps Miss Victoria ought to be very careful. She might not stand a chance against Ian's Scottish charm.

Daniel noticed that he wasn't the only one watching Ian with interest. Several ladies carried on whispered conversations behind their fans as the well-dressed man they'd formerly considered to be a nothing more than a gentleman's gentleman walked by.

Daniel stepped outside and looked for his carriage, thought a moment and dismissed the idea. The evening was still dressed in half-light, and the Chautauqua school was only a short walk across the beautifully landscaped grounds. He and his fiancee would stroll back to the hotel. Yes, they'd enjoy a moment of privacy before being subjected to the scrutiny of the three hundred or so guests who would be dining in the hotel this evening.

Whistling a merry dance-hall tune, Daniel picked up his pace. He wondered what his fiancee would be wearing this evening. He wondered too about Phillip. He wondered a great deal about Phillip.

Eight

"**W**ALK? You really expect me to walk in these pointed-toed torture contraptions that you call shoes?" Portia's ankles refused to stand upright as she stumbled around the dormitory in the white satin evening shoes that Bertha and Fiona had buckled on her feet.

"Of course you can walk. Just pretend you're Sarah Bernhardt or Lily Langtry making a stage entrance," Bertha instructed.

"I'd do better to pretend I'm one of those tommywalkers in Mr. Barnum's circus." Portia gritted her teeth and forced her ankles to stiffen.

"No, Portia. You can't stalk about like that. Glide, you're a swan. You're beautiful."

"I'm no swan, Fiona. I'm the ugly duckling. Oh, won't you reconsider? This is your chance, Fiona. I don't like the man, but at least he's an American. Edward Delecort isn't for you. You're an actress. He's a lord."

A look of pain flashed across Fiona's face. "No, you're wrong about Edward," she said stubbornly.

"I'm not wrong, Fee. What do you know about that kind

of man? I won't let you disgrace yourself by becoming his
—his mistress."

Fiona's lips tightened. "You don't know, Portia. For once
you've run into a situation that you don't understand and
you're scared. I think that it may be *you* that you're worried
about, and you needn't be. Mr. Logan will be pleased, I
promise you. Tonight, you're the you that you've never
been," Fiona said desperately. "Come, look in the mirror."

Fiona pulled her sister to the window where the early evening light cast a softness about the coming night. "See here,
in my looking glass."

Reluctantly Portia took the hand mirror and glanced at her
reflection. Her reflection? No, it was Fiona's face she saw
looking back at her, Fiona at her most beautiful. Her hair
had been swept on top of her head and laced with pale pink
and green velvet ribbons. Her eyes were sparkling. Her face
was flushed. She looked as if she'd just been given a standing
ovation and it frightened her.

Portia had spent all her life separating herself away from
a sister who was her duplicate. Fiona had developed into
Fiona, the beautiful. She'd become Portia, the caretaker.
Now, looking at the reflection in the mirror, Portia had disappeared and she didn't know the woman she was looking
at.

"Don't you see?" Fiona gave her sister a quick hug.

Whoever this person was, Portia knew that Fiona and Bertha had created a miracle. The former costume had been
transformed into a stylish confection of lace and flowers. The
cream colored gown was cut low at the neck, and finished
off at the shoulders with great, gauzy, puffed sleeves sewn
with pink roses and green brocade leaves. Over Portia's protest Bertha had cinched her into a corset that drew her waist
into an unbelievably tiny hourglass shape. Now the skirt
hugged her body in the front and gave way to a pleated
fullness in the rear.

The picture was of overwhelming elegance. Portia couldn't

assimilate the reflection she was seeing. She was completely bewildered and she lashed out in her confusion.

"Even if I could walk, Fiona, I couldn't possibly sit through dinner with my belly button pressing against my backbone. You've strangled the breath out of me!"

Portia knew she was being cross. But she was unsettled. She was totally out of her element and being out of control was new to her, new and frightening, even if she hadn't had the specter of Daniel Logan ever present in her mind. It was as if Portia was no more and this new creature was taking her in a direction that she'd never been.

Through the open window came the sound of music and laughter. The troupe had fallen into the spirit of the gay activities. Even without any money at all the roustabouts could walk about the grounds of the hotels and the resort areas along the Dummy Line. For the first time in their travels they were to perform at a place where the performers would be entertained on the same level as the guests.

"Portia are you ready?" Captain MacIntosh knocked and entered the room. "Oh, my goodness, Fiona, you did decide to accompany Daniel this evening."

"No, Papa," Portia said sharply. "I'm Portia as you very well know. Don't josh me."

"I'm not joshing. I'm just . . . surprised. I knew that you two were alike, but Portia, my dear, tonight, you're stunning. Standing there in the light, you're like a work of art. Words fail me. I cannot describe . . ." His voice trailed off and even one who did not know her father would see the color drain from his face.

"Papa, are you all right?" Portia forgot her shoes and her clumsiness and hurried to her father's side. "Oughtn't you to be in bed?"

"My God, even the voice. You sound like her. You are very beautiful, my child, very beautiful indeed. Your mother would be proud of you tonight, for you look exactly like she did the first time I ever saw her."

"Mother? I look like our mother?"

"You are my darling Kathryn, standing there gloriously in the moonlight." Horatio's voice was reverent. And he held Portia's hand so tight that she knew the rare emotion her father was revealing was real. "She was the grandest lady I ever knew, Portia. Tonight you would do her proud. Madam?" Horatio bowed. "I'll walk you to the stairs."

"Wait, Portia." Fiona hurried to catch up. "Your gloves. You must cover your hands." She handed Portia a pair of white elbow length gloves with three buttons at the wrist.

Still under the spell of her father's words, Portia slid her hands into the gloves and held them out for Fiona to fasten the loops.

It was a vision of the mother she'd never known that accompanied Portia down the steps and into the parlor where Daniel Logan was waiting. When Portia caught sight of the roguish dark-haired man holding out his hand, she knew how her mother must have felt when she caught sight of Horatio for the first time as well.

"Good evening . . . Daniel."

"Fiona?" Daniel was equally dazed. He'd accepted and appreciated Fiona's beauty the night before, but this evening she was absolutely stunning. There was a new excitement about her, a mysterious ethereal quality that surpassed his expectations. But beneath the proud beauty of the woman standing before him, there was something more, something fiery shimmering beneath the surface. And that unnamed element took his breath away. "My dear!"

Daniel took her hand and raised it, holding her fingertips for a long intimate moment before he touched his lips to them. Her eyes seemed bluer, more intense. Her hair, less honeyed, more vibrant. And her smile held the promise of intrigue and passion.

"Is Phillip going to allow us to be alone tonight?" Daniel had to hold on to himself with every ounce of control to keep from kissing those lips now parted breathlessly.

"Yes."

"Yes?" Daniel repeated her soft-spoken reply. Had she whispered because she was agreeing that she too felt the wonderful tension between them?

"Good evening, Daniel," she said, adding, "You look very grand tonight."

"I look grand?" he repeated. "I'm looking at a vision of Ophelia, the reincarnation of Miranda, the embodiment of Bathsheba and Cleopatra, and you're offering me compliments?"

"My goodness." Portia giggled as she realized the mistake Daniel was making. For a moment she'd been caught up in the magic of the moment. She'd been Sarah Bernhardt. She'd been Lily Langtry. She'd been Kathryn. Then she'd giggled. It hadn't taken long for her to remember that Daniel wasn't seeing Portia; he was seeing Fiona. She'd have to remember that, keep reminding herself that this was a performance, a waking dream that she had to get through without turning it into a fantasy.

"Yes," Daniel said in a slow, deep voice, "I see your goodness, your beauty and your charm, my darling fiancee. And tonight there's more. I'm not sure what, but by the time this evening is over, I expect to know." He tucked her arm under his and held her hand lightly. "Shall we go?"

Portia shivered. Once she'd passed through that doorway, there would be no turning back, and she was very much afraid that she would never again be the Portia she'd once been. She wasn't even sure she wanted to. The night was a blank script, with words yet to be written. And this was only the first scene.

"I hope you won't mind walking across the lawn," Daniel leaned his head lower and asked. "The night is so lovely and the luminous lights across the grounds are very beautiful."

"Walking? Oh . . . of course not." At least she had Daniel to cling to. She was doing very well until she forgot to concentrate on her feet. She caught a loose pebble with the narrow heel of her shoes and stumbled. Daniel held to her arm and caught her with his other hand before she could fall.

"Oh!" Portia's face flamed. It was happening again. He was holding her the same way he had that first night in the rail car, his free hand holding her firm flesh. She knew he could feel the racing of her heart for she could feel it thumping against his fingertips.

Daniel's heart wasn't any calmer. He'd thought the woman in the parlor was Fiona, a different, more vibrant, alive Fiona. But she wasn't. As soon as he'd caught her he'd been certain. The breast he was holding, the tawny-gold hair, this was Portia, his Portia and he wanted to pull her close to him and whisper that he was glad.

Hold on, Daniel, he cautioned himself. *You'll frighten her and you'll never regain this moment.* With great control he managed a light laugh, steadied her, and began to look around with great concern. "Must be a hole here. Dangerous. I'll just mention it to the hotel manager. Wouldn't want any of the guests to injure themselves."

Portia took several shallow breaths and managed to calm her heartbeat and restore some semblance of propriety to her person. She was grateful to Daniel for the moment to compose herself. "I'd say so. There might be guests who wouldn't be quite so sure-footed as you were in coming to my aid."

"You didn't injure your ankle, did you?" Daniel continued to hold Portia's arm.

"No. I don't think so, but," she added with great inspiration, "I doubt that I'll be able to dance this evening."

It wouldn't matter. If Portia couldn't walk, he'd carry her, anything to have an excuse to put his arms around her. He'd work out something. "If you're sure, we'll continue. Our table is probably ready."

It was, and the evening was easier than Portia had anticipated. She soon learned that she wasn't expected to join into the conversations of the male well-wishers who stopped by to congratulate Daniel on his engagement, or drink a toast to the coming wedding. And the females—well she simply smiled and nodded her head at their simpering comments.

She couldn't have said what she ate, mainly because she barely ate. Though her gloves were sheer, she was unaccustomed to wielding fork and spoon wearing a covering on her fingers. She didn't dare remove them or Daniel would know immediately that she was an imposter.

One exquisite dish after another came and went, and the wine steward refilled their glasses even before they were empty. The lacing of her corset, already so tight that she could barely breathe, became a torture. Every breath she took forced her breasts higher above the drape of her gown. And every time Daniel glanced at her she felt a flush of red flame up her neck toward her face. She'd never been so tense in her entire life. Going on stage would never be a problem again.

"Penny for your thoughts, Fiona."

"I . . . I was wondering why you would choose to pretend that I'm your fiancee when you have so many beautiful ladies to select from." Portia's voice wavered and, embarrassed by the hungry gleam in Daniel's eyes, she dropped her gaze to the crystal dish of cut flowers in the center of the table.

"Ah . . . Fiona, don't you know how very beautiful you are? Not one of the women here turn such a delicate shade of pink when I smile at them." Daniel reached out and touched her cheek with his fingertip.

Portia shivered and pulled back, hastily raising her wine glass to her lips. The glass was empty again, and again she didn't remember having tasted it.

The wine steward immediately appeared and poured a fresh glass.

Portia took a hasty sip.

"You might want to go a little easy on the wine, darling. It's more potent than it looks," Daniel suggested, leaning across the table to stay her hand a moment.

"I'm quite all right," Portia insisted, jerking her glass back in confusion. "Are you worried that I shall become tipsy and embarrass you?"

Portia looked around. She couldn't see anybody staring at her. Was she making a spectacle of herself? Hastily she set the glass on the table and jutted her chin forward.

"Of course not, Fiona, darling. You could never embarrass me. The guests are probably convinced that I'm treating you badly. Stop frowning or I shall have to kiss you to make your lips look happy again."

Portia caught her breath. He wouldn't. Not here in front of the guests. Daniel leaned intimately forward. He would. Quickly she forced her lips into a smile.

The words that came from between those smiling lips were anything but happy. "If you try and kiss me, Daniel Logan, I'll bite you and that's a promise."

"Oh, I believe you, darling. I still have the print of your teeth on my hand from the first time *you* put me in my place."

"Oh?" Portia looked at Daniel with wide eyes full of mischief. She really wasn't angry. She was—she was—she didn't know quite what she was. The man across from her was the most infuriating person she'd ever met. Yet, she was enjoying herself. He was fun to talk with and without a doubt he was the most handsome man she'd ever seen. "I'm sorry, Mr. Logan. That was truly inexcusable of me."

Daniel's face softened, his eyes locking with hers in a challenge. "I'm not at all sure you mean it, but I'll accept the apology in the spirit in which it's given."

Daniel leaned back and took in a deep breath. Best that he make the conversation less personal. The tension between him and Portia was potent. In another moment he'd lean across that table and claim those lips. He didn't believe that Portia would struggle for long and even the struggle would be glorious. *Whoa, Dan. Impersonal, remember?*

"Tell me about your troupe, Fiona." Daniel waved off an approaching guest and gave her all his attention.

Gratefully, Portia focused on a subject that she would discuss without conscious restraint. "What do you want to know?"

"Tell me about the theater, where you've been and what you've done?"

"Oh, we've been everywhere, from San Francisco to Seattle, from Kansas City to Philadelphia. We even had an engagement once in Johnstown, before the great flood."

"I remember hearing about the Johnstown flood," Daniel remarked, recalling the disaster caused by the great rains that filled and weakened the dam. Thousands of people had been swept away when the dam broke. "Where else have you played?"

"Once we performed in Washington D.C. in the very theater where Mr. Lincoln was killed. But the most important stage was Mr. Daly's theater in New York City."

"Is this the first time you've played in a resort area like the Sweetwater?"

"Yes, though Papa booked us into a place in the Catskills once. But there was some misunderstanding when we got there and we . . . weren't able to work out the details."

"Those things happen," Daniel agreed, thinking uncomfortably about how close the Captain had come to finding the same kind of closed door here at the Chautauqua. "Tell me more."

"We managed to find a theater nearby and we gave a performance that drew some of the visitors from the resorts. It was difficult, but we managed. Speaking of resorts," Portia said casually, "my father did have all the details worked out for us here, didn't he?"

"Why would you ask?" Daniel wondered what brought on her question. He'd made it clear to Mr. Lane that their arrangements were to be kept confidential.

"Well, a Mrs. Bartholomew stopped by our room. Her husband is a preacher. She seemed rather upset that a company of wicked stage actors were to perform at the Chautauqua. She said that we weren't on the printed schedule, so I just wondered."

Daniel groaned inwardly. A preacher. Well, he wasn't

surprised. He'd had experience in handling them. From the time the mines were staked out the saloons and gambling halls moved in. Behind them came the men who preached brimstone and fire outside the saloon. A contribution to God's work had been effective then; maybe he'd have to make another here.

"I wouldn't worry, Fiona. There must have been some oversight. Henry Grady himself envisioned the theater, opera, grand musicals, performed for those who wish to broaden their minds. That's why the stage was constructed."

"I only hope some of these people come. I can't believe that any of the guests of the Sweetwater would be interested in our little production of Romeo and Juliet."

Remembering the free tickets he'd guaranteed, he replied easily, "Oh, I wouldn't worry about that. I understand that there are hundreds of people who come out each day from the city on the train. Those people were to be the original Chautauqua audience. My guess is that you'll have a full theater. Now tell me more about your life."

And Portia talked, describing their travels and their conquests. She didn't mention their defeats, but Daniel knew that in the last few years there must have been many. He didn't stop her. When she talked about her life, she forgot to be nervous or to hold back, and he caught the glimpse of Portia, the stubborn young girl, and Portia the proud woman. And there was a fire inside both of them. Unlike Fiona who approached life more delicately, Portia reached out and embraced it, and reveled in the excitement it gave.

"Tell me about your mother," Daniel said.

"My mother was a very strong woman. She always made everything right, even when it wasn't."

"You must be very much like her."

"That's what the Captain said tonight. I never knew. I mean, he said that *I* look like her. Me!"

Daniel heard the wistfulness in Portia's voice, the wistfulness of a child for the mother she'd lost. He wanted to reach out and comfort her. But he knew any movement to do so would break the spell of her confidence.

"Were you very young when she died?"

"We were ten years old. She died giving birth to a little brother. The doctor said she should never have had another child. We buried them both beside a little country church in Virginia."

Ten years old, Daniel thought, *almost the same age as when my mother died. My sister was only three then*. "Was your mother an actress?"

"She was a dressmaker, in a small shop in Boston. My father belonged to a traveling stage show. She saw him in a play and went back stage to meet him. When the troupe left town she went with him. She became his leading lady. She cooked, made costumes and looked after the troupe. My mother was the most important thing in my father's world. They were the original Romeo and Juliet. I remember watching them when I was very small. They loved each other, very much."

"A very brave woman, your mother, to recognize what she wanted and have the courage to go after it. I think, my dearest one, that you must be a very strong woman, too." This time Daniel didn't stop to think. He simply took her hand in his and held it.

Her animation wilted and for a moment she looked so sad that Daniel was sorry he'd asked about the mother she'd lost. For a time the woman he was dining with had forgotten that she was acting a role. She had become a charming, exciting woman, and the time had passed swiftly.

Portia glanced around, distraught for a moment, then turned back to Daniel and gently removed her hand from his. There was a suggestion of unease in the way she sat up a bit straighter.

"And you, Daniel, tell me about your life. Do you have a family?"

"No, not for a long time. My father was a prospector in

California until the gold played out. Later he moved on, ending up in Nevada. My mother was the daughter of another miner. They were never very successful and my father finally gave up trying. My mother did what she could for a long time, until my sister died. One night my father disappeared and not long afterwards, my mother . . . died too.''

"How sad. And left you all alone? How old were you?"

"I was seven. But I survived. I didn't have a choice. Good heavens, Fiona, how did our conversation get so dreary? Let's have more wine."

Daniel signaled the waiter and watched as their glasses were filled once again. Portia didn't want more wine, but she too needed the distraction to cover the emotion threatening to spill over and make their conversation more intimate. Blast the man. She didn't want to feel compassion for him. "Tell me, how'd you get to be so rich, Mr. Logan?"

Daniel thought about his answer for a long moment. The string quartet played softly in the background. Muted laughter and low conversation faded away. There seemed to be only the two of them, caught up in the golden glow of the light of the candles on the table and the luminous globes inset in the polished wood panels of the walls of the dining room.

He signaled for his after dinner cigar and twirled it in his fingers before he answered. "Do you want the official version, or the truth? As my fiancee, you may have either."

"Truth?" She caught his eyes and the question he was asking became more than a question. He sat with his head cocked slightly, one eyebrow lifted, his tension obvious in the stillness of his waiting. He was offering her honesty that demanded honesty in return, an honesty Portia wasn't ready to give. She laughed nervously.

"Oh, since I'm a pretend fiancee, I want the glamorous version, of course. I'm an actress, Daniel, and an actress only deals in make believe and illusion." Her long lashes lowered dramatically, then lifted to show eyes widened with resolution. "And there are times, Daniel Logan, when illusion is preferable to reality."

"All right, Fiona. Let's find a more private place and I'll tell you about Daniel Logan, and let you decide." He signaled for the check, signed his name, and rose, solicitously assisting Portia to her feet.

It didn't take but a step for her to realize that either the floor was wavering or she'd sprained both ankles instead of just one. She took another step and stumbled slightly, taking advantage of Daniel's arm. If she fell in the middle of the Sweetwater dining hall the whole world would know she'd had too much to drink.

Daniel caught the misery in her eyes and understanding her dilemma, made a show of arranging her satin cape about her shoulders as he slid his arm around her waist and nearly carried her through an open doorway onto the balcony overlooking the lake. "Ah, Fiona, darling," Daniel said with a grin, "I do believe you are a bit tipsy."

"I am not!" Portia stamped her sore foot, winced and would have fallen had Daniel not caught her in his arms. "It's just that my ankle is swollen."

"Don't, Fiona. Don't ever act with me. You're not on the stage now, you little witch, so don't pretend. You matched me glass for glass back there, with a few more in between. I don't think you're accustomed to drinking. I think I'm going to have to carry you." He swept her up and walked boldly down the steps past the startled onlookers and deposited her gallantly in one of the carriages waiting by the door.

"Daniel Logan, put me down! Whatever will those people back there think about us?"

"They'll think that you just like my arms around you. The women will wish it were them, and the men, ah, darling, don't ask me what the men are thinking now. I don't think you're ready for that. Take us around the lake, driver."

Daniel settled back with his arm across the back of the open carriage. Portia looked up and saw his eyes filled with mischief. He was openly staring at her and as their eyes met his expression turned into something so powerful that she couldn't look away. Every part of her body caught fire and she shivered uncontrollably.

As her evening cape slipped from her shoulders, Daniel caught his breath. At that moment he wanted to kiss her more than he'd ever wanted anything in his life. The night and the music only added to the magic of the moment. The gentle sounds of the water beside them, the soft, sweet scented spring air rustling the leaves of the trees above them, even the moon washing the clouds with luminous softness, all seemed to surround them with an awareness that opened up such a pleasure as he'd never known.

Portia felt if she were inside Daniel's thoughts. The same magic touched her, bringing such an awareness of sensation that she'd felt as if she were taking in the very air that he was breathing out. Her defenses began to crumble as she gave way to the magic that arched between them. All thought of Fiona lay somewhere behind them. She wondered what it would be like to be kissed by a man, wondered and felt her pulse quicken at the sight of the man beside her.

Daniel shifted his arm, bringing it away from the back of the carriage to press her gently toward him. Portia felt helplessly trapped by his touch and she looked away shivering with anticipation. What would she do if he tried to kiss her? She was sure that Fiona had some experience with being kissed. But not Portia. Not until Daniel.

"What's the matter, Po . . . Princess, are you cold?"

"Eh, no. I mean—"

He'd bent his head close to hers so that when she turned to answer him his face was only inches from her lips, and her protest died as he said, "I'm going to kiss you, little one." He said it gently, and she knew she wouldn't stop him; she wouldn't even try.

"You are?" She whispered, and he heard the wonder in her voice. All he had to do was slide his arm lower and take her in his arms and . . .

Her lips parted in bold anticipation. She swayed toward

him and closed her eyes, waiting. Daniel groaned, and pressed his lips against the softness of hers.

Daniel had known passion. He'd known lusty women who took as much as they gave. He'd known women who pretended to be shy as they teased a man to distraction, but Portia MacIntosh was none of these. What started with sweetness and wonder quickly ignited an unexpected passion that rocked Daniel to the core. He forgot his plan to bring their relationship to an end this night, and gave himself over to the delicious taste of her.

Her breasts brushed against his chest and he heard the rustle of her dress and the soft sweet mewing sound she was making as all resistance melted away and she pressed herself against him. He let himself imagine, just for a second, the feel of her beneath that tightly laced corset, the sight of her glorious hair spread across his pillow, the scent of her body lush and ready for love.

Shocked at her natural response, Daniel drew back for a moment, gazed into her eyes and lowered his head again. Somewhere in the back of his mind he was aware that he couldn't stoke the flame of her passion without being caught up in the blaze. But he couldn't stop his lips. His mind might have fought and won a logical battle, but his lips answered her invitation and he kissed her again, God help him. He felt her response, then her shy acquiescence as she opened herself up to him like the bud of a rose unfolding to the sun.

For one brief moment the tension between them burst into an explosion that seemed to rock the carriage.

"Damn!" Portia gasped.

Daniel began to laugh. The evening fireworks display had begun and the sky overhead had turned into a magic display of colored lightning.

"Well, you give some spectacular kisses, madam."

Portia was stunned. She looked around. What had happened? What had she done? She'd practically thrown herself at the man who'd taken over their lives. What had she been thinking of? That was the problem, she hadn't been thinking. She'd been hypnotized by the devil. She'd almost . . .

"How dare you? You force me to have too much to drink. You get me tipsy and then you . . . you . . . kiss me and try to take advantage—"

"Now, now. I didn't take advantage of you, Fiona, darling. If anybody kissed anybody, you kissed me. And I guess you could say that we set off a spontaneous combustion. Just look at the heavens."

Portia looked up, aware for the first time of the skyrockets splattering the velvet sky. "Oh." She'd never seen such fireworks. For a moment it took her mind from the madness she'd just experienced.

For a time she sat, spellbound by the display, holding tight to Daniel's hand. She knew that what she was watching was nothing compared to what she'd felt when Daniel kissed her. She knew it, but she wouldn't think about that now. Tomorrow, next week, next year, she'd take out the memory of his kiss and allow herself to experience its wonder.

When at last the fireworks were over, the carriage moved slowly off into the silence toward the Chautauqua dormitory. At the entrance, Daniel assisted Portia from the carriage and held her hand as they walked to the door.

"Good night, my love," Daniel said softly and lifted her hand to his lips. "Parting is such sweet sorrow that I shall say good night till it be morrow."

She looked up at him in surprise. "You do know Shakespeare, don't you?"

"I know . . . many things, little one, and I think that there is much that I don't know as well." He leaned toward her, touched her lips lightly with his own and stepped back. "Good night, mystery lady. Thank you for a lovely evening. I'll see you tomorrow."

"Uh . . . No! I mean I . . . we won't be meeting with you tomorrow. Rehearsals begin in the morning and performances begin at seven-thirty in the evening."

"But I never did tell you about my past," Daniel said,

holding on to her hand. He didn't want the evening to end. He wanted to hold tight to the moment and to Portia as well.

"I think I already know more about you than I ought to know," Portia answered softly, twisting her hand and pulling it away. "I think you're a dangerous man, Daniel Logan, and I don't think I want to be your fiancee."

"Oh, but you are, darling girl. And I have no intention of releasing you from that promise. But, I'll leave you to your troupe—for now. Sweet dreams, Princess. Dream of me."

Portia whirled and ran inside, closing the door gently behind her. Daniel's final words were covered by the click of her heels as she glided across the parquet entranceway.

Daniel listened until the sound of her footsteps hushed. Across the lawn the music drifted on the night air. But here, at the Chautauqua, there was a kind of mystical quiet that fed the silence. *I'm damn sure that I won't sleep, and I'm no prince either. I'm just a man who's gotten himself in way over his head.*

Daniel Logan cocked his head rakishly as he walked back to the carriage. Hell, he'd been at worse places and he'd gotten himself out—or in. Too bad there wasn't a balcony on the fair Portia's bedroom window. He sniffed the summer air and shook his head. With roses planted everywhere, there wasn't even a trellis. Ah, well young Romeo was right about one thing, the parting had been very, very sweet. And there was always tomorrow.

Tonight? Tonight he had some serious poker to play. He'd better hurry. Why then did he linger by the Chautauqua dormitory, mooning over a mere girl?

Because she wasn't a mere girl and he'd rather be here with a woman who wore men's clothing and pretended she was her own brother and sister than anywhere else he could think of.

Nine

DANIEL strode thoughtfully back across the lawn. Half way over he stopped, turned and walked back toward a stand of pines near the main entrance to the white-walled Chautauqua school.

"Ben, are you here?"

There was no answer. Daniel cursed. He walked farther into the shadows and out into the light on the other side, calling the name more loudly.

Still no answer.

Back toward the hotel, Daniel moved, quickly now, his mind considering the possibilities. Ben Moore was one of the ten Pinkerton men Daniel had brought along and infiltrated throughout the hotel staff and Chautauqua school summer students. Ben had been assigned to keep an eye on Horatio MacIntosh until he was relieved. He wasn't where Ian had said he'd be.

Coming toward the hotel from the far side, Daniel stopped and looked around. Beyond the porch Daniel caught sight of a man hugging the shadow of a giant magnolia. He walked slowly toward the great waxy leaved tree. "Ben?"

"Sir!" the man answered, waiting in the darkness.

"Why are you here? You were told to stand by the Chautauqua and keep an eye on that acting troupe and the Captain."

"I am, sir. He's in the hotel. Should I have stopped him?"

"In the hotel, you say? Blast! The game. Surely he's not found the poker game. No, I don't want him stopped. I simply want to know where he goes and what he does. Where's Ian Gaunt?"

"I don't know sir. I saw him earlier with a lady. They were—walking about the grounds. But I haven't seen him lately. Do you want me to stay here?"

"Yes!" Daniel snapped, hurrying past Ben's hiding place and onto the porch. He was worried. If Horatio had found the poker game that William Trevillion and Simon Fordham were organizing in Simon's room there was no way he could protect him again. Blast the man. Didn't he have any concern for Portia and Fiona?

Daniel walked quickly past several guests who called out greetings, climbed the stairs to the third floor and knocked.

"Come in."

Daniel opened the door, glanced around and breathed a deep sigh of relief. Horatio MacIntosh wasn't there.

"You're late, son," William Trevillion said heartily. "But I guess I wouldn't be in too big a hurry to say good night to my fiancee if she looked like the lovely Fiona. Come and sit down."

"Drink, Dan?" Simon Fordham noted Daniel's refusal as he sat down across the table. "Do you know these other gentlemen?" He introduced two Atlanta businessmen, a man from Philadelphia who was scouting a possible railroad site for the railroad tycoon and financier, Jay Gould, and Milton Forest, an assistant to the governor.

Daniel managed to do well enough to stay even for the next hour, while he subtly pumped the men around the table. He couldn't see William Trevillion as a thief; his bulk alone would prohibit any quick exit from the scene of the crime. The fact that William played a little desperately could be attributed to the fact that, except for his money, the man was clearly out of his class.

Simon Fordham and Milton Forest, whom he had previously met, were wealthy enough not to need the money and they played carelessly. The two Atlanta men discussed their business associations and movements so freely that Daniel quickly dropped them from his list of suspects.

Daniel lost the next two hands to Simon Fordham as his concentration waned. He couldn't get Horatio MacIntosh off his mind. He wasn't well enough to be wandering around. If he wasn't in the poker game, where was he? Better still, where was Ian? He was supposed to have joined them.

After one more hand, Daniel stood. "Sorry, gentlemen, I don't seem to be in the mood for cards tonight. I'll ask you to excuse me."

"A late date, perhaps?" Simon asked with a not so secret leer.

"Only with the sand man," Daniel said with an elaborate yawn. "I'm just not up to your late hours. Good night, gentlemen. Oh, and William, if you'll try to remember not to sniff when you're worried, you won't give it away that you're bluffing."

Daniel smiled as he heard the men discussing William Trevillion's sniffing. He shouldn't have said anything, but the man was a bad enough card player to lose without broadcasting a bluff.

Daniel started down the stairway to the floor below, heard the sound of feminine laughter and ducked behind one of the large potted palms spaced out along the hallways.

"But Miss Victoria," Ian was saying in a worried tone, "won't your mother be alarmed at the lateness of the hour?"

"Ian, don't you think you could call me Victoria?"

"Yes, ma'am, Victoria, but I expect I'd better say good night. It's very late. Almost everyone has retired for the evening. I wouldn't want your father to get a false impression of my intentions."

"Fiddlesticks, Ian. I don't care what Father thinks. I'm

the only one concerned about your intentions. I thought surely that you'd ravish me in the moonlight." Victoria pouted in disappointment.

"But Miss Trev . . . Victoria. That wouldn't be proper."

"Ian, I've spent the last three years being proper and it didn't get me what I want. I don't think I'm going to worry about that anymore. I know that it's terribly forward of me, but I think that I like you very much, Ian Gaunt. Aren't you going to kiss me goodnight?"

Daniel couldn't resist peering around the palm.

Victoria was standing beside the door to her room, with her back to the wall. She was holding the lapels of Ian's dinner coat, pressing herself against him as she looked up at him with adoration in her eyes.

Daniel groaned. Ian didn't have a chance. He ought to interrupt his friend, rescue him, but he'd let Ian enjoy the kiss that Victoria was intent on giving before he announced his presence.

"Kiss you? Here in the corridor? Oh, no, Victoria. I wouldn't dream of compromising you."

Victoria sighed. "Thank you, Ian, dearest. I do feel very safe with you. I know that I can let you have one good night kiss without being frightened that you will try to take advantage of me."

"You can?"

Victoria lifted herself to her toes, parted her lips and slid her arms around Ian's neck. "Kiss me, darling Ian, please? I shall positively die from disappointment if you don't."

From where he was watching Daniel knew that Ian hadn't intended it to happen, but he was kissing Victoria Trevillion. From Daniel's point of view Miss Victoria wasn't participating in some safe little good night kiss. Ian might not know much about rich young girls like Victoria, but surely he knew enough about women to recognize that this was a very intimate kiss of invitation. Then, maybe he didn't.

Daniel decided that the time had come to interrupt.

"Oh, Ian. Sorry, old friend," Daniel said in elaborate

surprise. "I wouldn't disturb you, but I've been playing cards with Mr. Trevillion and I think you'd better close this off. I fear he may be coming along behind me."

"Father?" Victoria looked stricken. She glanced at Daniel, reached up and whispered in Ian's ear, pushed open the door behind her and slipped inside like a shadow running ahead of its source.

"Thanks, Dan," Ian said, shaking his head in confusion. "I don't know quite know how I let that happen. I didn't intend to—I mean she . . ."

"I know. Miss Victoria Trevillion is a determined young lady. She has the look of a woman ready to fall in love, Ian, and I'm afraid she's picked you as the recipient of her affections."

Ian groaned and ran his fingers through his hair anxiously. "What should I do, Dan? I don't seem to be able to treat her like a lady."

Daniel threw his arm around Ian's shoulder and led him down the hallway to their suite. "Ian, for some reason that makes no sense to you, Miss Trevillion doesn't want you to treat her like a lady. And I'd say from the looks of you that you're ready to oblige her in every way."

Ian blushed and shifted his hat to cover the part of him that betrayed his interest.

"I'm sorry, Ian," Daniel said seriously. "I shouldn't tease you. But if Victoria interests you, why not let yourself enjoy the girl."

"She's quality, Daniel, a real lady. I'm not in her class."

Daniel opened the door and switched on the incandescent lamp on the table beside the door. "Ian, I just spent the last two hours playing cards with her father. I don't know what Miss Trevillion is telling the world, but William made his money in moonshine and pigs. I don't know what his name was originally, but I doubt it was Trevillion and the only quality he has is what he's bought for his daughter."

"But . . ." Ian took off his coat and flung it toward the coat rack. "What shall I do? She wants to see me again."

"Then see her, if you like. For now, go to bed and dream about the lovely Victoria. But, Ian, be careful. She's probably a virgin and she's ready. If she has her way, you'll end up married to the lady before you know what's happened."

"Married? Oh no, Daniel. I have no intention of getting married. Why, what . . . how . . . I mean, I wouldn't know what to do with a wife."

"Somehow, I don't think we need to worry about that, my man. Victoria seems intent on helping you figure it out."

Daniel laughed at his friend's distress, and stepped out onto the terrace, glancing across the tree tops to the dormitory window. The space was dark now and he couldn't see a thing. But he felt a quiver run down his spine and for a moment he wondered if Portia were standing there staring back. After a long time, he stepped back inside, leaving the doors open to allow the night air inside.

"By the way, Ian, have you seen Horatio tonight?"

"No, should I have?"

"Not necessarily, but I ran into Ben outside and he said that the Captain was inside the hotel."

"Well, he could have been here and I might not have seen him," Ian admitted, sheepishly. "Victoria wanted to go for a moonlight boat ride and we spent some time on the little island in the middle of the lake. I suppose he could have come in while we were gone."

"Island in the middle of the lake?"

"Yes, it's a nice place to watch the fireworks."

"Of course," Daniel agreed smoothly. "And it's very private," he said under his breath, wondering if the kiss he saw in the hallway had been the first exchanged between the two. Probably not, Daniel decided and felt his own loins quicken at the thought. Perhaps he'd take Portia for a midnight ride on the lake. Perhaps he was in as much danger as Ian.

"Dan, I suspect that Horatio could be with Lady Evelyna. I saw them together earlier today and neither she nor her son was in the dining room for dinner."

"Lady Evelyna and Horatio?" Well, that was an interesting development.

Daniel switched off the lamp, made his way through the darkness to his bed and undressed. Sliding between the sheets, Daniel forgot about Captain MacIntosh. He thought about Victoria kissing Ian and he thought about kissing Portia in the carriage.

Poor Ian. Victoria had cast a spell on him. He didn't have a chance. Poor Daniel. He wasn't sure that he did either.

"Where is Portia?" Rowdy asked.

"I don't know," Lawson Paine, the second male lead, answered crossly.

"Fiona's the one who's usually late," commented another player.

"First the Captain gets sick. Then we get a call to be here at daybreak," Lawson expounded dramatically. "Then the Captain leaves to take the waters and Portia sleeps late."

One member of the troupe after another grumbled and moved about the large room adjacent to the stage that they'd been assigned as a rehearsal hall.

"Well," Bertha stood up and announced with put-upon conviction, "I'll just slip up to the dormitory and have a look-see. You fellows unpack the props and set up the stage. And don't forget what I told you about calling Portia Phillip when that Mr. Logan is around."

Bertha walked back across the open expanse of ground in the center of the Chautauqua complex and entered the dormitory building. She was worried. They might be staying at a fancy resort, but nobody had to tell her that there was something odd about this booking.

Of course all those swells up at the Sweetwater were living on Easy Street, but she wasn't sure that they'd be the ones to attend their performances. Suppose nobody came? They needed work, a long spell of it if they were going to recoup any of their losses.

With the Captain ailing and the troupe already in dire

circumstances, she was counting on Daniel Logan. He was going to be their ticket to success, one way or another—that is if Portia and Fiona didn't fool around and bring everything down around their ears. At the top of the stairway she found Portia, dull-eyed and listless, leaning against an open window overlooking the drive.

"You look terrible, Portia. Didn't you sleep at all last night?"

"Not much. Was that Papa I saw leaving?"

"I expect so. He's only just gone."

"And who was that in the carriage with him?"

"I believe I heard him call her Lady Evelyna."

Portia jerked her head toward Bertha, winced and shifted into an exaggerated pantomime of slow motion. "Ohhh!"

"Oh? I see," Bertha observed shrewdly. "A bit too much to drink last night?"

"Of course not," Portia protested sharply in an unusual show of temper. "I just didn't sleep well. Are you spying on me?"

"Certainly not. And the only way you can sleep well is to go back to bed. What you mean is that you didn't sleep enough. I heard you come up those steps. But it was a long time before you came to bed. Trouble?"

"Maybe."

"Want to talk about it?"

Portia took a deep breath and closed her eyes wearily. "No, not yet, Bertha. I just had some thinking to do. How did the Captain meet Lady Evelyna?"

"She came here with young Edward yesterday, to fetch your sister. Then last night, all four of them had dinner together at one of them other hotels."

"Papa left his sick bed to have dinner? Why didn't you stop him?"

"Me, stop the Captain? Besides, he swore he felt fine. And Fiona promised to watch after him. But, I am a little worried, Portia. Fiona came on home about ten o'clock. When I went to bed, the Captain was still out."

Portia groaned. She didn't have time to deal with the Captain now. Not with Daniel Logan holding her hand every chance he got, and—kissing her. The fate of the troupe was hanging on her keeping Daniel happy. And she still hadn't come up with any plan to repay Daniel for her father's gambling debt. Portia's head felt as if there were a marching band rehearsing inside, and her stomach was protesting vehemently with the rest of her body.

"Is the cast assembled?"

"Just like you ordered. Though I'm not sure that any of them have ever seen the light of day this early, not unless they were just getting to bed. Lawson Paine may look as bad as you, but he's there."

"Fiona?" Portia started slowly down the stairs. She'd have earned high marks in deportment if she'd been practicing walking like a lady with a book on her head.

"Yep, now there's a surprise for you. She's flitting around, smiling and singing, like a hummingbird looking for the honey pot. But how are we going to rehearse without the Captain? It's hard to do *The Tempest* without Prospero."

"We won't do *The Tempest*, Bertha. We'll do *Romeo and Juliet*. Papa doesn't need the practice anyway."

"Better be careful when you're talking around here," Bertha cautioned as they entered the large hall. "It's spooky the way the sound carries."

"The hall we've been assigned was constructed because they were going to offer musical instruction for the students of the summer college. It's built to enhance sound."

"Then why ain't they offering any?"

"According to Papa, after Mr. Grady's death the contributions to the project began to dwindle and this summer there are no visiting musical instructors."

"Morning, Portia," Rowdy's voice boomed across the large room, setting off vibrations in Portia's head. She closed her eyes and stopped for a long minute until the pounding began to dissipate.

"Rowdy, what'd I just tell you?" Bertha frowned and looked around anxiously. "Not Portia, Phillip."

"Sorry, I forgot."

"That's all right," Portia said softly, waving Bertha off with a faint motion of her hand. "Good morning, everyone, please have a seat. I'd like to talk to you."

"Oh, my, you do look awful." Fiona came to Portia's side and put her hand on her sister's forehead. "Are you coming down with something?"

It was only a short minute later that Daniel opened the door to the rehearsal hall. Portia looked up and made her way unsteadily toward him.

"Good morning, Phillip," Daniel said pleasantly.

Portia winced. Why was it necessary for him to shout? "Good morning," she whispered, trying not to look at the man who'd plagued her dreams all night.

"What's the matter. Aren't you feeling well?"

"No! Yes. I'm fine. Please, let's not continue any discussion on the state of my health. We're assembled as directed. Follow me." Portia closed her eyes and breathed deeply and forced herself to turn back to the members of the troupe, now wide-eyed and silent.

"Please, quieten down. I have something to say to you," Portia began bravely, trying desperately to remember to lower her voice appropriately.

"Performing at the Chautauqua College will be an opportunity to recoup a season that has, up to now, been a . . . disappointment. As most of you know, we've come under new ownership, temporarily, of course, but nevertheless, we have to please, not only our audience, but—"

"Me." Daniel Logan stepped forward and surveyed the tattered group of actors and stagehands, most of whom, he understood were one and the same. A bit player in one scene might be a main character in another and move scenery in between. He sensed their antagonism and knew that they were ready to tear him apart at the slightest urging from Portia.

"The MacIntosh Shakespearean Acting Troupe belongs to me now. I'm Daniel Logan. Good morning." Daniel doffed his bowler hat and replaced his look of no-nonsense sternness with a lazy conspiratorial smile.

"It is true that I now own the troupe, temporarily of course." He nodded at Portia. "Please don't worry that I intend to cause you any trouble. I simply wanted to meet all of you."

Portia took a deep breath. "Fine, the tall man with the red hair is Rowdy, who in addition to being a member of the cast is our main stagehand and gaffer. Standing next to him is Lawson Paine, our current star who manages to avoid most of the stagehand work."

"And I'm Bertha." The motherly woman stepped forward with a warm smile. "I do a little stage work, but mostly I make the costumes and keep everybody in one piece." Bertha finished Portia's task of identifying the actors one by one.

"I am very glad to meet all of you. Good morning, Fiona." Daniel walked over and smiled at Fiona with pleasure. "I'm pleased to see my leading lady looking so vibrant this morning. The resort's amenities appear to have agreed with you. I was a bit worried after what happened . . ." He shot a glance at Portia, whose eyes were wide with fear. ". . . last evening. I trust you slept well?"

"Uh, yes," Fiona agreed quickly, much too happy to quarrel about anything this morning. "I had a glorious evening. But, do go on, Mr. Logan," she urged quickly, taking in Portia's look of dismay. "We would all be very interested in learning your plans, wouldn't we . . . Phillip?"

"Phillip?" Rowdy's question slipped out before he could stop himself.

"Do sit down and be quiet, Rowdy Bolling," Fiona lashed out in a surprising show of authority. "My *brother*— Phillip—and I would like to hear what our new owner has to say."

Thank you, Fiona, Portia wanted to say. Fiona had never

given the impression that she spent much time thinking an issue through, but this morning, she'd redeemed herself once and forever. After a few pointed looks and a whisper or two all the actors made an effort to say something where they could call Phillip MacIntosh by name.

Daniel was forced to invent little pieces of stage business to cover the whispers and loyal conspiracy of Portia's troupe. For once Portia was content to hang back and let someone else run the show.

Daniel watched as Portia closed her eyes. She stood, stiff-backed and erect. The French sculptor, Bartholdi, could have used her as a model for his Statue of Liberty. That she was not at her best this morning was more than evident and Daniel had to adopt a stern expression to keep from laughing at her discomfort. He suspected that their morning rehearsal would be short and to the point.

"Wouldn't you like to share your thoughts with the group this morning, sir?" Portia's sarcasm wasn't lost on Daniel. The hair that had been gloriously entwined with velvet ribbons last night, was now hanging in limp wisps from beneath her cap.

"As a matter of fact, I would, thank you." He had only planned to introduce himself and reassure the troupe, discuss his immediate plans directly with Portia. But Portia's attitude worried him. He didn't know what to expect when they met this morning, but he felt resentment, anger, and resignation in her voice. The anger and resentment he had expected, but the resignation smacked of giving up and he hadn't expected that.

"As you know the theater where you will perform is large. Having been used for church services and lectures up to now, the lighting is poor. You'll have the regular oil stage lamps of course, and I've arranged to add some of the new luminous lamps lighted with electricity. This will mean that you'll be under closer scrutiny than you've been before."

"Does that mean that the audience will see our mended

costumes, worn-out shoes and wigs that should have gone to their makers long ago?'' Portia knew her voice was sharp and critical, and she didn't know why.

She ought to be grateful that Daniel was assuming the responsibility for the group publicly. But everything was all wrong. It ought to be her father up here directing their actions, not this black-eyed devil who stirred her senses by stepping into the room.

''You're right about the wigs, anyway,'' Daniel agreed. ''They're pretty awful. Nobody in their right mind would choose to look that bad.'' His voice and attention were directed toward Portia.

Portia gasped. Surely Daniel wasn't referring to Phillip. Or was he? She risked a glance at Daniel. He lifted one eyebrow slightly and a grin twitched conspiratorially about his upper lip. Could he have learned the truth? Did he know that Phillip was a woman? Daniel Logan wasn't somebody's fool. Portia felt like an animal caught in a trap.

''Therefore, Miss Bertha,'' Daniel went on smoothly as if he hadn't seen Portia's questioning glance, ''I'm arranging for you to have an assistant. Mrs. Lavinia Farmer, a local seamstress, will assist in making new costumes as soon as possible. She'll bring along some local help to repair the costumes you have now and begin at once on new ones. This will give you four days before the first performance to get everything in working order. If you need more people, she'll get them.''

''For pity's sake!'' Bertha was wide eyed with awe.

''This afternoon you'll go into Atlanta with Mrs. Farmer to select the necessary fabrics.''

''But . . .'' Bertha was stunned. She looked at Portia as if to seek her approval. When Portia's nod of resignation was given, Bertha waddled over to Daniel and gave him a big hug. ''Bless you, young man, but we'd have a hard time stitching up new costumes that quick.''

''Not on one of Mr. Singer's new pedal sewing machines. I understand that they have one in Atlanta and I've made arrangements for you to pick it up. Now, could I have another one of those hugs?''

In less than five minutes Daniel had already won them over. Portia held back a tear of bitterness. She knew she was being foolish, but it hurt for someone else to be able to come in and do what she and Papa had wanted to do, and been unable to, for so long.

"And do you have an answer, Mr. Logan, for how we can expand a twelve-man troupe into a cast of hundreds for this stage?" Lawson Paine voiced the concern that Portia had been wrestling with.

"Not for the first performance, Mr. Paine, but I have an answer for the second. Phillip and I will discuss it later."

"Phillip?" Rowdy's under his breath scowl carried across the room as perfectly as if he'd projected it.

"Yes, Phillip, as my personal assistant, will carry out my plans and supervise the changes. I expect all of you to make suggestions, but Phillip has full authority. And there will be no changes made without—his approval."

Fiona, giving Rowdy a sharp elbow to the rib cage, answered for the group. "Certainly; my brother has always been in charge," Fiona said with such positiveness that the other crew members nodded their agreement. "And those of you," she looked at Lawson with a serious expression, "who want to remain here at the resort will do well to remember that."

"Fine, then we understand each other." Daniel nodded and said in an ordinary tone that managed to suggest he hadn't noticed any of the undercurrents of tension, "I've arranged hot tea and coffee and sweet buns for the group every morning. What is the first order of business, Phillip?"

"I'd like to know first," Portia dropped her voice and took on the proper character for playing Phillip, "just how long our contract runs. The play selection and costuming depends on the amount of time we're booked."

"It is my understanding that, though the Sweetwater is open year round, the Chautauqua is a summer school running only from June through August. I'm not certain how you'll want to handle the selection of plays, but I suggest some kind of rotation perhaps, of three plays. I'll leave that up to you, Phillip.''

Three months of solid work, food and lodging in one place. Portia heard the gasp from the troupe and looked around, trying to focus her attention on Daniel's question. Her head ached, her mouth was so dry that she could barely speak, and she felt as though her body were slowly turning into a hardened mound of wet clay, being pounded by some ambitious sculptor.

"Tea," she managed weakly. "Tea and then unpack the props for *Romeo and Juliet*. We'll run through the blocking this morning."

Daniel moved to the door and snapped his fingers. Immediately two uniformed waiters brought in trays of sweet buns and a rolling cart with hot coffee and tea.

Daniel filled a cup with hot strong tea and handed it to Portia. "I think you'll find that this will help with the headache."

"How'd you know I have a headache?" Portia snapped before she realized what she was saying.

"I see that I'm going to have to give you lessons in drinking, Phil. Anybody could recognize the signs of a hangover. You should take lessons from your beautiful sister. A lady never overindulges in the drinking of spirits, even if the occasion is one of . . . *amour*."

"I'm not suffering from a hangover, Logan," Portia snapped, caught herself and became rigid once more. "And I'm not," she repeated woodenly, "not a lady. I just have a touch of . . . indigestion this morning."

"It's a hangover, Phillip, and believe me, I know the feeling well. Must have been some evening. I'm curious. Was it what you expected it to be?"

"Yes! I mean no. I mean, I didn't know what to expect."

Not only had Portia learned about a part of herself she hadn't known existed, but she'd learned that the carefully constructed perimeters of her life were made of cardboard. Somehow Daniel Logan had succeeded in merging Portia and Fiona into one entity and Portia was having trouble knowing who this new person was.

The members of the troupe were busy carting the props through the door and onto the adjoining stage, covering their conversation with noise.

"I didn't know what to expect either," Daniel admitted, "but the woman I was with last evening was delightful. I not only enjoyed her company, but I like her, very much. I'd like to be with her alone again, in the moonlight. If it weren't for all these people, I'd take her in my arms and . . ."

"You would? I mean, Daniel. Please, I'm sure that whatever you and Fiona shared is private." Portia closed her eyes and stood very still. Though her head was pounding she knew that part of the throbbing she felt was from hearing Daniel's words of desire for Fiona. "Fiona is charming company. But I hope that you remember, Fiona is a real lady."

"Of course. Fiona is wonderful, more special than I ever dreamed. I think that I'm going to find my engagement more exciting than I'd ever imagined. And you, Phillip, did you share your evening with someone special?"

"Oh, yes—no! Oh, why don't you mind your own business? You may own my troupe, but you don't own me."

To her great astonishment, Portia felt the threat of tears rise up in her throat. Oh, dear God, she couldn't cry. Fiona cried, not she. She wouldn't start here, not now!

"Christ's foot! What are you doing sleeping in my velvet robe?" Lawson's angry shout took the top of Portia's head off and effectively stopped her tears.

"What's wrong, Lawson? And please, don't shout."

Inside the costume crate, sleeping soundly, was a small, dirty little boy. At Lawson's nudge, he opened his eyes and sat straight up, fear widening his eyes as he took in the crew of actors gathered around the box.

"Who are you?" Lawson demanded, then turned to the others. "It's a dirty little boy, a ten-year-old vagrant."

"He's just a child, Lawson. You're scaring him," Portia said crossly and started toward him.

"Now, you all get back," Bertha admonished. "You're frightening the poor lad to death. Get away, all of you."

"It's all right," Portia whispered, partly to reassure the boy and partly because her head couldn't stand anything louder. "What's your name?" Portia held out her hand and waited. "I won't hurt you. Come with me and we'll have some milk and sweet bread."

At the mention of food the child forgot his fear and took Portia's hand. She helped him step out of the trunk and knelt down to get a closer look. A runaway, the last thing she needed now. "I think he's sick. He seems to have a fever."

"Just look at my costumes. Wrinkled, soiled," Lawson said, lifting the cloak and throwing it over his shoulder while he rummaged in the open trunk.

"Let me see him!" Daniel quickly checked the boy, touching his skin with the back of his hand. "I'm afraid you're right, Phillip. No telling what's wrong with him. You all carry on with your rehearsal, I'll take care of the child. Come with me, boy."

"No." The child's voice was weak but determined. "Want to stay here." He clung to Portia's hand desperately.

"All right." Portia let out a sigh. The sooner she took care of the boy, the sooner they could get on with rehearsal. "We'll find someone to take care of you." She poured a cup of milk and handed him a roll. He took a few sips of the milk but the roll seemed more than he could handle and he stuffed it into his pocket.

"Fine," Daniel agreed. "Phillip, you come too. We'll take him over to Dr. Garrett. You all get on with your work. You can manage without Phillip, can't you, Fiona, darling?"

"Certainly, Daniel."

They'd done *Romeo and Juliet* hundreds of times and Portia knew that come curtain time in four days, they'd manage, one way or another, but she ought to be here, not trailing after Daniel Logan in the middle of the morning. What with her father taking the baths with Lady Evelyna, Fiona's surprising move to take over rehearsals, and Daniel Logan's revitalization plans, Portia felt that she was losing control of everything.

At that moment the child lifted his head, flashing pale blue eyes over her in a worried expression. Portia felt an unexpected wave of protectiveness wash over her. She couldn't turn her back on him. At least somebody needed her.

"Where are we going, Dan?"

"Just across the grounds. Dr. Garrett has his offices opposite the hotel."

"I hope so. I don't think this boy can walk very far." Portia's voice came out as more cross than masculine. She couldn't seem to contain the frustration that Daniel's take-charge actions provoked.

"We're almost there." Daniel looked down at Portia with concern, more concern than he'd expected. He placed his hand on the boy's head, comforting him with his touch. She was surprised at the gentleness he was showing. He seemed quite anxious over the boy and Portia found herself worrying too.

Mrs. Anderson, Dr. Garrett's nurse, said that he was free, and noting the child's flushed face and feverish tossing about, took them back into his examination room immediately.

Dr. Garrett came forward immediately. "Who is the boy?"

"We don't know," Daniel explained. "He was hiding in a costume trunk. Must have slept there last night."

"The trunk was opened yesterday," Portia said, "and he wasn't inside then. He must have heard us coming this morning and closed the lid to hide," Portia observed.

"You're saying that he doesn't belong with the acting troupe? That's odd. He seems so attached to you."

"No," Portia answered. "I've never seen him before. What's wrong with him?"

Dr. Garrett took the child and placed him on a black leather covered table. The doctor looked worried.

He lifted the child's shirt and peered intently at the child's skin. "Ah, yes. I think we're looking at a case of plain old-fashioned measles. But he's pretty sick, and he's going to need care. On top of that, he's probably contagious."

"What kind of care, Dr. Garrett?" Daniel asked, the seriousness of the situation lining his face and deepening his voice.

"Don't worry, Mr. Logan, you aren't respoonsible for this little ragamuffin. I'll find someone to look after him until we can find his family; perhaps Reverend Bartholomew, one of the ministers on the Chautauqua staff, would take him in."

"No!" Portia said quickly, "I met his wife. I don't think that she'd be very good with a small child. And I wouldn't want to expose the entire dormitory to measles."

"You're right," Daniel agreed. "Don't you have hospital facilities here?"

"Only the sanitarium, and I'm afraid that a child wouldn't fit in with alcoholics and opium addicts."

"Then I'll arrange something," Daniel said with authority. "We'll leave him with you for the moment, if we may. I'll make the necessary arrangements and return."

"If I may be allowed to make a suggestion, Mr. Logan," Mrs. Anderson interrupted stiffly, "I know a woman who might take the boy in."

"Very good. Does she have children, I mean does she have experience in dealing with children? I know that measles can be fatal."

"Martha Ethridge raised three boys, alone, without any help. She can cope with one little boy. But I suppose I ought to tell you that she is a bit outspoken."

"What Mrs. Anderson means," Dr. Garrett explained, "is that Martha Ethridge is our local suffragette. She has the community up in arms over her determination to give women the right to vote. I'm afraid she's adamant about the issue."

"As am I," Mrs. Anderson added fervently.

"I don't care if she runs a saloon," Daniel said easily. "All I'm interested in is her kindness and her nursing ability."

"She'll do a good job, Logan. Now, Mrs. Anderson, get down off the soap box and fill a pan with cool water. We have to bathe this child." Dr. Garrett dismissed Portia and Daniel and turned to the boy lying quietly on the examination table.

"Certainly, Doctor. That should bring his temperature down. Oh, Mr. Logan, please close the drapes on your way out. With measles we must protect the patient's eyes."

Daniel released the window ties and let the drapes fall. The room went dark and the heat was already becoming intense as they left the small two-room house.

"Are you sure you want to take on a child?" Portia didn't understand Daniel's decision. Why would he be so concerned about a dirty little boy? Was there no end to the man's need to be in charge?

"I'm sure. I'll go now and make arrangements. Will you have Bessie ready to go into Atlanta? Ian will pick her up, fetch Mrs. Farmer and accompany them on the train into Atlanta to pick up the supplies. I'll meet with your stagehand later to make arrangements for new scenery."

"And you'll serve lunch to the crew, provide new clothing for my family, sweep the grounds and direct rehearsal. Fine. Anything else, sir?"

Daniel caught himself. He'd quickly fallen into the habit of assuming that Portia would be like Ian, agreeing with his decisions without question.

But Portia wasn't Ian. Watching the ramrod stiff back and the deliberate gliding motion of her steps, he realized that not only was Portia unwell, but she was feeling rejected as well. He hadn't thought about what he was doing. Taking charge was his natural reaction to a situation.

Now he paused. The troupe had been Portia's responsibility for a long time, probably since the death of her mother. She made the decisions, handled the problems and planned their strategy. Now, everything had changed. Her father had handed over the troupe and the care of both his daughters to

Daniel. Portia was forced to become Phillip and suddenly the old Portia wasn't needed anymore.

Portia. He'd tried to avoid thinking about her. He'd tried to go along with her ruse that she was Fiona's brother Phillip, hoping that eventually she'd trust him enough to tell the truth. But she hadn't. Looking at the misery in her eyes, he knew that what he wanted to do was take her in his arms and comfort her. In spite of her tough talk she was only a girl, unspoiled, innocent. He was much too old for her, too worldly. He understood that. It was up to him to see that there were no more lapses in deportment. It was up to him to protect her, most of all from himself.

Sure, a little voice chortled. *And that kiss she gave you last night was innocent? You're the enemy who has awakened the dragon. You'd better make up your mind how you're going to handle the new Portia MacIntosh before she devours you.*

"I think we ought to talk, Dan," Portia began bravely. "I'm sure that you mean well. But you really don't understand the responsibilities of running an acting troupe. If my father asked you to oversee us it was because he was ill. He's already much better and I insist that you let me get on with my duties as manager of the MacIntosh Shakespearean Acting Troupe."

Though he was inclined to comply with her request Daniel knew that there were too many ways she could find out what he'd done to guarantee the troupe's success. That on top of everything else might be too much.

"I wish you wouldn't insist on being in charge, Phillip. I gave your father my word. You need me more than you think, and I'd like us to work together. Everything would be much easier if we could get along, don't you agree?" Stiff? Yes, but playing on her father's request was the only thing he could think of that would stop her.

They'd reached the entrance to the Chautauqua.

"Work together?" How dare he? His condescending attitude was the spark that set off a flare of temper. "Work together, when we both know that you cheated my father into gambling away our livelihood? I think not, Logan. And I'll thank you to stop forcing me—my sister—to accompany you about the resort. You have your life and she has hers. The engagement must end.''

Daniel sighed. She wasn't ready to tell him the truth. She'd rather continue to be Phillip than to face the fact that the sparks flying between them every time they met were brought on by more than just jockeying for position of authority. Maybe it was just as well. As Portia he wouldn't be able to keep his distance from her. As Phillip, she'd erected a natural barrier between them. He'd honor her choice for both their sakes.

Still, Daniel had to make her see that she was wrong about Horatio. "I'm sorry about your father, Phillip. But the truth is that he isn't well. He was supposed to stay in bed and I've been told that he left his room last night. If we can't trust him to take care of himself, we'll have to do it for him.''

"My father is both reliable and trustworthy. Once he regains his health he'll take care of us as he's always done!''

Portia knew that her protesting was a lie. Horatio MacIntosh had never been either one. He lied when the truth made more sense and he'd been known to lift a wallet or a piece of jewelry now and again if they needed money, or the notion struck him. But he was her father. She loved him. She was only ten when she'd promised her dying mother that she'd take care of them both. It hadn't been easy, but up to now she'd managed.

Horatio's little games were often amusing minuscule sleights of hand that were her father's way of tweaking the noses of the swells who might look down on an acting troupe. But he'd never done anything seriously wrong—never..

"I think I know who takes care of who, Phillip. But, are you sure that he's all right? His health is too important to take a chance on.''

"I'm surer of him than I am of you, Daniel Logan. Who was that man you were talking to last night after you left Portia? He was hiding in the shadows outside the hotel.''

Daniel started. She'd seen him checking with Ben. He

didn't like that. Ben was supposed to stay out of sight. Of course Ben was to have kept Captain MacIntosh out of trouble too, but he'd lost the man.

"Just a guest," Daniel said casually, "out for a stroll and a smoke."

"He wasn't smoking. I'd have seen the glow of his cigarette or his pipe."

"Maybe he's like you, Phillip, and prefers a chew. Speaking of chewing. I've had the hotel lay in a supply of good tobacco, especially for you. I do have to leave you now. I have several errands to take care of."

"Good!" Portia tried to keep the relief from her voice. She felt rotten and the constant tension from being alone with Daniel was more than she could take. Maybe she ought to join her father at the Springs. Maybe those dreadful waters would take care of her discomfort. Maybe they'd make her forget the feel of Daniel's arm around her. Maybe if she had a plug of chewing tobacco she'd actually take up the nasty habit. Maybe.

Ten

FIONA had disappeared. Rowdy said that the Captain was having lunch with the Countess, and Bertha had been gone all afternoon. The thought of food gave Portia stomach butterflies and after she had tried and given up on a nap, she left the complex and walked down toward the lake. Her head pounded, yes, but it wasn't entirely from the wine she'd drunk the night before.

The real problem was Daniel Logan. Portia was simply disintegrating into some fluid mass of confusing emotions. And it was all because of him. For the first time in her life her mind and body refused to cooperate and she didn't know how to resolve the problem. There was nowhere to turn.

With her hands in her pockets she left the path and strode blindly across the grounds beneath the trees, almost stepping on the couple lying arm and arm on the blanket beneath the limbs of the spreading oak.

"Oh, sorry. I didn't know anyone was here."

"Portia! Are you spying on me?" Fiona sat up, rearranging her gown defiantly as she stared angrily at her sister.

The slightly built handsome man with Fiona turned red in embarrassment at Portia's presence. "I hope you don't misunderstand, Phillip." He looked at Fiona, a question on his face. "Uh . . . ma'am?"

"It's ma'am, Edward. I don't have a brother. This is my sister Portia, who is leaving—now!"

"Believe me, Fiona," Portia explained wearily, "I didn't even know you were here. I'm not following you. But I hope you know that this can't continue. You are an actress and Edward is a Lord. All he's doing is dallying with you. Use your head!"

"Please, Miss Portia," Edward came to his feet and holding Fiona's hand, pulled her up with him, "I'd like you to know that I . . . I . . ." His Adam's apple bobbled as he swallowed loudly. "You're wrong about me. I wish to marry Fiona."

"That's out of the question, Edward. Fiona has responsibilities. She is the leading woman in the troupe. She can't desert the family. We depend on her."

"But, Portia, I love him." Fiona's lips were trembling, but she refused to back down. "I love him and I won't let you make me give him up. Do you hear me. I won't. *I won't.*"

"Hell fire and little fishes!" Portia looked at the determination on Fiona's face and knew that she was spoiling this for her sister. But she pushed away the doubt in her mind. "How can you talk about love? You don't know anything about men. How could you know that you're in love so soon?"

That wasn't the question she should have asked. But it was the question she needed desperately to have answered. Could two people meet and fall in love instantly? What did it feel like? What if one felt it and the other didn't?

"Oh, yes, Portia." A change came over Fiona's face. She seemed to glow. "You know instantly. When you look at that certain person there is a tingle that starts in your toes and runs all the way up your backbone to the top of your head and you just want to be with that person, forever."

Fiona turned back to Edward, leaned against his chest, and continued, "Isn't he wonderful, Portia. He wants to take me back to England with him. He's going to make some of Mr. Edison's wonderful luminous lights like those in the hotel, and he's certain that London will want them immediately. Oh, Portia, we're going to get rich!''

''I don't mean to make you unhappy, Fiona, but you know what will happen if you and Lord Delecort blow our cover that you're Daniel Logan's fiancee. If he turns us out, what will happen to Papa and the others? If you make Daniel Logan angry, a great many people will be hurt.''

''I don't care,'' Fiona protested tearfully. ''If you'd ever been in love, Portia, you'd understand how I feel. Why don't you just go tell Daniel the truth?''

''I can't. It might worry Papa. I can't help you if it hurts him.''

Papa. It wasn't only Papa that she was protecting by continuing with the disguise, it was herself. She felt as though she were being split down the middle. Half of her was the old Portia who knew who she was and where she was going. The other half was this new person, emerging like a butterfly coming out of a cocoon. She was twisting and turning, trying to stand, and she wasn't yet strong enough to fly.

Portia looked at her sister. She didn't have the right to cause Fiona unhappiness. For all she knew, after what happened last night, Daniel Logan would turn them out anyway, no matter what Fiona did. It was she who had changed the simple acting role into another dimension. And it would be she who was responsible for the consequences.

''All right, Fiona, while we're here. Be happy, but for a while longer, please be happy out of sight of the other guests. I'll work out something.'' She turned away, knowing that before she was even gone they were in each other's arms again.

If what Fiona described was love, she knew that wasn't what was wrong with her. She wasn't happy. She felt wretched. There was no wonderful feeling running up her backbone. When Daniel Logan had kissed her his touch had been like the jolt of a cannon ball. She'd been consumed with fire and she'd felt some great yearning that she could not put a name to. Even now there was a shivering unease that hovered beneath her skin, skin that felt hot and tight, and she wanted to fling herself into the lake to cool her body.

Portia continued to walk, arriving finally at the site of the famous Salt Springs, the basis of the resort area. It had been the Springs that had drawn the people to the area to begin with. She stood on a platform built among the rocks and watched the water boil to the surface. There was a salty, mineral taste to the air. The water itself looked like a thundercloud, a silvery clear thundercloud, spewing icy fog into the summer air.

"Would you care to take one of our vapor baths, sir?" An attendant stood at Portia's shoulder. "You appear to be a bit under the weather. The mineral water will cleanse the body's impurities, aid in indigestion and if you have a problem with drink or opium, you'll be much improved."

Was it that obvious that her thoughts were impure? Portia tore off her cap and slapped her thigh in distress. "Hell fire! Can you tell about my impurities by looking at me?" She was so startled by that possibility that she didn't realize that she'd released her hair to cascade down her back in a riot of color.

"Impurities, no sir. I'm sorry, ma'am, I thought you were a gentleman." The attendant looked embarrassed. "But we do have a separate section for ladies. If you'll follow me."

"No thank you, not today," Portia said hurriedly. "I just have a slight headache and I wanted to breathe the air."

"Then at least drink a glass of the lithium water. I promise you'll feel better."

Portia forced herself to drink the mineral water. It must have been her imagination, but the taste didn't seem as strong. It was almost refreshing. And surprisingly enough by the time she returned to the dormitory she was feeling better. Her stomach was calm, her head easy and her body relaxed and ready for a nap.

Portia wasn't certain yet what she'd do about Fiona. But

her infatuation with Edward Delecort couldn't be allowed to get out of hand. An English Lord couldn't possibly be serious about marrying her sister. Besides, Fiona was too important to the troupe. She was a member of the family and she couldn't desert them. Portia would see to that.

Maybe pleading Fiona's extreme fatigue so that Daniel wouldn't expect her presence tonight was a mistake. Maybe she'd only been thinking of putting space between herself and Daniel, not Fiona at all. Well it was done now. Tomorrow she'd worry about what they'd do next. Tomorrow.

Parting is such sweet sorrow. We'll part . . . until the morrow. But in her thoughts the lines were being spoken by Daniel Logan. She was Juliet, and she wanted Daniel. Oh, lordy how she wanted that man.

Eleven

"**O**H, Mr. MacIntosh! Phillip is it? I'm speaking to you, young man."

Mrs. Reverend Bartholomew. She was bearing down on Portia as she walked across the Chautauqua grounds. Every time Portia saw her she was more convinced that the woman had descended from the ostrich family. Her ample bosom seemed to get ahead of her skinny legs and her chin jutted upward as though she were permanently tipped forward.

"I want to talk to you, young man. I insist that you stop."

Portia stopped and waited. Why not? The way she was feeling she should have expected such an encounter. But this time she intended to put the woman in her pious place, quickly and permanently.

"How may I be of assistance, Mrs. Bartholomew?"

"I want to know what you've done with that poor helpless child?"

"What I've done? I haven't done anything with anybody, not yet."

"But I distinctly heard two of those disreputable looking men on your crew talking about finding a sick child hidden in one of your trunks. They seemed to think that you'd taken him in. And I want you to know that we don't intend to allow it."

"We, who?"

"Why the members of my missionary society. We are morally bound to instruct the heathen and care for the sick. It's God's will."

"I don't have the boy, Mrs. Bartholomew, but it seems to me that if God wanted you to have him, he'd have put him in *your* trunk. Now, please excuse me, I have work to do."

Portia fought the urge to give physical expression to the biblical expression, *smite thine enemy*. The woman was doing what she considered the right thing. Except that if she got her hands on that boy, she'd have to fight Daniel Logan to do it. Good luck to her. Portia turned away, stopped and turned back again with a devious smile. Why not? After all, she was her father's daughter.

"Oh, Mrs. Bartholomew, ma'am, if you really consider rescuing the boy to be your Christian duty you might discuss the matter with Mr. Daniel Logan. He's a guest at the Sweetwater. I believe that he's taken the boy in."

"Oh, the gentleman who has his own private railcar? Mr. Lane in the school office may have mentioned him to me, as a possible contributor to our cause." Mrs. Bartholomew couldn't conceal her momentary chagrin. It was obvious that Mr. Logan's interference had caught her off guard.

"Oh, yes," Portia said, in her most innocent schoolboy voice, "I'm sure that Mr. Logan would be most interested in making a contribution to your cause if you ask him. He is always interested in helping people."

"Oh? I don't suppose that you'd put in a word with him, in behalf of our missionary work, would you? I mean, you do have some connection to the gentleman, don't you?"

Portia suspected that Mrs. Bartholomew was torn between feathering her religious nest and giving in to the temptation of indulging in pure gossip.

"Oh no, not me. It is my sister, Fiona, who is affianced

to Mr. Logan. You must have heard of Fiona, the stage actress.''

Portia felt a smile twitch her lips. Let Mrs. Bartholomew wrest control of the child away from Daniel if she could. Poor Mrs. Bartholomew.

Portia thought of the boy and wondered if she'd done the right thing. Why wish that woman on anybody? But Daniel Logan? Well he deserved it for taking over like some tyrant.

Picturing Daniel and Mrs. Bartholomew facing off made Portia's devilish action more acceptable. Ha! The woman didn't stand a chance. Daniel Logan would either swallow her whole or charm her silly. Soberly Portia reached the conclusion that her own position was not so very different from that of Mrs. Bartholomew. She was standing square in the middle of the lion's den, and Daniel was slowly ingesting her, one wicked glance at a time.

Still, she couldn't get the child off her mind. Poor little boy, he'd been pretty sick. She didn't know anything about children, but she'd recognized the fear in his eyes. And she found Daniel's concern confusing. Why would he care about an orphan?

Why did he care about any of this? It didn't make any sense. From time to time she'd allowed some needy soul to join their entourage, staying long enough to get back on his feet, or, as in Bertha's case, become a permanent member of the troupe. But the process of belonging took longer for her than it did for Daniel.

Fiona had always accused Portia of focusing her entire being on the family, never allowing herself to see anything or anybody beyond. Not Daniel Logan. He seemed to have no boundaries. He was a man of instant decision, instant action, instant results. And he'd become instantly involved in their lives. Everything about the man disturbed Portia.

By the time Portia got back to the stage work area, Rowdy and the others were busy applying fresh paint to the scenery. She grabbed a brush and worked with them until lunch time.

Afterward they put away their supplies and returned to the dormitory to get ready for the evening meal.

Gone were the days of simple bread and meat, if they were lucky, in a tavern, and straight to bed. Here, they were forced to mind their manners and present a civilized face to the other residents of the Chautauqua. Tired and hungry, the troupe quickly made themselves presentable and hurried down to the dining room, leaving Portia blessedly alone.

Drawn to the window Portia stared at Daniel's room, wondering if he were watching her. The spectre of him met her at every turn. She tugged her cap tightly on her head and turned to leave. But sometime during the afternoon there had been an addition to their quarters, a large oval mirror in a free standing frame, a mirror that reflected too clearly the scruffy, unmatched garments she was wearing.

Fiona was right. She was a disgrace to the family. She looked like she belonged with that orphan child. When had she let herself become so threadbare? Maybe she'd looked like that all along and she'd just never taken the time to notice. It had never mattered before. No wonder Fiona was so concerned.

Portia wasn't ready to become a lady, but maybe she could look more presentable at the dining table. Quickly, before she changed her mind, she tore off the boy's clothing and pulled on one of Fiona's spare petticoats, only one; she had no intention of being totally uncomfortable. In the chifforobe she found a simple day dress of soft pink and pulled it over her head. Running a comb through her hair she caught it in the back with a black velvet ribbon. The natural curl in her hair made a red-blond cascade that satisfied Portia's taste. Not fashionable, but at least she looked like a girl.

Girl. She pondered her reflection in the mirror. She wasn't Portia disguised as Fiona the woman, not the Fiona of last night. She was simply Portia the girl. That was new to Portia and for now that's all she wanted to be.

Her heart beating with apprehension, Portia walked down

the dormitory steps to the dining room on the first floor. Her pulse thudded wildly in her chest. What was she doing? All she wanted was to finish this engagement and get away from this place. Her courage failed her and she stopped at the door and looked inside. Good, her father and Fiona were already at the table. Suddenly she wasn't hungry. She'd just skip dinner this evening.

"Portia? Is that you?" Rowdy gave a whistle that brought a blush to Portia's cheeks.

Too late; she'd been seen. She'd have to go inside and eat. Feeling as if she'd walked on stage in the wrong costume, Portia walked across the dining hall toward her family.

"Portia, you look beautiful. Having two such lovely daughters purely makes my heart sing." Horatio rose and made an elaborate production of seating his first born child at the table.

"It's about time you stopped looking like a ragamuffin," Fiona said with a frown that clearly expressed the recognition of her dress.

"I'm glad to see you've decided to return to the fold, Fiona," Portia said sharply. Compliments weren't customary and she felt everyone's eyes on her. "What's the matter, Edward, have to run home to the castle?"

"That's not fair, Portia," Fiona said quietly. "I came to check on Papa. Isn't it wonderful," she went on with a glance that dared Portia to continue, "he's feeling much better. He insists that we all drink a glass of this mineral water."

"I've had mine already," Portia said crossly, knowing that she was behaving badly, but unable to stop herself. "Where have you been all afternoon, Fiona, while the rest of us were painting scenery?"

"Oh, I'm sorry about that, Portia. I didn't expect the paint to arrive so soon. Mr. Logan said it wouldn't be here until morning."

"You were with Mr. Logan?" Portia didn't mean to sound so sharp. She cleared her throat and took a swallow of mineral water to cover her confusion. "I mean, that's good."

"Well, yes. He came by and we discussed a temporary

refurbishment plan. We decided to apply a fresh wash on the sets for *Romeo and Juliet*. By the time we decide on the next show, we'll have totally new sets and costumes.''

''*We* did? How nice of you to take an interest in production, Fiona, particularly since you weren't around to help implement those plans.'' Portia was miserable.

''Fiona, don't worry about our doing the work,'' Rowdy interceded. ''I could have come for you, but Portia turned up and helped us finish.'' He turned to Portia with a frown. ''What's wrong with you, Portia? We knew where to find Fiona if we needed her.''

Portia's ''I see'' was limp. She hadn't told anyone where she was going. She'd only wanted to get away. The silence magnified Portia's misery.

Horatio cleared his throat and looked around the table. He felt Portia's confusion and wished that he could help her. For so long she'd been the mainstay of the family, using their need for her like a suit of armor. Now the need was being diminished by both Daniel and by Fiona's emerging independence. Now Portia had to find herself at an age far past the time most girls did. And there was no easy way for her to do it.

He could direct the attention away from her. ''So, Fiona, did you have a nice afternoon with Edward?'' Horatio asked as he added a biscuit to his plate and passed the dish around the table to Portia.

''Yes, Papa, there are two other hotels down the road, fine hotels. Of course they aren't as fine as the Sweetwater, but they're very grand. Edward and I . . .''

''I thought you were told to stay out of sight,'' Portia interrupted sharply.

''I'm sure she did, Portia.'' Captain MacIntosh poured a glass of mineral water and handed Rowdy the pitcher as though he expected Rowdy to follow suit.

Rowdy looked suspiciously at the Captain, shook his head, then quickly passed the pitcher to Fiona.

''By the way, my daughters,'' Horatio went on smoothly,

"We're going to have a distinct honor. Evelyna tells me that later in the summer Mr. Joel Chandler Harris is going to be one of the guest lecturers at the Chautauqua. He's going to read some of his original works."

"Evelyna?" Portia pursed her lips into a frown. Her father's newest infatuation was the next order of business she intended to address. But that had to take place privately. She'd already said too much before the crew.

"Harris? You mean the man who writes those children's stories about the animals?" One of the other actors spoke up. And before long there was a lively discussion of the quaint tales delivered by Uncle Remus, the beloved old black man that Mr. Harris used as the story teller.

Portia picked at her food, took a few more swallows of the mineral water and let the swirl of talk carry on around her. She was simply tired, she told herself. She'd never found herself outside the center of the circle before. She didn't care about ready-to-wear clothing, or silk stockings, or the new Sherlock Holmes detective stories. And she didn't know what she was doing wearing Fiona's gown, playing at dressing for dinner.

For the first time Fiona seemed more attuned to the activities of the group than she. She was the one who should have been there to direct the stagehands, not Fiona. She would never have gone off and left the hands to paint without supervision. Yet, they'd managed fine. When she'd arrived the work was nearly finished and she couldn't find any fault with their effort.

Abruptly Portia shoved her chair from the table, stood up and whirled around. Muttering an "Excuse me," she fled from the dining room, past the Reverend and Mrs. Bartholomew who were just entering.

"Well, I never." Mrs. Bartholomew scowled. "There's another one of them. Did you see that? It's perfectly obvious from the way that dress hangs that she's wearing no corset, and only one petticoat. Actresses, the devil's own handmaidens!"

"Be charitable, Frances," her husband admonished. "She looked as though she might be in distress. She could need our guidance. We must pray for her, Mrs. Bartholomew."

"Papa, what's wrong with Portia?" Fiona asked with concern in her voice. "She's acting very strange. Do you think that she's becoming ill too?"

"No. She's . . . what happened is very hard for her, daughter. You two are growing up. I hadn't realized that. I guess I hadn't realized that at all. I think that she's very concerned about us. She's given us so much, Fiona. Now we need to give her time."

Horatio finished his meal quietly. He'd only been half right in his explanation to Fiona. *The situation is more than hard for Portia,* he wanted to say. *You aren't a little girl for her to supervise any longer. And she's run into a strong man, who is usurping her place before she has time to make a new one. She's becoming a woman and she's fighting it every step of the way.*

Had he been right in telling Daniel that Portia and Phillip were the same? He didn't know. Maybe all of this would blow up and the life they'd had together would end badly. But he was tired of traveling, tired of the responsibility and no matter how much he pretended, he knew that he couldn't continue as they had in the past. Dr. Garrett hadn't told him anything he didn't already know. He only hoped that the direction in which they seemed to be moving was right for his family.

"You've taken on what?" Ian dropped the dressing gown he'd been folding and stared at Daniel in disbelief.

Daniel bent down and retrieved the garment. "An orphan child, a small boy, about six or seven, I'd say."

"Well, why not? How foolish of me to question one 'catch colt' when you've already taken over an acting troupe, a wily old thief and his two daughters, one of whom goes around pretending that she's some tough from a Tenderloin street corner. Only one little orphan? Dog bite me, that's simple."

Daniel couldn't help himself. He burst out laughing. For all the years he'd known Ian, he'd never heard him resort to slang.

"Ian, the boy has measles. He'd been living with his grandmother who died last week. He's very sick at the moment, but Dr. Garrett assures me that he's over the worst of it. We don't have facilities here to take in young boys, but I've been told that a Mrs. Ethridge has a soft heart and if we pay for his keep she'll give him a good home."

"You mean that's all I have to do, don't you?"

"Well, no, Ian. I didn't mean to imply that I expect you to make the arrangements, though I suppose, in spite of what I might say, that's what I do, isn't it?"

"No, Daniel. You're just accustomed to taking charge. You're the leader and I'm the follower. I've worked for you for too many years to change our patterns now. I don't mind, really I don't. I just had my mind on . . . something else and you caught me by surprise, that's all. Where is the boy now?"

"At Mrs. Anderson's house. She's Dr. Garrett's nurse. She would keep him, except she has to run the doctor's office. I suspect she runs the doctor too. This Mrs. Ethridge who's taking the boy in is a real suffragette. Thinks women ought to be allowed to vote."

"So do I," Ian commented dryly. "At least some women."

"Some women, as in Mistress Victoria Trevillion?"

"Certainly not. Victoria wouldn't know a politician from a scalawag. She's the kind of woman who needs a man to care for her."

"A man like you, Ian?"

"Really, Daniel! Well—maybe. Victoria is an impressionable young lady who is allowed far too much freedom by her father. I'm sure that I'm simply a challenge to her. What would she want with a stuffy old man like me?"

"I can't imagine why any lady would want a wealthy, handsome, loyal man for a husband, Ian. I certainly can't."

Ian was a fine looking man. Proper, yes, but he had a

kindness about him that he'd learned to shield just as Daniel had. Victoria had improved her standing in Daniel's eyes by her keen observation of, and sensitivity to, his friend. And Daniel suspected that in spite of his protesting, Ian returned the feelings.

"Husband?" Ian echoed in surprise. "Now just a minute. Just because I've been fortunate to have had dinner with the lady for two evenings . . ."

"And taken her for boat rides, bicycle rides, and for long private walks away from the hotel, without either her mother or a companion being present? Doesn't that strike you as a bit unconventional, Ian?" Daniel covered a smile with a questioning fatherly attitude.

"Aside from being uncomfortable with the other guests, her mother isn't well. Victoria explained that to me. And I do believe that her mother thinks that Victoria's maid is accompanying us during the daytime."

"And why isn't she?" Daniel was finding it hard to keep his amusement hidden. Ian might have an intimate acquaintance with Belle's dance hall girls, but the determination of one simple society girl seemed to have escaped him entirely.

"Well, Victoria knows that I would never compromise her reputation. Besides, her maid is much too silly. Victoria couldn't be expected to tolerate such a country bumpkin. I mean, the maid doesn't even know how to ride a bicycle."

"Doesn't ride a bicycle? Of course not. No doubt she couldn't be trusted with the vote either, could she?"

"Certainly not." Ian's relief at the change of subject was more than apparent. "But I do think there are women who could become sufficiently informed to make those kinds of decisions," he hastened to add. "There are many who do already."

"Yes," Daniel agreed seriously, "like Portia. If she were of a mind to, she could handle politics. She'd have made a great prospector, Ian. Can't you just see her, working right along side of her man? Belle would have liked her too."

"No doubt. But Portia isn't a lady, Daniel. And I think

my friend, if you're seeing yourself as that man, you're forgetting how far you've come.''

"Maybe I have. And maybe I ought not to. Life isn't nearly as much fun as it used to be, Ian.'' Daniel walked out onto the terrace and glanced across the tree tops toward the dormitory. "I miss the excitement of dealing with the miners, the challenge of the elements, the taking of risks. Being wealthy is being secure, but it's damned dull.''

"That's just because there isn't much you haven't accomplished,'' Ian said quietly. "That's why you're chasing jewel thieves for the Pinkerton brothers, for the pure challenge of outsmarting the crook. You certainly don't need the risk, nor the money. You don't even work at it. You just sit back and wait, knowing that sooner or later the thief will give himself away.''

"I've been lucky. But risks, Ian, risks are what makes life interesting, taking a gamble and assuming the responsibility for your actions. We're so successful now that the only risks we take are in deciding what frock coat to wear.''

"Maybe, but there are some who take risks without studying the consequences,'' Ian remarked with a twinge of concern in his voice.

"Oh? Did you have anybody special in mind?''

"Yes, Edward Delecort. He seems taken with Fiona MacIntosh and I'm a bit worried about the girl.''

"Ah, Ian, there you go again being stuffy. What's wrong with Edward and Fiona? They're obviously smitten with each other and have been from the moment they laid eyes on each other. As a matter of fact, he's going to marry her, as soon as they can resolve the problem of her leaving the troupe without a leading lady.''

"Then you already know?''

"Absolutely, Edward came to me the morning after they met and asked me to release Fiona from our engagement.''

"Then why are you still carrying on the charade?''

"Oh, Fiona is no longer my fiancee,'' Daniel said with a smile, "Portia is the woman I'm engaged to.''

* * *

The Chautauqua dormitory window was dark. Daniel felt a sense of disappointment. He'd only intended to shock Ian with his explanations.

Who was he fooling? It wasn't the challenge of the acting troupe, or the jewel thief, or the child that had filled his mind, blocked his concentration, and had him pacing the length of his terrace. It was Portia. Ever since he'd kissed her he'd set off a kind of almost forgotten, unrestrained excitement.

As a child he'd watched the prospectors work with a frenzy when they smelled the presence of gold. They'd work around the clock, without food or sleep until they'd dropped from pure exhaustion. As he grew older he'd learned that there were other kinds of excitement. Belle taught him to read and write. She taught him to plan a course of action and keep his emotions hidden until that plan had been achieved.

Belle's girls had taught him about passion and the ways of love. Daniel had reached out and embraced every new thing that came to him with the same kind of restrained frenzy as those miners. He became the manager of Belle's Virginia City saloon, then of her general store, and finally of the hotel they'd built together. He'd been sad when Belle retired. He'd cried in private when she died. Afterwards he'd left Virginia City and moved to New York.

Now, those years of excitement and the drive to succeed seemed almost a dream. Except for Ian, he'd never allowed himself to be close to anybody else. Caring hurt too much —until he'd met Portia and she'd brought back a need that he'd thought he'd locked away forever.

Ian was staring at Daniel with an odd look in his eyes. After a long moment he cleared his throat. "Eh, Dan, I wonder if I could talk with you a little more, about Victoria."

"Sure, what's on your mind?"

Ian turned and walked out on the balcony. "I'm meeting her for an evening coffee, Dan, and I'm . . . I guess, what I'm trying to say is that I'm a bit uneasy with the way things seem to be going."

"Oh? How's that?" Daniel followed his friend out into the darkness, sensing that Ian needed that anonymity to open up.

"It's Victoria. She . . . we hold hands. Her foot plays with my ankles beneath the tablecloth at dinner. I can't seem to keep any distance between us. One way or another we seem to always be touching. And it's having an unsettling effect on me."

"Whoa, Ian. You're no schoolboy. You've had your share of women, though you're discreet beyond reason. What's the problem here?"

Ian rubbed his hands together. He couldn't admit it to Daniel, but he seemed to have lost his sense of propriety. The little familiarities that he was describing were keeping him constantly on edge and he was very confused.

"It's just that my intimate experiences have been with a different kind of woman. Victoria was schooled in England where she and a companion toured the Continent before returning. She's been reared as a lady but she's no simpering, silly little hothouse flower. I like her. I'm afraid I like her very much and I don't know what to do about it."

"Ian, I don't know why you're asking me. At the moment I may be as uncertain about how to handle a woman as you. I mean Portia is driving *me* crazy and I . . ."

Ian let out a deep breath. "I suspected as much. A fine pair of worldly men we are."

"Maybe, but one thing I'm sure of, when a man and a women are right together, they don't need anybody to tell them what to do. Maybe we both need to stop fighting the inevitable, my friend. I suspect Victoria wants a great deal more than coffee and I'm damn sure you do. I'm going for a walk. Don't wait up for me," Daniel said. He grabbed his coat and let himself out the door.

"I shan't," Ian called after him. After a moment he flicked off the room light and slipped into the hall. He'd wondered how he could explain his assignation to Danial. He'd half hoped that Daniel would find some reason to interfere so that he couldn't get away.

Traveling with Daniel had introduced Ian to wealthy society girls. *Hands off* had always been the signal they'd given. Silly games, simpering laughter and downright uncomfortable little expectations had kept Ian from seriously considering any of them. He'd always preferred the ordinary folks. They were what they were and the rules were clear.

But Victoria had taken one look at him on the hotel porch and she'd turned him every which way for Sunday since. Being constantly alone with her had assaulted his senses unbearably. Her rich, warm laughter was contagious. She liked compliments. She said that his old world manners intrigued her. She seemed intent on pursuit and when he was with her, he couldn't resist her.

Then she'd kissed him in the hallway. The kiss was not the innocent kiss of a young maid; he hadn't expected that. If Daniel hadn't come along and interrupted them—Ian blushed as he recalled his ungentlemanly response. He ought to have asked Daniel's advice then. But Daniel had seemed so preoccupied that Ian hadn't found the right opportunity to voice his own problem.

Now he was doing it again, falling in with Victoria's unorthodox plans by walking softly down the corridor toward her room at midnight. He wasn't sure how she planned to get away to meet him so late.

He wouldn't admit it to Daniel, but he had fallen in love with Victoria. He was wrong for her, much too old and too reserved. But she was magic and he knew that he couldn't stay away.

Ian came to a stop adjacent to the potted palm. What was he thinking of? Victoria might not know what she was inviting, but he did. He was the man and he knew that a proper lady should never suggest a midnight rendezvous. He stood in the corridor, wracked with indecision, only a second away from retreating down the hall to the safety of his room.

From nowhere two arms suddenly slid around his neck and jerked him into a darkened alcove beyond the plant. "Ian, I thought you'd never come."

As the arms tightened around his neck, any misgivings Ian might have had vanished with the touch of Victoria's eager lips. The dinner gown she'd been wearing when he left her an hour earlier had been exchanged for something silky and deliciously bare.

"What about our coffee?" he finally managed to say.

"I don't think you want me to go downstairs half undressed do you?" Victoria said with a wicked growl, tweaking the hair on his chest.

Ian looked down at his open shirt and missing cravat in confusion. "Victoria I'm sorry. I can't imagine what I was thinking of. I would never . . ."

"But I would, Ian. And I want to, with you, now, tonight." She released the ties of her dressing gown and the sides fell open.

The alcove was dark. But the incandescent light in the hall illuminated her nude body with silver. Her breasts were full and peaked and Ian knew that no matter what happened, he would do what she wanted. Damn the consequence. She'd heated his blood to the point of no return. He knew that making love to Victoria was improper but he couldn't refuse her invitation. "Victoria," he growled hoarsely, "where?"

"My maid's room, in here." She turned the knob in the darkness behind her and pulled Ian inside.

"Where is your maid?" His shirt was gone. His pants were being unfastened.

"In my bed of course. Kiss me Ian Gaunt, or I shall die from wanting to be in your arms."

Daniel wandered beneath the trees, carefully avoiding any late night strollers as he walked. It came as a surprise when he heard his name whispered from the shade of the magnolia tree at the corner of the hotel porch.

"Mr. Logan? Is that you?"

It was the undercover Pinkerton agent. ''Ben, what are you doing here again?''

''It's that Captain MacIntosh. He's in the hotel again.''

''Where? Have you looked for him?''

''Don't know. He isn't in the poker game, I managed to bribe a waiter. If he's playing billiards, I couldn't see him. What shall I do?''

Blast the man! He was harder to keep up with than a new silver strike. ''Just keep your eyes open, Ben. I have other men on the premises watching. I suspect that I know where the good Captain is.''

Daniel knew that Horatio and Lady Evelyna had been spending a good deal of time together and Daniel was worried. They seemed an odd couple. He needed a full report from the Pinkerton office on the Countess.

''Just stay put, Ben, I suspect he'll turn up.'' Daniel turned away, stopping short as he heard the furtive crunch of a footstep behind him in the darkness.

''Who's there?'' Daniel swung around in time to catch sight of a slight young woman in a pink dress running away in the moonlight. As she ran the ribbon in her hair came untied and spilled a mass of yellow hair down her back. Yellow—fool's gold, he thought as he ran after her, an imitation of the real thing, something precious that could lure a man to his death. He picked up the pace.

''Fiona! Wait. What's wrong?''

''Fiona?'' Portia stumbled. *So he thought she was Fiona. Well, why not? Only once had he seen Portia wearing anything but boy's pants*. She regained her footing just as Daniel reached down and caught her arm in his large hand.

''Why are you running away from me, little one?''

''Who says I'm running from you?'' Portia jerked her arm from his grasp and looked up at him with sparks in her eyes. ''I'm just out for a walk.''

''It's very late for a walk, alone.''

''I couldn't sleep.'' Her back stiffened and without being aware, her small hands made tiny fists.

"Why? Are you distressed, darling?"

"Of course not. Do I look distressed?"

"You look," he said huskily, "excited, as though you've just been kissed. "Are you . . ." he amended his question to, " . . . did someone bother you?"

This wasn't Fiona. He was certain of that now. The girl standing in the moonlight before him, like a brave candle flickering in the dark of night, was Portia. She was breathing heavily, and the warmth of that breath against his face drew him like a moth to a flame. She held her slim young body arrow straight, shoulders squared, radiating her passion with every flickering breath.

"Bother me?" She planted her hands on her hips and dared him to argue. "Certainly not! I wouldn't know how to . . . I mean, you're the only man who's ever—kissed me."

Daniel smiled and lifted his hand to her cheek, caressing it lightly with one fingertip. "You know how, darling, you kissed me and you kissed me very well. And I think that you want me to kiss you again."

Her anger was replaced by wariness and she took a backward step. "Never. I'm—I'm a lady and a lady doesn't kiss strangers!"

"But, my darling fiancee, we aren't strangers, are we?"

Even in the moonlight he could see the flush in her cheeks and the stubborn tilt to her head. Daniel inhaled deeply. Blast, she was beautiful. He had a sudden desire to reach down and touch the breast quivering with every breath she took. Instead, he slid the finger up her cheek to catch a strand of hair and push it back from her forehead.

"Are we . . .?" He almost said Portia, caught back the words and lowered his head.

Portia felt a twisting sensation in her stomach that was more severe than any physical pain she'd ever experienced. Being near the man hurt. But the hurt was delicious and she felt herself swaying toward him. Was she going mad like those patients in the sanitarium across from the Springs?

Daniel's finger curled around her ear, beneath her chin,

sliding down her throat to pause for a long moment before moving back to lift her face.

Portia was shaking all over. She felt as if her very skin was on fire and the heat rippled through her like the waves on a pond pushed by the wind.

"Please, no." She tried to speak. "You make me feel like a willow tree in a storm, Daniel. You mustn't . . ."

"Yes, my darling, yes. I must."

She could have lowered her head, but she didn't. He was going to kiss her. And she'd let him. She wouldn't run away like some schoolgirl. Tonight she was Fiona MacIntosh, and Fiona would allow her fiance one sweet kiss, just one, and then she'd turn away.

But Daniel's face was so very intense. He was frowning. His lips were parted as if he were in great agony, agony that she was causing. More than that, he seemed dazed, like a mighty warrior caught in the spell of a sorceress, unable to stop himself from carrying out her wishes. And what she wished was that he would kiss her now.

A cloud darkened the night sky, and Portia was sure that she'd simply been swept up in a wonderful dream. As Daniel's arms pulled her close it seemed natural to move against his warm, hard body. His kiss was slow and wild. Portia gave herself over to it, feeling the heat flare, jolting her lower body.

She pulled back, her eyes wide with wonder.

"What's wrong, darling? Did I frighten you?"

"I felt . . . I mean the heat. I'm burning up. I feel all quivery and I can hardly stand."

Daniel let out a deep breath and tried to speak in a reasonably controlled voice. "I think I understand the feeling."

"But you couldn't. It's frightening. Oh, Daniel, now I'm so warm and still I'm shivering. I can't breathe. I must be sick."

Daniel couldn't hold back his laughter. "Oh, darling, I don't think so. Here, take my jacket." He took his time removing his jacket and placing it around her shoulders.

"Now come over here and sit down in this swing." He led her across the grass to a swing hanging from the limb of a giant water oak.

"Oh, yes—I think I do need to rest." Portia pulled the coat about her tightly and sat down. When Daniel lowered himself to the bench beside her she felt a second shock run through her body. "See, there it is again."

Daniel slid his arm along the back of the swing and let the weight of his body move them back and forth. "You're all right, lass. I promise. Lean back against me and let me try and explain."

Portia, stiff as frozen clothes on a line, allowed herself to lean back, but she couldn't relax. "Explain."

"If your mother had lived, she would have been better able to tell you these things than I."

"Leave my mother out of this, Daniel. Explain. Why am I burning up one minute and shivering the next, if I'm not sick?"

"It's what happens sometimes, when a man and woman kiss."

"Nonsense. We often have to kiss on stage and this doesn't happen. I've never seen anyone shiver and burn up from a kiss."

"It's a bit more than that, darling. It has to do with the man and woman and how they feel about each other. When a kiss is right, sometimes the couple want—I mean their bodies want more."

"More?"

"Yes. Let me demonstrate." Daniel dropped his fingertips to her shoulder and turned her toward him.

"No, remove your hand." Portia slid from his touch, but she didn't turn her face away.

"All right. That's probably best. When a man and a woman kiss," he lowered his head and touched his lips lightly to hers for only a second, "their bodies give and receive certain signals. Do you feel them?"

Portia hid her shock well as she analyzed the faint trembling that followed his touch and decided that if this was the signal he was sending, she didn't have anything to worry about.

"Yes. But that wasn't what I felt before. Therefore, I think you're wrong, Daniel." She jumped to her feet and smiled happily. "That just proves that you don't know everything."

Daniel reached out, took Portia's hand in his and jerked her down into his lap, covering her small mouth with lips that released all the passion he'd held back moments earlier.

His sudden move and the warm, insistent invasion of his tongue shocked Portia's senses, sending her spiraling into a dizzy rush of feeling that drugged her brain and turned her body into a raging inferno. She pulled her hand from his grip and tried to push against his chest. Instead her hands found bare flesh that convulsed beneath her fingertips. His skin was firm and strange, and its texture excited her. For a moment she was so absorbed by the response her touch was invoking that she almost didn't feel his hand skim her breast.

Then his tongue was skating across the inside of her mouth as his hand moved intimately inside the neckline of her dress capturing the stiff peak of her breast with fingers of fire. Without knowing that she was doing so she arched herself against him, filling his palm with her breast. She cried out under his devouring mouth.

What was happening was darkly wicked and exciting and Portia knew that whatever he was trying to prove to her was having an equally intense response in himself. Her hands rippled across the smooth expanse of his back. She could feel his muscles twitch beneath his silk shirt. Abruptly, his mouth left hers and traveled to her neck, where she could feel the rapid exhaling and inhaling of the heat of his breath against her chest.

His hand encircled her exposed breast for a long delicious moment then began repositioning her inside the dress that had somehow been opened to his touch. He lowered his head briefly and nuzzled the nipple through the fabric of her dress, then leaned back and shifted her position on his lap.

Daniel groaned. Portia's eyes were half-closed, cloudy

with passion, her lips still parted, inviting him to claim her once more.

It was then that she became aware of the throbbing protrusion from his body against her. She was aware too of the answering throb of her own body.

"I guess, Mr. Logan—Daniel . . ." she managed to say as she pulled away and began trying to adjust the bodice of her dress. "I'm aware that you know a great deal more about this sort of thing than I do." There was no point in trying to pretend that she didn't know what had happened or how right he'd been about bodies and signals.

Running her fingers through her tousled hair she tried unsuccessfully to still her breathing and ignore the disheveled state of Daniel's dress. He wasn't going to be of any help. Though she couldn't bring herself to look at him she was certain that he was laughing at her. Finally she stood up, tugged her dress back into place and swept her hair defiantly behind her ears.

"I hope that you will understand when I say that this must not happen again. Obviously you know about women and how to . . . arouse them. I, on the other hand, have no knowledge of men. The lesson was a valuable learning experience that I shall have to think about."

Portia straightened her shoulders and held out her hand, determined to keep it from trembling. "Good evening, Mr. Logan. I can find my own way back. Thank you."

"You're welcome." Daniel's voice cracked huskily. "I think the lesson learned was mutual." He stared at her stupidly for a moment as she continued to hold out her hand before he offered his. If she'd bitten him again he wouldn't have been surprised. When she merely clasped his hand, shook it firmly and turned away, he began to smile.

"Good night, darling. Tell your twin that I expect—him —in my quarters at ten o'clock in the morning, sharp."

There was barely a stumble as she absorbed the thrust of his words. Then he wondered what he was trying to prove. Whatever it was, it might be that the lesson was proving to be more personal than he'd intended. When he stood he found that his legs were rubbery. His shirt studs were missing entirely and he had no idea where he'd lost his cravat. The only remnant of their passion was a black ribbon lying in a patch of moonlight, a ribbon as velvety soft as Portia's breast. The smell of honeysuckle lingered sweetly in the air.

Daniel didn't see Ian when he went to bed. It didn't occur to him that it was after midnight and Ian wasn't there. For he was filled with a longing for a small slip of a girl who had turned his insides into warm brandy and charged his mind with the fire of those incandescent lights that sizzled like sunlight in the shadows.

Twelve

IT was barely eight a.m. when Ian shook Daniel rudely awake.

"Get up, man. He's done it."

"Who's done what?" Daniel pushed himself up against the down pillow and stared sleepily at his associate. Ian was still dressed in his evening clothes, or partially dressed. His shirt was half buttoned. His tie was hanging around his neck and he was holding his frockcoat by its collar. "Did somebody rob you?"

"Not me, Daniel; Lady Delecort. The jewel thief broke into her room last night while she was asleep and took the diamond necklace she wore at dinner."

"Blast! I was afraid of something like this. Do you know any details?"

"No. I only just heard about it when I was—was coming down the corridor—earlier. The hotel detective is in the room next door, making inquiries. You'd better dress. I expect him here next."

Daniel came to his feet and reached for a pair of trousers. He plunged his feet into the pants and threaded his arms into the dressing gown that Ian was holding for him. His mind was furiously cataloging what he'd been told. Some time after Lady Delecort had retired a thief had entered her room and taken her diamonds.

Perhaps the theft had occurred while he was with Portia. With the hotel under surveillance by his men the theft had still occurred. Who was the elusive thief? Portia! Could he have been wrong about Portia? Why had she been running away from the hotel, wearing a dress? Perhaps he'd intercepted her escape. No! He refused to believe that. She certainly hadn't had the necklace on her. After the intimacy of their embrace he could reasonably swear to that. But how about Horatio? Portia could have been serving as some kind of look-out. Maybe she'd been a decoy, luring him away from the hotel intentionally.

Daniel's heart sank. How could he have let the very thing happen that he'd been sent there to prevent. Damn! Blast!

There was a knock. "Hotel Security, please open up."

Ian dropped his hands resolutely and opened the door. "Yes?"

"Are you Mr. Daniel Logan?" The florid faced man standing in the doorway flexed his arm, calling attention to the awkward bend of the elbow that signaled a break that had not healed properly. "We've had a little problem here in the hotel and I'd like to ask you some questions."

"Certainly." Daniel stepped forward. "I'm Daniel Logan. This is my associate, Ian Gaunt. And you are?"

"Hill Jackson, hotel detective. Mr. Blake, the proprietor, has authorized me to make inquiries." The man didn't offer to shake hands and neither did Daniel. There was an air of animosity about him that seemed uncalled for.

"What seems to be the trouble, Jackson?" Daniel stretched and rubbed his sleep-filled eyes as the detective walked in and looked disdainfully around.

"The Countess of Hidemarch was robbed last night."

"Sorry to hear that. And how may we be of assistance to you? God, I could use some coffee."

Ian closed the hotel room door. "I've already called down for coffee, Daniel."

"I wondered if you happened to see anything—unusual?"

For a moment Daniel thought of Portia, then cleared his mind. It wouldn't be smart at this point to allow the detective any hint of his involvement. "No, not that I'm aware of. What time did the robbery take place?"

"Sometime after midnight when the lady retired. What time did you turn in, Mr. Logan?"

"About twelve thirty, I imagine."

Hill Jackson walked slowly around the sitting room, peered into Daniel's room and moved slowly around past the terrace to the door that led to Ian's room. "May I?" He put out his hand to the knob and waited for Ian's nod of consent.

"Certainly," Daniel said, impatient for the man to conclude his interview so that he and Ian could get to work.

"Well, well. Either Mr. Gaunt is a very tidy guest, or he hasn't been to bed." The detective turned back to Ian, studying the odd state of his dress more carefully.

Daniel, too, noticed now that Ian appeared to have thrown on his clothes hurriedly, the same clothing he was wearing last evening, except for the cummerbund which was missing.

"Neither," Ian replied stiffly. "I was away last evening. But I assure you that my activities had nothing to do with any robbery."

"That was you I saw coming down the corridor while I was entering the room next door, wasn't it?"

"I'm afraid so," Ian admitted, drawing himself up even more stiffly.

"Care to tell me where you spent the evening?"

"I . . . I'd rather not, Detective Jackson. It would be most indiscreet."

Suddenly Daniel understood. Ian had been with the lovely Victoria. It was Daniel's turn to say, "Dog bite me, Ian. You were with a woman!"

Ian's look of misery was answer enough.

"Now, look here, Detective Jackson—may I call you, Hill?" At the law officer's reluctant nod, Daniel put his arm around his shoulder and walked him toward the terrace.

"You see, Hill, it's like this. There is a young lady here in the hotel who has decided that Ian would make a fine husband. You know how these women work in a place like this. Ian hasn't had much experience with women. I'm afraid that he's allowed himself to fall into her trap."

"Sure, I've seen 'em. But we've had a robbery and I have to investigate. It's my job, a job that I mean to keep."

"Of course. But you understand that Ian is of the old school. He'll protect this young lady with his last breath, so I'm going to have to figure out a way to prove his story without compromising her reputation. Or, it's off to the church with Ian."

"Of course this introduces another possibility," the law officer said, sliding Daniel's arm from his shoulder. "If Mr. Gaunt wasn't here, I have no proof that you were either, do I?"

Daniel groaned. "No, I suppose not. But the only thing that does is put both of us in the same shoes as half the guests in the hotel, doesn't it?"

"Maybe." Hill Jackson nodded, looking from Daniel to Ian and back again. "But I intend to get to the bottom of this, so don't either of you decide to leave right away."

"Don't worry, Detective, I haven't finished my business yet. We'll be here."

Once the door closed, Ian dropped into the ornate velvet chair and covered his face.

"I don't know what to say, Daniel. I'm not sure how it happened. She wanted to go for a late night coffee. It seemed to be an exciting adventure to her and she has such a way about her."

"Where did you go for coffee, into Atlanta?" Daniel shook his head in concern. "Ah, Ian, didn't you know what she was up to? No, of course you didn't. When a man falls in love he goes deaf, dumb and blind.

"Love? That's foolish, Daniel. I mean . . . I—we were simply . . ."

"What, Ian? What did you expect when she set up a midnight meeting?"

"I guess I didn't think at all, Daniel."

"What happened?"

"After you left for your walk I went back down the hall toward her room. We were to meet at the palm tree by the alcove. She—she'd talked her maid into sleeping in her bed. Her maid's room opens into the alcove. Victoria was waiting. We . . . she wasn't dressed for going anywhere."

"A spider, Ian. She spun a web and you walked right into it. Was she a virgin?"

"Really, Daniel," Ian protested, red-faced at the implication. "Of course she . . . I mean certainly . . ." His voice trailed off miserably. "Yes, she was."

"And now, you're engaged? She must have been desperate to pull such a stunt."

"Why yes, we *are* engaged. I plan to marry her. I truly want to, Dan. Any gentleman would be honored. Why does that bother you?"

"Ian, I know what you're about to do. What I want to know is what you *want* to do."

Ian rose and walked slowly toward the terrace. After a long time he spoke. "I know what you think, Daniel, but it isn't true. Victoria confessed everything. The Trevillions aren't really quality folks, Daniel. Mrs. Trevillion doesn't show herself much because she's very uneducated. She's afraid that she'll make a gaffe and ruin her daughter's chances."

"Smart thinking. It must run in the family."

"Victoria has been very honest with me. They aren't old money from New Orleans as they've pretended. They are from Memphis where her mother's family was in trade. Mrs. Trevillion inherited several businesses along the river front. Mr. Trevillion has made a fortune raising pigs. An honorable background, but one that might be considered less than genteel.

"Victoria is very much afraid that even though she's beautiful, wealthy and has been educated in the finest schools, none of that will matter if people examine her background closely. One way or another, she wants to be somebody. I admire her spunk, even if our being together was originally part of a plan rather than from love. I told her that I was no catch."

"Now, just a minute, Ian. The last time I looked there were at least a dozen eligible bachelors here. Victoria may be a scheming wench, but she has good taste. She chose you out of all the prospects. That makes her pretty smart in my book."

"Well, it didn't seem to bother her that I got my start as a bartender. She seems to think that makes us just about perfect for each other, Dan. She . . ." Ian said shyly, "says that she loves me."

"And it's obvious that you're in love with her, Ian. I'm happy for you." Daniel frowned. "You didn't tell her about our assignment here, did you?"

"Of course not, Daniel. I feel bad enough about that as it is; if I'd been more responsible, this might not have happened. What do you want me to do now?"

"Maybe both of us lost sight of our objective for a moment, Ian. Right now, I'm going to pay a little call on Captain Horatio MacIntosh. It seems that he's managed to slip out of the dormitory and into the hotel for two nights in a row. Just where he's been might prove very interesting."

"You don't really suspect Captain MacIntosh, do you?"

"I don't want to, Ian, but I have to consider the possibility that he's the thief. I have to suspect the whole troupe, except perhaps Fiona. And for all I know she may be the most skilled actress in the group. It all seems too convenient. Maybe they all belong to the same gang. The Countess and the Captain. Maybe they travel the resort circuit together, the Countess on the inside and the Captain on the outside. Maybe the theft was just a blind."

"But the troupe? That seems to be rather a large contingent for a gang to carry around from place to place, don't you think?'' Ian said quietly, watching Daniel's face as he paced about the room.

Of course, Ian was right. Daniel stopped his pacing. But if the real thief was someone else, he was smart enough to make use of the end result.

Mentally Daniel ran down his list of characters, as it were. The Captain and the Countess playing patty-cake. Edward and Fiona falling in love at first sight. The lovely Victoria setting a trap for Ian, effectively occupying his concentration, and Portia—Portia had turned his own mind into pure mush. While the hotel is turned into a hotbed of passion, the thief settles in and makes off with a necklace right under all their noses.

Even Shakespeare couldn't write a script to compare.

The breakfast cart arrived. Quickly Daniel shaved and dressed, drinking his coffee as he completed his toilette. His mind raced with the possibilities. The hotel would make good the Countess's loss because the Sweetwater belonged to the Jewelry Alliance by whom the Pinkertons were employed. It had been his job to prevent any further jewel thefts while he identified and arrested the thieves. For now he was no further along than he'd been when he arrived.

Toilette complete, Daniel lifted his hat from the coat rack and began sliding his fingers into gray suede morning gloves. First, he'd talk with Ian, then with Horatio.

"Ian, about last night. You're thirty years old. If the girl is what you want, marry her. If not, I'll help you get out of the situation. For now, go to bed. I need a fresh mind from you this evening."

The closing of Ian's door was the only answer Daniel got as he left the room and started down the stairs. Several people called out to him as he made his way through the lobby, each eager to discuss the excitement.

This time, Daniel avoided the rehearsal hall and made his way straight to Captain MacIntosh's dormitory room. After a knock he was told to enter. Inside the Captain, wearing a red velvet dressing gown, was having a full breakfast at a table by the window.

"Oh, Logan. Won't you join me?"

"Captain, how did you get room service in a place where they think that more than tea and dry toast is a sinful waste?" Daniel asked in amazement.

"Oh, it was just a matter of making friends with the cook. Always pays to make a fuss over the staff."

"Of course, the cook." Daniel removed his hat and gloves and sat down at the table with the bewhiskered actor. "I'm afraid that we have a slight problem, Horatio."

"Oh, Portia? Fiona? Are they in trouble?"

"Neither Portia, nor Fiona, Captain." Daniel took a deep breath. He'd considered several approaches and rejected them all. There was only one way to find out what he wanted to know: ask. The direct approach might prevent his proving his case, but at least he'd scare the Captain off and prevent Portia and Fiona being exposed as accomplices.

"Then what?" Horatio put down his cup and waited.

If the old crook was guilty, he was doing a good job of pretending innocence.

"There was a robbery at the hotel last night, Captain."

"Oh? Who was robbed?"

"Countess Delecort. The diamond necklace she was wearing at dinner was stolen, while she slept."

Captain MacIntosh's fingers tightened on his cup. "Evie was robbed? When? Is she all right?"

"Sometime after midnight. And yes, she's fine. What time did you leave her room, Captain?"

"So, you know."

"I know that you two are setting a poor example for Fiona and Edward."

"I see." Horatio made no attempt to conceal the truth. "I left her suite between twelve and twelve-thirty. She had removed her jewelry earlier. The last time I saw the necklace, it was on her dressing table. Am I a suspect?"

"Only by me, Horatio," Daniel admitted. "Did you steal it?"

"No, but I could have. And I suppose you know that or you wouldn't be here. Did she tell you that I did?"

"I haven't spoken to Lady Delecort. I'm afraid that the hotel detective has decided that my associate, Mr. Gaunt, and I are more likely candidates."

This time Horatio's surprise was genuine. "You, Logan? But didn't you tell them that you were with Portia?"

"How did you know that?"

"I'm afraid I saw you, on my way back to the dormitory. You were—sitting—in the swing."

"Oh." Sitting in the swing? They had been kissing. He'd been, God only knew what he'd been doing, when Horatio saw them. "I don't know what to say, Captain. I didn't intend that to happen."

"Just as I didn't intend to meet Evie," Horatio said simply. "Of course I'm a lot older than you. And Portia is my daughter. I didn't say anything because I didn't want to have to issue an ultimatum until Portia decides how she feels."

It was Daniel's turn to say, "I see."

"Under the circumstances I know that you hold our fate in your hands. I also know that Portia would do whatever she thought was necessary to save the troupe."

"What you saw, Captain, was entirely my fault. Portia shouldn't be held responsible."

"I hope that you know, Logan, Portia has never been with a man before, in any way. You're probably the first to ever hold her hand. I am still her father and even if it costs me the troupe, I won't allow her to be hurt."

"Hurting Portia is the last thing I'd ever do, Horatio. I care about her, more than I want to."

"And what do you intend to do about it?"

"The same as you, I guess; wait for Portia to decide what she wants from me."

"That's fair enough, Logan," Horatio agreed. "Portia has

held this family together all her life. We care about her too. I think we'll all wait for her to decide what she wants."

There was a quick knock on the door as it opened.

"Papa, I'm on my way to the lion's den to make my report."

Portia was adjusting her cap to cover her curls as she entered the room. She lifted her head and caught sight of Daniel sitting across from her father. Did he see? No, she'd already shoved the last strand beneath it before she knocked.

"Oh, I didn't expect you here, Daniel. Is something wrong?"

"Lady Delecort was robbed last night, Phillip," Daniel said quickly.

Portia's gaze swung to her father in a panic. "Papa?"

"I'll give you the same answer I gave Daniel. No. I did not take Evie's necklace."

"Evie? Oh, Papa, I asked you not to go over there. I knew that would only bring trouble. That woman isn't interested in you. She's just slumming. Now look what's happened. Give me the necklace." Portia held out her hand.

Horatio stood, shoved his chair away from the table, and answered Portia as only Hamlet could have done. "My daughter, I know that you have had cause to suspect me in the past. But of this dastardly deed, I am not guilty. I would thank you to take your mistrust elsewhere. Now I have to ready myself to take the waters. My condition, you know."

Portia burst out laughing and began to applaud. "Very good, Papa. Very good indeed. Now, swear to me on the memory of my mother that you didn't lift the jewelry."

With a pained expression that convinced Daniel, if it didn't convince Portia, Horatio took Portia's hand, swore his innocence, and led her to the door.

"Now, take Daniel away and let him tell you who the hotel detective really suspects."

Outside Horatio's door, Daniel and Portia faced each other uneasily.

"What did he mean, Daniel. Who do they suspect if not my father?"

Daniel started down the steps. "I'm afraid that they suspect either Ian or me."

Portia gasped. "But you couldn't have . . ." She broke off. She had been about to say *because you were with me*. But Daniel wasn't with Portia, he was with Fiona. Except that Fiona had been with Edward while his mother was being robbed. Oh, the situation was becoming much too complicated.

"No, I couldn't have. I was with—a fiery little vixen who stirred my blood and set me to pacing my bedchamber for half the night. But you'd know about that, wouldn't you Phillip? You'd know about a man wanting a woman?"

Stirred his blood? Portia turned and stumbled down the stairs into the sunlight.

"Uh, no, I don't know much about women. I'd think that they all might affect a man that way, wouldn't they?"

"Well, there are some special women who affect a man more than others. I'm afraid that this particular one is likely to get herself into big trouble if she doesn't find a good man to take her to bed—soon."

This time Portia couldn't conceal her distress.

Fiona. Daniel was standing there telling her that *Fiona* needed to be bedded. But it wasn't Fiona he had kissed; it was she. Would he put his threat into action? What on Earth would Fiona do if he kissed her as he'd kissed Portia in the moonlight?

Did Fiona respond to Edward's kisses the way she did to Daniels? She wished she had someone to talk to about what was happening to her. How did a woman control herself, keep a man from getting around her and forcing her into a compromising situation? Did they even try? For all she knew women felt and reacted the same way as a man; they just did it privately. Did Fiona allow Edward to touch her? Did she feel as if she were bursting into a thousand pieces when he did? Those thoughts were shattering every ounce of her control and she knew that she was lost.

Daniel didn't seem to notice her confusion. He was standing there, his hat in his hand, bouncing it against his knee. She searched his face, but it was so difficult to decipher. Dare she probe his statement of his feelings further? Could she make a logical decision if she had the facts?

Portia was shaken. Her chest seemed constricted and she was finding it hard to breathe. Her skin was burning in the heat of the sun's rays. She needed to move into the shade, away from Daniel's innocent man-to-man remarks. But she needed the truth more.

Boldly she spoke, throwing caution to the winds. "Did she, the woman, express her feelings for you?"

"Not in words, not yet, Phillip, but sooner or later—she will."

"Could she be mistaken? Could she believe that you care for her, when you don't?"

"She could. She doesn't have any notion what feelings she arouses in a man. She might not know that her actions speak louder than her words."

Portia caught back her words of denial. He believed that he was describing Fiona. He couldn't know that it was Portia who was trembling even now from the remembering. Drawing in a deep calming breath, Portia forced herself to consider how a proper brother might be expected to respond in such a situation.

Making her tone as calm and masculine as she could make it, she said, "I realize that your engagement to my sister is only a sham, Logan, but until the arrangement is terminated, I expect you to treat Fiona as the lady she is. Do I make myself clear?"

Fiona he had no problem with. It was the woman, stiff-necked and proud, before him that Daniel was having difficulty withstanding. Daniel had known passion, but outside of caring for Belle, he'd never known the kind of obsession that Portia created. He'd tried to analyze this strange power she held over him.

But Daniel was growing weary of this subterfuge. He was ready to put Phillip away and bring Portia out into the light so that he could tell her how he felt. Though he wasn't yet sure that it was love, it was something. But this was Phillip, not Portia, who was waiting for an answer. And if he didn't get away, he was likely to reveal that he knew the truth.

"Certainly, Phillip. I shall endeavor to regard Fiona as a lady in every instance. You need not fear for her safety in my hands. Now, I will have to ask you to excuse me this morning. I have some business in Atlanta that I must tend to. Please carry on with your duties as usual."

Daniel placed his hat on his head, gave it a jaunty tap and turned back to the hotel. Portia watched him walk away, too emotionally exhausted to reply.

"Oh," Daniel stopped and turned back. "Tell Fiona that I will be away this evening so she won't have to join me for dinner. But I'll expect her to meet me after your performance tomorrow evening."

"Why?"

"To celebrate her triumph as the fair Juliet. Ian tells me that a boat ride on the lake is a lovely way to spend an evening."

"But . . ."

"I'll wait at the dormitory door."

Daniel didn't dare look back again or he would have covered the distance between them and taken Portia in his arms no matter who she was pretending to be. Her face had gone white with confusion. Both anger and fear coursed through his veins. God, she was so young, so vulnerable.

At least he had to be away for the next two days. For now, he had to distance himself from Portia before he gave in to his urges to make love to her. He was no better than Victoria. She wanted a man and she chose one. Without a conscious commitment, he was guilty of the same thing.

Now that he had a new hotel guest list he had to go back

to Atlanta and telegraph the home office for more background information. So far he hadn't seen anything or anybody suspicious. Stealing one necklace seemed out of character for the thief; not the usual *modus operandi*. Daniel had about decided that this theft was a red herring.

Daniel picked up his pace.

Portia watched him walk away. By now he was too far away for her to refuse to obey his instructions. She knew that any argument was hopeless anyway. Apparently the authorities didn't know about her father's light-fingered history yet. Daniel could say that he and Mr. Gaunt were suspects, but she knew that her father would make a far better choice. And she couldn't take a chance that Daniel might tell them about Horatio and "Evie."

Portia walked down to the lake, deep in her thoughts.

She didn't believe that Daniel was a thief. He made her furious, but he was kind and caring. Men in general had never impressed her as more than trouble that needed controlling or rescuing. But Daniel seemed to know who he was and where he was going. He was always totally in control and she doubted if he ever needed anybody. There was an unspoken energy about the man that quite simply made her feel alive.

But wait: what about the man in the shadows, the man Daniel had been plotting with. She'd heard him say that they'd been working too long to let something happen now. Was all this nonsense about looking for a wife just some carefully plotted sham to cover his real purpose in being at the Springs?

Portia was confused. The lake was calm in the morning sunlight. She stood there for a long time, her stomach churning as she considered what Daniel had said. She was distressed about her father and the troupe, but the truth of the matter was that it was Daniel, the man, who disturbed her.

It was too bad that Daniel wasn't the thief. Then he'd be arrested and she'd be rid of him. But, wait. She was beginning to get an idea. If Horatio wasn't the thief, then someone else was. Maybe the authorities were right. Forcing herself to put aside the strong feelings she had about the man, she considered the possibility that Daniel really was the thief. She had seen him talking to a stranger in the shadows. She knew how persuasive he could be.

Suddenly Portia felt heady with the idea. If she could prove that Daniel had the necklace, she'd be able to force him to return the troupe in exchange for her silence. The authorities didn't really have to be told. He'd return the necklace but that wouldn't matter. She'd have rescued the troupe and taken control again.

Portia took a deep breath and felt the beginning of a confident smile. Everything made more sense now. Being a thief would explain his presence at the resort. He was simply using the troupe and a fiancee as a diversion. She'd almost allowed Daniel to distract her totally. But if he thought that he'd use her or her family for any further distraction, he was sadly mistaken.

An instinct told her that Daniel hadn't been untouched by their kisses. If he could use her, she could use him. As long as he felt this desire for Fiona, he would protect the troupe. And they could still use his help with finances. Except that now, Fiona couldn't be allowed to go out with him any more. It had to be Portia.

Fiona couldn't be exposed to Daniel's kisses. They were too powerful, too delicious. But what was more important was the fact that she had to stay close enough to Daniel Logan to prove his guilt. No matter how much she—no matter how difficult it would be, Portia had to protect the people she loved.

At least she wouldn't have to see him for almost two full days. She'd be able to look after her duties as she normally did, without interference. No more midnight walks across the hotel grounds. No more wicked kisses in the moonlight. In the meantime, she'd have a talk with Fiona. There was one thing she had to understand before she formulated her final plan. She needed to know if being in love made you crazy. She needed to know—quick.

Thirteen

T HE theater was filling up with a good cross section of hotel guests and Chautauqua attendees. The stage was washed with light along the apron that extended out beyond the curtain. The extra incandescent lights being installed for later productions were not yet in place.

"Looks like your ticket give-away is working," Ian said as he eased into the seat next to Daniel.

"Yes, and I'm worried that with everyone away from the hotel, our thief will strike. In spite of my suspicions of the Captain, I still don't know who the thief is. I've telegraphed the names of the guests on our list to the home office. They will cross check the names with the guest list at Saratoga Springs.

"Too bad we don't have one of those new telephones Tom Edison invented," Ian observed. "We could get an answer right away."

"That will come soon enough. A wire that you can talk through from one place to another. Motor cars to take you cross country. This is the time to live, Ian. The world is changing. Anything new from the rest of the men?"

"Nothing. Our man at the train station says that nobody

we're considering has left the hotel and nobody else has come in looking suspicious.''

"That means that the thief isn't finished yet. I was afraid of that. Lady Evelyna's necklace was only a dry run, to test the waters. What else have you done?''

"Ben has instructions to stick to Horatio like glue. If he takes Evie home, Ben will be under the bed.''

"I hope he isn't easily embarrassed,'' Daniel commented absently. "Maybe I'm losing my perspective, but I don't actually think the Captain is our thief. Stealing a necklace from the Countess would be dumb. He'd be an automatic suspect.''

"Maybe it wasn't so dumb. He probably figured that we'd think like that. And again, maybe you don't want him to be the criminal,'' Ian suggested quietly.

"I know. I wish I hadn't allowed myself to get to know them personally. That's why I decided to bait my trap. Otherwise the thief is going to strike again and this time, I'll have to admit I have no idea that we'd be able to stop him.''

"What kind of trap are you baiting?''

"While I was in Atlanta I learned that Jay Gould and his daughter, Helen, will be in town at the end of next week. He's coming in to look over some railroad depot sites. They had planned to spend one night and leave by train the next morning for Savannah, but Helen wants to see the Sweetwater. They've decided to come in a day early and make a side trip to the Springs. What we'll do is—''

"Wait, Daniel,'' Ian interrupted, "here's Victoria and her father.'' Ian rose, held out his hand to clasp Victoria's fingertips, and brought them to his lips.

"Good evening, Logan, Ian,'' William Trevillion said, tucking his thumbs into the pockets of his vest as he glanced around. "*Romeo and Juliet*, eh? Quite a shindig for an old farm boy like me.''

"Father, do sit down and quit playing the country bumpkin. This isn't the first theatrical performance you've attended and Daniel and Ian already know you're a shrewd businessman.''

Victoria smiled at Daniel and allowed Ian to lead her to the seat joining his.

"Would you look at that woman, Vickie? She really is something, isn't she?" William Trevillion was returning the disdainful gaze of Mrs. Frances Bartholomew and she and her husband as they made their way to their seats in the second row.

Daniel smiled. He wasn't surprised to see Brother Bartholomew. At first he'd been furious with Portia for telling Mrs. Bartholomew that he'd arranged care for the sick boy. It hadn't taken long for him to realize that Mrs. Bartholomew considered it her Christian duty to censor the troupe. She was set to make trouble if he couldn't change her mind. His suggestion that she and the Reverend enjoy the free tickets for the play was followed by a more than generous donation to their missionary cause. The donation worked wonders in appeasing her concern.

A moment later Edward Delecort and the Lady Evelyna swept regally into their seats and the gas lights along the wall dimmed. There were no musicians to provide the proper mood. After a moment Horatio stepped out from the wings and stood in the silence until the crowd hushed.

In a rich melodious voice Horatio offered a prologue which set the stage for the story of two star-crossed lovers, Romeo and Juliet.

The curtain rose and the play began. The audience never knew that the lovesick young Romeo was being played by a woman. Portia presented the lad simply and sincerely. Fiona as gentle Juliet took the stage and suddenly the theater was transported to Shakespeare's Verona. Two hours later Daniel came to his feet with an audience who'd been captivated with the beauty of the tale.

"I take it back," Ian said, raising his voice to be heard over the applause. "They are magnificent. If we were back in the West, the miners would shower them with gold dust and chunks of silver."

Daniel found it hard to speak. He'd read most of the Shakespearean plays and seen a number of them on the New York stage. He'd laughed and discounted as bragging the Captain's claim that his troupe was as good as any of England's Haymarket Theater players. For once Horatio hadn't exaggerated.

Charlatan, impoverished rake? Yes. Thief? Maybe. But whatever the man was, he was unquestionably a very fine actor. Daniel had never seen a better Lord Capulet. Fiona was the classic ingenue. Lawson Paine made a perfect Mercutio. And Portia? Now that she'd seen her on stage he understood how she could be so convincing as Phillip without worrying about being found out. Her naturally husky voice and slim build coupled with an instinctive talent had been carefully honed to the right combination. On stage she became her character. That talent had served her well, both on stage and off. Only Daniel knew that beneath that wig and those male clothes, Portia was very much a woman.

Ian left with the Trevillions. Lady Evelyna and Edward stopped for a brief discussion of the merits of the play and departed. Soon only Daniel was left, sitting in the shadows, watching as the sets were struck and the props removed to the adjacent hall.

In the darkness, Daniel's expression grew troubled. What was he doing, waiting for a woman; no, a girl not yet stirred to full awakening? Though he hadn't intended to like her—hell, like wasn't even the truth. He was infatuated with Portia MacIntosh. She'd stolen into his life with such lack of guile that he hadn't realized how important she would become. Now, the first thought of his day was Portia. And so far, he'd managed one chance encounter after another, each leaving him more frustrated than the last.

He was a man of experience and he knew better than Portia where their passionate kisses could lead. He'd known women who sold their bodies. He'd seen others give their love to a man, only to be left behind, broken and alone. He couldn't let himself go any further with Portia. She was ready to become a woman and her body knew better than she that Daniel could be the one to take her.

He'd allowed himself far too much liberty with a woman who was totally inexperienced and much too passionate. Her father was showing signs of slowing down. Her sister had fallen in love. Everything was a threat to Portia now and she was vulnerable. He could overcome her objections and make love to her. But until he decided what he wanted, he wouldn't allow himself to make love to Portia.

Daniel was an honorable man. And Portia deserved marriage, even if that was probably the last thing she wanted. But marriage was something that Daniel had avoided. He tried to visualize Portia hosting an important dinner in his New York hotel. No, she'd hate that. The only place he could see Portia was standing knee deep in a stream panning for gold. And mining was the life he'd left behind.

Behind the stage Portia assisted in the storing of their props. She avoided the stage area. Daniel's eyes followed her from somewhere in the darkened theater and she found that instead of being her normal careful self, she had turned into a clumsy scullery maid.

"Aren't we done yet, Portia?" Fiona glanced around anxiously.

"No! There are the—the costumes. We need to check them."

"Since when?" Bertha stood in the wings, her hands on her hips. "Haven't I checked the costumes for the last ten years without any supervision, Portia MacIntosh?"

"Yes, but there's Papa. We still have to . . . to see about Papa." Portia left the rehearsal hall and started across the Chautauqua grounds. "This was probably tiring for him, the first performance since his illness set in."

"Papa has already left the theater," Fiona snapped, hurrying beside her sister. "He's having a late supper with Lady Evelyna. And Edward is waiting for me."

"I'm sure that Mr. Logan would expect us to . . ."

"He doesn't expect *us*," Fiona interrupted. "I think that Daniel Logan is expecting you to have dinner with him, and you're just finding excuses not to go. Isn't that right?"

Portia came to a stop in the shadows by the dormitory wall, stricken by Fiona's honest appraisal of the truth. She was afraid and she was tired of trying to conceal that fear from her sister. Portia MacIntosh, who never let anything or anybody frighten her, was truly scared.

"Oh, Fiona, I don't know what to do. I don't seem to be able to . . ." To Portia's surprise, tears welled up in her eyes and her throat choked with the pressure; "to . . ."

Only seconds later Fiona's arms were around Portia and Portia was allowing herself to be comforted. "Portia, what's wrong? I'm so sorry. I've been so happy with Edward that I hadn't noticed that you were troubled. Oh, that's not true. I did know, I just didn't want to recognize it. Please, tell me."

"It's Daniel Logan. He . . . kissed me. I mean, he kissed you, more than once, and I . . ."

"You liked it, didn't you?"

"No! Yes. I mean I don't know. I'm so confused. Every time I'm around him I want to scratch his eyes out and then I end up letting him touch me."

"And what's wrong with that? Edward kisses me, and touches me. And it's wonderful, Portia. We're so much in love that it hurts. Why shouldn't you feel something for Mr. Logan?"

"Because I can't, Fiona. I won't. I don't belong with a man like that. I'm not a lady, Fee. I don't even want to be. Besides, I promised Mama."

Fiona drew back and stared at her sister in the dark. "What do you mean, you promised Mama? What did you promise her?"

"I promised her that I'd look after you and Papa. And I haven't even done that very well. Look at us. Papa's lost the troupe. We're dependent on someone else for our livelihood. We can't even make decisions about what we're going to do."

"Oh, Portia, you're wrong. Mama never expected you to spend the rest of your life caring for us. Things change.

People change. Maybe it's time that *we* think about changing too. Have you ever considered the possibility that Daniel Logan might be falling in love with you?''

"Love?" Portia pulled herself from her sister's arms and turned away. "You don't understand, it isn't love he feels. He explained that; it's body signals. And, oh, Fiona, it isn't *me* his body wants—it's you."

Daniel stood in the shadows outside the dormitory waiting. He'd made up his mind. Until he finished his assignment, he'd conduct himself as a friend, an employer. He wouldn't kiss Portia, or touch her except in the most proper way. He'd set his trap for the thief, make the necessary arrangements to return the acting troupe to Horatio and go back to New York. He'd put some time and distance between himself and Portia before it was too late.

Most of the other members of the crew had left the building, ready for ice cream, popcorn balls or some of the new soda water drinks. Still Portia hadn't come down.

Finally, just as Daniel was ready to enter the building and climb the stairs to search, he saw her step through the doorway into the light of the gas lamps on either side.

All Daniel's plans were swept out of his mind when he saw her. Like a lamb being led to slaughter she stood, dressed in a simple shirtwaist of white linen and a plain skirt of dark blue. Like a school girl, Portia had pinned her hair into a soft swirl of curls and garnished it with a severe black bow. There was a worried frown on her face as she waited.

All Daniel wanted to do was sweep her up in his arms and find the nearest swing so that he could hold her in his arms and tell her not to worry. But he wouldn't. He'd already made up his mind that tonight there would be no physical contact. She was an employee, in his care, and he'd treat her with respect.

Just some refreshments and a simple boat ride over to the island. They'd watch the fireworks and talk about his plans for the troupe, nothing more.

"Good evening, Fiona. You look lovely this evening." Daniel couldn't keep himself from taking her hand and bringing it to his lips. In her despair, she had forgotten her gloves and he could see the evidence of years of painting sets and physical labor.

"I'm very tired, Daniel. Do I have to—I mean, couldn't you please excuse me tonight?" Her voice held a touch of desperation as she pulled her hand away and held it up in a gesture of self-defense.

Daniel could see all the uncertainty of her feelings in Portia's eyes. She was caught up in the emotion that arched between them like a fragile leaf spiraling in the wind. He never should have kissed her. He shouldn't do it now. But as he lowered his head, he knew that his determination was wavering like the fine mist from the Springs.

Portia's eyes widened with fear. Daniel stopped, reminded himself of his promise to conduct himself as a friend, and placed a light kiss on her forehead instead. "Don't be afraid, my little one. I won't tire you. I only want to discuss my plans for the next play. I think that I've hit on a fine idea."

"Oh?" Portia allowed Daniel to fold her arm beneath his and walk toward the waiting carriage she hadn't noticed before. "Where are we going?"

Daniel assisted Portia into the carriage, marveling once again at how different she was when she was alone with him. On stage she was Romeo. Around the grounds she was Phillip. But once she was attired in a simple gown she was a lovely young woman.

The horse walked slowly down the wide path, between mounds of roses and geraniums and sweetly scented shrubs. From the hotel came the sound of an orchestra playing *Lorena*. Beside the drive a trio of violinists struck up a soulful rendition of *The Girl I Left Behind Me*.

Tonight Portia didn't worry about her dress or whether or not she would give herself away as a fraud. If their little tryst in the swing had fooled Daniel, she had no doubt about her ability to continue the performance. The question was, did she want to tell him the truth? Two days ago she was ready to tell Daniel that the woman he'd kissed was Portia, not Fiona.

Now, what purpose would it serve? Even if he knew the truth, nothing would be altered. He insisted on having a fiancee and she'd made the agreement so it was up to her to go through with it. Besides everybody else was happy, and what right did she have to sacrifice their joy for her benefit. Another nagging thought skirted the surface of her mind. She didn't want Fiona to know how far their kissing had progressed.

Portia listened to the music, unaware of the half pensive, half frowning expression on her face, until Daniel spoke. "You look worried, Fiona. Please don't be, on my account."

She seemed startled out of her reverie. "I guess I am, Mr. Logan. We're heading in some new direction and I don't seem to be able to do anything to change it. I feel so helpless."

"I know this must be difficult for you. That's what I want to talk to you about, an idea I have that might provide additional cast members and some private income for you and the troupe."

"Private income? You mean money that would come to us, not you?"

The carriage came to a stop and Daniel stepped to the ground, taking Portia's hand to assist her. "Yes, directly to you. Come along."

Caught up in his words, Portia allowed herself to be led to the boating dock and assisted into the small wooden craft. Daniel stepped down into the other end and took the wooden oars in his hands.

"How? What is your plan?"

The beauty of the night was lost on Portia. Light laughter echoed across the water. The sound of music wafted with the midsummer breeze. But Portia was immune to her surroundings. Instead she leaned forward eagerly.

Daniel smiled. His plan to imitate Ian's romantic moonlight boat ride had been foolish in the light of his new plan to deal with Portia as an employee. As it was turning out, the boat ride was not being appreciated. Portia could be in the middle of Grand Central Station for all the difference it made.

"All right, my lady, have you decided which play you'll do next?"

"Yes, *Twelfth Night*, but how can that make money for the troupe?"

"Well, the hotel always has a masquerade as part of the summer entertainment. I propose that we incorporate the play with the masquerade and make some of the guests a part of the cast."

"I don't understand."

They had reached one of the man-made islands left in the middle of the lake when the site had been excavated. The boat came to a gentle stop on the sand. Daniel fastened the oars and stepped to the shore, lifting his hands to assist Portia.

Heedless of his offer, Portia crawled eagerly to the front of the boat and slung her leg over to the shore, righting herself without assistance.

"Tell me what you have in mind, Mr. Logan." Portia looked around, mindful for the first time of where they were. "Why have you brought me out here? Are you afraid someone will hear?"

"No, Fiona. I've brought my fiancee on a moonlight boat ride. This is supposed to be an acceptable romantic treat for lovers."

"But—we aren't lovers, Daniel."

"I know, but we still have to keep up the pretense, don't we? Now come along. We'll find a bench where we can watch the fireworks."

His fiancee? Of course. Daniel was taking his fiancee for a romantic tryst in the moonlight. This was only for the benefit of the other guests, not because he wanted to be alone with her. Or maybe it was just a means of keeping her away from the other guests.

Portia sighed. Fiona couldn't be right. Daniel could never be interested in someone who'd just climbed out of a boat as if she were some shabbytown hoyden. She didn't know why she was even worrying about that now. Daniel had mentioned money for the troupe. Horatio couldn't have more than a few dollars left, and she knew that sooner or later, her adventurous father would break loose.

Watch the fireworks? Portia lifted her skirts to keep them dry, and nodded. "Fine, Daniel. Do let's find a bench. Then you can tell me about your plans. By the way," she added impishly, "have you mentioned them to Phillip yet?"

"Not yet. I haven't seen him since the closing curtain. But I do want to let him know what a fine job he did with the role of Romeo. I could almost believe that he'd really experienced the torments of being in love."

In love? Daniel couldn't possibly know how right he was about Romeo drawing emotion from the torment of emotional upheaval. Never had the words flown so easily from her tongue. Even Fiona had seemed caught up in the magic.

"Eh, yes. Phillip is very talented, as are all the MacIntoshes. I'll tell him of your admiration."

"Not necessary, Fiona. I'd rather tell him myself." Daniel spotted a bench near the water's edge and directed her there. "I believe that we'll have a good view from here."

View? Fireworks? Portia curbed her impatience. Such silly prattle. When was the man going to explain his plan? Portia arranged her skirt and straightened her back. The spot Daniel had chosen was well away from any of the other guests. Between the bench and the water was a bonfire which tinged the shallow waves with orange. Toward the other end of the island another fire sent sparks into the night sky.

"Yes, this view should be very nice, Daniel."

"Now, about my plan. Or, would you rather me wait and discuss this with Phillip?"

"Daniel! Tell me the plan."

"All right. How many major characters are there?"

Well, there are the twins, Viola and Sebastian who are shipwrecked on the island of Illyria, each believing the other to be dead. Viola is the role—Portia plays. She falls in love with the Duke of Illyria. She finds out that he needs a page, disguises herself as a boy and gets the job."

"And does Horatio play the duke?"

"No. The duke must be a younger man. That's Lawson Paine's part."

"I see," Daniel mused, "go on. Portia plays Viola. What role do you play?"

"Fiona is the fair Olivia, whom the duke secretly loves."

"Why secretly?" Daniel didn't know why he was asking these questions. He was well aware of the plot. He'd read and re-read most of Mr. Shakespeare's plays in the last two days while he was working out the details of the trap he'd mentioned to Ian and trying to stay away from Portia.

"Because Olivia is in mourning for her brother who was also lost in a shipwreck, she refuses to see the duke. He is forced to send his page Viola to plead his love. Viola, madly in love with the duke, pleads with words from her own heart. The words are so eloquently spoken that instead of falling in love with the duke, Olivia falls in love with the young page, who of course is really Viola."

"So which role does Horatio play?"

"Horatio is Olivia's uncle, who is arranging her marriage to another man. Rowdy plays her household manager who is also in love with Olivia, and Bessie is her maid."

"Go on, what happens?"

"Viola is again sent to Olivia to relate the duke's feelings. But Olivia refuses the duke's attention, falling more deeply in love with the soulful words of the handsome young page.

"By this time, the true suitor, arranged by the uncle, sees that Olivia is in love with the page, and challenges him to a duel. Meanwhile, Sebastian, who was separated from his twin sister Viola in the shipwreck, finally arrives in Illyria."

"Of course," Daniel said lightly. "Sebastian fights the duel instead of the sister disguised as a boy. Then what happens?"

"Olivia asks Sebastian to marry her, thinking that he is

the page, sent by the duke. Sebastian, bewildered, but delighted, agrees. And the duke—''

Daniel finished the sentence for her. ''The duke realizes that it is Viola he loves. What she doesn't know is that he figured out much earlier that she was a girl. That's when he realized that he was falling in love.''

''No, the duke didn't know of the deception,'' Portia protested, wondering if her father had had some sinister plot in mind when he chose this play. It was uncomfortably close to what was happening to her. This wouldn't be the first time her father had pulled such a trick. He'd think it amusing that they were doing a play that reflected real life.

''At any rate,'' she went on quickly, ''if you want to do *Twelfth Night*, we can cast the other major roles, but we don't have enough actors to play the parts of the party guests and the townspeople. There aren't speaking roles, but with all those lights and that large stage, we're going to look a bit slim.''

''So you need more bodies. Perfect!''

Daniel considered the situation. The play was a perfect choice because of the twins Viola and Sebastian. The idea of Portia disguising herself as a young man because she'd fallen in love with the duke was intriguing, and he wondered at Horatio's choosing it. The *Twelfth Night*, the climax of a season of celebration, would tie into the hotel's festival very well.

''Yes, but even if you could recruit locals to fill the minor roles, it isn't that easy. So, let's not build air castles, Daniel. You may be very good at whatever it is you do, but you don't know the first thing about directing a theatrical troupe and I don't have time for foolishness.''

Immediately Portia was ashamed of her ungrateful outburst. Whatever else Daniel Logan might be, he was a generous owner. Bessie and Mrs. Farmer were already repairing their costumes and were ready to begin sewing the new fabrics right away. And he'd promised to provide whatever they needed.

"You're right. I am being too mysterious. This is what I propose. Some of the hotel guests will play the roles of the townspeople and the family. By involving them in the play it will fill the theater while giving you time to recruit other actors. The audience will forgive their friends any errors without ridiculing the troupe."

"Time?" Portia's response was incredulous. "How many people do you expect us to add?"

"However many you need. And don't think that I'm entirely ignorant of your problems. There was a time when I did some stage work. Not this of course, but I have some knowledge." No point in explaining that his stage experience had consisted of being the master of ceremonies for the musical numbers provided by Belle's dance hall girls.

"Why would you even want to do this?"

"Because it will tie in nicely with the ball I intend to give for Jay Gould, the wealthy New York railroad man and financier, and his daughter Helen who will be here next week. We'll let the guests take part in the play and the cast will then be invited to the ball. Mr. Gould and his daughter should find this an exciting bit of entertainment. What do you think?"

"I think that you're quite mad," Portia answered in her most disapproving tone. There was no way that she would allow Papa and the crew to mingle with the guests at the hotel. There'd already been one robbery. Suppose there was another? No, it wasn't safe. Besides, what would she do about Fiona? There was no way she could keep Fiona and Edward apart.

"Perhaps, Fiona, but the hotel will pay a handsome fee to your father if you will present the play as part of the entertainment at the ball."

"You mean do the play at the hotel?"

"Yes, an abbreviated version of course. We could call it a dress rehearsal, done with only black stage sets that will not change from scene to scene."

"Like a charade?"

"Like a charade, and your troupe will of course be dressed

in keeping with the theme. Even now, Bessie and Mrs. Farmer are sewing the costumes. You'll be provided with real gold and jewels to make the presentation more authentic.''

"Real gold and jewels?" Portia's heart sank. Now she was certain that Daniel was plotting something. Real jewels? What was the man up to? "Why would you want us to do this, Daniel?"

Because it will surely bring out the thief, Daniel wanted to answer. "I know," he answered instead, "that you are concerned about the loss of direct income and the end of the summer is weeks away. I should think that two hundred dollars would be helpful to all of you."

"Two hundred dollars?" Portia threw her arms around Daniel's neck in unconcealed joy. "Oh yes, thank you Daniel! I mean—" She removed herself from his arms, whirled around and stood staring out toward the dying fire. "I'm sure we can work out something."

A circle of silvery stars suddenly shot across the sky and the night came alive with the explosion of color and sound. Standing by the fire, tightly hugging herself with her arms, Portia knew that nothing she could hear would drown out the erratic beat of her pulse that came from the simple touching of Daniel's body. She sighed.

Between blasts Daniel heard her sigh and fought to hold himself back from recapturing her in his arms. Kissing Portia MacIntosh was becoming addictive. Neither the lithium water, nor the sanitarium down the road had a cure for that kind of sickness. He ought to know, he'd drunk a gallon of the mineral water in the last few days.

Daniel came to his feet and stood beside Portia as the display came to an end. Without talking, he offered his arm and they made their way back to the boat and across the lake to the dormitory. Outside the doorway he gave a simple bow.

"Thank you for a lovely evening, Fiona. Please tell Phillip that I'll expect him at ten o'clock in the morning. We have to begin making plans immediately. Will you inform him?"

"Yes, I'm sure he'll be there." Portia took a step back

and waited. She felt incomplete somehow, as if she'd been promised a sweet and it hadn't been presented. "Good night, Daniel."

"Good night, Fiona, and thank you."

"Thank me? For what?" She was delaying. She ought to turn back through that door and go to bed. Daniel had acknowledged her unspoken request and hadn't tried to touch her, not since that first chaste kiss on the forehead.

Daniel took a step closer. "For being a good sport about agreeing to perform the play in the hotel. I mean I know that you don't normally handle the details. I should have left that up to Phillip, but I wanted to know what you would think about the plan."

He was simply working out the details of their employment, just as she would expect him to do. Certainly she could show some appreciation for his efforts. He wasn't really a cad. She'd known from the first that her father hadn't truly been cheated. And she didn't want to believe that Daniel was the hotel thief!

"Thank you, Daniel. I've learned a great deal about being a lady. I've never been a fiancee before and probably never shall again. I thank you for your confidence."

"Oh, but you're wrong." Daniel grinned. "You are more a lady than those phonies back at the hotel. Look at the Trevillions, they're a good example. Mrs. Trevillion's family made their money in trade along the Mississippi. Her husband made his raising pigs. They send their daughter off to Europe, then pretend to be something they're not in order to find a husband for her from among the real gentry. I'll bet you that most of them are just like you and me. The only difference is that you're honest about what you are and you're smart."

"Honest?" Portia gulped. Whatever she was, honest wasn't it. Smart was safer to deal with. "Nobody's ever told me I was smart before."

A summer breeze caught Portia's hair and pulled it from the clasp of the bow, winding it across her cheek. The same breeze ruffled Daniel's hair rakishly across his forehead. He reached out to touch Portia's face at the same time she lifted her fingertips to his. Their hands caught and held for a very long minute.

"Fiona?"

"Daniel?"

They spoke at the same time, laughed and dropped hands again.

"Good night, again, Daniel."

"I know how Romeo felt," Daniel said huskily. "Parting is sometimes—hell." Abruptly he drew Portia to him, kissed her hard and quick, then released her and turned back into the darkness.

Under her breath, Portia whispered, "Ah, Romeo, parting is such sweet sorrow. And he was right. Hell fire and little fishes, we have to meet tomorrow."

"Evie, I wonder if you know how much it has meant to be with you." Horatio dropped a card on the stack and picked up another.

"You mean without having to pretend to be a cross between Dr. Feelgood and Mr. Barnum? I don't know why you aren't dead from a heart attack, or in debtors prison somewhere, Rashie, dear." Lady Evelyna picked up the card Horatio discarded and began to spread her hand on the table. "Gin! That's twelve thousand, three hundred and two dollars you owe me."

"Care to try for double or nothing?" Horatio lifted Lady Evelyna's hand and kissed her palm. "Or had you rather find some other payment plan."

"Horatio MacIntosh, if it weren't for Edward, I'd marry you and stay right here to keep you on the straight and narrow path."

"What does Edward have to do with us, Evie? He's a grown man now, and I rather think that Fiona has taken him in hand."

Lady Evelyna stood up and threaded her arms into the sleeves of her silk robe. She walked to the open door and stepped out onto the balcony. Horatio followed her.

"There is something you don't know, Rashie, about me. I think I'd better tell you the truth. I'm not really a countess."

Horatio turned Evelyna to face him. "That's all right, darling, I'm not really a captain. And I'm not wealthy either. It doesn't matter a fig to me or to Fiona what you are. I think I'm beginning to care for you and I didn't think there'd ever be another woman in my life."

"Oh, Edward really does have a title, or he will one day. You see, Edward is Lord Delecort's only child. He recognized Edward as his legal heir last year. Edward is twenty-one now. He will have to return to England and assume his official duties soon. I only brought him to America because I wanted him to know where I came from before it was too late."

"Where you came from? But Evie, I thought you were a real English lady."

"Sure, straight out of a pub in Boston. My father is the proprietor of the Lucky Duck Saloon. Edward's father, Lord William, owns a fleet of ships. He came here twenty-five years ago on business. We fell in love. When he left, I went with him.

"I don't expect you to understand. But we were in love. He was already married to a woman much older than he. It didn't matter. I never regretted it. Lord Delecort is old now and ill. He knew that I was homesick. So he insisted that I return to my family a wealthy woman."

Horatio caught Lady Evelyna's hand and squeezed it gently. "I knew another lady who left her family and went with the man she loved. She was a fine lady, too."

"Your wife?"

"Yes. I came into town with a traveling tent show. She came to see the play with her friends. I looked out into the audience and saw her. We fell in love at that moment. Three days later she left town with me. We were together for twenty years."

"Allistair loved me too, but in truth, we never married. His wife died last year, but by then it was too late. I'm sorry, Horatio, but I am a fraud. My name is really Evelyn Petty."

"Sorry? I'm not. Don't you see, it was destiny, Evie. Two old frauds who've found each other. Stay with me, Evelyn Petty."

"Are you sure, Horatio?"

"I'm very sure, Evie. It's time I found somebody else to keep me in line. It's time I let my children go."

"I know, Rashie, I must do the same. Edward will return to England. He won't care about what people say. He'll be happy there with Fiona as his wife. It won't matter so much that I'm not along."

"And Fiona, will he make her happy?"

"Edward is kind and caring. He loves Fiona. As the Countess of Hidemarch she'll have everything she could ever want. If she can keep Edward from spending his fortune on telephones and incandescent lights."

Horatio slid his arms around Lady Delecort's ample figure and drew her close. "Then maybe I should say, poor Evie. Because you know I'll never have anything to offer you except my name."

"That's enough, Rashie. But there's one thing I have to make plain right now. I won't share you and I won't put up with any tomfoolery. We're two of a kind and I understand you, very well."

"How do you feel about acting, Evie? I think you'd make a splendid Lady MacBeth."

"Maybe, but I think you'd make a better retired actor than I would an actress. Rashie, you don't have to worry. I may not have a true title, but I'm not poor. Lord Delecort made a very generous settlement on me. And Edward inherits everything. You see, I'm not just a guest here at the Springs, I plan to buy one of the other hotels."

"You own a hotel?" Horatio's mouth dropped open. For the second time in his life he'd fallen in love. And this time the woman turned out to be a fraud like himself. That was a wonderful irony. But now, he was finding out that she was truly wealthy and that was a turn of events he hadn't counted on.

"I do. And I've decided to stay on here, permanently. What do you think? Will you like being the proprietor of a resort?"

"Evie, I can't think of a finer life for two old frauds. What do you think of Lord Horatio? That has a nice ring."

"I think I like Captain MacIntosh better, Rashie. Have you ever been on a ship?"

"No. Don't tell me that you own ships, too."

"Only one, darling, only one."

"I've never been a rich man before, Evie. You're going to have to show me what to do."

"Oh, Rashie, don't be silly. You most definitely know what to do. For right now, you can start with turning off the lights."

"No darkness tonight, Evie, darling. For the first time in a long time I plan to go into a venture with my eyes wide open. That is if you're sure that you want a worn out old fool like me for the rest of your life."

Evelyna Delecort let her dressing gown fall to the floor in a cloud of silk. "Horatio MacIntosh, I wouldn't have it any other way."

Fourteen

"MISS Fiona—good morning!" Ian looked surprised. "Are you alone? I mean, was Daniel expecting you here this morning?" Ian stood back hesitantly, allowing Portia to enter the parlor.

"No, he's expecting Phillip. But Phillip is busy. He sent me to make his morning report. Will you tell Mr. Logan that I'm here?"

"But he isn't here at the moment. He had an early morning meeting. I was to tell Phillip that he'll be back shortly."

"I see. Thank you. I'll just wait."

"Fine. I hope you won't mind waiting alone. I'm meeting Vickie for breakfast this morning."

"Vickie?" Portia couldn't hold back a tiny smile.

"Miss Trevillion," Ian said with a blush. "But I'll be glad to wait with you, if you'd feel uncomfortable about being here alone."

"No, you go on ahead. I'll be fine."

After Ian left Portia wandered about the sitting room, wondering why she'd come to Daniel's room as Fiona. As Phillip she could maintain a distance between herself and Daniel. But for the last three days when she'd come to his quarters

• 223 •

Daniel had been relaxed, casual and it had become more and more uncomfortable to ignore his man-to-man talk. It wasn't Daniel's fault. He thought he was dealing with another man and Portia was learning that men were much more informal than women when they were alone.

She'd been afraid that the next visit might find her employer totally nude instead of partially dressed, like the last time. She could never maintain her disguise if she were faced with delivering her report to a Daniel Logan without clothes. Being Phillip was no longer safe. Being Fiona wasn't safe either. There didn't seem to be a Portia anymore and she didn't know what to do.

Curious, Portia wandered into Daniel's chambers. The covers had been thrown back, as though he'd just left the room. His red brocade robe was flung across the pineapple carved post at the foot of the bed. Across the top of an ornate cherry chest of drawers were his comb and brush, his mustache cup and straight razor. The tag of a yellow silk tie hung from a half opened drawer. She pulled it through the opening and rubbed it against her cheek.

The smell of him engulfed her. The silk was soft against her cheek. She closed her eyes and the picture of Daniel in the moonlight appeared unbidden in her mind. It was so real that it was almost as if he were really there. He was strong and rugged, and Portia sighed. How would it feel to really be Daniel's woman, to feel his lips on her body, teasing, touching. She'd had no warning of the wonderfully strange feelings that a man's touch could arouse. Even now she felt that prickly little sensation in her lower body. Her throat tightened and she forced her eyes open.

This obsession with Daniel Logan had to stop. She'd come to make her report as Fiona rather than Phillip to keep those kinds of thoughts away and here she was standing dreamy eyed in his bedroom, touching the things that had touched him.

Guiltily she opened the drawer to replace the silk. Pushing it to the back of the drawer her fingers touched something,

something cold and smooth. She pulled back the stack of clothing to reveal a half open jewelry case. Nothing unusual about that, she reminded herself, except that one of the pieces of jewelry belonged to a woman.

There was probably a good explanation for Daniel having a gold necklace set with rubies along with a man's diamond ring and a pocket watch inscribed with a rose and the initials A.L., Portia told herself with little conviction.

Why? Where did Daniel get the necklace? She dug through the case. There was the necklace, the ring he'd won in the poker game that first night, and the watch, nothing else. Why was she so concerned? Did she expect to find Lady Evelyna's necklace hidden beneath his underwear? Of course not.

No matter what she'd told herself, Daniel couldn't possibly be the thief, and even if he was, why should she care? If this necklace had been Lady Evelyna's she would have used it to secure the return of the troupe. But this was gold and rubies and Lady Evelyna's necklace was set with diamonds. Whatever Daniel was doing with such magnificent jewelry was his own business. But what was Daniel's business?

Dumbfounded by her discovery and the train of thoughts her mind was taking, Portia didn't hear the door open. She didn't hear Daniel walk across the sitting room and into the bedroom.

"Darling, I was expecting Phillip this morning—what are you doing . . ." Daniel saw the necklace in one hand and the watch in the other. He was stopped short by Portia's incredulous gaze.

"Daniel, I didn't mean to . . . I shouldn't have pried. Where did you get these?"

"They belong to me," Daniel said.

"Did you steal them, Daniel? Please, you can tell me."

"Steal them? Of course not. Why would you think that?" And then he understood. She thought he was the thief. He started to smile, caught sight of her stricken expression and narrowed his lips seriously.

"My darling girl, I did not steal either the necklace or the watch." He took the pieces from her and replaced them carelessly in his drawer. "The necklace was made from the first gold that I ever mined. The rubies were added, one at a time over the years as a kind of measure of my success."

"You must be very successful," she whispered, feeling both foolish and relieved.

"If you measure success by wealth, I suppose you'd say that I am. But the watch means more to me. It belonged to my father. It isn't even valuable. Never did keep good time—always runs twenty minutes fast. I deeply appreciate your concern, but you mustn't worry about me. Now, suppose you tell me why you are here instead of Phillip?"

Daniel took her hand and led her away from the chest into the sitting room. Why had she left Phillip behind and come to his room as a woman? He could see that she was confused. Her blue eyes were dark and wary. Perhaps she was afraid of him. The very thought set off a need to reassure her. He wanted to put his arms around her and protect her, to wipe away her uncertainties and tell her that he'd make things right.

Portia couldn't face Daniel. Why had she come? Suddenly, masquerading as Fiona seemed foolish. She wasn't safe alone with the man no matter who she was. Simply because he was near her, she felt the prickling feeling change into a gush of warmth that flushed her skin with heat. She'd deliver her report and leave. Even if Daniel was a thief she couldn't turn him in. She'd have to think about what to do.

"Phillip is busy this morning, Daniel," she said hurriedly. "Papa sent me to tell you that Lawson Paine is sick. We need to begin rehearsals this afternoon but we don't have another actor to play the part of the duke. We may have to cancel the performance, or delay the production until Lawson is well enough to perform."

"Lawson ill? What's wrong?"

"Dr. Garrett thinks he may be coming down with the measles."

"Damn!" Daniel swore without thinking. Canceling the performance would involve canceling the masquerade ball.

His trap was already set. This couldn't be allowed to happen. "Couldn't you substitute another play?"

"Well, we could continue with *Romeo and Juliet*, but I'm afraid that the subject of that play doesn't lend itself to a joyous masquerade ball."

"You're right. I'll have to think of something. Go ahead with plans for rehearsal this afternoon. I have another actor in mind."

"You have? Who?"

"Me."

"You'd play the duke? Mr. Logan, I hardly think that you could learn the lines by the time we open. And we don't have the time to teach you about the stage."

"Fiona, I have a confession to make. The reason that I could quote those lines from Shakespeare is the same reason that I could defeat your father in a poker game. I have a photographic memory. Since I was a boy I've been able to see something and remember it. All I'll have to do is read over the script again."

"You can read the script and learn the lines—just like that?"

"Yes, with a little help from you. I don't know about the delivery, but since this is a performance being given as part of a festival, the guests shouldn't mind a few mistakes. If you will go over the script with me I believe that you'll feel a little better about the idea. I wouldn't want the troupe to look bad before the visitors who will be attending the ball if I can avoid it."

Portia groaned. She had the same fear. It wasn't enough that they were introducing a new play. They would have to deal with an inexperienced actor when they were probably appearing before their most distinguished audience. As Viola she would be the actress forced to deal with Daniel. He'd be playing the part of the duke, the man Viola was secretly in love with. Even if Daniel mastered the role, Portia wasn't sure that she could do it.

Still, she was an actress. Papa had always been a perfectionist. *Twelfth Night*, even with its amateurs, would be no exception. She'd simply have to do her job, even if it would tax every ability she had.

"All right," she decided, "I'll send Phillip back to rehearse with you, Daniel." She made a move toward the door.

"I thought you said that Phillip was away from the grounds. I fear that it will be too late by the time he returns. It will have to be you."

"But the room is too small to get a true idea of the projection of your voice. We'll use the stage."

"No! I mean, that would be embarrassing. I don't want to get on the stage until I'm sure that I can deliver my lines. Come with me. We'll find a spot that is private."

Without quite knowing how it had happened, Portia found herself in a carriage with him driving down a country road away from the hotel grounds.

Daniel didn't speak and gradually Portia found herself relaxing. Maybe it would work. Even if it didn't, Daniel would be forced to assume the blame for their failure. The guests wouldn't dare criticize him.

There was something peaceful about the morning. Bright sunshine made a patchwork quilt of light and shadow on the pine-covered lane. Birds swooped back and forth across their path, some chasing intruders away from nests of new-laid eggs, some carrying fat worms to babies already hatched. But it was the sweet smell of wildflowers that swept along with the summer breeze that gave Portia the most pleasure.

"God's in his heaven and all's right with the world," she whispered softly.

"Perhaps," Daniel answered, reining in the horse and directing him off the road beneath a mammoth water oak tree. Daniel sat in the silence, holding the reins lightly in his hands.

"Oh, I didn't mean to say that."

Wearing the same pink dress she'd worn that night in the moonlight, Portia seemed very small and unsure of herself, sitting on the end of the bench as far away from him as she could sit. She was looking at Daniel, her eyes wide.

"Why not, little one? I think perhaps that the Garden of Eden must have been much like this, before it was changed."

"I . . . I don't know much about the Garden of Eden, except that there was a snake who tempted Eve. Hadn't we better get started? I mean we have a lot to do before we have to get back to lunch."

"Oh, but we don't have to get back to lunch. I had the hotel pack a picnic for us." Daniel swung down from the carriage, tied the horse to a limb and lifted a basket from behind the seat.

"When did you arrange this?"

Daniel continually surprised Portia. Had he planned this all along? No, that couldn't be. He wouldn't have taken Phillip on a picnic and he hadn't known that it would be Fiona who would come to deliver the report.

"When I called down for the carriage, I asked for the lunch then. The kitchen prepares lunches each morning for those who want to picnic on the grounds so they just placed a basket in the carriage. Here, let me help you down."

"No, I can get down by myself." Portia swung her feet over the side of the wagon and started to slide to the ground. If she hadn't been in such a hurry she wouldn't have caught her feet in her petticoat and Daniel wouldn't have had to drop the basket and catch her.

"Blast! Petticoats and corsets are the devil's own torture traps!"

"My sentiments exactly," Daniel agreed, lifting Portia to a standing position. "I prefer my women without them."

Portia raised her head and caught the full force of his gaze, intense and wild. His voice had gone husky and she could feel the pounding of his heart where her breasts were pressed against him. Blast him, always touching her. She felt the rise of heated emotions, fueled by his touch. No, not this time. She wouldn't let him reduce her to a mass of uncertainty. Not again.

"Your women? Oh! You are a thoroughly despicable man,

Daniel Logan. Let me go! How many women do you have anyway?''

Daniel smiled. *Ah, Portia*, he wanted to say. *The only woman I want, I don't have.* "Now, darling. Don't be jealous. I was simply agreeing with you. Why would that make you cross?"

"I don't know, Daniel. I don't understand why you make me turn into some fishwife." She lowered her eyes, and tried to staunch her rapid breathing.

Daniel watched the sweep of her lashes as she closed her eyes. There was something poignant about her, standing here, allowing him to hold her. There was a hint of desperation about her and that was as disturbing to him as it must be to her. He never wanted her to look at him with that kind of resolution. Yet he too was caught up in the tension of the moment.

She was resting her head on his chest. His fingers were still holding her elbows, not as tight as they had been when he caught her. What was he doing? She was waiting as if she expected to be kissed. And, dear God, he wanted to kiss her. He wanted to tear those hateful petticoats from her body and press her down against the warm earth. But he couldn't. He'd promised himself that he wouldn't allow the madness of his thoughts to go any further.

"Listen Po . . . Princess," he said, his voice edged with tightness, "I'm not so strong a man as you think. I don't want you to trust me, or give in to me because you think that you have no choice. You aren't one of my women. I never want you to think of yourself that way. I care about you, my gypsy girl, and I don't quite know what to do about it."

Portia felt her fear turn into something warm and tender. For the first time she was beginning to realize the real power she held over this man. He was trembling. She could feel his tension beneath her cheek as she leaned against his shirt. She didn't know how to respond, but she knew that he was waiting for an answer.

"Maybe I am beginning to undersand, Daniel. And I do thank you for your restraint. Couldn't we just not do or say anything—personal? I mean I'm sure that I don't know how to play games or do any of those silly things that I hear women talk about. I wouldn't know how."

Portia raised her head and looked at his face. His hair was falling across his forehead in that familiar way. His eyes seemed troubled, and she wanted to kiss them the way her mother used to kiss her eyes asleep when she was a very little girl. Funny, it had been a long time since she'd thought about that. Remembering brought her mother back and made her feel safe. She smiled.

"I don't know, my dear. Not doing anything may be very hard," Daniel said, stepping back and taking her hand. "You see, I like you very much, just the way you are. I don't think that I'd want you to ever do any of those silly women things."

In the silence the creek made a sudden gurgling, laughing sound and Portia felt the weight lift from her mind. She took a deep breath. The day was good. Life was good. Why couldn't she, for once, leave all her doubts behind and enjoy this man?

"Can we take off our shoes and wade in the creek?" Portia separated herself from Daniel and ran down to the water's edge.

"Perhaps, if we walk down just a short distance." He pulled the branches back and waited for Portia to proceed down the path. "I was told that there is a deep pool where you can go for a swim if you want."

Portia caught her breath as she stepped out into a clearing completely surrounded by trees and brush entwined with green, sweet blooming vines. The shallow band of water widened and grew quiet as it made its way into the hidden lagoon and moved out again beneath the cool shadows on the other side.

"Oh, it's beautiful, Daniel. So beautiful. We can . . ." She caught back the words she was about to say as she remembered suddenly why they had come. "We can rehearse here without anyone hearing. Shall we sit here on the bank and begin?"

Daniel opened the basket and withdrew a bottle which he tied to a small bush and dropped into the cool water. He placed the basket in the shade beneath a tree and pulled out the battered copy of the script he'd been studying. Portia was right. Rehearsal was the reason for their coming here. *The play's the thing*, he reminded himself, not a pleasant outing with his lady.

"Fine. Do you need to see the script, Fiona?"

"No. I know them all. Just start with the duke's first lines."

Daniel opened the playbook and began to read. His voice was beautiful. Portia quickly realized that Daniel had all the makings of a fine actor. His sense of timing was better than Lawson's and not once did he sound as though he was delivering the Gettysburg Address.

Portia closed her eyes, reciting the lines from memory. When the duke entreated his page, Viola, to plead his love for the fair Olivia, Portia found herself understanding as never before the despair that the young woman must have felt. Poor Viola had fallen in love with a man who was totally devoted to another. By the time they reached the half-way point in the script, Portia had forgotten her misgivings and gave herself over to the emotional intensity of the play.

When Daniel dropped the script and implored Viola to remove her masculine clothes and "let me see thee in thy woman's weeds," Portia had the odd sensation that the plea was genuine. She couldn't answer him. The lines flew right out of her head and she sat staring at him in bemusement.

Daniel laid the script down and closed his eyes. *Easy Daniel. The time has come to force Portia to emerge. Don't scare her.* "Tell me the truth, Princess, what do you think? Will I disgrace Mr. Shakespeare's words?"

"I think that you read the words as if you wrote them, Daniel," Portia answered breathlessly. "I'm very impressed."

"And I'm very hungry. What say you we take a break, have lunch and maybe talk?"

"Yes. I can see that you don't need me to help you learn the lines." Her voice seemed to hesitate in her throat. She forced herself to look at the man whose dark eyes had turned a volcanic black in the shadow of the pine tree under which they were sitting.

Lunch she could deal with, but the talking? That was scary. There was something about this place that seemed almost spiritual and she felt a quiver of unease ripple down her backbone. "You are a remarkable man, Mr. Logan."

Daniel came to his knees and took Portia's hand in his. He lifted it, pressing his lips against the soft cotton of her gloves. "And so are you, little one. I think that I am going to enjoy being in love with the passionate Viola."

Through her gloves she felt the touch of his lips. The forest seemed to glow with warmth as he continued to hold her hand. Beside them the creek sang musically as it dived over a rock and slid down its slick gray surface into the little pool below. Violets strewn by the unknown hands of some woods fairy colored the carpet of green grass with splotches of lavender. Above the sky was unfurled like a blue flag, dappled with cottony tufts of white.

"The passionate Viola? What makes you think that she's passionate?"

"I'm sure she is." Daniel leaned forward, pulling Portia toward him.

He is going to kiss me, Portia thought dreamily. *And I want him to.* She felt her lips part and she caught a quick desperate breath. How wonderful it would be if it were really she that Daniel wanted to kiss. But it wasn't Portia Daniel wanted, it was Fiona.

"No. You mustn't kiss me, Daniel." She sprang to her feet and moved to the water's edge. "I didn't come here for that. You've got to stop kissing me. We're here to rehearse. And there's lunch. You promised me lunch."

Daniel groaned and made a move toward her. "So I

did, little one. Lunch it is. Let me get the wine from the pool.''

No, she didn't want him to move any closer, to see the flush on her face. "That's all right, Daniel. You get the lunch, I'll get the bottle." She turned around, dropped to her knees and leaned forward to fish the wine from the pool. Daniel had secured it with a length of cord tied to a small bush at the edge of the bank.

Kneeling by the pool Portia could see her reflection in the water. As she leaned forward she sucked in a quick breath as she took in the picture of the woman looking back at her. Her eyes were open wide. Her hair was tousled wildly and her face was bright with excitement. The woman she was seeing wasn't Portia. But she wasn't Fiona either. This creature was alive with a joy, a passion that Portia had never experienced, and she was hypnotized by the picture.

"Need any help?"

Daniel's voice drew her back to the present, startling Portia into action. She pulled the bottle from the water and tried to untie the knot.

"Blast!" She couldn't loosen the cord. It was the gloves. She stripped them from her fingers. But the cord had absorbed the water and the knot had tightened.

"Here, let me." Daniel called out from where he was unpacking the lunch.

Portia gave one last impatient jerk to the tether. The small bush to which it was anchored came out of the soil by the roots so unexpectedly that Portia lost her balance and tumbled head first into the creek.

It happened in a second. The icy water closed over her head. Portia opened her mouth to scream. The wail turned into a glub. Portia had never learned to swim. Frantic now she flailed her arms and legs as the water pulled at the hem of her dress and dragged her down. The more she fought the further out into the pond she moved and the deeper she went. Helpless panic swept over her. She was going to die.

She opened her eyes in the clear water and saw the bright

sunlight dapple the rippling water like a prism. Portia began to kick her feet and move her arms. She wasn't about to die now. Her lungs were bursting when she felt herself moving toward the surface. Just as her head reached the surface she was grabbed by two hands that jerked her entire upper body out of the water.

"Portia! Portia, are you all right?"

Portia coughed emptying her lungs of water as she took in a deep sweet breath of air. Daniel was holding her close, lifting her into his strong arms. Whimpering, she clasped his neck, burrowing her face into his chest. Her head whirled with shock and her chest ached with trying to breathe. Daniel was there, holding her. She was safe. Though her eyes were closed now, she could feel him, smell him; her lips parted against his neck and she could taste him.

"You're all right, Portia. I've got you."

As her ragged breathing began to slow she opened her eyes and Daniel's worried face came out of the blackness. "Yes, I'm all right. I'd have been all right in the first place," she insisted bravely, "if it hadn't been for this blasted dress and petticoat."

"I don't doubt it for a moment, darling." Daniel made his way across the pool, climbed up the bank beneath the trees and dropped to his knees, still holding Portia in his arms.

Portia felt her breath quicken. She couldn't pull her eyes away from his. She smiled at him, a shy, tentative smile as she struggled with the need to thank him. There was a look in his eyes that she'd not seen before. He seemed unsure of himself as though he were asking and she didn't know how to answer. "Daniel," she whispered, then wished she could call back the word.

The air, the very sunlight that filtered through the trees and mottled his face with light seemed charged. Portia felt as though she were seeing him for the first time. He was a man who'd cared for her family, teased her and forced her to examine her inner self. She was no longer some tough-talking molly and he was suddenly shy.

The silence stretched between them, the unasked question hanging in the silence. A bird trilled softly from the tree top, answered softly by its mate in the brush. Portia's eyes swept timidly down his face, examining his mustache, the tightly corded muscles in his neck and his lips, quivering slightly under her gaze. To her family she'd always been the caretaker, feeding on their need for her. To be needed by Daniel—and without knowing how, she sensed the unspoken need in his eyes—reached deep inside and touched a secret part of her.

Portia was changing. Lying there in Daniel's arms she could feel herself opening up like the petals of a flower unfolding or the clouds spreading and allowing the sunlight to pour through. She wouldn't fight the wonder any more. Boldly, Portia slid her arms around his neck and kissed his face. His mustache was scratchy but she liked the feel of its abrasive touch against her skin. His skin had a light taste of salt about it and she felt him shiver as she pressed herself against him.

He laid her back on the cushion of pine straw and leaned over her, his dark eyes blacker than the sky at midnight.

"I'll never let anything happen to you, my little love. I wouldn't want to do without you." And his mouth found hers. This time when he kissed her he couldn't hold back and she opened herself up to him giving him her answer with such trust that she knew there would never be uncertainty between them again.

They came together in a burst of sunlight in an afternoon touched with magic. As if in a dream, Daniel unfastened her dress and peeled it back, following his fingers with his lips. Beneath the onslaught of the fire he wrought Portia gave herself over to her frantic need to touch and feel and be touched.

Daniel was kissing her and she was arching herself against him, asking, pleading for him to give her something she didn't understand. Her hands were inside his shirt, touching that wonderful masculine chest that had driven her crazy as she'd watched Daniel walk about his room half dressed. And then his shirt was gone and she could feel the wiry tingle of his chest hair touching her bare breasts.

A dreamlike awareness let her know that Daniel had caught the hem of her skirt and was lifting it over her head, but she was swimming in such a wash of sensation that it was as if this place were itself a dream. There it was again, that sharp ripple of heat that ran up the inside of her legs and churned in her lower body like water just ready to boil.

"Oh, my love," Daniel whispered, "you are so very beautiful."

Dimly she was aware that Daniel had pulled his body away from her and she made an attempt to wiggle back into the cocoon of touch and feel that had surrounded her. His kisses were deeper and harder and she felt the movement of his lower body. Then he was back, his rough strong body touching her as she'd never been touched before. His hands were playing at her breasts setting off delicious sensations that seemed to burst beneath her skin like fireworks exploding in the night sky.

Daniel felt her trembling all over. He knew that he'd taken her across some forbidden line of awareness, of sensation out of control. She lay naked beneath him, her arms clasped about his neck, her fingertips digging helplessly into his skin. She was giving herself to him, allowing him to touch her in places no man had ever known before. Daniel's own heart was pounding so that he could no longer think rationally. Loving Portia was madness, but he couldn't stop.

When he'd seen her disappear beneath the water and watched the churning of the creek as she struggled, his heart had stopped. It was in that moment that he knew that he loved Portia. He'd stripped off his shoes and coat and dived in after her. Now he felt her flesh mold herself to his touch. She was his, and they belonged together.

"I thought I'd lost you," he said between kisses.

His hands left her swollen breasts and moved down the body arching itself against him. For a second she resisted when he slid his hand between her legs and then she gave a muffled cry and opened herself up to him. He urged himself to go slow as he felt the hesitant trembling. Suddenly she went still beneath his touch. She didn't know what he was doing but she wasn't pulling away. For a long minute he simply moved his finger in and out, as his tongue and his body pressing against her thigh duplicated the movement.

Caught in the wonder of the sensations Daniel was creating with his touch, Portia was electrified with feelings. She had never known that two people could be together this way. Vaguely she knew that the promise of this had been there from that first night. She'd been around men all her life but never had there been such awareness, such tension, and now such intensity of need. Her body knew and overruled her mind. She felt Daniel hesitate as he touched a barrier with his fingertip. Her body felt him shudder as he removed his hand and brought it back to take her in his arms.

When he moved over her she felt a different sensation. Her body seemed to scream out, to vibrate with some unnamed anger. And then she felt it, the intrusion into that sea of swirling sensation. At the same time Daniel's mouth slanted across hers, demanding, taking, urging her to return his boldness until she felt his tongue delving into her mouth. His mustache teased and caressed as all her senses came screaming to life. Her nipples ached. Her body was melting from the inside and she felt herself begin to quiver as though she were freezing and burning up at the same time.

"Daniel?" Her voice was choked with need.

Portia felt the heat of him, throbbing against her. At the moment she thought that she would die, he moved swiftly, pressing his hot flesh into her with a trembling intensity that became more forceful in the degree of his control. She felt the power of his need and reveled in the knowledge that she had brought him to this trembling state. And then he was inside her. Her body shuddered as it experienced the sharp hot pain that came with the fullness of their joining together, and her heart went crazy.

The explosion of sensation that followed was terrifying as they moved together toward some giant trembling abyss. She held back, tightening her muscles into a rigid dam, even as she matched Daniel's thrusts. She could feel the pressure growing. She was at the edge and she couldn't hold it back. Portia felt the heat skyrocketing until it exploded, fanning out from her secret core to the tips of her toes and fingertips in a thousand little jolts of fire that stunned her with its intensity.

Portia opened her eyes to the sight of the pained expression on Daniel's flushed face. As he realized that she was watching him he changed the frown into a loving smile and rolled to his back carrying her with him. "Ah, my little gypsy," he whispered, kissing her and drawing her close. For a long time they lay, her head against his breast, his hand cradling her bare bottom as he held her against him. She didn't want to think about the consequences of what had just happened. She only wanted to lie there and feel the wonder that still touched them.

She'd never dreamed that something like this could happen. She'd truly never known that men and women felt like this when they mated. The concept of having such feelings for all one's life was inconceivable until now. Three weeks ago, the idea of her ever lying with a man would have been laughable. Now Daniel had come into her life and taken over.

Daniel was lying so still that he could almost feel the confusion of Portia's thoughts, for they were mirroring his own. She was such a surprise, such a passionate woman-child. His thoughts were filled with wonder at what had happened and scorn for himself for allowing it.

What had he done? He'd fallen in love with an innocent girl and he'd made love to her. What kind of man was he? Her father had asked him to take care of her, and he hadn't been able to keep from loving her. He knew that he ought to say something to take away the questions she must be asking, but he didn't know what to say.

He knew now that from the moment he met her he'd felt

more than just responsible. That first night when she'd punched him and bitten his hand, he'd been infatuated. Until now he hadn't admitted that his infatuation could be more than plain male lust. She had such spirit, such enthusiasm, such vitality. She was alive in a way that he understood. And now, he'd changed her forever. His long fingers tightened on the warm flesh of her buttocks. Even now, knowing what he'd done, he couldn't stop responding to the very touch of her.

Portia wondered when Daniel would speak. She sensed that he'd been as moved by what had happened as she had been. He'd called her name with such emotion. *Her name— Portia! He'd called her Portia!*

In a flash she sprang to her feet and stared down at him marshaling her confusion into sudden, overwhelming fury. "You knew! You knew all along, didn't you? You called me Portia."

"Yes, I knew." Daniel wished he could call back his words. He'd taken away Portia's shield of protection by his action and there was nothing he could do but admit the truth. Ah, but she was magnificent when she was angry.

"How?"

"I knew from the beginning," Daniel began. "It was easy. You and Fiona look alike, but there is an inner fire about you, my darling Portia, that I could never mistake."

"Don't call me darling," Portia snapped. "And I'm not yours. I belong to nobody but myself. It's Fiona who is your fiancee, not I."

"No," Daniel corrected quietly, then quickly went on, "it's you, darling. I understand why you changed places with Fiona."

"How? How could you possibly understand?"

"Horatio explained. He realized the responsibility he'd heaped on you. And he was afraid that this time the problems he'd caused might be too much, even for you. I agreed to step in, and we used your concern for his health to keep you from fighting my taking over."

"You knew and you let me go on making a fool of myself? You . . . you cad! You black-hearted devil." Portia drew back her hand, ready to strike Daniel with all the frustration she felt. "Why didn't you say something earlier?"

Daniel caught her wrist. "I wouldn't do that, darling. Remember what happened the last time? How would the duke look with a broken nose?"

Daniel bit back a smile. He truly hadn't meant to call her Portia. But he'd completely lost every shred of control. Now he was holding her wrist as she stood over him, completely nude, her nipples still swollen into hard little peaks. And the angrier she became the more he wanted her. Daniel felt himself stir and harden before her open gaze and he could do nothing to stop it.

"Oh! You're . . . changing," she said, her eyes widening in amazement.

Daniel came lazily to his feet. It had happened and there was no way to take it back. Where they went from here he couldn't imagine. "Yes, that's what happens when two bodies are right together. They send out signals of longing."

She pulled her hand away and took a step back, keeping her eyes on his erection. "Do you mean that every time we are together this will happen?"

"Probably. It's happened almost every time so far."

"With Fiona too?"

"No, just you."

"Well, I'm angry with you, Daniel Logan. I don't think I trust you. How do I know that you won't do that again?"

"You don't."

"But why me?"

"I haven't figured that out yet. Maybe because you're not one of those silly fibbergibbets who go around pretending that she doesn't feel anything when a man touches her. I can't promise that I won't do that again. But I will promise that I won't make love to you unless you want me to."

"You won't?" Portia wasn't sure that his answer pleased her. She didn't know what she felt or why. She ought to be angry with Daniel that he misled her, that he'd pretended that he thought she was Fiona. But, truthfully, she couldn't be angry when all she felt was a great sense of relief that the charade was ended.

"I won't," he promised.

Portia swallowed hard. He was so big, so handsome. If she admitted the truth, she'd confess that she wanted to know more about what they'd just shared. She might never know a man again. This afternoon was her one magical chance to be the woman that Daniel seemed to think she was. She forced herself to accept the fact that Daniel was like everything else in her life, temporary. He was right in calling her "gypsy." Long ago she'd learned that tomorrow would come and they'd move on, just as they always had. Tomorrow she would be what she really was. This afternoon she'd be what she wished she was.

"May I touch you?" Portia said and wished she hadn't.

"I don't think that's a good idea, my gypsy girl. I'm having a hard enough time staying in control."

"You are? Why?"

"Portia, surely you must feel something of what my body is showing you. You're a very passionate woman. That's not something that you hide. Look at your breasts."

Portia glanced down at her body. She knew that she should be embarrassed, but curiously she wasn't. Her body was something she'd never paid much attention to, other than to wish at certain times that she was a man. Now she saw that her breasts were standing erect, her nipples were hard little rose colored orbs. They tingled. She touched herself and felt the instant response as little valleys of sensation ran away beneath her fingertips.

"I never knew," she whispered. "I just thought they were there to nurse a baby. But when you put your mouth on them they got all puckered and tingly. Do you feel like that when you're touched?"

"Oh, Portia, you don't have to touch me to make me feel all puckered and tingly. All you have to do is talk about it.

Now, come along and I'll show you another way to make it go away." He held out his hand.

Portia hesitated for a long time before lifting her fingers to touch his. "Will this time feel like the last time did?"

Daniel groaned. "God, no. Nothing will ever feel like that again. This is just a necessity, for both of us. What we need is some of the lithium water, but this will have to do." He turned toward the pool.

"You aren't going to make me go back in that water, are you?" Portia pulled back in fear.

"I'm going to carry you in, here at the edge where it's shallow. We'll wash ourselves and cool off. Don't worry. I won't let anything happen to you. Trust me."

This time Daniel's groan was internal. Trust him? How could he ever ask her to trust him again after what he'd just done?

"All right, Daniel." Portia walked close and put her arms around his neck, bringing her body against him.

"Uh, that wasn't exactly what I had in mind." Daniel lifted Portia in his arms and stepped down in the water, conscious of his erection rubbing against her bottom as he walked. When he was waist deep he dropped Portia's legs and allowed her to slide down into the water.

Trust only went so far. The memory of what happened was too strong. Portia couldn't make herself remove her arms from around Daniel's neck even though her feet were touching the bottom. The touch of his body hair caressing her was intensified with the gentle ebb and flow of the water. And the erection caught between them seemed to become larger instead of shrinking.

Portia leaned back to question Daniel. The arching motion that had to occur in order for her to look up at him increased the pressure of her lower body against him. "What is supposed to happen?"

"It's . . . I'm supposed to . . . shrink."

"How long is it supposed to take, Daniel?"

"Forever, if you keep doing that."

"What?"

"Pushing against me. You see," he said drawing in a long breath, "the cold water is supposed to take away the desire. But it isn't working."

"Oh, I'll try to move away." Cautiously Portia released her arms, holding to Daniel's upper arms as she stepped back. The ground was soft, the mud squishing between her toes. She was doing it. Everything was going to be all right. It was, until the bottom dropped off and there was nothing there. With a squeal, Portia flung herself forward, wrapping her legs around Daniel's body, impaling herself on that part of him that was throbbing with desire.

"Oh!" Portia felt Daniel's arms slide down and catch her bottom. She didn't know whether it was his motion or her own body's involuntary movement, but suddenly he was inside her and she was assailed with new sensations of response.

"You promised," Portia said from between clenched teeth.

"I didn't do this, darling, you did. And if you won't be still, I'm not going to be able to stop."

She wasn't sure whether she spoke or not. But she knew that her body wasn't listening to her urgent commands. It had discovered a missing part and found the place where it should go. The water only added to the sensations that ripped through her body as she tightened her legs around him.

"Portia, my darling Portia." Daniel tried to hold back. He truly did. He tried to lift her away only to feel her tighten her muscles to hold him inside. And then it was too late as wave after wave of delight spiraled through their bodies like the rush of the creek hurtling into the pool.

Collapsed against his shoulder, Portia was holding on to him in spent release as he walked toward the bank. "That wasn't what I had in mind, darling," Daniel said quietly. "Not only did I break my promise, but I can't be sure now that I can be trusted at all."

"It wasn't you, Daniel." Portia felt as though she were floating. She leaned against him. "I did it." She took a deep breath and tried to corral her thoughts. Finally, she raised her head. "But, you're wrong, Daniel. You have to be. After today, we won't allow it to happen again."

"Ah, Portia, if it were only that simple. Don't you see? Even now I want to kiss you. All we have to do to fan the flame is . . ." He leaned forward and touched her lips. The responding shiver was answer enough for both of them.

She gasped. "You're right, Daniel. We can't be trusted. I never knew the power of love—loving. It's like opium, isn't it? What do other people do?"

Daniel dropped her onto the grass and turned away. How could he explain what he was just beginning to understand. This was an important moment between them. He had to be very careful in his answers. Honesty was important to Daniel, but so was his responsibility to explain the choices without either embarrassing or pressuring Portia. He was in love with her and because of that knowledge he wanted to make everything all right. But how?

Daniel covered his confusion by arranging their clothing across the bushes to dry in the sunlight. He stepped into his underpants and tied the strings. Wet or not, he couldn't allow himself to become aroused again. They needed to talk and every time their bodies communicated they were swept up in a passion that wouldn't be stilled.

"There are three kinds of people, little one; those who give in to their desires as we just did, satisfy them and part. There are those who refuse to acknowledge them and bottle up their emotions so deep inside that they eventually become completely stifled. And there are those who marry and if they're lucky, they spend the rest of their lives enjoying making love."

"Oh." Portia allowed herself to consider what Daniel had just said. She could hardly refuse to acknowledge the feelings they both shared. It was too late for that. And she couldn't allow herself to consider marriage. That left only the first explanation, that of giving in to their desires and parting.

There was something so final about the word "parting." Yet, she was not so innocent that she didn't know the consequences of giving in to desire.

"I don't think we have any choice, Portia. We'll get married. We are already engaged." He knew this wouldn't be easy for her and he didn't want to frighten her. "The time has come for me to take a wife. And I think we may be well suited." Daniel's voice was emotionless. It was as if he were making a list and marriage was the next item to be crossed off.

"Don't be silly, Daniel. You don't want to marry me. I never expected you to. I could never make a proper wife and besides, I can't leave my family. They have to come first."

"Why? Why can't you do something for *you*, Portia. You feel something for me, I know that you do."

"Perhaps," she admitted, coming up behind him, groaning as she felt the twinge of soreness between her legs.

"What's wrong?" Daniel forgot his intention to keep a distance between them and turned toward her, catching her upper arms in his hands.

"I'm just a little sore." She winced.

"I'm sorry. The soreness will go away."

"Yes, and so will you, Daniel. I understand and I don't hold you responsible for what happened. I truly don't. I wanted you and I won't deny it."

"But, Portia, suppose there is a child?"

"A child?" Molly Watson, one of the young actresses had fallen in love with one of the actors. Three months later she'd learned that he was married and she was going to have a child. Horatio had fired the man. Molly had stayed with the troupe until the child was born. Then she'd married the son of the woman who ran one of the boarding houses where they frequently stayed. Poor Molly. Portia hadn't understood Molly's foolish actions then. Now, she realized she was no different from Molly.

"There won't be a child, will there Daniel? I mean does a woman always get that way? It doesn't seem fair."

"No, not always. And you're right, it isn't fair."

"Then we shall wait and see. If I were to . . . I mean, have a child, well, I shall just have a child. I would make no demands on you."

"But the child would be mine too. I couldn't walk away from my own child, Portia," Daniel said with a sharpness in his voice. The honesty wasn't going the way he'd expected. He was losing her and he didn't want to. "I should never have allowed this to happen," he blurted out.

"I think that I must accept at least half the responsibility. I'm not going to pretend that I didn't feel the same things you did. Our bodies seem to have some kind of power over the other. I understand now, so many things. And I thank you for making me examine myself, Daniel. But that's all it can ever be."

"Stop being so noble, Portia MacIntosh. Don't you understand that I've just asked you to marry me, and I've never done that before in my life?"

Bravely Portia turned away. *You can play the role of Juliet, Portia. You've learned about love this day. He doesn't have to know that you're dying inside.* "Thank you, Daniel, but I must refuse." There was no use in being modest about her movements. There was nothing about her that Daniel hadn't examined, intimately. Portia pulled the still damp petticoat and camisole over her head and turned back to the lunch.

"And you expect me to accept that?"

"The only thing I expect of you now, Daniel, is that you fill our cups with cool spring water so that we can eat."

Daniel stared at her composure in disbelief. For the first time in his life he didn't know what to say. He was more confused than she. Portia was admitting her desire, accepting half the responsibility for their loss of control and what was more, she'd been as wild and passionate as he was.

The thought of having Portia in his bed every night for the rest of his life was mind-boggling. Even now, Daniel wanted to rip those damp clothes away from her body and make love to her again. But it was not going to happen. She was filling their plates as though they'd never made love. He was being rejected.

Her blonde hair was drying in the sunlight, making wild ringlets across her head and down her bare shoulders. Dusky rose nipples still peaked against the thin fabric of her camisole and a strap slid off her shoulder. She looked like some mythological sorceress sprinkled with gold dust.

Daniel found himself following her instructions and scooping up the icy spring water with their cups. Portia had filled their plates with bread and cheese and grapes. They ate silently. By the time she'd placed slices of sugar cake on their plates Daniel knew that they had to talk. In spite of her calm acceptance of the situation, nothing was settled.

"About Phillip," he began.

"What about Phillip?" Portia bit off a piece of cake, wishing desperately that she didn't have to reveal any more of the truth. At least as Phillip she had some protection from her own self.

"That's what I need to know. Portia, will I have to deal with Phillip now?"

"What do you mean?" Portia swallowed the cake and waited, her mind whirling with new confusion.

She wasn't ready to confess the whole truth. And Daniel knew that the deception had to be finished. He had to peel away every layer of her insulation if he wanted to reach her.

"Well, I had planned to invite Phillip to accompany Ian, William Trevillion, and myself to take the waters, have a massage and have our bodies oiled in the morning. That should be a real learning experience for your brother."

"But you can't. Phillip . . . Phillip doesn't . . ." And then she understood. Daniel knew everything. He'd known that she was Phillip too.

"Oh, I think it's time that Phillip learns what you've learned, don't you?" Daniel smiled that wicked daring smile she'd come to expect. "I mean he's as innocent as you, Portia. I have a lady already lined up to teach him about life."

"You fiend! You know it all, don't you, Daniel Logan!

You knew that Fiona wasn't me, and you've known all along That I'm Phillip. You walked about your room half nude, forced me to drink hard liquor and smoke cigars, knowing that Phillip was really a woman."

"Yes." Daniel caught her hand, turning it up so that he could plant a kiss in her palm. "And I'm truly sorry about that, Portia. Forgive me. All of this started out as a kind of game that got out of hand, as much for me as for you. Phillip was your shield, just as you and your troupe were my shield. You were my fiancee, and in protecting me from the other guests, I told myself that I could better keep an eye on your father."

"But why? That makes no sense, Daniel. Why would you want to do that? You're a wealthy man with influence and position. Why would you care about the troupe or my father?"

"I'm wealthy now, Portia. But there was a time when I didn't have money, or anyone to care for me. There was a wonderful woman who took me in and made me belong. When I saw you in that rail car I saw that same desperation in your eyes that I felt so long ago. I couldn't turn away."

"And the boy in the trunk?"

"Yes, the child too. I don't blame you for being angry with me, but you intrigued me from the start. Once your father made me promise to go along with your little deception, I quit worrying about the whys and enjoyed the challenge. Then I got caught up in my own little game and let it go too far."

"Yes, we both did." Portia withdrew her hand and studied Daniel for a long moment. "I think we'd better get back to the Chautauqua before they send out a search party for us."

"But we haven't decided anything yet, Portia."

"Oh, but we have. We know that we can't be together. We can't be trusted, either of us. Every time we touch we seem to set off sparks that neither of us can control. So, this is the end of the engagement, and the end of Phillip and his daily reports. Don't you see, it has to be this way."

"No I don't see." Daniel protested. He'd never considered

that the wench would turn him down. He'd offered to do the proper thing. Being married to Portia had started to appeal to him long before they'd made love; he just hadn't admitted it to himself. He'd even let her come between him and the job he'd come here to do.

"We'll see each other at rehearsals only." Portia turned away and began to gather up the picnic. "From now on, any reports you need will come from Rowdy." She paused and her voice softened. "We've had this day, Daniel. But there won't be any more. I've understood that from the beginning. We'll move on and so will you."

And then he did understand: everything in Portia's life had been temporary—her mother, her lifestyle, her pleasure. How she must have felt as a child, moving from place to place, seeing normal families live normal lives when she'd had to grow up overnight. How could he change her mind? Maybe he couldn't, but he was going to try.

"Perhaps you're right," Daniel agreed. "Maybe we should stay apart for a while." For the moment he'd go along until he finished his assignment and talked to her father. Responsibility for her family was too deeply ingrained in Portia for her to consider giving it up for her own happiness. He could understand and accept that, for now.

Their clothes were almost dry. They pulled them on, each trying not to look at the other. But what would they say when they got back to the hotel? It was obvious that something had happened. There was nothing to do but bluff it out and tell part of the truth. Portia had fallen in the water and Daniel had rescued her. That was all. There was no way that anyone could know different.

They rode back in silence. At the Chautauqua door, Portia slid down from the carriage and dashed inside. With any luck she'd avoid any of the troupe members, for they would be on stage by now. Good, she'd guessed right. The lobby was vacant. She hurried up the steps to the second floor and stopped. Her nemesis faced her.

"Good afternoon, Miss MacIntosh. I have convinced my

husband, Reverend Bartholomew, to petition the director to reconsider your being allowed to perform the rest of the summer. I felt it only fair to inform you.''

"On what grounds, Mrs. Bartholomew?"

''Morals, Miss MacIntosh. The entire family is totally immoral and undesirable. Just look at you.''

Portia raised her eyes and smiled. If she was going down, she was going down in style. She wasn't her father's daughter for nothing.

"Mrs. Bartholomew, have you and the Reverend ever been swimming in a creek?"

''No, of course not. I would never wear one of these revealing bathing costumes.''

"Neither would I, Mrs. Bartholomew, neither would I. You see I've just found out that it's much more fun swimming nude. I highly recommend that you try it sometime.''

Fifteen

REHEARSAL for *Twelfth Night* began as a sober affair. From the moment Portia came on the set the crew felt the underlying tension. The announcement that Daniel would be playing the role of Duke Orsine only added to the unrest.

It was the hottest part of the day. The heavy velvet drapes were pulled back to allow every hint of air to come inside. The stage lay in shadows for nobody wanted the contributing heat of lit lamps. By the time Horatio took his place in the front row, the entire crew had been infected by apprehension.

"Buying costumes and new scenery is one thing, Portia, but are you sure that Daniel Logan can play the part?" Fiona asked, giving voice to the silent question of the others.

"I'm sure. The man has the kind of mind that simply has to read a thing and he has it committed to memory."

"But his delivery, my daughter, will he be able to present the lines without becoming a posturing peacock?" Horatio's resonant voice carried to the back of the theater where Daniel was standing in the darkness.

"I think so," Portia answered quietly. "He's an amazing man. I believe that he could do anything he set his mind to."

Daniel started down the aisle. Something about Portia's

tone bothered him. She'd fought Daniel's intrusion into her life every step of the way. Now she seemed resigned to his presence. The spark of her defiance was dimmed and he wasn't certain that he liked what he was seeing.

"Thank you for your confidence," Daniel said as he reached the stage, "but I'm afraid I'm not an actor. I will need all of you to help me."

They worked through the afternoon, explaining the little tricks of the stage, working with voice inflections and the subtle nuances that Horatio employed so effectively.

Portia forced herself to walk through the role without allowing herself to respond to the man. Viola's love for the duke took on new meaning as Portia acted the part of his page and followed his instructions to plead his love for the beautiful Olivia.

Rehearsals progressed through each scene until they reached the final portion of the play. When the duke took Viola's hand and forced her to look up at him, Portia felt her heart compress into such pain that she did not have to force the look of dismay across her face.

She was very near the breaking point. Spending hour after hour in close confinement with the man she'd just made love to was more unsettling than she had ever imagined. She'd thought that it would be simple enough to put the afternoon behind them. It had happened and that was that. But it wasn't to be.

Every time he spoke she felt an ache. She thought she'd been prepared to stand beside him, play her part as she'd done a hundred times before. But this was different. Playing the role was painful because she wasn't acting anymore. She was a woman in love with a man she couldn't allow herself to love.

"Portia, ah, Phillip," Horatio belatedly corrected from the wings. "Are you all right? You seem awfully intense."

"I'm all right, Papa." But she wasn't. She was coming apart at the seams and there seemed to be nothing she could do to stop herself.

"Loosen up. How can you expect Daniel to respond properly when he's talking to a fence post."

"It's all right, Father, call me Portia. Daniel knows that there is no Phillip. I'm sorry. I'll try to do better."

"It's all right, Portia," Daniel said under his breath. "It will all work out."

She didn't dare look at him. The tension in his voice only made her own nerves tighten. How was she going to deal with Daniel for the next few days?

Portia sidled casually away and perched on a box which was serving as a brick wall. Only a little longer and she'd be able to get away to find a private spot and think about what had happened between the two of them. If only she could get through the last scene with Daniel.

"All right, cast, let's get on with the scene. Portia, take your spot. Sebastian has just discovered that Viola, his lost twin sister, is not drowned, but is instead disguising herself as the duke's page. Sebastian confesses that he's been mistaken for his sister, and in her stead, has fought a duel and won the lovely Olivia.

"Now, Daniel, you stand about a step away from Viola and face her. You've learned that the loyal Viola is not a boy. She is a kind and loving woman and you want her. Viola, this is what you've been waiting for. The duke is about to declare his love for you, Portia. Let us begin."

Daniel cleared his throat and began. His low voice was tight with strain as he recited his lines, "Give me thy hand; And let me see thee in thy woman's weeds."

Portia allowed him to take her hand. She lifted her eyes, caught sight of the emotion Daniel was trying to control and felt her heart begin to beat erratically. It took only the touch of his hand to bring back the feeling. She was once more beside the pool. And she was seeing Daniel as he had been then, laughing, beautiful, desiring her.

Declare his love? No, it couldn't be true. Daniel had said they'd be married. But he hadn't said that he loved her. He'd taught her how to be a woman, but it had been without those words of love that rolled from the tongue of the duke when he thought of the fair Olivia.

In that moment Portia knew that whatever she had inside herself to give had been claimed for all her life. Saying that she'd stay away from the man didn't make the feelings go away. He wasn't a creditor who could be put off until next month, or a contract to be negotiated. It was more than that. He'd crept inside her mind as well as her body and like Violet, she'd fallen in love. What she hadn't understood is that love didn't make or ask for promises. It simply was. She loved Daniel Logan and love hurt when it wasn't shared.

"Draw her close, Daniel," Horatio instructed. "Look at her. Let the audience know that you are seeing her for the first time, with eyes of love."

Daniel tightened his grip on Portia's hand. He saw the panic there and wished he could say something to reassure her. "Easy," he whispered.

"No! I'm sorry," Portia cried, whirled around and ran from the stage.

Daniel started after her.

"Let her go, Daniel." Horatio put a hand of restraint on Daniel's shoulder and held him back. "She has to work her way through this herself. Fiona will see to her. In the meantime, Bessie will read their lines while we continue."

Daniel held himself back and watched as Fiona ran down the aisle after Portia. Funny, the roles had reversed. It was Fiona's strength that Portia needed now, not his. He was helpless to find a solution for her. He had none for himself.

"Ian, can't we go somewhere away from all these people?"

Victoria Trevillion leaned against Ian's shoulder, lifting her eyelashes prettily as they walked casually across the lawn.

Beside the path couples were playing croquet. White-suited gentlemen and ladies in crisp shirtwaists and dark skirts looked like puffs of cotton balls dancing across a background of emerald green.

Ian caught Victoria's upper arm and tucked it beneath his

own, effectively using his elbow as a barrier between them. It was becoming harder and harder to restrain Victoria Trevillion's eagerness to be close. Ian doffed his bowler to an approaching couple as they moved around the graceful limbs of a weeping willow tree.

"Afternoon."

"How do you do?"

The response was automatic. The curious gaze of the couple moving past them wasn't.

"Vickie! Do behave yourself," Ian admonished under his breath. "What will the other guests think?"

"Oh, Ian," Victoria protested with a light laugh. "Who cares? You're going to marry me, aren't you?" She paused, glanced around and pulled Ian through the branches beneath the tree where she clasped her arms around his neck and stood on tip-toe waiting. "Well aren't you?"

"I haven't spoken to your father yet. Until I've done so, nothing is official."

"Oh, Ian, why must you be so stuffy. Don't you want to kiss me, Ian?"

"Of course I do, but I'm not. It isn't proper, Victoria. Will you stop this. Haven't we already—?"

"Only once. Oh, Ian. I want to touch you. I want you to touch me." Her hands slid down from around his neck and cupped the burgeoning area, now announcing his body's willingness to do her bidding.

Ian put out both hands and caught Vickie's arms, holding her away from him with a grip of steel. "Vickie, please. I don't think that this is a good idea. We're out where anybody could happen by."

"But, Ian, you won't come to my room. And you make us go where there are people around. I want to be alone with you. Ian Gaunt, I've been looking for a husband for three years and I didn't see anybody I'd have, until I met you."

Vickie parted her lips. Her breath came in quick little puffs that inflamed the skin beneath Ian's chin. She began to sway back and forth, moaning softly. And then Ian's arms were around her, lifting her up to reach his lips and he knew that he was lost. As they moved back beneath the curtain of green, Ian felt himself being pulled to the ground.

"Victoria, we must stop this," Ian protested, fighting the assault being made by her full pink lips as he tried to remain sitting upright. He knew if he allowed himself to lie back on the ground he'd never be able to resist.

"Why? It's wonderful. I love you and you love me. Tell me you like kissing me, Ian. Tell me that you love me madly. Tell me that we're going to be married right away and travel the world making wonderful, glorious love."

"Yes. Yes, I do love you. We're going to be married right away," Ian admitted, swept away by her joyful passion. He couldn't refuse her. He couldn't resist her. She was the joy that he'd never known. She was life. She was love. She was—unfastening his trousers and pulling herself to his lap.

"No, Vickie. Not here. Suppose someone comes."

"Hush, darling Ian, I know it is scandalous for a lady to sit on a gentleman's lap. But," she raised herself, arranged her skirt prettily about her and lowered herself. "You see, grass makes me break out in big red splotches."

Ian gasped. He was inside of her and she was simply sitting, smiling over her shoulder at him in a way that would look completely normal to anyone who might happen by. Only he could see the passion smoldering in her gaze, see the parted lips and feel the gentle, slow undulations of her body as she moved herself.

"Are you disappointed in me, Ian?"

"Never, Vickie." He was lost to the moist heat of her body. Tensing his muscles he willed his body not to respond. His best intentions were in vain. Without a responding movement on his part he felt the rising tide of his desire. Unlike Victoria, he was finding it difficult to hold back the threat of his climax. Only the sound of footsteps gave him the control to dam the eruption.

Beyond the veil of leaves he caught sight of a couple, pausing for a moment not three feet from their hiding place.

Victoria had to be aware of their near discovery. Yet, Ian felt her rise slightly and plunge back to force his penetration even deeper. Her mouth opened and Ian knew that she was running on the edge of danger.

Just as she began to tremble, he turned her toward him and kissed her, catching her moan of pleasure with his mouth. And then he too was lost. All he could do was hold on and feel the rush of emotion wash over them both.

Afterwards, Victoria leaned back, resting her face against his chin, breathing more slowly now that her passion had been spent.

"Victoria," Ian whispered, spent in the aftermath of their lovemaking, "what am I going to do with you?"

"Marry me, Ian, tomorrow."

"But don't you want a big wedding, a reception, with all your family and friends present?"

"Not me," she said softly. "I just want to be your wife. Oh, Ian, don't you want me?"

"Want you? I've never wanted anything more in my whole life. It's just that, well, we need to talk, Victoria. I have something to tell you."

"You aren't already married are you? You told me that you aren't married, Ian." Victoria leaned back, stricken at the possibility. She felt their bodies separate and the movement made her afraid. Reaching beneath her skirt, she made adjustments to her undergarments, replacing them before she moved to the ground beside Ian. As she arranged her clothing, Ian took care of himself. By the time she'd composed herself and looked up, his hat was in his lap and he was frowning.

"No, I'm not married, Victoria. In fact, I'd never thought to marry. The fact that you want me still astounds me. I don't understand it. I don't understand it at all and I think I must."

"Why?" Victoria lowered her head and stared at a determined ant moving across an exposed root.

"Victoria, I'm told that I may not be too hard to look at, but there are others here at the Sweetwater who are more pleasing to the eye. I do have the means to support a wife, but there are certainly other prospects with family and position. Why would a beautiful young woman like you choose me? I think I have to understand.''

Victoria watched the ant reach the other side of the root, turn and start back in the direction from which he'd come. She knew the time had come for truth. Ian was as carried away by their love-making as she had been. She couldn't be mistaken about that.

What had happened between the two of them had come as a great surprise. Loving a man was not the painful duty she'd expected. Granted, the invitation to her bed had been calculated, but the great pleasure she'd experienced had totally changed her motivation. Where she'd wanted Ian for her family's sake to begin with, now she wanted him for herself. She'd fallen in love with this reserved, silent man and she couldn't continue her deception any longer.

''All right, Ian. I'll tell you the truth. I set out to seduce you. From the moment I saw you on the veranda I picked you as the man I wanted to be with. It was all part of my plan.''

''What plan? I don't understand. Why would you . . .'' He couldn't say the words. Why would she give herself to him like some lady of pleasure? What did she hope to accomplish?

''I want to marry. I need to marry a wealthy man who won't ask questions.''

''Need . . .? Are you?'' He couldn't ask the question. Looking at the pain in her eyes he found that the answer wasn't even important.

''With child? No. I'm not with child, my dearest Ian, unless you've given me one.''

Ian sucked in his breath. *Unless he'd given her a child.* Was that possible? Could she in fact already be carrying his son? The thought of Victoria, plump and full breasted, suckling his child made his loins stir and he felt himself harden. Even now, he wanted her with every ounce of his being.

''Victoria, I don't know what secret you hide beneath those

great dark eyes but you didn't need to seduce me. I wanted you from the first moment I saw you. There is nothing you can tell me that will change that.''

"Not even if I tell you that you aren't the first man I wanted to marry? There was someone in London, someone I thought I was in love with, until he found out about my family. I only hope that you will understand.''

"Understand what? What is there about your family that could possibly make me not want you?''

"My family is penniless. They sent me to Europe, hoping that I'd marry a nobleman. Instead our engagement was broken and he married someone else. But he never . . . I mean, I never allowed him to . . .''

"Victoria, darling, I know that you never made love. Men can tell about these things.''

"Oh, I'm so glad. I wasn't sure." Victoria took Ian's hand and faced him, ready to continue with her confession. "Afterwards, I came home and found out how near we were to being in the poor house. So, I decided to shop for a husband where the rich and famous play. Saratoga Springs proved unsuccessful. So, we spent the last money we have in the world to come to the Sweetwater so that I could trap a rich man.''

"Is that all?" Ian made no effort to hold back his sigh of relief.

"All? No, I suppose it isn't. As you've probably guessed, my parents aren't quality people. My mother hasn't come out of her room because we couldn't afford to buy her a proper wardrobe. My father thought it was important for him to make a show of wealth so we spent what we had on making the two of us look as if we have money. I'm sorry.''

Ian caught Victoria's hand and forced her to move closer. "My dearest one, I want to say something, indelicate perhaps, but the truth. For I never want any dishonesty between us again. Will you listen?''

"Of course, Ian. Say whatever you like. I deserve it.''

"I can't claim to be a rake, but I've known women, both

quality and those who have been forced to live in—other ways. One thing I do know, your responses to me have been the expression of a rare and exciting passion. I do not believe that you have the experience to fake what we've felt. You may have set out to deliberately trick me, but I think that we've *both* been caught up in your snare."

"You're right, Ian. I didn't expect it to be—so wonderful. Mother didn't know what I planned to do, but she always said that being a wife was a duty, not a pleasure. I didn't know."

"Long ago, in Nevada, I vowed that I would never marry unless I loved the woman. If I loved her, it wouldn't matter to me who she was, or what she was. I never expected the woman I'd love would be such a brave and beautiful lady."

"Love? You mean that you can love me after what I've told you?" Victoria raised her head and widened eyes swimming with tears of disbelief.

"I love you, Victoria Trevillion. But before we go any further, I should tell you that I am not what I appear. I made my money in saloons, bawdy houses and gambling halls. A true gentleman I'm not, and there may come a time when you will be ashamed of my past."

Victoria flung herself back into Ian's lap, unmindful of the hat that cupped the evidence of Ian's unrelenting desire for the black haired wench planting wide kisses across his face.

"Oh Ian, my darling Ian, my father is a pig farmer. My mother's father owned houses of—ill repute along the Mississippi."

"I know about your family." Ian gave himself over to Victoria's kisses, allowing himself to believe that perhaps she might not withdraw herself from him now that she knew his past.

"You knew my father was a pig farmer?" Victoria reared her head back and caught Ian to her breast in a moment of unbridled joy. "And you still want me?"

"I'm a charlatan, Victoria, not a gentleman. Do you still want me?"

"Oh yes, now, here beneath the trees." Victoria slid from Ian's lap and pulled him over her. "I love you, Ian Gaunt. If I am in the family way, can we still . . . you know?"

"I certainly plan to. Sometimes, I'm told that it takes a while to become a father, even when you're married."

"Not you, Ian. I can tell. You're very powerful. You're like the ocean, strong and silent. That is, you're very . . . very . . ." Her words were lost in the wonder of the touch of his lips on her bare breasts. "Oh, Ian. I do love you."

"And I love you, Victoria. Those are words that I never expected to say. We'll be married right away," Ian promised, pressing himself against her, forgetting for the moment where they were.

"When?" Victoria wriggled suggestively beneath his strong hard body.

"Tomorrow, tonight, this afternoon," Ian whispered incoherently. "I'll find Daniel and make the arrangements. Daniel, blast!" Ian raised up in alarm. "I was supposed to deliver a message to Daniel this morning and I completely forgot about it."

"Forget Daniel," Victoria coaxed, sliding her hands between them to touch that part of him that had pressed against her so intimately.

"Ah, Vickie, look what you've done to me, totally distracted me into forgetting my assignment." Ian got up and pulled the reluctant Victoria to her feet. "I love you and we'll be married, but there is something I must do."

"But, Ian—"

"Don't fret, darling. Let's go back to the hotel. You make the necessary arrangements for a wedding dress. I'll arrange to have funds advanced to pay for your mother's wardrobe and anything else you need."

"But, Ian, I want you. I want us to get married and have a wonderful honeymoon." She pushed herself against him once more. "I don't care about dresses and ceremonies."

"Darling, I want that too. And we'll have it—soon. But

I have business to take care of first. Let me escort you back to the hotel.''

Victoria smiled. "To my room?"

"No. No more of that until we're married, my dear. Please tell your father that I will present myself later to formally ask for your hand in marriage."

Reluctantly Victoria agreed. Even as she picked leaves and grass clippings from their clothing, her heart was singing. The big, stern looking man beside her was going to be her husband. She was going to be Mrs. Ian Gaunt and they'd have all their lives to be together. For now, she'd have to wait—maybe.

"I'll come to you tonight?" Victoria teased. "I could disguise myself as a dance hall girl and you could teach me how those ladies please a man."

Ian rolled his eyes at the latticework of tree limbs overhead. What was he going to do with this passionate vixen? He'd awakened a monster who had no intention of restraining herself. He groaned—and smiled. He was restrained enough. He never wanted Victoria to hold back. He might even teach her some of Belle's girls' wanton ways.

"Ahhh!" He took a deep breath, caught her arm properly in his and stepped out from beneath the tree. He didn't even want to think what hell he'd have to go through forcing her to wait until they were married. He wasn't sure he even wanted to try.

Sixteen

NEVER in her life had Portia felt such inner turmoil. She left the rehearsal stage in sheer panic, running down the drive away from the Chautauqua, past the lake, away from the Sweetwater. Now the late afternoon sun was beating down on her, the heat sucking at her skin, forcing her to take great gasping breaths of air.

The road she was following ran along the railroad track between the Sweetwater and the end of the main line in Austell. On her right was the bottling operation where the mineral water was stored and shipped across the entire country. She passed the smaller resort hotels, the boarding houses and several merchants displaying fresh foods and supplies for purchase by those who rented the tents and small cabins on the grounds of the Chautauqua school. Everywhere there were people, both locals and guests, staring curiously at the young woman dashing wildly down the road.

Sweat beaded on Portia's forehead. She wanted to scream out. She wanted to go back in time before they'd ever come to this place. She wanted her life to go back to what it had been before—before Daniel Logan. Why was all this happening?

"Miss MacIntosh! Miss MacIntosh!"

A carriage pulled up beside her.

"Good afternoon, Miss MacIntosh."

Portia ignored the female voice, wishing that it would go away. She didn't want to see anyone, talk to anybody. She just wanted to be alone.

"Please, won't you get in out of the sun?"

Portia came to a stop, breathing heavily. It was no use. The intruder had no intention of going away. Portia turned her face toward the woman driving the carriage. "Lady Evelyna?"

"Call me Evie, girl, and get in before you faint."

Portia found herself following instructions.

Lady Evelyna drove the carriage expertly. She didn't ask why Portia was running down the road as though she were being chased by demons. She simply drove, turning off the main road, letting the horse find his way along in silence. After some time she pulled up, held the reins loosely in her hand and waited.

"Want to talk about it?"

Portia glanced up guiltily. They were parked beneath a large oak tree, beside a rippling stream. From the direction of the water's flow, Portia guessed that it might be the same swiftly moving creek where she and Daniel had . . .

"I don't know," she said quietly. "I'm not even sure why I ran away like that. Everybody must think that I'm losing my mind. I don't know what's wrong. I'm usually much more reasonable."

Evelyna Delecort looked at the young woman and sighed. She wished that she had some idea of what Daniel Logan had in mind for the girl. Horatio had been certain that they were meant for each other, that all he had to do was set the stage properly and Portia's position would be established for the rest of her life. From where she was sitting, Evie wasn't sure that Portia wanted to live until tomorrow. Well, she'd stepped in, she could hardly make things worse.

"Only one thing I know of that turns a woman's thinking inside out and makes her doubt her own mind—a man.''

Portia didn't answer. But the quiver of her lips told Evie that she had hit on the problem.

"Do you love him, girl?"

"No! Of course not. Fiona says that being in love is wonderful, that it makes you happy, that you want to be together always. I don't feel like that at all. I hate him. No . . . I don't hate him, I just don't want to feel the things I feel when I'm with him.''

"You and Fiona are very different, aren't you?"

"Yes, I suppose. She's gentle and good. The world seems to soften when she's around. She's sunshine and flowers.''

"And what are you, Portia?"

A dragonfly darted across the water and lit on a branch, hovering silently as its wings fanned the air steadily. Only the sound of the creek disturbed the silence. Portia felt her tension draining away and she considered Lady Evelyna's question.

"I'm not sure I know what I am now. I always thought that I was strong, organized, able to take care of business. Until I met Daniel Logan. Now, I don't know anymore.''

"I wonder if you realize that what you've just described is what is *expected* of you, not what you are. You said that you are organized, that you take care of business. That's admirable. I understand that. But what about underneath that firm, in-charge facade? What are you, Portia MacIntosh?''

"I don't know. My life is suddenly different. I see and feel things that I never knew—wonderful, powerful, scary things that I can't control. A part of me seems to be melting away and I don't know how to get it back.'' Portia's voice had dropped to a whisper, a painfully tight whisper.

"Look out at the water, Portia," Evelyna said, placing her plump hand on Portia's arm. "The surface is tranquil, smooth where there are no barriers. Then look what happens where it comes up to a rock. It churns and boils its way around the rock. Once beyond it's quiet again, but you know that the current is there, just below the surface, ready to explode again.''

"I don't understand." Portia turned away from the creek and raised blue eyes filled with confusion.

"I think you're like that creek. You've encountered a barrier, Portia. You, not your father or your sister. Daniel is your obstacle and you're churning your way around him. Falling in love is a bit like that creek over there. It can be smooth and happy like Fiona and Edward, or it can be volatile and exciting, like you and Daniel. It's all a matter of what we're made of, my dear. There comes a time, if we're lucky, when we find our obstacle. Do you want to bask in the sunlight, or run with the lightning?''

Run with the lightning? Portia caught her breath as she recognized the truth of Lady Evelyna's description. Every time Daniel touched her she felt as though she was exploding inside. "But that can't be love," she murmured. "It's too intense, it hurts, it's . . .''

". . . the most wonderful feeling in the world if it's shared by the man. Is it, Portia? Does Daniel Logan feel the same way?''

"Yes. No—I don't know, Lady Evelyna. I think he feels obligated to marry me. But I don't want to be an obligation. I could never marry a man like him, live in a big hotel and serve tea. I'd die.''

"Why not?''

"I just couldn't. I'm an actress, a gypsy, always moving along. Nothing in my life has ever been permanent except Papa and Fiona and me. I can't lose that. I don't know how to be anything except what I am.''

"Portia, let me tell you a story about another gypsy. When I was a girl, younger even than you, I fell in love with a man who was so far above my station that I didn't even understand what his position in life was. Not only was he a titled gentleman, but he was an earl. Nothing mattered. We were in love and that was enough. I ran away with the man I loved and we shared more than twenty-five years of the kind of loving that most women never even know about.''

''But, look at you Lady Evelyna, you're a lady. And you fit into his world.''

''Portia, Edward's father was a married man, and the Minister of Culture to the Queen of England. I couldn't marry him. Can you imagine how I felt when I found out what his position was? To him, station in life didn't matter. But it mattered to me. I decided to learn to be what he wanted. Though he could never acknowledge my presence, I wanted him to be proud of me.''

''But you're called Lady Evelyna?''

''William always called me the Countess. He had a number of titles and properties. Hidemarch was given to him by the Queen. He gave that title to me. The title was merely honorary but he always considered it real. We lived at Hidemarch when he could come to me. Edward grew up there. As a child he never knew that he was illegitimate. By the time he was sixteen William had recognized him as his heir and the successor to his titles.''

''He must have loved you very much, your William. But this is different, Lady Evelyna.''

''Not so very different, Portia. When I ran away with William, I was only seventeen years old. My father ran the Lucky Duck pub in Boston. And I'd never even been to school.''

''You?'' Portia glanced at Lady Evelyna in astonishment. ''But you . . . how did you do it?''

''William taught me. But he wouldn't have cared if I never learned anything. You see, we were each other's barrier in the stream, pulled toward each other again and again. It was wonderful. It didn't matter that he was a nobleman and that I was a serving girl, we were magnificently in love and that was all either of us cared about.''

''Magnificently in love. I'm afraid that the only comparison between that and what Daniel and I seem to share is the painful, stormy part. That can't be love. It's dreadful. It's more like—like having the measles, most of it.''

"Perhaps, but now that you've felt that feeling would you want to do without it?"

And Portia knew that was the question she had to answer, the decision that had precipitated her flight from the theater. Did she want that kind of sweet agony for the rest of her life? In truth, she'd been so busy caring for everyone else that she had never thought about a man at all. Now the reality of what had happened came back to her, more dazzling than any play or any daydream.

And the blinding truth was that loving Daniel had been like running with the lightning. Once seared by that heat, she would never be the same again. Maybe she and Daniel were meant to be together.

Yes, I want Daniel, she wanted to say. Instead she gave Evie the answer she knew to be true. "I wanted a mother, but my mother died. I wanted a real home with a yard and flowers. I wanted to go to school like the other children and get a spanking when I misbehaved. But none of that was meant to be. My family needs me too much."

And that truth had sent her away from Daniel's arms. She was the moth who had broken free of the flame, only to discover that her wings might never fly again.

"Do they need you, or do you need them, Portia?"

"Of course they need me. You don't understand. Fiona is scared of the dark. When I was ten years old I promised my mother that I'd look after Fiona and Papa."

"Ah, Portia." This time Evelyna reached out and pulled Portia into her arms. "Your mother never intended that you should sacrifice your life for your sister and your father. She was a passionate woman who took a chance on life and love. She wanted your father and he was all that mattered. If she were here, she'd tell you to do the same."

"But, Fiona—"

"Has Edward now."

"And my father. He isn't well. Who'll look after him?"

"Me." Evelyna pushed Portia away and caught both her hands. "Horatio and I understand each other, Portia. He is tired and ready to stop traveling. After William died I had nothing left in England. Everything belongs to Edward. Now I've come home to stay. I never thought I'd find someone like your father. Our coming here was meant to be. We'll be all right."

"What shall I do, Lady Evelyna, I don't know anything about loving a man like Daniel."

"Just be yourself, Portia. Let Daniel know what he has to look forward to and don't make it too easy for him to get it."

"I'm afraid that it's too late for that," Portia admitted in a small voice. "He already knows."

"Umm, gone that far has it? That scoundrel."

"I—we don't seem to be able to be around each other without . . . I mean . . ."

"You don't have to explain, Portia. That's pretty obvious to everybody. He watches every move you make and the hotel guests have seen so little of him that they think he's taken rooms in the Chautauqua dormitory. You've got him going every which way for Sunday, girl."

"I do? Is that good?"

"It can be. I think I'm going to have to interfere a little, in view of your not having the benefit of a mother's guidance. Lord help me if I'm wrong, but I think that Daniel Logan is having just as hard a time as you are. He's a man used to having his own way. Maybe he needs to fight again for what he wants. And maybe you're the one to teach him."

"Hah! I don't think that I can teach him anything. He's too—too full of himself."

"Well, it's a pretty old-fashioned approach, Portia, but a man doesn't always know what he wants. It's up to the woman to show him."

"But I'm not sure that I ought to want him. I'm not sure that I want to live in his world either."

"Who says you have to live in his world, girl? Make a new one for both of you."

"Where have you been, Daniel?" Ian met him at the door to their suite, a tight little grimace announcing his displeasure.

"I've been rehearsing for the new play. And then I went for a long walk. What's wrong?"

"We have guests—Lord Delecort and Miss Fiona."

Daniel stepped inside and lifted an eyebrow in question.

"Sir?" Edward Delecort cleared his throat and took a deep breath. He tightened his hold on Fiona's arm and pulled her forward. "Fiona and I would like a bit of advice."

Daniel found it difficult to look at Fiona's face without thinking of Portia. The hair was different, yet the same. While Fiona's was like sunlight, Portia's was more like a nugget of gold that caught the light and winked its worth to the finder. Portia's eyes were a deep warm brown that sparkled with anger one minute and passion the next. Seeing Fiona there in his parlor made him long for Portia even more than he'd done for the last three days.

"Certainly, Edward."

"We want to be married, right away."

"I see. And how may I assist you?"

"Well," Fiona said shyly, "it's Portia. She won't want me to go to England. With Papa being ill and my leaving, the troupe won't . . . I mean it will just destroy my sister. And I don't want that."

"Yes, I can see that you have a problem, Fiona. But, I'm not certain what you expect from me."

"It's this, sir. We were wondering if you intended to return the troupe to the Captain as you promised, or if the engagement you've announced might be a real possibility. I mean," Edward stumbled, turning red with embarrassment, "we think that perhaps you and Portia really care about each other. If that is true, Fiona and I could be married more easily."

Well, Edward had stated plainly the problem he'd been

wrestling with for the last hour—what to do about Portia MacIntosh. He started to answer, caught the look in Fiona's eyes and changed what he was about to say.

"What Portia and I feel is between us. But I don't think that she is interested in marriage."

"Maybe not," Fiona agreed, "but she is very disturbed about you. I've never seen her pace the floor and I haven't heard her cry since Mama died."

"Cry!" Daniel jerked his head away in a gesture of despair. "Portia was crying?"

"I think so. Last night she hid her head beneath her pillow, you understand, but I heard. And I know that she's not herself. You saw how she ran away this afternoon. I've talked to Papa and he says that I should go with Edward. But I don't want to hurt Portia. I can't."

"When do you want to leave?"

"We'd like to be married right away," Edward said, "but Fiona feels that she should honor the contract that the troupe has with the Chautauqua. We want to announce our plans now so that the others will have a chance to make other arrangements. In September we'll return to London. I have obligations there that I must assume."

"I understand, Edward. And I appreciate your concern. At this point I don't have a final answer. But don't let anything interfere with your plans," Daniel said, adding, "I expect to be in a position to decide about—many things soon. Let us get through the performance and the ball on Saturday and by that time I'll have a solution—one way or another."

Once Fiona and Edward left the room Ian turned anxiously to Daniel and held out a piece of paper. "William Pinkerton telegraphed the list of guests from Saratoga Springs and I thought you'd like to see it."

Quickly Daniel scanned the names. "Lady Evelyna and Edward. William Trevillion and his family. And nobody else matches?"

"Nobody else does, Daniel. As a matter of fact there are several names on the list that I don't recognize at all. But look, this is the interesting thing. William also sent the list of guests from the Crown Hotel there, and that does give us another match."

"Oh? Who?" Daniel quickly scanned the second sheet. Silas Fountain of Fountain Shipping Lines, at both Saratoga and the Crown. Odd, I don't recognize that name. Have we ever met Mr. Fountain, Ian?"

"No, Daniel. And as far as I can recall, I've never heard of a Fountain Shipping Lines either."

Daniel searched his photographic memory. As a rule, sooner or later he could bring a name or person into focus if he'd ever seen him before. Not this time.

"Even so, Ian, if Silas Fountain was at both the Crown and at the Springs, he doesn't appear to be on the Sweetwater guest lists. How does that help us?"

Ian made a little gesture of disgust. "Daniel, where is your sharp edge of deduction? If the Fountain Shipping Lines don't exist, then Silas Fountain must be an alias. Therefore he could be here. He could be anybody. But I have a strong feeling that he's the thief. And by now he must be getting ready to make his move."

"Someone is; of that I'm certain, Ian. That's why we have to be ready. That's why I arranged that the ball be a masquerade. We can conceal ten men to watch and nobody will know that we're setting a trap."

"What makes you think that the thief will make his move at the ball? Wouldn't it be smarter to rob the guests' rooms while they're away?"

"And miss the Lodestone rubies?"

"You're going to use the necklace you had set with your own gold and rubies? But Daniel, that was the gold from your first strike!"

"And the rubies I bought over the next ten years. Belle always thought I was crazy for buying rubies, but to me they were the symbol of my having made my fortune. They were for the memory of my mother and my sister. And every time I made more money, I added a stone.''

"Well, you're taking a chance, but it ought to bring out the thief all right. Suppose you lose it?"

"Such a piece of jewelry is only important to the woman who wears it and the man who gives it to her. If I lose it, it's gone. Have we heard from Mr. Gould?'' Daniel turned and started back to the hotel. He wanted to bathe and change. He'd bring Portia back to the hotel for dinner. That way he could study the guests in light of the new information.

"Yes. Gould and his daughter Helen will arrive in Atlanta, transfer their private car to the Georgia Pacific Line and reach the station in Austell about noon. They will be ferried to the Sweetwater in time for a private dinner with several influential personages, after which they will attend the ball being given in their honor.''

"And they depart the next morning?"

"Yes, they will return to Atlanta where they're to be hosted by Mr. William Inman and other Atlanta dignitaries. They leave the following day for Savannah.''

"Fine. Make certain that everyone knows of their arrival. Their name will set the trap, my rubies will be the bait and we will catch a rat.''

"I hope you're right, Dan. I confess that I'm ready to bring this to an end.'' Ian pulled out his gold pocket watch and flipped it open with a carefully manicured thumbnail. "Daniel, there's something more that I'd like to discuss with you. Do you have time now?''

"Certainly, Ian. Can we talk while I bathe and dress for dinner?'' Daniel glanced involuntarily across the grounds to the darkened dormitory window. Portia would be backstage now, getting dressed for the performance, directing the stage hands, overseeing the stage properties. Portia . . .

He'd spent several hours thinking about what had happened between them. It had come as something of a surprise to discover that he really wanted to marry her. They had nothing in common except a firm wish to be in charge on both their parts. But he found himself remembering her loyalty, her honesty as she asked to touch him, and her great passion. What more could a man ask for in the woman he wanted to spend his life with?

He could see them together, not in his New York hotel, but in the wilderness, in a small rough cabin beside a roaring winter fire, making love. Alaska and Portia both called to him in a way he'd not felt in a very long time. Exciting, passionate, each with great promise to one who understood what was being offered.

"Dan?" Ian interrupted his thoughts with an urgency that made Daniel aware of the importance of his conversation.

"I'm sorry, Ian. What did you want to talk about?"

"It's this. I know that this may come as a surprise, but Vickie and I are going to be married."

"You're what?"

"I love her, Daniel. And I'm going to marry her. I'd like you to have dinner tonight with us and Mr. and Mrs. Trevillion. I've already spoken with them and they've agreed. This will be in the nature of the announcement of our engagement."

"Are you sure, Ian? I haven't said anything except that I like Victoria, but I'm not certain that she is what she appears to be."

"Are any of us?"

"True enough. But you could be making a mistake."

"I could be, but I'm not. And you're right, Dan. The Trevillions aren't what they appear to be. When I picked up William Pinkerton's report it also contained a check I asked him to run on the family."

"And?"

"Victoria had already told me that her mother has kept to her room because they couldn't afford clothes for her. They are almost out of funds. I know that William made his original money in pigs and that when the city of Memphis cleaned up the river front, Mrs. Trevillion's fancy houses that she'd inherited were closed down. They spent every cent they made on Victoria's education and preparing her to find a rich husband. Now, they're practically destitute.''

"But Ian, how can you be sure that she really loves you? Maybe you're just the . . .''

"Fool she's settled on to bail them out?" Ian finished. "Possible, probable even. But you see, Daniel, it doesn't matter. I love her and I never thought that would happen. I know the truth and I can make her happy. This life has been good to me, but Victoria has made me see that there is more.''

"Yes, I can understand that, old friend. The life we live is pleasant, but it becomes more boring every day. We've become pompous and over-full of ourselves, haven't we?"

"In a word, yes.''

"Portia won't be joining me this evening; she needs to get rested for the performance. But I will be happy to join you. Ian. I am very happy for you.''

"Did you say Portia?"

"Yes, and Ian, it's Portia now. Phillip is no more!''

"Good, Daniel,'' Ian said sincerely. "I'm glad that you and Portia are through playing games. I think that you belong together. Now, I'll leave you. We're taking Mrs. Trevillion to see Romeo and Juliet.''

After Ian left Daniel went to his room and removed the necklace from its hiding place. He hadn't put it in the hotel safe because he'd feared that the thief might strike there first. Fingering the heavy gold setting, Daniel remembered his determination to put away something that would be a symbol of his achievement. Now the necklace was complete, but without the proper woman to display it, the jewels were only pieces of glass.

Portia would wear it in the final scene of the play. Perhaps, just once, Mr. Shakespeare wouldn't mind a bit of creative alteration of the final scene. He'd bring the entire cast on stage, costumed as they might have been for a great feast. The clown would then sing his final joyous song to proclaim the ending of the tale. The Sweetwater wasn't Ilyria, but

Daniel was convinced that The Bard intended the story to have a happy ending.

And Portia would wear the rubies. She'd give them the fire they demanded and reflect its heat. The necklace had been waiting for her, just as he had.

Seventeen

DANIEL paced back and forth on the veranda. It was growing late. Surely he hadn't misunderstood the message Rowdy delivered after the performance. No, Rowdy definitely had said that Portia would meet him in the main dining room for dinner after all.

He could see Ian and Victoria, along with her mother and father, already seated in the center of the room. Mrs. Trevillion had been a pleasant surprise. She was a gentle, sweet-looking woman who obviously loved her husband and daughter very much.

For the third time in less than five minutes Daniel looked at his watch. As he closed the cover and dropped it back in his pocket a hush fell over the dining hall. Every eye in the restaurant turned toward the doorway behind Daniel. He swung around.

Standing, side by side, like a mirror vision of each other, were Portia and Fiona. Even Daniel was speechless. He'd known that the two girls, no, he corrected himself, *women*, were beautiful, but never in his wildest dreams had he imagined the impact of them together.

Portia in icy lavender and Fiona in palest green, both were

gowned in satin brocade cut low across the bustline and gathered at the shoulders in a flounce of sleeve. Tiny, nipped in hour-glass waists were caressed by the shiny fabric that fell in unfettered flounces to the floor. There were no bits of lace, no flowers, no sewn-on pleats to divert attention from their faces. Only the hair styles and adornments were different. Fiona had wound velvet leaves and pearls in her hair. Portia had simply drawn her strawberry-blond curls high on her head, allowing a few wisps to caress her cheeks and forehead. It wasn't until she turned her head that Daniel could see the creamy white gardenias pinned beneath the mass of curls.

At that moment Portia smiled and lifted her chin dramatically and held out her gloved hand. "Daniel, darling?" Queen Victoria couldn't have made a more regal sweep across the restaurant than Portia leading the way.

"Portia?" Daniel could only stare in bewilderment. The swell of Portia's breasts peeked invitingly above the edge of the dress, moving as she breathed.

"Daniel, we're blocking the passageway. Shall we sit down?" Deftly she slid her arm beneath his and clasped his forearm with her fingertips.

"Oh, of course. This way."

But Portia had already seen Ian pulling out the chair beside him and smiling in invitation. "Close your mouth, Daniel darling, you look as if you've just seen a ghost. Don't I please you?"

"Good evening, Portia," Ian was saying, "Edward, Fiona. I'd like you to meet my fiancee, Miss Victoria Trevillion and her parents." Ian completed the necessary introductions smoothing over any awkwardness. Soon they were conversing easily, everyone except Daniel who'd gone from surprise to anger, and seemed to grow more disturbed by the minute if the scowl on his face was any indication.

"So, tell me, Miss MacIntosh," Mr. Trevillion began. "Oh, I beg your pardon, I suppose I'll have to say Miss Fiona now that we know that there are two of you."

Fiona started to answer, realized that Mr. Trevillion was

directing his question to Portia and began to smile. "Maybe you'd better explain, Portia."

"Yes, I suppose I'd better. Actually, Mr. Trevillion, I'm Portia. That's Fiona next to you. She's going to marry Edward sitting opposite you. The name change was a kind of joke on Daniel. He only learned this morning that we'd been— teasing him."

"Teasing?" Daniel lifted an eyebrow. "Is that what you called what you were doing this morning, darling?" He took Portia's hand and planted a kiss on her fingertips, a wicked, suggestive kiss that announced plain enough that two could participate in whatever game she was playing.

"Now, now, Daniel, mustn't be cross. Do I understand that this is an engagement party, Ian?" She turned to Ian, tugging lightly at her hand, trying unsuccessfully to remove it from Daniel's iron tight grip. "How exciting. Are we having champagne?"

"Indeed," Edward interceded, and called to the waiter. "I think a celebration is in order."

"What lovely gowns you're wearing," Victoria said. "I must find out the name of your dressmaker."

"Of course." Portia lifted her free hand in a gesture of agreement, all the while pulling the other hand still being held by Daniel, beneath the table cloth. "Can you believe that they're both ready made? Lady Evelyna took me to a little dress shop along the rail line. All we had to do was remove all the trim."

"You've been shopping with Lady Evelyna? How interesting. I'm glad to know that you got over your distress." Daniel's remarks were accompanied by a tighter grip of his hand. "Isn't that how women always get over being angry at their men, by spending money? I'm fortunate that my fiancee is able to afford to indulge her whims."

Portia leaned toward Daniel, snapping open the fan that had been attached to her wrist by a thin strap. "She had the bill sent to you. She insisted that you wouldn't mind. Do you, darling?"

Behind the fan, Portia leaned closer, touched her lips to Daniel's, and fluttered her eyelashes. She'd expected him to be surprised at the new Portia, but the degree of his astonishment went beyond anything she might have planned. At least she'd shocked him into letting go of her hand.

"What are you up to, you little wench?"

"Daniel! Please. You're not going to be one of those dreadful penny-pinching husbands are you? Do pour me some champagne. I feel very merry."

"Allow me to propose a toast." Edward stood, holding out his glass. "To the eight of us, those who are married, and those who are about to be, let us drink to love and happiness."

Glasses were raised in accord and each sipped at the amber liquid, bubbling in the crystal glasses. All except Daniel, who stared at his glass in consternation.

"I say, Dan," Ian queried, "aren't you going to drink to our mutual good fortune?"

"Good fortune? Of course. As a matter of fact, let us share that joy with everyone. I love parties . . . and games." Daniel came to his feet. "Attention! Attention everyone!"

Throughout the dining hall one guest nudged another until everyone grew silent.

"Ladies and gentlemen," Daniel said with a broad smile, "please join me and my dinner companions in a toast to celebrate our upcoming weddings. Miss Victoria Trevillion has agreed to become the bride of my associate, Mr. Ian Gaunt; Miss Fiona MacIntosh and her intended husband, Lord Edward Delecort, and Miss Portia MacIntosh who is to be Mrs. Daniel Logan."

Glasses were raised and a round of cheers and applause followed. When Daniel held up his glass again, the crowd grew quiet once more.

"And I have another special announcement. In honor of this grand celebration, and the visit of my old business associate, Mr. Jay Gould and his daughter, Helen, I should like you all to attend a masquerade ball on Saturday evening here

at the hotel. Ladies, you must deck yourselves in your love-
liest gowns, and claim your most elegant jewels from the
hotel safe, and come masked to our Twelfth Night Festival.''

This time the applause was even more enthusiastic and the
conversation rose to a fevered pitch. "Jay Gould?" Simon
Fordham appeared at Daniel's shoulder. "I'll be glad to see
the old crook. He took me to the cleaners in his Erie Railroad
deal. What about you, Daniel?"

"I never take that kind of risk with my money, Simon.
Gold and silver are my passion, that and a little gambling
now and then. Will you still be here on Saturday?"

"I wouldn't miss your ball for the world." Simon was
talking to Daniel, but his eyes never left Portia. "Congrat-
ulations, Miss MacIntosh, I never thought anybody would
snare this rapscallion. But I can readily see why he finally
succumbed. May I have the pleasure of a waltz at the ball?"

"Certainly, Mr. Fordham. I would be pleased to dance
with you."

"Portia won't be dancing, Simon," Daniel said sharply.
"She . . . doesn't dance."

"Too bad," Simon said with regret in his voice. "Well,
I shall simply have to content myself with sharing a glass of
punch with her instead." Simon nodded his head toward the
table. "Good evening, ladies."

"Daniel, dear, you must not be concerned that I'll disgrace
you at the ball. Lady Evelyna and Edward have volunteered
to teach me to dance. After all, as your wife, I'll need to
learn all the feminine graces, won't I?"

"Wife?" This time Daniel's voice was so choked that
Portia had difficulty understanding.

"Of course, darling, fiancees generally end up by being
wives, don't they? You know, wives—those women with
whom men share their . . . secrets."

Portia then turned to speak to Ian, slipping her hand innocently beneath the tablecloth in search of her napkin. When
her fingertips wandered secretly across to Daniel's upper thigh
she felt his muscles jump. The sudden intake of breath that

accompanied his uncontrolled reaction was obvious to almost everyone.

"Oh, darling, are you all right?" Portia withdrew her hand and placed it on Daniel's forehead in concern. "You look feverish." She stared in concern at the frown gathered between his brows.

"I'm not feverish. There is nothing wrong. I'm simply . . . hungry. When are these blasted waiters going to bring our food, Ian?"

"Don't fret, Dan, our food is here. Victoria, you will like the trout I've ordered. It was caught this morning and transported to the hotel in ice so that it would be fresh. And there are new peas and potatoes, straight from the garden."

"Ah, Ian," William Trevillion said, shaking his head, "fish is fine, but if you want good eating, there's nothing like a young roasted pig. Mrs. Trevillion here sets a fine table. Though Victoria is more into all these French dishes."

"Papa, please. I'm sure that Ian doesn't want to hear about roast pig. When I was in Austria we ate the most wonderful little cakes with spun sugar icing."

"I'm partial to fish and chips, myself," Edward commented. "Nothing like buying them straight off the fire from a street vendor. I'm sure that you're going to love visiting London, Mr. Trevillion."

"No thanks. Until you fellows catch that Jack the Ripper fellow, I think I'll just stay here."

Neither Portia nor Daniel could in fact eat much of the trout, nor the soup, nor the desert that followed. Daniel grew quiet, watching her with dark eyes that seemed somehow disappointed.

Portia was beginning to feel the start of a headache behind her eyes. This wasn't working. She had followed Lady Evelyna's plan faithfully, trusting that following a script would make her actions authentic. It wasn't working. Trying to be a lady wasn't difficult, it was the knowledge that she was acting that made her ashamed.

Edward began an animated discussion of the wonders of

science and the thresholds about to be crossed. "I just read about the world watching Oscar Wilde's *Dorian Gray*, the first moving picture in New York City. We have power plants and electric lights now, and the world is about to change."

"As long as they don't fool around with baseball," William Trevillion commented, "they can do whatever they like."

"You aren't talking, Daniel. Perhaps you'd like a glass of mineral water," Ian said with a question in his voice. "It might make you feel better."

"Say, speaking of feeling better," Mr. Trevillion commented, "one of the gents staying here told me about some new syrup that will really pick you up. A druggist right here in Georgia invented it, calls it Coca Cola. You ought to buy into it, Daniel. Never know, it might turn out to be big."

"No, thanks, I don't invest in anything that I don't understand."

"What do you do, Mr. Logan?" The question came from Mrs. Trevillion.

"I'm afraid that I don't do much of anything now, Mrs. Trevillion. I have two hotels, one in Virginia City and the other in New York. And I have land and mining claims in Alaska."

"Alaska?" Portia forgot for a moment to be the charming minx she was playing and allowed her interest to show.

"Yes, I have a number of properties in the Klondike. I'm considering checking them out after I leave here. This kind of life," he glanced around at the other hotel guests, "has grown a bit tiring recently. You'd love the ice and snow in the Klondike. You'd have to learn to shoot so that you could protect yourself from the bears."

"Bears?" This time Portia's interest wasn't an act. She'd seen bears in the traveling circuses and she'd felt their frustration at being caged. To see one in the wilds must be a truly wondrous sight.

"Yes, bears and the native Eskimos who hunt them and wear their skin to keep warm."

"Like the Indians?"

"Yes, only these people are friendly. They live in houses made from blocks of ice." Daniel and Portia could have been the only ones at the table. Her eyes sparkled and she leaned forward, listening raptly to his descriptions of the natives and how they lived. For a time they were able to talk quietly, oblivious of the conversation swirling around them. And he realized with a start that she was honestly interested in the country and its people.

By the time the meal finally ended, Portia had dropped her flirty pose. She was both tired and charged with energy. Realizing that she'd lost sight of her plan to show Daniel and herself that she could fit into the circle of guests she excused herself, prepared to end her failed off-stage performance and flee into the night. But Daniel was having none of that.

"Portia, my dear, shall we try the ballroom this evening?" Under the guise of assisting her from the room, Daniel's arm slid around her waist. This time it was Portia who gasped.

"Oh, thank you, no. I've had rather a long day. I think I'll retire." At least that statement wasn't a lie. The morning seemed a hundred years ago.

Portia lowered her head, fighting the instant leap of her heart at his touch. "Please excuse me, Daniel. I'm sorry about this evening. It was a mistake."

"Why?"

"I don't fit in this kind of surrounding. I can't be Fiona. I really don't want to be."

"And I don't want you to be," Daniel whispered in her ear, his lips touching her ear lobe. "I much prefer the gypsy woman I made love to this morning. If you're really tired, I'll take you to my room for a rest."

"Your room? No! I mean I believe I would like to dance after all."

"I thought you would."

This time it was Daniel who played games. Between the lobby and the ballroom on the top floor he found a dozen ways to touch Portia. By the time he took her in his arms for the first dance her nerves were strung out in a fine thread which threatened to snap.

"What do you think you're doing?" Portia snapped, trying to put the proper distance between them.

"This is called courting, darling. The man uses every opportunity to touch his lady. Smile now, or the world will think we're quarreling."

"But, Daniel—" This time her concern was genuine. "There is something I think you should know."

"What is it?"

"I really don't know how to dance."

"You don't have to. I'll teach you. I'll direct you with my hands. Just loosen up and let me show you."

She did and before she realized that she could, they were whirling around the ballroom. The music was lovely. The mirrored walls reflected their graceful movements. Masses of flowers filled the air with sweet perfume and Portia began to lose herself to the loveliness of the evening. She didn't resist him, succumbing instead to the magic as she pressed herself recklessly against him.

As the music came to an end Portia realized that they had danced themselves out onto the terrace. Potted plants formed shadowy spots of privacy where other couples were whispering softly. Inside, the orchestra struck up a lively polka. Daniel dropped his hand from Portia's back and led her away from the merrymaking inside.

"You're very beautiful, Portia," he said. "You constantly surprise me. One minute you're a drill sergeant issuing orders, the next minute you're an innocent child and tonight you're a grand lady." His arm went around her waist, a tremor shaking his body as he held her. This great need for a woman was new to Daniel.

"Am I?" His words both thrilled and worried Portia. She felt as though she'd been cast in a new play. She was walking through unfamiliar lines, learning a new character, only this time there was no dropping the role when she stepped into the wings at the end.

"Oh yes; you *are* a surprise."

"And you don't like surprises?"

"You're right. I like to know what will happen. Otherwise I might make a mistake."

"And would that be awful, if Daniel Logan made a mistake?"

"I don't know. You may be my ultimate test."

Portia moved away, stepping further into the shadows before she realized her mistake. What she needed was light, the protection of being in the company of others.

"Am I a mistake, Daniel? Are you sorry about what happened between us?" She shouldn't have asked the question. His answer, no matter what it was, would be too intimate. She made a move back inside.

Daniel caught her arm and turned her back to face him. The light of the moon cast a silvery sheen to Daniel's face. His eyes, the color of blackest night, were sheathed by thick spiky lashes. Brows drawn in slashes of deep concern totally unnerved her new-found courage. She wanted to retreat into the ballroom where people and activity would hide her confusion. Yet she was drawn to Daniel by some overpowering compulsion that she could neither understand or explain.

"A mistake?" Daniel finally echoed, reminding Portia of her question. "I don't know. When I'm away from you I tell myself that you're too young, too innocent. I don't want to be involved with anyone, certainly not a gypsy girl who bloodies my nose and uses her teeth as a secret weapon. But then I see you and all I want is—this."

His arms were around her. He was kissing her, touching her, setting her aflame with the heat of his touch. And she knew that his kiss was what she wanted too.

The fragrance of the man and the night wrapped around her, and she breathed deeply of it, floating in the hazy pleasure of his touch.

When his hand touched her breast she realized that she was doing exactly what she had planned to avoid. She'd known that if she allowed him to get too close she wouldn't be able to control her own desire. Dinner, a little flirting, a touch here and there, and good night. That had been her plan, the plan that hadn't lasted to the second dance.

"Daniel!" She pulled herself from his grasp, breathing deeply as she straightened her dress and glanced around. "Let me go! We agreed this morning that we couldn't trust ourselves. I have no intention of getting myself with child. We agreed that this wouldn't happen again."

"But Portia," Daniel said, his voice deepening with emotion? "I told you that we'd be married. Marriage is a move that I've—contemplated of late. It's time that I settled down. I want you." Daniel's head lowered over her, his mouth moving across the rise of her breast hungrily. "That's a damn sight better reason for marriage than most of the ones I know."

"Daniel Logan, there's one thing you might as well learn right now. Nobody tells me to do anything. It seems that my family doesn't need me anymore. I may, or may not marry you. But if I do, it will be because I choose to. And I don't think that I choose to take a husband who doesn't love me."

Portia slid deftly around Daniel, intent on getting away.

"Stop, someone's coming." Daniel moved his arm around Portia and pulled around the corner, deeper into the shadows behind an urn of flowers.

Footsteps moved toward the urn and paused. After a moment a second set of steps followed.

"Did you hear?"

The voice was a low murmur.

"Yes. Jay Gould and his daughter will be here."

"Generous of Logan," the voice whispered. "He's even giving a masquerade ball complete with all the finest jewels on display for our convenience."

"Then it's settled. Saturday evening?" The second voice was indistinguishable. It was difficult to tell whether the speaker was a man or a woman.

"Yes. I'll do it then."

After a long silence, one set of steps began to move away.

Daniel, unable to identify either speaker, began to move quietly to the side of the urn, motioning for Portia to be silent. Portia didn't know what Daniel was up to, but she knew that this was her chance to get away from his overwhelming presence.

As Daniel moved around one side of the urn, Portia broke to run the other way. Her mad dash took her directly into two waltzing lovers who had danced out the door and fallen into a passionate embrace. The collision knocked the young man to the floor. His partner whirled around, banging into Portia in her haste to avoid discovery by the onlookers gathered in the doorway, and disappeared around the corner.

Portia glanced up, caught the wrath of Daniel's expression as he pulled the young man to his feet. She fled across the terrace, coming to a sudden stop as she reached the doorway. Raising her chin, Portia stepped regally between two gentlemen watching the dancers, and disappeared inside.

By the time Daniel had apologized to the young man, Portia was gone. He hadn't been able to catch a glimpse of either of the nocturnal speakers and Portia was nowhere to be found. Only one gardenia, its petals bruised and turning brown, lay in a patch of moonlight where it had fallen wounded to the floor.

Eighteen

OTHER than for rehearsals, Portia took great pains to avoid Daniel for the next few days. She made no effort to play the role of the lady during the time they were together, choosing instead to revert to her usual masculine dress and attitude.

But her normal sense of well being didn't return. The boy's clothing chafed at her breasts as it never had before. For the first time she felt awkward in returning to the role she'd always assumed. It was with both a measure of relief and a bit of pique that she accepted Daniel's apparent wish to avoid being alone with her as well.

She managed also to avoid her father's attempts to discuss the stalemate between her and Daniel. Fiona offered no new advice. Lady Evelyna stayed in the background. Even Mrs. Bartholomew left her alone.

Portia went through her normal routine, fulfilling her responsibilies, as if she were drugged. Sleep was becoming more and more of a stranger, visiting her only in the last hours before dawn, making her pale and tired when she finally woke.

For Fiona, falling in love was a wonderful happening, a

joyful event. For Portia it was a tragedy with no final curtain to end the pain. Perhaps it would have been easier if her mother had lived. She might have prepared Portia for the turmoil she would face and the torment Daniel would cause. Alternately she cursed Daniel Logan and wanted him with such overwhelming desire that she couldn't think of anything else. What was she to do?

At least the play was coming together nicely. The extras and guests taking part learned their lines and their places competently enough to pass, if not entirely professional. New costumes and sets were finished. Bit by bit, everything meshed for the abbreviated performance to be given in the ballroom on the night of the masquerade ball.

"Portia." Fiona danced into the dormitory room one afternoon, her face flushed with excitement. "You should see Mr. Gould's private railcar. He calls it Atalanta and it's the most palatial thing you've ever seen. It even has its own observation room, a kitchen and a parlor. They tell me that Atalanta was a mythological Greek huntress who had lost her freedom when she stopped to pick up the golden apples her lover had dropped. Isn't that exciting?"

"Then they're here," Portia said listlessly. There would be no turning back now.

"Yes. You'd never think that he could be that wealthy. Mr. Gould is a little man, with a gray beard and a great frown. He looks like a—a shopkeeper."

"How is a wealthy man supposed to look?"

"Like Edward," Fiona said promptly. "And—Daniel."

Daniel. Portia groaned inwardly and sprang to her feet. She moved to the window automatically, looking across the grounds toward Daniel's balcony. The window was her secret connection with him and she seemed bound to it as firmly as if he were calling out to her.

"Oh, Portia, I'm sorry. I didn't mean to distress you. Actually, Mr. Gould doesn't look rich; his daughter does. They say that even though she has beautiful jewels and a magnificent wardrobe, she's wonderfully kind and caring.

She travels with him and looks after him, just like you do for Papa.''

"Are the costumes for the last scene ready?" Portia had fought Daniel's plan to bring the entire cast back on stage for the final song. Mr. Shakespeare's play promised a great festivity signifying the marriage of Sebastian to the fair Olivia and the pledging of the Duke's love for Viola. But the scene was offstage, told by the clown's final song of joy. Daniel had been insistent that the entire cast wear their richest gowns and jewels and assemble behind the clown. At the end of the clown's song, they would then circulate among the guests in full costume.

"Oh yes, Portia. I can't wait to see your gown. The dress is crimson and black, shot with threads of gold. You'll be magnificent as the duke's lady," Fiona added.

"Edward and I went for a walk about the hotel. The decorations are magnificent," Fiona chattered gaily. "There are flowers everywhere. And the lights are covered with little paper lanterns that give off a hundred different colors. Daniel has dressed the musicians as court jesters, traveling bards and minstrel men. I understand that the hotel is providing the guests with costumes. Oh, Portia, I've never been so happy!"

Fiona whirled around the room, her arms clasped about an imaginary partner, her happiness shining in her eyes for all to see. Portia managed a half-smile, afraid she might let the unbidden tears hidden behind her eyelids escape.

Noticing Portia's stricken look, Fiona came to a stop and caught her sister's hands. "Oh, Portia, my other half, I'm so sorry that you're hurting. I'm an insensitive clod. Tell me what I can do."

"There's nothing anyone can do, Fiona. Daniel Logan is *my* problem and I have to solve it."

"Portia, I truly don't understand why he is a problem. It's obvious to everyone that he's mad for you. And I know how you feel about him. Why is it wrong for you to fall in love?"

"I can't be in love, Fiona. I'm not like you. I could never allow a man to control me. I know myself. Daniel might think that he wants me, but he would soon grow tired of my stubborn ways. Being my husband would become so distasteful that he'd find someone else and I couldn't bear to have him leave me, too."

"How wrong you are, sister. I'm not leaving you. Neither is Papa. We'll always be your family. Just as Daniel will always love you, if your love is true."

"But loving hurts. I'll never be what Daniel wants."

"I think that you're exactly what Daniel wants. Anyone can see that you and Daniel are alike. You're both stubborn, opinionated, bossy and filled with an inner excitement that shines whenever the two of you come together."

Fiona's voice dropped into a gentle persuasion. "Let us consider the situation, logically. Daniel is in his thirties and he hasn't married. Why?"

"Because he has had no need, I suppose."

"Exactly. He certainly can't have lacked opportunities. So if he is single it's because he hasn't met a woman he can't turn away from. Yet, the first time he sees you he comes up with a plan to make you his fiancee."

"That was necessary. to allow him room to conduct business."

"Perhaps, but have you seen him make any attempt to conduct business, or for that matter to end the engagement?"

"No, unless . . ." Portia's thoughts raced back to the necklace in the drawer. What kind of plans did a jewel thief make and would she be aware if he'd made them? "No, and I don't understand that."

"That's what I've been trying to tell you, Portia. You absolutely captivated him at the engagement party. You were wonderful and it wasn't difficult for you to turn him inside out. The man wants you. And you want him. You're just both too stubborn to admit it."

"That's what Lady Evelyna said too. Maybe I do. Maybe it is the life he leads that scares me to death. I don't know who I am anymore. I wish I knew the right way to go."

"Portia, when the time is right you'll know and you'll do

the right thing. You always know what's best for the rest of us. You're just having to learn what's best for *you*. In the meantime, what you're going to do right now is get ready to celebrate the Twelfth Night. Daniel has arranged for us to use one of the hotel rooms as a dressing room. Everything has been moved there."

Once more Daniel and Fiona had made the necessary arrangements that hadn't even occurred to Portia. She'd been too confused over her feelings toward Daniel.

"You know that the Twelfth Night was originally part of the Christmas celebration," Portia said crossly, and followed her sister into the hallway. "This is the middle of summer, we ought to be doing *The Tempest*."

"Funny, that's almost exactly what Daniel said a while ago, except he thought we ought to be doing *Taming of the Shrew*."

"Are you sure about this, Daniel?"

"This may be the only thing I am sure of, Ian. From the time you gave me the message that Gould was coming I've had doubts. Maybe I'm the wrong man for this job. Maybe my edge is dulled and I'm being led down the garden path."

"You're being led down the garden path, all right," Ian agreed, biting back a smile, "but it isn't the jewel thief that's doing it. Are you going to take the necklace with you now?"

"Yes. I don't want Portia to know about it until she's dressed for the last scene. That way she won't turn belligerent on me and refuse to wear it."

"Aren't you worried about losing the necklace?"

"Yes, it is a risk. But maybe the loss of the jewels is less of a danger than the risk of losing Portia if I don't get this jewel thief out of the picture. Until the matter of the thief is settled, I can't make any plans."

"I see. Well, it's too late to back out now. You've set the trap well. All we have to do is keep our wits about us. By the way, I have something to show you. I'd like some advice."

"Oh?" Daniel forced himself to pay proper attention to the small box Ian was holding. "What is it?"

"Well, it isn't an it, it's two. I couldn't decide which ring is right for Victoria and I wanted your opinion. Whichever one I don't choose I can return."

Ian opened the small box to reveal two smaller ring boxes. The first one contained a diamond as large as a pea, sparkling like one of the new electric lights in the ceiling overhead. The second gem, a ruby, set in heavy gold, was less spectacular, but the instant Daniel saw it he knew it wasn't right for Victoria. The ruby was meant for Portia. It matched the necklace as if they'd been designed as a set.

Without realizing that he'd done so he took the ruby ring in his hand and stared at it with perplexed concentration. A ring signifies an engagement. He'd never even considered buying one for his fiancee. A ring meant commitment. It brought reality to the illusion. As he fingered the smooth stone, he knew the ring belonged on Portia's rough little hand.

"I take it you're enamored with the ruby," Ian said dryly. "I thought all along the diamond was more like Victoria."

"Yes. Yes, you're right, the diamond is the perfect choice for Victoria, Ian. The ruby needs a different sort of woman to wear it, a woman of fire, a woman who isn't fine and delicate, a woman who is a survivor."

"From the look in your eyes, old friend, I have the impression that you know such a woman."

"Yes. And I have to find a way to stake a claim on her. Ian, what shall I do? I'm in love with the little spitfire and she won't have me. She's like the icy mountains of the Klondike, constantly alluring and just out of reach. That's it." He paused, then hit his head. "Why didn't I see it?"

"What? What do you want to do? You're not making a lot of sense, Daniel."

"I'll take her to Alaska, away from the theater and her responsibility, away from make-believe, away from the kind of life where everybody is pretending to be something they aren't. I want to marry Portia and spend the rest of my life

with her. Now I know why I bought the land in the wilderness.
It was for the two of us. We'll go to the Klondike."

"Well said, but perhaps premature. It isn't me you must
convince, it's the lady. Maybe what you ought to do is be a
bit subtle, sell her on the country."

"Sell her? How in hell do I do that? Even though her
family is off to another life, Portia isn't going to leave the
life she's leading now without a struggle."

"Maybe not, but forcing her won't work. You see what's
already happened when you try. I suggest you put that ring
in your other pocket and get to the dressing area. The celebration is about to begin. You've sprung your trap. I only
hope you don't end up losing the necklace, the ring, and the
woman."

From the opening scene to the final abbreviated duel fought
by Sebastian for the hand of the fair Olivia, the masked crowd
went from the height of joy to the depths of despair at the
plight of the lovers and the duke's blindness to the truth.

Daniel was superb as the duke. There wasn't a dry eye in
the ballroom when Viola, masquerading as his page, substi-
tuted her own feelings for the duke, and pled the cause of
the Duke of Ilyria for the hand of the fair Olivia. As the play
ended with the duke finally recognizing Viola as the woman
he loved, applause broke out, temporarily halting the action.

Only the cast noticed the change Daniel made in the duke's
final speech when he said,

> *"A passionate new beginning shall be made*
> *Of our dear souls. Meantime, sweet Portia,*
> *We shall not part from hence. Come;*
> *For so you shall be, while you are a man;*
> *But when in other habits you are seen,*
> *You are Daniel's love and his fancy's queen."*

Daniel reached inside the pocket of his costume and removed the necklace, placing it around Portia's neck and fas-

tening it from behind. He clasped his hands around her waist and held her as the clown stepped forward and began to sing his final song of joy.

"What are you doing?" Portia whispered through lips clenched into a smile. "This isn't in the script."

"It is now. I put it there. Don't you like my gift?" That's why I had this gown designed for you, to match the necklace. You are truly a queen, my Portia. And tonight, I am the king."

"Aren't you taking a chance, Daniel? Suppose somebody steals it? Suppose the thief is here. Oh, Daniel, please, put it away."

"That's what I'm counting on, love. Now smile."

On the final note of song, the entire cast bowed to an audience already bursting into violent applause.

"Portia darling, relax and let yourself be a queen. If the evening goes according to plan, the thief will never steal again." As the orchestra began to play, Daniel gave Portia a quick kiss on her cheek and bowed at the waist.

"Now, my lady, the Duke of Ilyria would dance with his fancy's queen." Before Portia could gather her wits about her, Daniel swept her away across the polished floor.

"I've never seen such splendor," Portia said breathlessly as Daniel whirled her about the room. "Where did the guests' costumes come from?"

"They are exact copies of those worn to Alva Vanderbilt's costume extravaganza about ten years ago. She had all her guests pose for a photograph and we managed to find a copy. See, there's a Puritan Girl, and a Matador."

"And an Arab prince. Look, there is Lady Evelyna dressed as Electricity. Even with a mask I'd recognize her instantly. She's carrying a lit torch. I'll bet Edward rigged that up."

"That costume was originally worn by Mrs. Cornelius Vanderbilt. But there is the one I like best."

Daniel spun Portia around so that she could see the woman dancing with a man who'd come as a Dresden Figurine. Portia couldn't be certain, but she thought the pastel, white wigged figure was Edward.

The woman with him was a gypsy. Her hair was tied back with a scarlet scarf. Around her neck was strand after strand of beads. In her hand she held a tambourine.

"Those beads look real," Portia whispered.

"I'm certain that they are," Daniel answered. "It's working—just as I planned. Now, Portia, I have to leave you. There is something I must do. So if I appear to be disinterested, please know in advance that this is not the case."

"Why? What are you doing, Daniel? I think that there is more to this ball than you've admitted. Please, promise me that you won't do anything foolish."

"I see that you've mastered your dancing lessons, Miss MacIntosh." The first dance piece ended. The tall pirate appearing at Daniel's side was Simon Fordham. "And I insist on claiming your charming fiancee for the next waltz."

Daniel turned to Portia. "I'd be delighted, Mr. Fordham." Portia gave the pirate her hand and followed his less than smooth lead across the polished floor. When the music ended they stood for a moment with Edward and Fiona. Fiona yawned prettily and said, "My, it's getting late. What time is it?"

Simon Fordham reached for his watch fob, stopped and shook his head. "Fancy that, I must have forgotten my watch. But I'm sure it's much too early for you to retire, Miss Fiona. Certainly not until I've claimed one dance. May I?"

Fiona frowned but allowed herself to be led away by Simon Fordham, wagging her finger at Edward in unspoken warning that she should not be abandoned for long.

After that Portia lost all track of whom she was dancing with, giving herself over to learning the fox trot and the latest folk dancing with her various partners. But she was conscious always of Daniel's presence. He seemed to stay close by, his hair falling across his forehead in that familiar rakish spill.

Each time she looked over her partner's shoulder she caught his eye.

Portia was grateful when her father finally claimed her attention. "I'm afraid that I can't keep up with you youngsters anymore," he confessed leaning on Portia's arm.

"I'm ready for a glass of punch anyway," Portia said quickly. "Let's walk on the porch and catch our breath."

With the Captain's hand on her arm, Portia made her way to the refreshment table set up on the terrace. Just as they reached the edge of the dance floor, Daniel and Helen Gould whirled into their path. Horatio stumbled into Daniel, swore and steadied himself.

"Ah, Portia, tonight has made me know that I'm growing old. The time has come for me to consider my declining years."

"Phoo! Your declining years. Such nonsense! By the end of the summer you're going to be your old self and there'll be no stopping us now that we have new sets and costumes."

"No, Portia." Horatio took two glasses of punch and led Portia to a quiet spot near the rail. "The old life is coming to an end. God knows, I don't want to give it up. I'll miss the traveling, the socializing, the matching wits with the gentry. With Fiona getting married and Daniel and you—"

"There is no Daniel and me," Portia snapped. "The engagement is only a pretense, Papa, a pretense that will end —soon."

"Oh? That isn't what Daniel said when he came to ask for my permission to marry you."

"He did what?" Portia's mouth flew open. She couldn't begin to protest such an incredible statement. Why would he do such a thing? His proposal had been the right thing for a gentleman to do, but she'd refused. Why was he continuing the charade? She couldn't marry Daniel Logan. She wouldn't marry Daniel Logan. Enough was enough.

Portia whirled around, intent on discussing Daniel's high-handed action. As she turned she found herself looking straight up into Daniel's dark eyes.

"You asked Papa for my hand in marriage? Why?"

Horatio slid his hand from beneath Portia's arm and moved back toward the ballroom. Daniel glanced at the old gentleman, waited until he was out of hearing range before beginning a hesitant explanation. He hadn't realized that what he was about to say would be so difficult. Ian had given Victoria her ring and she was already wearing it. Daniel swallowed several times before finally gathering the nerve to state his case.

"I've grown weary of the life of the rich. Marriage is a good idea for both of us and we're well matched. I have mining claims in Alaska and it's time that I returned to the business of real living. I don't expect you to find Alaska as appealing as I do. The life there is hard on women. But I will try to make you happy. I want children and I believe that we will suit each other. I've bought you a ring."

"Oh, you have! You've decided that we'll marry and then you'll go off to Alaska to mine gold. You want children and I'll do as a wife. You expect me to be pleased with your proposal?"

"Well, I'd hoped you'd be. What do you want, Portia?"

"I want . . ." She stumbled over the words she'd never allowed herself to verbalize. "I want to be needed, I think. But most of all I want someone to love me. The trouble is, I'm not sure any longer who *I* am."

"You've always been whatever those you loved wanted you to be, Portia. You only know who you've *been*. I know who you *are*. You're the spitting tiger who won't allow anything to disturb her cubs. You're the wild eagle swooping out of the sky to snare his prey. You're the storm beyond the horizon. And you're going to marry me."

"That's how you see me?"

"You've always thought of yourself as the other part of Fiona. You're not. I think, my gypsy girl, that you're the other part of me. I want to stake my claim, darling. Will you accept my ring?"

"Oh, Daniel. You overwhelm me. I can't think straight when I'm with you. But one thing I do know is that I can't take your ring, unless I know the truth. Where did it come from?"

It wasn't the ring Portia was concerned about. She was beginning to understand that Daniel was serious about having her. In truth he knew her better than she knew herself. That made her afraid. There was a danger about him that she feared. Blindly she searched for its source.

Daniel reached into his pocket. "To tell the truth I don't know. I didn't buy it—not exactly. Someone else did." He couldn't tell her that Ian had bought the ring. She was already ready to bolt. He was handling this badly.

Someone else did? Just when she'd decided that he wasn't the thief he was giving her a ring that was stolen, probably from the same person who'd owned the necklace she was wearing. For years she'd had to look after Horatio and his sleight of hand. Now she was in love with another thief. Her heart twisted. She didn't know what to say. As she struggled for words she caught sight of the puzzled expression on Daniel's face as he dug in his pockets.

"It isn't here. The ring, it's gone. It was there when I was dancing with Helen Gould, I felt it. Now it's gone. Is he baiting me? First the thief takes a single necklace and now my ring is gone? That doesn't make sense."

"Thief? You think Helen Gould is a thief? Come now, Daniel. I don't care if you're not wealthy, Daniel. I'll marry you if you want me, just don't lie to me, anymore. Is the necklace stolen?"

"Lie to you?" Daniel broke out laughing. "Oh, Portia, my love. I told you that I'm not a thief. I bought this necklace and paid for it, one stone at a time. The ring came from Ian."

"I'll understand and forgive you," Portia said primly. "All you have to do is return the jewels. I haven't lived around the Captain all these years without recognizing . . ." Her voice trailed off. *Without recognizing the moves of a thief,* she almost said, as the picture of her father bumping into Daniel flashed into her mind. She'd just heard him bemoaning that he was growing old, that his life was changing. He hadn't been able to resist trying his luck one more time. Or was it one more time?

"Papa!" She twisted out of Daniel's grip and ran back toward the ballroom just in time to see Horatio dancing with an Egyptian princess with so many chins that she would probably never miss the jeweled necklace he was about to purloin.

Daniel, fast behind Portia, saw the same thing. As Portia reached one side of the dancers, Daniel reached the other, cutting in on the pair so smoothly that Horatio didn't know he'd been caught until Portia whispered her warning.

"Give it back, Papa."

"Give what back?"

"The ring you took from Daniel, my engagement ring."

"Ah, how'd you know?" Horatio's dismay wasn't so much from having to give up the ring, as admitting that even his quick fingers were slowing. As Horatio grinned and produced the ring box, the music ended and Daniel came from across the room toward them.

Daniel's face was stern as he tried not to smile. The old crook was just having fun, yet he was about to blow the plan he and Ian had so carefully set up. He had to stop Portia before Horatio's little deed spoiled everything.

"Why, Father?" Portia was saying.

"I'm sorry, my dear. I was just feeling sorry for myself, I guess. Here I am, losing both my daughters. The life I've always known is coming to an end. I just couldn't resist proving that I haven't lost my touch. I was going to give it back."

"Oh, Papa." Portia threw her arms around Horatio. "I'm so sorry. I wish I could make things like they were."

Daniel came forward, Lady Evelyna in tow. "Horatio, I'm afraid that I'm very tired," Evelyna said with a sigh in her voice. "Will you take me to my room?" She put her hand on Horatio's arm and leaned into him with a gentle smile.

"Of course, Evie," Horatio said, separating himself from Portia with a show of his old good humor. "Give her the ring, boy, before you manage to lose it permanently."

"No chance of that, Horatio," Daniel said loudly, using the opportunity to call attention to his plan to catch the thief. "All these jewels, including the necklace, will be put in the hotel safe tonight, to protect them."

Portia watched her father leave the room, deep in conversation with Lady Evelyna. She could see Fiona and Edward, lost in the rapture of their love as the music started again and they waltzed around the floor. Lady Evelyna would comfort Horatio. She understood and she cared. The Captain would be in good hands. As for Daniel, there was still the unsettled matter of a marriage to be discussed.

"Now, may I have this dance, darling?"

Daniel's tall, broad-shouldered body was still clad in the red velvet jacket, black breeches and shiny soft boots of the duke. His dark eyes were intense, giving off unmistakable sparks of heat that showered over Portia like stardust from Prospero's magic wand, as he slid the ring on her finger.

Portia meant to refuse. She meant to insist that they discuss his outrageous plans. Yet, from the moment she saw the ruby on her ring finger she'd been caught up in the magic of the night. Now she could only nod and lift her arms to encircle his strong neck.

Daniel spun her smoothly across the floor and out the door onto the terrace. She arched away from him, trying desperately to stave off the ummistakable attraction she felt every time she came near the man.

She tried to jerk away, drawing in a deep, calming breath. *Not this time* she thought. He was not going to get around her fury by touching her. She'd learned the power of his touch. But Daniel had anticipated her move and before she could gather her emotions he'd swung her around and pinned her to the wall in the darkness.

"Don't, Daniel . . ." she whispered, trying desperately to move away from the pressure of his body holding her captive against the wall. "Why would you speak to my father about marrying me without my permission? If I marry you, I'll be the one to decide. Do you understand?"

"Of course, Portia."

Portia realized that her struggle was having a rather opposite effect. Not only was she unsuccessful in wresting control away from Daniel, but the obvious swell of his masculinity was having an uncontrollable effect on her own body. "Please, Daniel. Remember where we are. What if we're seen?"

"What if we are? I doubt that there is one person in the hotel who doesn't know that I want to kiss you." He pulled her closer.

Like mercury in a thermometer, Portia's blood rose so quickly that she suddenly felt light-headed, swaying unsteadily against Daniel. "Why are you doing this? You make me crazy. I can't think when you're holding me, when you're . . ."

"I don't want you to think. *I* don't want to think. I believed that once I'd had you I'd be able to forget about you . . . but it's worse now. Whatever I'm doing, I want you with me. I can't sleep. I've worn a path beneath that dormitory window. There isn't even a blasted vine for me to climb."

"Oh, stop, Daniel. Please stop. I don't want to hear this. You have to stop kissing me." But even as she spoke her own breath was coming faster and she felt her traitorous body molding itself against Daniel.

A trill of laughter came from nearby and Daniel jerked up his head, glancing around. "Come!" He pulled her into the curve of his arm and around the corner of the building.

"Where are you taking me?"

"Someplace where I can do this." And his lips were hard against hers, claiming her with an intensity that she couldn't have fought off even if she'd wanted to. He forced open her lips, violently, plundering the very breath from her body.

"You're mine," he swore, his lips trailing down her neck, leaving a path of scorching heat in their wake as he reached and claimed her breast.

She couldn't hold back the moan of pleasure that swept through her. His lips left her breast and claimed her mouth again. She could feel his heart thundering against her and she knew that she was lost. Then, just as suddenly as he'd claimed her, Daniel groaned and stiffened, ceasing his relentless assault on her mouth.

"Portia," he whispered hoarsely, "if speaking to your father was a mistake, I'm sorry. His approval seemed to be the proper thing to do and I thought that if I had that you might understand that I am serious about our marrying."

"Why, Daniel? Why would you want to marry me?"

Daniel released her and stepped away, leaning against the wall in silence. "Damned if I know, Portia. I know that you're going to drive me mad, that living with you will be one argument after another. If I tell you to stay at home, you'll leave. If you want to do one thing, I'll want you to do another. But we're right together, my darling, and you know it."

"Yes, I know. It frightens me, Daniel. I don't know if we can be together without destroying each other."

This time when he turned and pulled her close, she didn't fight him. His kiss was a gentle promise, a tender side to Daniel that she hadn't seen before. She couldn't fight him anymore.

When he finally pulled away they were both trembling with the heat of their desire. And the measure of their control was a different kind of promise.

"I could kiss you again, Portia, kiss you and touch you until you go wild from wanting me. But I won't do that. I'll only ask you, will you come with me, Portia? Now? Will you let me make love to you?"

Portia gave a helpless sob. She couldn't fight him. He was right. All he had to do was touch her and she was his. Whatever she'd been before was no more. Daniel had put his brand on her and with or without his ring she belonged to this man. She could give no other answer than the truth.

Simply, without reservation, her need for him stripping away her attempt to hold on to the last shred of her past she said the only thing she could.

"Yes."

Nineteen

DANIEL paused to whisper a few words in Ian's ear. "Keep an eye on things for a while, will you, Ian? Portia and I want to talk, privately."

Ian looked at his old friend with amusement and said, "Talk huh? From the looks of you I can understand that. But what about our friend, the jewel thief?"

"Nothing to worry about yet. He won't strike until all the jewels are in the safe. We have plenty of time."

Daniel caught Portia's hand and pulled her through the mass of dancers into the hallway, past the steam baths and mineral water room that occupied half of the top floor. They then ran down the stairway to the next floor to the corridor leading to Daniel's room.

A quick kiss at the doorway swept away the last remnant of Portia's hesitation and in a moment she was inside, and in Daniel's arms.

"Are you sure, Daniel? Don't do this if you aren't certain. Because if I marry you I'll never let you go."

"I'm sure, Portia. How can you doubt my feelings for you?"

"Because you've never said . . . I mean you've never told

me—" But she couldn't say the words. She was no more able than Daniel to give voice to the truth.

"Do I have to tell you what you already know?"

He crushed his mouth over hers, with a violence that slammed her heart against her chest. "Yes. I have to understand. I want you to be honest with me."

His hands swept into her hair, dislodging the coronet of artificial braids that Bessie had pinned to her own mass of unruly hair. Soon the hairpiece was gone as were the pins, and her hair spread across her bare shoulders.

"Then understand this, my lady, you're mine. You're never going to know this with any other man. I'm not going to let you go and I'll follow you to the ends of the Earth if you run away from me."

Portia groaned and lifted her arms about Daniel's neck. She was past knowing, or caring. All she wanted was this man for all her life. She began to tear at his clothes, pulling buttons away, sliding his jacket from his body, allowing herself to touch the hard, lean plains of his chest.

Her bodice was open and Daniel was kissing her breasts, taking them in his mouth, tugging at them with such greed that she could only arch her back to give more. There was no turning back. They would be together as only a man and a woman could be.

Then he lifted her in his arms and strode across the parlor to his bedroom, slamming the door behind him. Laying her on the bed, he quickly stripped her petticoats and undergarments from her body. Standing in a pool of silver moonlight Daniel slowly began to remove his boots and the skin-tight breeches of his costume.

On the bed Portia watched in rapt wonder. Daniel was the most beautiful man she'd ever seen. He stood over her, hands on his hips, his manhood thrusting forward in a pulsating, trembling quiver.

Beneath him, Portia cupped her breasts in her hands, rubbing her nipples in slow, painful ecstasy. "Daniel?" Her voice was hoarse with desire.

Daniel knelt on the bed beside her, brushing her hands away with his lips. Portia had filled his mind, invading his senses until he was mindless with wanting her. This time he would move slowly, he promised himself as his lips and hands ranged over her body. When Portia reached timidly to touch him, Daniel forced himself to hold on with a control he hadn't known he had.

"Oh, Daniel," Portia moaned, using her hands to urge him to move over her. "How can this be?"

But Daniel refused to take her. He'd only begun to tantalize and explore. With his lips he memorized her breasts, the soft smooth skin of her stomach, and the inside of her thighs, following the trembling trail of nerve endings to the honeyed core of her sweetness.

Portia gasped. "Daniel, what . . . ?" The flash of heat that he ignited with his mouth spiraled into an intense burst of fire lifting her to such heights of pleasure that she thought she might die.

Beneath his touch Portia began to writhe. Her pleasure was an exquisite torture that was more than he had ever known in a woman. He was conscious that every wave of sensation was brought about by his touch and his rapture was a thread of desire pulled thin to the breaking point.

Flinging her head back, she let out a moan of delirium that signaled her point of no return. Afterward she collapsed and sighed. In the moonlight Daniel could see her smile of contentment. Like a kitten she burrowed her head into the pillow, stretching her neck and arms in happy gratification.

"Oh, Daniel. I didn't know loving could be so—wonderful."

Still hard and throbbing with need, Daniel delayed his own release in his need to hold Portia. She turned eagerly to him, cradling herself in his arms, kissing him, telling him with her touch that she was supremely happy and that he was responsible.

The joyous touching of Portia's lips quickly fanned Daniel's own flame to such depths of desire that he could no longer hold back. He moved over her, pressing himself into her. His thrust was meant to be slow, to ready her body, build her desire so he wouldn't cause her pain. His concern was unnecessary for she received him eagerly, wrapping her legs around him, holding him inside.

He caught her bottom in his hands to regulate their rhythm. She moaned, and the violent roar of their coming together soon exploded into a shattering frenzy of delirious release.

This time, Portia held him, gently kissing his forehead, drawing little circles on his back with her fingertips. She didn't want to admit that for the first time in her life she felt safe. Being held in his arms gave her such a feeling of protection. Still afraid that it wouldn't last, she refused to think about tomorrow. The cool air from the window carried the smell of blossoming flowers and cooled the dampness of their bodies.

When Daniel began to move away, Portia protested. "No."

"But I'm too heavy. You're such a tiny thing, such a little . . ."

She hadn't wanted to fall in love. She hadn't wanted to become intimate with a man. Daniel understood that. But Daniel knew that sooner or later she was going to admit what he'd learned tonight: Portia and Fiona shared the same birth, but he and Portia were the real soul mates. They belonged together, because only when they were joined did either of them feel complete.

"Portia, there is something I want you to know." Daniel pulled Portia into the curve of his arm and took a deep breath.

"Yes." Portia felt as if she were floating in warm air.

"When I said that we would marry—no, that's wrong. I want to marry you because I love you, very much."

"Oh, I'm so glad. I love you too, Daniel. I don't ever want to make you unhappy." She burrowed her head beneath his chin and planted little kisses down his neck.

"Just keep loving me, Portia. There's something else that

I have to say if I'm being honest with you, about why I'm really here, about my search for a wife.''

Portia caught her breath and grew very still. "Why you're here? You mean you *were* looking for a wife?''

"No. A wife was the last thing I was searching for. I came here to catch a thief.''

"To catch a thief? I don't understand, Daniel.''

"My darling fiancée, I'm here on the trail of a jewel thief who set the Saratoga Springs Resort Hotel office on fire and robbed the safe. I'm a Pinkerton detective.''

"You mean you aren't a wealthy silver miner?''

"Oh, I'm a silver miner all right, and a detective, and I am wealthy.''

"Then the necklace really is yours?''

"It was. It belongs to you now. And so does the ring. After tonight, I'll have caught the criminal and then we'll find the Reverend Bartholomew and get married. What about that, my little one?''

"Daniel Logan, if you call me little one again I'll bite you. But this time it won't be on the hand. In fact,'' her fingers left his back and threaded their way between them toward his lower body. "I might do it anyway. Would my mouth feel the same to a man as what you did to me?''

She began to wiggle down in the bed.

"*Feel the same*?'' The picture of what Portia suggested was making Daniel's heart twist in his chest. Her touch brought an immediate response so overpowering that he had difficulty answering. "Yes. I mean, no. I mean it is wonderful, but I don't think that I'm quite ready for that—yet.''

"Oh?''

But he was ready, definitely ready, and afterward Portia proved her point to his ultimate satisfaction. She was no longer a girl. She was a woman, a woman who fell asleep in Daniel's arms, exactly where she belonged.

When Portia woke the patch of moonlight on the floor by the bed had shrunk to a long sliver of gray. She stretched and smiled, reaching out her fingers to Daniel in the bed beside her. It was time they talked.

He was gone.

Sitting up quickly, Portia pulled the spread around her and peered intently into the darkness. ''Daniel?'' There was no answer. The silence said that she was alone.

Why had he left her? How could he have stolen off into the night after what they'd shared. Stolen! That was it. She checked the bedside table. The necklace was gone. He'd said that after tonight he'd have the thief. He was a detective and he had a plan. Portia smacked her head with her palm.

He'd planned the entire evening to make certain that the thief would strike. That's why he'd made such a show of giving her the necklace and the engagement ring. That's why he'd invited Jay Gould and his daughter to the Sweetwater, and arranged the ball—so that everyone would wear their most elegant jewels and he'd force the thief to strike.

But he hadn't taken her ring. It was still on her finger. The last thing she remembered before she'd fallen asleep was his promising to love her forever. Then he'd left her in his bed where she'd be safe while he went after the criminal alone.

Portia sat straight up. Suppose something went wrong. Suppose something happened to Daniel. No! He was her life now. She should be with him. Portia slipped her feet over the side of the bed to the floor. Nothing would happen to Daniel if she could help it.

Quickly Portia dressed. It must be long after midnight. She had to find him. She tried to hurry but the costume was bulky and her fingers awkward. Finally she kicked the petticoats and vest aside, stepped into the brocade gown and fastened its hooks.

Tip-toeing past the closed door of Ian's room, Portia made her way through the parlor to the corridor and down the servants' stairs to the lobby. While the main stairway and the lobby were illuminated with the new electric lights, the back hall was pitch black. Good, she could find Daniel without being seen.

Floor by floor she crept through the darkness, her heart thumping wildly in her throat, her mind formulating and discarding plans. Every creak in the stairs seemed magnified in the silence until she was sure she would scream from the tension. As she reached the bottom floor she heard a sound.

Someone was there in the darkness below her, waiting, holding his breath in the dark. Trying to orient herself according to the arrangement of the lobby, Portia was certain that once she reached the bottom she could turn left and find the kitchen area. To the right should lead to the hotel office suite. Portia hesitated, straining her ears for some suggestion of where the other person was standing.

There was not a sound. Whoever it was he too had frozen. This eliminated the intruder being a servant. There'd be no reason for him or her to be hesitant. That left two possibilities. Either the person in the darkness was the thief, or Daniel.

She didn't wait any longer. Her eyes had acclimated themselves to the darkness. If Daniel was standing below her, she'd find him. If the person waiting was someone else, that meant that Daniel was in trouble. That possibility brought panic to her pulse. She couldn't lose Daniel, not now.

"Daniel?" she whispered, her throat so dry that she could barely speak, "is that you?"

Silence.

Portia swallowed hard and took the final two steps to the hallway. "Answer me, you rake. I know what you're doing and I won't let you do it alone." She hesitated, made up her mind and turned toward the office. "I love you, Daniel Logan, and we're a team. I intend to help you."

"Portia! Shush!" Daniel's stern whisper came from somewhere farther down the corridor to her right.

At that moment a door opened at the other end of the hall where she judged the hotel office to be. A black hooded figure tore down the corridor, brushing past Portia. As he passed he caught her shoulder, bringing him to a momentary halt.

"Stop!" Portia cried, reaching out to grab the stranger's

arm, trying desperately to hold on. "Come back!" she screamed, feeling him pull away.

"Get out of my way, you little fool, or you'll be sorry!"

Then the thief pulled out of her grasp, shoving her violently to the floor. Portia's head banged into the wood paneling with a thud that stunned her.

"Portia?" Daniel covered the distance between them in a second and was kneeling beside her. "You little fool. What did you think you were doing?"

"Helping you, Daniel," she replied in a dazed voice. "Daniel, he's getting away. Go after him."

But the man wasn't leaving the building. Instead he took the servants' stairs. Daniel hesitated, torn between giving chase and caring for Portia who seemed groggy from her fall. He heard the thief's footsteps stop. A door opened and then there was silence.

"Go on, Daniel. Hurry! I'm all right."

"All right. Go back to my room, Portia. Wait for me there." Daniel kissed her cheek, sprang to his feet and took off in a run. She heard him swear, and then there was silence.

She'd made Daniel lose the thief. He hadn't needed her help. She'd charged in to solve a problem just as she'd always done for her family. Except this time she'd failed. Not only was she unsuccessful in stopping the thief, but she'd made it possible for him to get away. She'd known from the beginning that Daniel didn't need her. Their bodies seemed to speak in some special language, but they couldn't stay in bed forever, but making love seemed to be the only part of their relationship that she was good at.

Portia took a deep breath and felt a pain at the back of her head where she'd hit. She closed her eyes. That was when she smelled it. *Smoke. Fire!* Daniel had said that the thief's modus operandi was to set fire to the hotel and rob the safe. *The Sweetwater was on fire.*

"Oh, no!" Portia forced herself to her feet and felt her way down the passageway until she came to its end. Quickly she opened the door, finding herself inside the office, as she'd surmised. A faint glow beyond a glass partition caught her eye and she rushed toward the door outlined by the light behind it. She jerked it open.

She was inside the manager's private office. Briefly she took in the open safe and the wastepaper basket where fingers of fire were licking at crumpled papers in the small container. Frantically she looked around. Always before there'd been a jug of that awful mineral water on every table. Now? Nothing. Without a thought she slipped out of her gown, wrapped the smoldering brass container in the voluminous skirt and flung it through the window, shattering the glass and allowing the burning paper to float to the ground where it burned itself out on the grass.

She'd removed the fire from the hotel, but what about the thief? If he got away Daniel would be held responsible. Realizing that the noise would attract attention that would demand answers she didn't have, Portia slid her feet over the sill and slipped out of the window, running furiously across the grounds to the Chautauqua dormitory, pausing first to gather up her scorched dress. She couldn't get back to Daniel's room without being seen. Maybe she didn't belong there anyway.

From the dormitory window Portia watched as a small swarm of men searched the grounds. She couldn't see Daniel. He must be inside the hotel. For a long time she stood watching. Her head ached. She wanted to cry, but her eyes were dry. She'd fallen in love with Daniel Logan and in one foolish moment born of that love, she'd ruined his career. He wouldn't want her now; she couldn't face his scorn.

Miserable, tired, and wallowing in self-pity, Portia crawled into her bunk, the twinges of her body reminding her of what they'd shared. Long after the sun nudged her wide-eyed stare she grieved for what she'd lost.

"Damn it, he got away." Daniel was standing in the second floor corridor threading his fingers through his hair in pure frustration. "He could be in any room in the hotel and I wouldn't know it."

"How'd it happen?" Ian asked quietly.

"Portia. I told her about the thief and why we were here." Daniel winced. He hadn't meant to be that honest with Ian, but it was too late now. "I left her sleeping and came down here to wait in the corridor as we'd planned. She woke up and must have gotten it into her head that I needed her help. Just as she crept down the back stairs the thief came out of the office and they collided. Portia got thrown to the floor and the man took off up the servants' stairs in the dark."

"Is Portia all right?"

"Yes. I sent her back to my room."

"Well, she didn't go. And it was a good thing. She discovered the fire that our thief built in the office trash can and pitched the fire, can and all, out the window. Stopped the hotel from burning."

"Why doesn't that surprise me?" Daniel said, shaking his head in chagrin. "She's some woman, isn't she, Ian?"

"Yep. I think she's just about what you need, Daniel. In the meantime, where do we go from here? The safe has been cleaned out and we are no closer than we were before."

Daniel swore, rubbing his eyes in exhaustion. "I don't know, Ian. I guess our first move is to talk to Hill Jackson. You have the men watch the grounds, the stables and the train station. I'll go and roust out our hotel detective."

"Daniel, I'm sorry. You lost your necklace and the ring and we still don't have our thief."

"Just the necklace, Ian. I couldn't put her ring in the safe." Daniel's voice trailed off as he stood there in the darkness. The memory of their making love brought a smile to his face that he couldn't hide. "I wonder if she bit him?"

"Bit him? Daniel, are you sure that you didn't hit your head in the scuffle?"

"I'm fine, Ian." Daniel straightened his shoulders and hid his smile. "Have the men search the lower floor as soon as it's light. Maybe they'll find something to identify the man we're looking for. I'll go and find Mr. Jackson.''

The Pinkerton men did find something. They discovered Portia's ruby engagement ring in the servants' corridor between the kitchen and the suite of hotel offices. Hill Jackson was incensed when he found that without being consulted, Daniel had engineered the ball and the wearing of the jewels in order to force the thief to make his move.

Only Daniel and Ian knew that the engagement ring hadn't been part of the contents of the safe. Only hours earlier, that ring had been on Portia MacIntosh's finger in his bed, in his suite. Now she'd either lost it, or taken it off and dropped it in the corridor. It didn't make any sense. Surely it was an accident. Portia had come to help him, charging into the darkness because someone she loved was in danger. Unless . . .

Suppose he was wrong. Portia was trying to help someone she loved, all right. But suppose it wasn't him? Could he have been fooled so badly? With a heavy heart Daniel managed to excuse himself and check his suite. The bed was empty. Portia was gone.

There was no other explanation. Portia had intended to keep him occupied while the robbery was committed. But her plan had misfired. She'd waked and found him gone. Now she was gone, too. Had he found his thief? No; he refused to believe it.

Daniel's success had turned into a pain that was ripping him apart. He'd loved four women in his life and he'd lost them all, his mother, his sister, Belle and now Portia.

''Damn!'' He refused to believe that she'd been using him from the first. She was honest and good. But she was loyal and he knew that her family came first. If she'd been forced to she could have set him up. He didn't know how she'd done it, nor who her partner was. All he knew was that his love hadn't been enough to stop her.

She'd outsmarted him.

The little minx. She'd loved him senseless. That wasn't a lie. Nobody could fake what they'd shared together. She'd been a virgin, an innocent girl who'd reached out and touched something inside him that had been dormant so long that he didn't know it was still there.

A girl, masquerading as a boy. A jewel thief, pretending innocence while she did what she had to do to save her family from ruin. "Damn!" He swore again. But this time his curse was accompanied by the begrudging hint of admiration. To be outsmarted by a girl. He nodded. He'd been beaten, and he'd admit it. What a woman he'd fallen in love with.

He'd just bide his time until he could get to her. They'd return the jewels quietly. Somehow he'd convince the authorities to drop the charges and convince Portia that she never needed to steal again. After all nothing would be lost and he'd make it worth her while. Then, he'd kiss her . . . Once he'd kissed her, she'd agree to his plan. Alaska might not be as exciting as stealing jewels, but it would come close.

By now, he was beginning to smile. Portia MacIntosh was like the Klondike, wild and untamed. She was passionate, caring, smart and he didn't intend to lose her, no matter what it took to convince her that they were meant to be together.

To Ian's consternation, Daniel told him to call off their men and send them to bed. He knew who the thief was and they'd straighten everything out in the morning. First he'd get a few hours of sleep. By that time the Chautauqua school would be up and then he'd have a little talk with Portia— that is, if they could talk without touching. Hell, he'd forget the talking altogether. Touching was their method of communication. And no matter what happened, he knew that they communicated very well.

Portia was still awake when the sun came up. She felt more tired and drained than she ever had in her life. She was deeply in love with Daniel Logan and she'd ruined his career. He'd lost the thief and all the jewels on her account. The thief was very likely laughing at them now. What she'd like to do was take MacBeth's dagger and cut out his damned heart.

There was no way she could make things right this time. Unless . . . Portia sat up. Unless she could find the thief herself. For a long moment she sat there, forcing herself to rehearse the scene with the man in the dark corridor. He'd been a tall man and he'd been strong. But he was shorter than Daniel. And the voice? It wasn't disguised. She'd heard that voice before, but when?

Portia's pulse was a telegraph line of staccato beats as she considered the possibilities. *She knew that voice.* She had heard it before. Recently. Daniel had the kind of mind that could read and remember. Well, she had her own talents too. She could hear a voice and bring it back to mind.

Quickly Portia cleaned her face and teeth. Running a comb through her hair, she stepped into one of her new dresses and shoes. One thing she'd learned in the last twenty-four hours was to plan her actions. The upcoming confrontation was to be the most important of her entire life and she couldn't afford to mess it up. For Portia knew that she was going to the Klondike. She'd always wanted to mine gold and hunt bear.

Twenty

PORTIA was half way across the grounds when she remembered whom the voice belonged to. At first she shook off the thought. The idea was too bizarre. But it had to be. She'd been an actress too long to mistake a voice.

Through the flower garden, around the rose mound and onto the veranda she strode, barely taking time to acknowledge the greetings of guests still reliving the merrymaking from the Twelfth Night Ball.

The lobby was empty and Portia was able to skirt the office and make her way up the steps without incident. A helpful maid divulged the room number she was seeking and she quickened her step.

Portia found the suite and knocked.

No answer.

She knocked again. "Hello inside?"

He was gone. But where?

And then she knew where he had to be. Quickly she retraced her steps, this time ignoring the calls from the breakfast guests gathering at the door to the dining room. She leaned down, unfastened her shoes and stepped out of them. She lifted up her skirt and ran down to the railroad tracks. She had to catch the first railroad car departing the springs, otherwise he might escape.

At the very last minute she reached the end car on the Dummy Line Railroad and swung herself on board in a flurry of bare legs and petticoats. She made it. Now, if she was right . . .

Minutes later she stood outside the private car and, using her best Fiona stage voice, polished and deeply suggestive, she called out, "Hello, inside? Is anyone there?"

The car door opened. Behind the man she could see valises flung hastily on the bed. He hadn't yet had time to unpack. The man's startled expression gave her a chance to slip inside.

"Good morning, Miss MacIntosh. Is there something you wanted?"

"Yes, as a matter of fact there is," Portia began, carefully choosing her words and tone of voice. While she was absolutely certain, there was still the very slight possibility that she was wrong.

She looked casually around, trying to formulate a question that might stall her need to be truthful. If she could distract him she could search. But that wasn't likely to happen. No, there was nothing to do but go for the answer, head on, without subterfuge.

When she didn't answer the man said, "Well, I'd appreciate it if you'd state your business. I've arranged to be attached to the 9:15 shuttle train. I have business in Philadelphia at the end of the week."

"Of course. I'd like to have this over with as soon as possible myself. Because of you I may have lost the only thing I care about in my life and I won't allow you to leave until you've handed over the jewels. I'll see that they're returned to the hotel. I will say nothing until after you're gone."

Surprise, anger, uncertainty all swept across the thief's face in waves of astonishment. "What on earth are you talking about, Miss MacIntosh? I'm a very wealthy man. I don't need to commit robbery to have anything I want. I must insist that you leave."

"I think you know what I'm talking about. You're the thief, Simon Fordham. I know it. That first night I sat in the next car watching you play cards through the window, I could only see three sets of hands, yours, my father's and Daniel Logan's."

"So?" Fordham regarded her through half closed eyelids.

"My father was wearing stage jewelry. Daniel was wearing his ring made from a silver nugget. You were wearing a large diamond ring. That ring went into the pot, a pot you lost. Now, you're wearing it again."

"So? I have many rings, Miss MacIntosh. Why would that make you question my financial status?"

"And you wore a chain from your vest buttonhole to your watch pocket but you couldn't give me the time. That tells me that you didn't have a watch. It didn't make sense that a man of your means wouldn't have his own jewelry or a watch. What time is it now, Mr. Fordham?"

The man scratched his whiskers and smiled. "That's where you've outsmarted yourself, my dear." He pulled the chain, dangling a watch from the fob. He flicked open the back of the watch and scowled. "The time is exactly 9:05. Damn your eyes. I thought that I had plenty of time. You and your questions are about to make me miss my train."

"No, Mr. Fordham. You still have time to get down to connect your car to the train. Your watch is twenty minutes fast."

"How would you know?"

"Because I recognize the watch, just as I recognized your voice. The watch belonged to Daniel Logan's father. The initials A. L. are engraved on its back. I can see them from here. The watch was in the hotel safe last night along with the other jewels. Daniel considered it priceless, though it doesn't keep accurate time."

"So, you figured it out. Pretty smart. Too bad, my dear. It looks as if you're going to have to come with me. Nobody will suspect Simon Fordham of having been a jewel thief. Simon Fordham is a very wealthy man. But a stage actress, who disappears the morning after a robbery will be a prime suspect."

As Simon reached behind him, locking the door and jerking free one of the ropes holding back the drapes, Portia realized that she'd made a bad mistake entering the car. "Is there really a Simon Fordham?" Portia's question was as much a stall for time as for information.

"Of course, my dear. Simon Fordham is my first cousin. He's very old and never leaves Vermont. My name is Silas Fountain. I never planned to be a thief, you understand. It's just that I lost all my money in that railroad deal with Jay Gould. And dear Cousin Simon has lived much too long. Once he dies and I inherit everything, I'll retire. In the meantime, I pick up a little extra spending money."

The question-asking ploy didn't work. As he spoke, Simon started toward Portia, swinging the silken rope in his hands. "As you said, I still have time to join the train. I'll just tie you up while I have the car attached."

"Why, Mr. Fordham? Why are you doing this?"

"To cover my tracks. Besides, you're a pretty little thing. I didn't pay much attention to you the night you rescued that old fool from our game. Later, when Daniel paraded you before all those old biddies I realized that I'd made a mistake, one I'm about to rectify. You won't be disappointed. I think that you'll enjoy our next stop. We're going to Savannah."

"I'm not going anywhere with you, Mr. Fordham," Portia said with certainty.

"Oh yes you are." Simon Fordham was surprisingly strong. Though she struggled, this time Portia didn't have the advantage of surprise and she was no match for a desperate man. It didn't matter. An escape artist had once been a member of their troupe and he'd taught Portia how to hold her hands in order to slide them out of the knots. There was nothing she could do about the gag that Simon tied about her mouth.

''Now, my little wildcat. You sit quietly and wait for me. Once we're recoupled, we'll get underway.''

Then he was gone. By the time she heard the click of the lock on the outside of the door Portia was free and the gag untied. She looked desperately around. The door might be locked but if she was anything she was resourceful. After a lifetime with a traveling theatrical troupe she could improvise. First, the jewels.

It didn't take long. Simon Fordham hadn't even tried to hide them. They'd been wrapped in a towel and laid in the bottom of a small valise. The necklace, Daniel's necklace was there. She tucked it into her pocket and replaced the rest of the gems in the towel. Then, for the first time, she missed her ring. She'd been wearing it when she went to sleep. Surely it hadn't been lost. But she'd worry about it later. For now, she had to get out.

For once in her life Portia wished she carried a parasol or a purse. At least she'd have somewhere to hide the gems. Then she had an idea. With a straight razor she found in Simon's shaving things, she cut down another of the tie-backs like Simon had used to bind her with. Stringing the necklaces, ear rings, broaches and rings over the cord like the pearls in a necklace she lifted her skirt, and fastened the cord loosely around her waist, allowing it to slip down her hips beneath her bloomers. The jewels would be concealed in the folds of her petticoat. Now she was ready for escape.

Ten minutes later she gave up. The windows were barred. The glass in the door was reinforced with steel and the walls were double paneled. Nobody would ever break into the car and she wasn't going to break out. Then she heard a sound, someone walking down beside the car. Simon Fordham was back. Quickly Portia dashed across the room, picked up a brass spittoon and stood behind the door.

For a long minute he fumbled with the lock before he

opened it and stepped hesitantly through the door. It was now or never. Portia thought about the gems, about her family, about Daniel, closed her eyes and swung the weighted container.

Crack! The man slumped to the floor and groaned, turning his head as he fell. *Please God, don't let me have killed him*, Portia prayed and dropped to her knees. She'd only meant to stun him enough to allow her to escape. She couldn't murder anybody, even a thief.

Then she recognized her victim. *The man on the floor wasn't Simon Fordham*. She'd know that rakish fall of black hair and that mustache anywhere. This time she'd done it. She'd killed Daniel Logan.

"Oh, no! Daniel, darling. Please don't be dead!" She turned him over and knelt over him. His heart, was it still beating? She pressed her ear against his chest. Nothing. Was he breathing? Yes. Frantically she untied his cravat and began to unfasten his shirt. "I'm sorry. I thought you were Simon Fordham. Please don't be dead. I love you. I can't live without you."

"It's almost worth the headache I'm going to have to hear you say that." Daniel opened his eyes and closed his arms around her, pulling her to the floor across him. His kiss was big and possessive and Portia returned it joyfully. After a long delicious moment Daniel pulled away.

"How'd you find me?" Portia sighed and nuzzled his neck.

"I'm a Pinkerton man, remember? Besides, there's only one honey-haired gypsy who races barefoot after a train and climbs on board. Are you all right?"

"Oh, yes, Daniel, but we'd better get out of here before Simon Fordham returns. He's the thief. I recognized his voice."

"Don't worry, darling. Simon walked out of this car straight into Hill Jackson, the hotel detective. Since Simon was in such a hurry to leave, Hill decided they'd go down to the jail and have a little talk about why."

"Did I hurt you?" Portia whispered, planting little kisses across his cheeks and nose.

"You mean from that blow on the head? No. But you seem to be sticking me with a pointed object, in a part of my body that doesn't need to be wounded."

"I'm sticking you? Sticking you?" Portia shifted her body and gasped. "Oh!"

As she clambered to her feet she reached down and caught the hem of her skirt, lifting it to her waist.

"Darling, as much as I want you, at this moment I think we'd better not get carried away. Hill Jackson or one of his men will probably be back here any minute."

"The jewels, Daniel—what shall I do with them?"

Daniel rose slowly, a curious expression on his face. "What do you mean, what should you do with them? Where are they?"

"Well, I was going to steal them from Simon Fordham and I . . . well—" She bunched up her petticoats and untied her drawers, allowing them to fall to her ankles. "I'm afraid that you're going to have to loosen the knot."

For the first time in his life Daniel was speechless. The little minx had adorned her body with jewels. "There isn't another woman in the world like you, Portia MacIntosh. What am I going to do with you?"

His gaze lifted to her face and she caught her breath. For a second she remembered the first night she'd hit him in a rail car, his own private car. That seemed like a hundred years ago. She'd been a cocky, foolish child then. Now she was a woman, a woman who knew what she wanted. She wanted Daniel Logan and whatever life he offered. There was something wonderful between them, something deeper than desire, than wanting to be close.

"I'll tell you what you're going to do with me, Daniel. You're going to take me to your car and make love to me. Tonight, all night, and all the nights to come. You're going to marry me, Daniel Logan, or I'm going to tell the world that you and I stole these jewels together."

"You would, wouldn't you, you bossy little wench? Always trying to run everything, never giving a man a chance to tell you that he's already arranged a wedding ceremony back at the hotel, that he's going to take you to the land of ice and throw you into the nearest snow bank." Daniel took a step forward, lifted Portia and threw her over his shoulder.

"What are you doing, Daniel? What about your head?"

"It's my heart I'm worrying about at the moment. Besides, I'm simply following orders, Portia. There are times when I intend to do just what you tell me to. Reverend Bartholomew and the ceremony can wait until tomorrow. By the way, Mrs. Bartholomew said to tell you that you were right about ladies wearing swim suits, whatever that means."

"It means . . . never mind, it isn't important, except perhaps to her husband," Portia said, trying not to feel Daniel's hand on her bare bottom. She couldn't control a little quiver of excitement.

"Something wrong, darling?"

"No, Daniel, except that now something is sticking my, me, well . . . a place you wouldn't want to be injured."

Daniel chuckled and turned toward the door.

"Wait, Daniel, my . . . bloomers."

He stopped, gave the muslin garment a kick, and sent it scudding under the bed.

"Don't worry, Princess," he said replacing his hand with his lips for one quick, wicked kiss. "I promise you, underdrawers are one thing you aren't going to need, now or ever."

Twenty-one

"**D**O stand still, Portia. I can't hook this corset with you fidgeting about."

Fiona gave a sharp tug to the back of the steel-boned garment that Portia was rapidly beginning to regard as a torture chamber.

"I don't understand why I have to wear this thing. If Daniel is determined that we marry, I don't know why he didn't just let Brother Bartholomew say the words in the chapel."

"Portia, what do you mean, *if* Daniel is determined? He loves you. This wedding is going to get top billing. You've drawn a full house. Even Jay Gould and his daughter Helen are stopping by on their way back to New York," Fiona chattered happily.

"Oh my, yes," Bessie agreed. "They say there hasn't been so much excitement since the elephant parade that opened that Piedmont Exposition in Atlanta."

"You like this three-ringed circus, Fiona? I'll change places with you. At least you've seen Edward. Daniel has been too busy for days to see me."

"Portia MacIntosh, Edward is mine and I won't have you say such a thing, even as a joke."

Fiona sounded angry, but Portia could see that there wasn't an ounce of concern in her manner. She'd become positively serene since it was decided that she and Edward would marry in the chapel on the family estate in England following the Delecort family tradition.

Portia caught her sister's hand and squeezed it lightly. "I meant that you and Edward could have all this pomp and circumstance. I wish," her voice turned wistful for a moment, "I wish Daniel and I could just be together, without getting married. Then when he finds out that I'll never make a proper wife, he could send me home. I could come back and look after Papa and the troupe and . . . everything could be normal again."

Bessie came to stand behind Portia, holding more white lace-adorned garments in her hands. "Be together? Without getting married? Hush! I'll not listen to such talk."

"Mr. Logan intends to make this wedding the most important social event of the season and you're a lucky young woman. Turn around and hold out your arms."

"Now what?" Portia let go Fiona's hand and grumbled crossly. She knew that she was just out of sorts and unable to voice her real concern. Where was Daniel? It had been two days since she'd even seen him. There'd been no more chance meetings on the grounds, no more rehearsals under his close scrutiny, no more stolen kisses. In short, he'd been so busy planning this blasted three ring circus for over a week that he hadn't had any time for her.

"Arms," Bessie reminded. "Hold them out. This is your corset cover. Over that goes the chemise and then we add the petticoats." Bessie threaded the garment over Portia's extended arms and moved around to fasten the tiny buttons in the back.

"Corset cover. No! By the time I get to the dress I'll be wearing so many clothes that if I don't die of asphyxiation, I'll die of heat prostration. I won't do it." Portia ripped off the offending corset cover and began to unfasten the white silk stockings she was wearing.

"Portia MacIntosh, you behave yourself!" Fiona threatened. "Daniel sent all the way to Atlanta for this wedding dress. It was being made for someone else. Daniel agreed to pay for the dressmaker to alter it for you, and to hire extra help to finish another dress in time for the other bride's wedding."

"No! No! No! I won't do it. I may have to get married, but I refuse to be something I'm not. If he wants to marry me, he'll take me like I am, or find someone else." Portia pulled on her familiar faded Chinese kimono and flung herself across her cot, covering her eyes with her arm. "Go away, all of you!"

Bessie and Fiona stared at Portia in shocked silence. Nobody had ever cajoled, bribed, or threatened Portia into doing anything. As they looked at each other in distress, there was a knock on the door.

"Excuse me, ladies." Horatio opened the door and stuck his head cautiously inside. He took one look at the situation and nodded. "I've come to speak with the bride for a moment, if I may." He indicated with a silent motion of his head that the room should be vacated and then sat down on the cot next to Portia's.

Portia tried to still her sniffles. She never cried. At least she never had, until she met Daniel. Fiona had turned into the Rock of Gibraltar and she'd turned into Niagara Falls.

"What's wrong, daughter?"

"Nothing, Papa. No, everything. No, I don't know. Am I doing the right thing? Why is it so hard to get married?"

"I don't know. I asked myself that question when your mother and I were married. One minute I wanted to run away and go back to the time when I was just a carefree young actor. And the next minute I thought about being without Kathryn and I was afraid that she would change her mind. The worst thing was that she wouldn't let me see her for two days before the wedding."

Portia sat up. "She wouldn't?"

"No, some silly superstition that I'd think she was more beautiful if I'd been away from her. That was utter foolishness. No woman was ever more beautiful than your mother on our wedding day, just as you will be for the man you love."

"Oh, Papa, you're the man I love." Portia flung her arms around Horatio's neck in a rare display of affection. "I don't want to leave you. Couldn't you come to Alaska with us?"

Horatio laughed. "No, Portia. You don't need me. I want you to know how very proud of you I am. Catching Simon Fordham was a very brave thing to do. You know that he and an accomplice have been responsible for a number of hotel robberies in the last two years. You could have been hurt."

"But I was afraid. I was afraid that . . . I mean I couldn't let you . . . or . . . Daniel be blamed."

"I know. You're always willing to protect the people you love. That's what love is, Portia. But, here, I almost forgot. Daniel sent you a wedding gift."

"A wedding present, from Daniel?" Portia took the small white box with the silver ribbon and laid it against her cheek. Daniel. How could she have been such a ninny? Of course she loved Daniel. And Daniel loved her. He'd loved her even when he thought that she might be the thief. He wanted her, a stage actress, when he could have picked anybody. And he wasn't avoiding her because he was having second thoughts. He was just observing some silly superstition in staying away from her. Of course she wanted to marry him. It was just all this marriage ceremony business that was so frustrating.

"Thank you, Papa. I'm going to miss you. Promise me that if you need me, you'll send a telegram right away."

"Oh, I won't have to do that, daughter. Daniel tells me that it won't be anytime before they'll have those telephone lines strung up between here and Alaska. I'll just ring you up. As a matter of fact, Evie and I are thinking about investing in the project."

"Oh, Papa, Alaska is so far away."

"Not from Daniel, my dear. He's your responsibility now, just as you are his."

"You're right." Portia sprang to her feet. "I'm going to be Mrs. Daniel Logan. I'll have to learn to shoot a gun, Papa. Oh, Papa, we'll live in the wilderness and look for gold. Once we get there, Daniel says I won't have to wear all these petticoats. I can wear men's pants, or . . ." Portia blushed and turned away, remembering the rest of Daniel's statement . . . *absolutely nothing at all*.

Portia kissed the Captain once more and walked him to the door. "Tell Fiona and the others I'd like to be alone for a while before they come back to help me dress. Will you, Papa?"

Her father nodded, kissed her on the forehead and left the room.

Portia looked down at the box, her gift from Daniel. She held it close to her heart for a long time before opening it. The two days away from Daniel had been the most miserable time of her life. She had known nothing about love, until Daniel had kissed her. Then he'd shown her the joy that could come from loving a man. Now she'd learned the despair of being separated. How had her father endured losing his Kathryn? He'd had his children and he'd loved them, but that wasn't the same. Now Papa had Lady Evelyna, Fiona had Edward, and she had Daniel.

Eagerly she ripped the wrappings away revealing an intricately crafted silver and black inlaid box. Inside the box was a long gold chain with a hook on one end and a key on the other. Beneath the chain was a sheet of folded paper. With trembling fingers, Portia opened the note.

My darling, Portia. This is a key chain meant to be worn by the chatelain of a castle, around her waist. She was entrusted with the nourishment and the care of all those who

dwelt inside. I give you this key as a symbol of my love.
Everything I have is yours, including my heart.

Daniel asked for the third time, "You've had the Pavilion
strung with lights?"

"Yes, Daniel." Ian watched his old friend pace anxiously
about the hotel parlor. "An arbor, just as you ordered, covered with green smilax, white gardenias and pink roses, has
been built in the middle of the floor directly over the glass
dome that covers the springs bubbling up through the rocks
to the surface."

"Good. I want Portia to see the springs. The night we
went dancing in the Pavilion the floor was so crowded she
couldn't have seen through the glass, even if the cavern had
been lit."

"You were very generous, Daniel. Having incandescent
lights installed among the rocks is a generous gift to the park.
You've turned the Pavilion into a fairyland."

"Will she like it?"

"She'll like it, Daniel."

Ian bit back a smile. He'd never seen Daniel so wrought
up. For the past two weeks Ian had had his work cut out for
him to prevent Daniel from moving Portia into his suite and
locking the door. Even then, there'd been secret midnight
meetings that lasted until sunrise. There'd been picnics and
scandalous private drives along Sweetwater Creek, which Ian
had hidden from the other guests by saying that he and Vicki
were joining the couple for the day. Of course, Ian admitted
guiltily, he and Vicki hadn't been entirely unappreciative of
the opportunity to be alone.

Finally, it had taken a serious talking to by Lady Evelyna
before Daniel realized that he should restrain his desire for
the woman he loved. He admitted that he had no patience,
if he saw Portia he wanted to *be* with her, alone. Out of
respect for Portia's reputation, he forced himself to take Ian's
advice and stay away completely for the last two days bending

all his efforts toward planning the wedding and finding local employment for the acting troupe.

Now, at last, his self-imposed absence was coming to an end.

By eight o'clock the Pavilion and Chautauqua grounds were overflowing with visitors and hotel guests. Daniel was resplendent in a formal black frock coat and close-cut black trousers with braided side seams. He wore a white ascot, white silk embroidered waistcoat and black patent leather button boots.

John Philip Sousa's band played splendid patriotic music, followed by the Chautauqua School Church Choir singing special wedding songs. Lady Evelyna, Edward, the Trevillions, Dr. Garret, Winston, the boy Daniel and Portia had befriended, and other special invited guests and members of the acting troupe circled the walls of the Pavilion, waiting eagerly for the arrival of the wedding party.

The first to arrive was Daniel's carriage, a handsome pair of white plumed dappled grays pulling a smart black open carriage. Daniel and Ian dismounted, nodded to Reverend Bartholomew and guests. Daniel took his place to the left of the arbor while Ian returned to the drive to assist the approaching bridal party.

Drawn by two white horses, Portia's white carriage was festooned with brightly colored ribbons, flowers and plumes. Announcing the bride's arrival, the band began a soft rendition of Mendelssohn's Wedding March. Fiona, resplendent in blue watered silk, trimmed with grosgrain ribbons and satin, carried a nosegay of roses and bachelor buttons. With her hand clasping Ian's arm, they moved inside and took their places on either side of the arbor.

Portia was hidden from Daniel's view as she climbed the steps. There was a collective gasp and the crowd fell back. Later, Daniel would swear that the springs halted their churning motion and the hall went silent at the moment when their eyes met.

Like an angel, Portia stood in her wedding gown of satin

and pearls. In her hand she held a white lace fan garlanded with gardenias and satin ribbons. Her golden hair was woven with pearls and a lace train cascaded behind her and across the marble floor like a waterfall. With the lights twinkling over her head and the late afternoon sunlight wrapping her with spun gold and silver, Daniel knew that Portia was the illumination he'd been reaching for, the treasure for which he'd searched all his life.

From the moment that Portia saw Daniel, all doubt disappeared. As she walked toward him, across the glass inset beneath her feet, she suddenly felt a calming presence wash over her and she wondered if the tale of the great healing spirit of the Springs could be true. Her heart began to sing.

She scarcely noticed the words being spoken until Reverend Bartholomew said, "Will you take this man, now and forever?"

"Oh, yes. I mean, of course I will." Of course she would. Why had there ever been doubt?

Daniel heard her answer and he knew that the empty space inside him had been filled, and forever wouldn't be long enough to show all the love he felt.

". . . love honor and obey." He grinned at the last one. Portia MacIntosh obey? Not in a hundred lifetimes. But her voice was strong, without faltering, not for the world to hear, but for him. At last Reverend Bartholomew pronounced them man and wife. When Daniel raised her chin and sealed their promises with a kiss, Portia knew that all she wanted was Daniel for all her life.

Afterwards, the well wishers threatened to crush the couple with their greetings and their joyous celebration. Suddenly Daniel swept Portia into his arms and charged through the crowd to the carriage. "Drive, man!" he yelled, settling into the back seat, with Portia firmly in his grasp. "Get us away from here."

"But, Daniel," Portia said hesitantly, "what about the reception, and the champagne and the cake?"

"Let Ian and Vicki cut the cake. I want to be alone with my wife. To the rail station, driver!"

This time Daniel's kiss was anything but gentle. This time Portia's response was anything but chaste.

Daniel directed the driver to his private rail car and dismissed him. Carrying Portia in his arms he left the carriage and climbed the narrow steps to the platform, into his private car.

"Oh, Daniel." Portia sighed, and burrowed her face into his neck. "Are we really married?"

"We're married. We have a paper signed by the very Reverend Willard Bartholomew that says so."

"I'm glad. I really did want our child to have a father."

Daniel stopped, kicked the door shut, and allowed Portia's feet to drop to the floor as he slid his arms beneath her back and held her. "Are you . . . I mean . . . are we going to have a baby?"

"I'm not sure, Daniel. There are so many things I don't know, so many things that I have to learn. But I truly want to have your children, darling." She slid her hands inside his coat and pushed it from his shoulders to the floor. Next she unfastened his vest and the shirt beneath, allowing them to fall together.

"Portia!" Daniel's voice was thick with desire. Quickly his hands sought the buttons on her wedding gown, swiftly removing the satin garment. As he slid the silk petticoat down her body his hand touched bare skin, warm, soft bare skin, encircled by a single gold chain. "You're not wearing anything underneath?"

"Absolutely not, Daniel, only my key. There are times when I choose to follow directions. No drawers, remember?"

And then he kissed her. His lips were warm and sweet. He explored her mouth as if he were kissing her for the first time. He threaded his fingers through her hair, holding her gently, tenderly, afraid that he'd frighten her with the depth of his feelings. And then all their clothes were gone and his fingertips were kneading the soft curves of her bottom as he lifted her against the throbbing part of him trembling between them.

A deep growl of happiness began somewhere in Daniel's throat. His breathing became erratic and his hands trembled with each thrust of Portia's body against him. He took a deep ragged breath and pulled away.

"Are you sure about the Klondike, Portia? Will you be happy in the wilderness without your family?"

"Daniel I love you. I understand now why my mother ran away with my father, and Lady Evelyna ran away with Lord Delecort. I *must* go with you, be with you. Together we are complete."

"I've already taken care of your father, and the troupe. If anything ever happens, you'll all be taken care of too."

"There you go again, taking charge. I don't care about being secure," Portia said. "If ever you decide to ask me, I'll say that all I want is you. And I don't think that I can wait much longer, Daniel. My body is practically screaming now."

Crooking a slanted eyebrow, Daniel lifted Portia and carried her to the bed, laying her across the pillows. "Your wish is my command, my little wench."

There might be a time for quiet discussion in the years to come. There might be a time when their lovemaking would be tender and leisurely, but not yet.

For a long time he just looked at her. Then he kissed her eyes, her nose. Her skin was smooth and sweet tasting as he kissed her face, her throat. When he took her breasts inside his mouth, she gasped and arched against him, filling him with joy. Rolling to his back, he brought her with him, lifting her, sliding her lower so that his erection filled the vee between her breasts.

She loved the feel of the soft hair of his chest against her face. Eagerly she pressed herself closer, holding her breasts together to form a cave of heat to hold his maleness.

They were both damp with perspiration, every nerve ending stimulated to the breaking point. Daniel's hands suddenly cupped her buttocks and lifted her, sliding her forward against his fullness, slowly up, and back down again. Over and over the tip of his male part teased her until Portia thought she would die of wanting him.

"Daniel, please, Daniel. I feel as if I shall explode."

"No, my darling, not yet. I want you to burn with desire, ride the crest of the fire, reach for the stars."

"Only if you ride with me," she panted, throbbing with the need to have him inside her.

All reason, all control were cast aside as he rolled over and lifted himself above. Never had such power been channeled into one entity as when Daniel moved inside her and felt her body fasten itself to him with white hot waves of desire. All of their senses were focused on each other. Their eyes met. Their lips parted in wonder.

And then the scalding fire inside her began to ignite setting off such a blinding heat that when the explosion came it tore them into a million fragments of pleasure, then put them back together again in a long, shuddering flood of joy.

For a long time he stayed inside her, waiting until the last vibration died away before sighing in contentment and collapsing beside her. He drew her into his arms, holding her with gentle pleasure.

"Portia, I never, ever, dreamed that a man could feel so much love for a woman. I never thought to marry. I saw my mother die, my sister, Belle, the woman who took me in. I was afraid to let myself love anyone. *I* was the actor on a stage, only half alive before you came and I never knew it."

"Will it always be like this?"

"I don't know, my darling. I don't know how long always will be. But for as long as I can see and touch and feel, I want to be with you."

"And I with you. I shall probably be a shrew to live with, Daniel. I'm so accustomed to being in charge that I don't know how to share. I'll probably fight you every step of the way and make you the most miserable man in Alaska."

"So long as you and I have this at night."

"Yes, oh yes. When I'm being very bossy, all you have to do is kiss me, Daniel, and you know what happens."

"Oh, yes, I know what happens when we kiss." He chuckled and kissed her behind her ear, down her neck and to her breast. "I think I know how to make peace with your wicked stubbornness. If not I'll throw you to the bears."

"Bears? You're teasing me aren't you? We won't really have bears to worry about, will we?" Her voice was muffled and uneven as she gave in to the pleasure of his touch.

"No bears, Portia, I'll keep a legion of Eskimo guards on bear alert."

"Eskimos? You mean we won't be alone?" Portia allowed a hint of regret to tinge her voice.

"Not in the daytime, Princess, but always at night."

"Good." Her fingertips released the shoulder she was clasping and moved lightly down his body until she found the part of him that was already beginning to swell. She encircled him with her small hand, exploring, touching, fanning a different kind of explosion.

"Ahhhh! Portia, go slow. I think that there is something I should tell you, darling."

"Oh? Am I doing it wrong? I want it to be good for you, Daniel. I intend to practice until I get it right, if it takes all night long."

"No, you're doing it very right. But I ought to tell you that the nights in the Klondike are sometimes six months long!"

"I know," Portia said with a wicked thrust. "And there's one thing I think you should know. I'm a perfectionist about everything I do. Do you think you can be patient while I learn?"

"I think so," Daniel said and thought with pleasure of all the nights to come. "But we'll have to see."

Daniel's blood stirred and he gave himself over to Portia's touch. She was so beautiful, so wild and untamable and she was everything he wanted for all the days and nights of his life and perhaps beyond.

AUTHOR'S NOTE

The Sweetwater Hotel and the mineral springs actually existed, as did Henry Grady's beloved Piedmont Chautauqua College. As many as 30,000 people a day visited the area, including the Vanderbilts, the Astors, Mark Twain, President William McKinley and Joel Chandler Harris. There is no proof that Jay Gould and his daughter Helen visited the resort at the time of our story, but they were in Atlanta as the guests of Samuel Inman, who was a financial partner in the resort, and they traveled on to Savannah afterwards.

The setting and the workings of the resort and the Chautauqua area are accurate, including the performance of Shakespearean plays.

Lithium water was recognized as early as the time of the Cherokees for its medicinal properties, on through the 1800s, by the Congress of Physicians, and is being marketed today by the current owner of the springs, Gleda James, without whose help this book could not have been written.

The Sweetwater Hotel burned in 1912, but Daniel and Portia could have been part of that gilded age, a time never equaled again, an era like those past—and those yet to come—that perished in the smoke of its passions.